The Wicked Phoenix

Elves of Vacari, Volume 1

T.A. McEvoy

Published by Theresa McEvoy, 2023.

Table of Contents

Tom Vick

Thank you, my wonderful boyfriend. I appreciate the time you took to read every draft of the book. My whole life has increased tremendously since we met. Your encouragement meant a lot to me, always having my back and letting me know I could do anything.

Various Locations in The Wicked Phoenix

Main Realm

- **Vacari:** A breathtaking realm where elves, humans, dragons, and merfolk have coexisted for ages.

Main City inside Vacari

- **Goldmoor:** The major city in Vacari where King Alex and Queen Jeanne ruled.

Cities inside Vacari

- **Crystal Vale:** Ruled by the wise King Manard, this city has allied with Goldmoor for years. Ong Swifthammer is a prominent warrior from this city.
- **Fel Thalor:** The home of the Druchii. Qellaun and his sister, Lyra, hail from this city, and the Druchii have sworn to serve Phoenix Shadowwalker.
- **Flameford:** The home of the powerful warlock, Phoenix Shadowwalker.

Forests inside Vacari

- **Purplefire Woods:** An enchanting forest bathed in purple hues near Goldmoor.
- **Emeraldwoods:** An enchanting forest with green-hued woods located near Crystal Vale.
- **Emberwooods:** An enchanting but perilous forest bathed in red and orange, situated near Fel Thalor and Flameford.

Hidden Sub-Realm inside Vacari

- **E'vahona:** The hidden realm of the Eladrin elves. A gift from the Goddess of Light, safeguarded with a hefty price. This is Keisha's home.

Sub-Realm inside Vacari

- **The Hidden Isles:** The location of the Noble dragons. To access The Hidden Isles, one must cross a magical barrier.

Kingdom inside Vacari

- **Coraluna:** The magnificent underwater kingdom of the Merfolk. King Oceanous watches over the kingdom and its inhabitants.

Lagoon inside Vacari

- **Serpent's Lagoon:** Queen Jeanne is imprisoned with various dangerous serpents, hydras, and evil dragons.

World Map

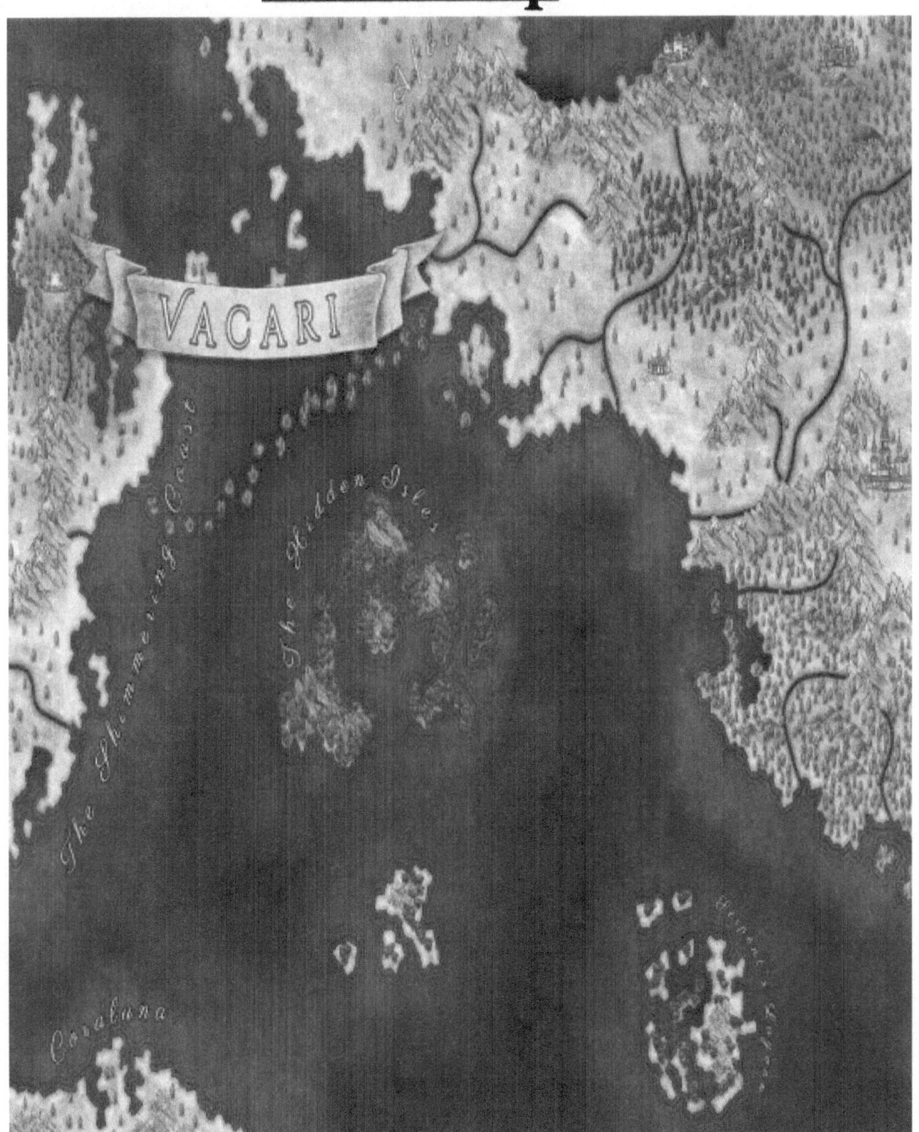

Character List

Main Characters:

1. Keisha - A courageous Eladrin archer with a strong sense of justice.

2. Ong Swifthammer - A loyal and skilled human warrior
3. Pumpkin - An adorable and mischievous young panther with a mysterious connection to Keisha.
4. Phoenix Shadowwalker - The dark and sinister human warlock seeking to unleash chaos and darkness upon the world.
5. Qellaun Deadcrusher - A powerful and fearsome Druchii of the Dark Alliance, serving Phoenix.
6. Lyra Deadcrusher - A cunning and skilled Druchii sorceress working for Phoenix

<u>Noble Dragons (Council Members):</u>

1. Gold Dragon (wisest and oldest) - Kimras, the leader of the grand council, carried an air of regal grace.
2. Silver Dragon - Silvara, the gentle and nurturing silver dragon, sat with an air of serenity that soothed even the most troubled spirits
3. Bronze Dragon - Dirona, the ancient and regal bronze dragon known for her unmatched wisdom.
4. Brass Dragon - Hespherus, the powerful and charismatic brass dragon whose eloquence could sway hearts and minds.
5. Copper Dragon - Caelum, the clever and mischievous copper dragon.

E'vahona Characters

Council Members:

1. Lord Karrenen - Revered throughout Vacari for his extraordinary mastery of magic, with unmatched command over the arcane arts.
2. Lady Elowen - A skilled diplomat with a keen eye for politics and negotiation.
3. Lord Galadon - A fierce warrior and defender of the Eladrin, renowned for his bravery.
4. Lady Lythia - A talented healer and empathetic counselor supporting the Eladrin community.

Infiltration Team

1. Seraphina-Eladrin Mage
2. Thalorin-Eladrin Mage

Evil Dragons

1. Red Dragon - Zylron, the once loyal red dragon whose allegiance to Phoenix

Druchii Forces

Kelru Palvoh -Captain of the Druchii forces
Caedon Parquette- Druchii Warrior

Divine and Significant Beings:

1. Kadona - Goddess of Light and protector of the Eladrin Elves

<u>Notable Figures</u>

1. Eldric-Keisha's father
2. Serena Keisha's mother
3. Maelgrim Shadowwalker-Phoenix's Shadowwalker's father

<u>Merfolks</u>:

1. King Oceanous - Ruler of Coraluna
2. Adrianna - Daughter of King Oceanous
3. Aqilus - Right hand of King Oceanous and Adrianna's mate.

<u>Crystal Vale Characters</u>

1. King Manard- King of Crystal Vale
2. Elna-Dark Ritual Expert of Crystal Vale
3. Rarum-Warrior of Crystal Vale
4. Idos-Mage of Crystal Vale
5. Orius-Mage of Crystal Vale
6. Zeveus- Warden of Mystical Connections.

<u>Goldmoor Characters</u>

1. King Alex- King of Goldmoor
2. Queen Jeanne- Queen of Goldmoor
3. Alaric-Representative from Goldmoor
4. Representative from Goldmoor
5. Taldor-Merchant of Goldmoor

Prologue

In the enigmatic realm of shadows, Qellaun Deadcrusher, a fearsome Druchii warrior, emerged like a specter of colossal proportions. His lithe, obsidian figure was draped in the essence of darkness, a living embodiment of the evil forces that held sway. His pallid complexion bore the undeniable mark of one who had ventured deep into the abyss, a stark contrast to the sinister inferno that smoldered within his crimson eyes, whispering tales of treacherous plots. A cascade of raven-black tendrils, akin to a midnight waterfall, framed a visage seemingly hewn from the very fabric of malevolence.

Clad in armor of ebon hue, it appeared as though the very shadows conspired to weave a protective cloak around him. Arcane runes, intricately woven into the inky fabric, pulsed ominously, a testament to his mastery over the mystic arts. His gloved hands, each finger adorned with wickedly sharp obsidian talons, lovingly caressed the hilt of a long, serrated blade—an instrument forged in the merciless crucible of their ruthless world.

With every measured step, Qellaun performed a ballet of deadly grace, a fluid testament to his lethal expertise. His very presence exuded an insatiable hunger for dominion, rendering him a formidable enigma in the service of Phoenix Shadowwalker.

Amidst the shadowy passages of Flameford, Qellaun, the precursor of malevolence, discerned the echoes of agonized wails and the frantic clamor of dark machinations. With a weary resolve, he embarked on the ominous path that led to the foreboding tower, the customary abode of Phoenix Shadowwalker.

The creaking door yielded to his indomitable will, narrowly averting a searing bolt of fire that tore through the entrance. His unwavering gaze remained steadfast, a beacon of courage even in the face of volatile sorcery. "My Lord, what sinister musings consume you?" he inquired, his hushed murmur tinged with reverence.

A warlock shrouded in enigma, Phoenix possessed tresses as silver as moonlight and eyes as abyssal as the deepest chasm. His features twisted into an impatient scowl, brimming with an aura of unassailable authority. "I grow weary of these ceaseless delays," he hissed unswerving determination. "The time has come to set our grand design into motion, to grasp dominion over Goldmoor."

Ever the devoted servant, Qellaun inclined his head in solemn concurrence. "Indeed, My Lord," he replied, unyielding in his allegiance. "The moment we have longed for approaches. I shall summon the Druchii to your side, and together, we shall embark on our journey to Goldmoor. The city shall tremble beneath your feet, and your name shall be whispered in fear and tremble in awe."

A sardonic smile curled upon Phoenix's lips, his eyes ablaze with an insatiable thirst for power. "Go forth, then, and rouse the Druchii for the impending tempest," he commanded, his voice resonating with arcane authority. "I shall join you in Goldmoor, where the initial tendrils of our conquest shall take root."

With a final nod of obeisance, Qellaun departed the tower, his shadowy figure swallowed by the ever-present obscurity of Flameford. The looming abyss of their ambitions extended far and wide, and the destinies of both master and servant were inexorably entwined in the impending maelstrom of their conquest.

Chapter 1

Enchanted Encounter in the Purplefire Woods

In the heart of E'vahona, Keisha, an Eldarin elf of ethereal grace, stood like a forest nymph incarnate, her very presence an ode to the luxuriant woodlands that cradled her youth. Her steps, delicate as a butterfly's wing flutter, seemed to resonate with a whispered sonnet to the verdant realm surrounding her. By her side, Pumpkin, her sleek panther companion, moved as if woven into the silent tapestry of the emerald domain itself.

Keisha bore the mystic artistry, a legacy passed down by her mother, Serena, a gifted archer whose aim had been as unerring as the love she held for her daughter. Keisha's fingers caressed the exquisitely crafted bow, once Serena's, and with every stride, she carried her mother's wisdom and the weight of her enduring legacy, a torchbearer of ancestral knowledge.

Golden rays from the sun filtered through the towering forest canopy, conjuring ephemeral dance patterns of light and shadow upon their meandering path. Like deep emerald pools, Keisha's gaze flickered upward to the cathedral-like branches above. Beneath the ancient arboreal sentinels, it was here that memories of her parents lingered like whispers of forgotten songs.

Her father, Eldric, a human mage with hair ablaze like wildfire and eyes as profound as the forest's heart, had instilled the arcane currents now coursing through her veins. Inheriting his eyes, Keisha beheld his wisdom and boundless love. Together, they had forged a home where love and magic had intertwined their destinies, like ivy embracing an ancient oak.

As Keisha continued her odyssey through E'vahona, she couldn't escape the sense of her father's latent magic resonating within her—a dormant power she had left unexplored since his passing. The reminiscences of her ancestral abode, now distant, held the elusive key to unleashing her dormant potential, like a sealed scroll waiting to be unfurled.

The love of her parents, her mother's teachings, and her father's arcane legacy converged, thrusting Keisha into her quest. Though her childhood home lay behind her, the enduring legacy of her parents carved a luminous path for her to follow, beckoning her to rekindle the long-lost magic dwelling within her like a phoenix rising from the ashes.

Drawing near a babbling stream, Keisha's curiosity beckoned her toward its crystalline waters. With a graceful extension of her slender fingers, she dipped them into the stream's cool embrace, savoring the refreshing sensation that coursed through her veins. Contentment washed over her as she retrieved her well-worn pack, each scar and marking a testament to countless odysseys. She filled her water container with practiced precision, and the soft click of sealing it reverberated through the tranquil forest, a ritual of preparation and determination.

Nestling securely within her pack, her trusty longbow and arrows lay vigilant at her side, like loyal sentinels of the forest. The dappled rays of the sun painted a mesmerizing path ahead, and an inexplicable urge compelled her to delve deeper into the woods, unveiling the mysteries hidden within its enchanted bosom, as if beckoned by ancient whispers.

Renewed in her determination, Keisha forged ahead on her journey through Vacari, guided by the echoes of her parents' memories and their enduring legacy. As she ventured deeper into the forest's core, the surroundings underwent a subtle transformation. She stood at the threshold of the fabled Purplefire Woods, where the air hung heavy with enchantment, and the ancient trees formed a natural gateway to the mystical depths beyond, like the entrance to a forgotten realm where dreams and reality intertwined.

Unwavering in her loyalty, Pumpkin moved beside Keisha with the same ethereal grace that had seen them through the realm of Vacari. Their bond remained unshakable, a testament to their cultivated enduring companionship. Together, they embarked on a journey deeper into the mystical heart of the forest, where the very air crackled with latent magic, promising revelations and trials in equal measure.

With unyielding resolve, she ventured closer to the forest's edge, crossing the threshold into the enchanting forest known as Purplefire Woods. In the distance, an alluring cascade beckoned with its melodious call, an ancient and irresistible refrain.

Drawing nearer, Keisha emerged into a concealed clearing, where the world unfolded in a tapestry of vibrant greens and sparkling waters. There, before her, a waterfall descended with a grace that seemed almost mystical, its crystalline waters merging seamlessly with a tranquil, deep stream. The sight stirred her elven heart, and a gentle smile graced her as she stepped closer to witness this hidden treasure.

The cascade's waters pirouetted like liquid crystal. Each drop was a radiant testament to nature's sublime artistry. A secret jubilation bubbled within her as she beheld this sanctified oasis. With an eager yearning to become one with its refreshing embrace, she slipped beyond a curtain of vibrant foliage. Her attire cascaded to the forest floor with an elven grace, unveiling her resplendent crimson hair and eyes as verdant as the heart of the woods.

Meanwhile, a solitary figure emerged further down the forest's winding trail: a dark-haired human, his piercing blue eyes mirroring the azure heavens above. The distant serenade of flowing water reached his keen ears, tugging at his senses with a blend of thirst and tenacity.

A sigh of relief escaped his lips as he stumbled upon the elusive water source just when hope had begun to wane. His eyes met those of his steadfast black steed, Thunder, an unspoken covenant forged between them. "Soon, my noble companion," he whispered, his voice laced with gratitude. He guided Thunder toward the alluring clearing with a steady hand upon the reins, where their fates intertwined with the beguiling waters that summoned them both.

Venturing deeper into the forest, the towering canopy gradually receded, unveiling a serene glade bathed in dappled sunlight. The tranquility of the place found the harmonious company of a melodic female voice that filled the air with enchanting harmonies akin to the whispered secrets of woodland spirits. A wistful smile tugged at his lips as he mused, "It seems I am not the sole seeker of solace in this concealed haven."

Amidst the serenity of the grove, his light-hearted laughter echoed through the air, causing the verdant grass to sway in joyful greeting. Yet, his mirthful disposition came to an abrupt halt as he arrived at the clear stream winding through the heart of the meadow. He blinked, half-suspecting that his eyes had conspired to deceive him. In bewildered disbelief, he rubbed his eyes futilely, attempting to confirm his vision, only to be met with the same mesmerizing sight.

Before him, across the stream, a tableau of ethereal beauty unfolded amidst the dappled tapestry of shadows and glistening waters. An Eladrin with fiery red tresses and porcelain skin, bathed in the golden caress of sunlight, was gracefully ensconced in the stream's gentle embrace. Her presence exuded a surreal, otherworldly elegance within this hidden sanctuary.

Whispering to himself, he couldn't help but muse, "Perhaps I should linger here a while, a mere observer. It has been far too long since I've beheld such an enchanting sight."

As he lowered himself onto the supple grass, intending to savor the captivating spectacle, a faint sound from his steadfast steed disrupted the tranquil moment.

The Eladrin's emerald eyes swiftly swiveled toward the source of the disturbance, locking onto the human's presence as he rested on the grass. Gentle yet tinged with caution, her voice inquired, "What brings you to this place?"

His laughter reverberated through the clearing, akin to a soothing melody. "What else, my dear? I am but an observer, here to partake in this place's beauty and its residents' grace."

She gestured toward a panther named Pumpkin, a creature that moved with the fluidity of shadows, beckoning the beast to engage. Pumpkin leaped lithely in front of the man, her sleek ebony form a testament to his feline prowess. The man instinctively stepped back, his hand inching toward the hilt of his sword, a wariness born of respect for the imposing predator.

The Eladrin, now carrying a hint of amusement, offered a cautious counsel, "I would advise you against any hasty moves. Pumpkin is bound to my will and shall remain docile unless provoked. Attempt to unsheathe your sword, and you'll find her quicker than your blade."

His gaze shifted to the vigilant panther, whose amber eyes held an enigmatic intelligence. Honoring the warning, he slowly withdrew his hand, acutely aware of the gravity of his choice. He returned his focus to the Eladrin, who glided gracefully towards the water's edge, her vibrant hair cascading like a fiery waterfall.

A mischievous smile teased the corners of his lips as he goaded, "Carry on, dear Eladrin. I am but a humble warrior, eager to witness more of your captivating allure."

In response, she cast a reproachful glare in his direction. "Avert your eyes, warrior!"

Undaunted, he let out a soft chuckle. "Why should I when I am graced with such an enchanting vista?"

A tension-laden exchange in the forest's heart unfolded, where two distinct worlds collided amid nature's splendors. Her fiery spirit blazed forth as she scowled at him, her command carrying the weight of an empress's decree. "Warrior, once more, I insist that you avert your gaze, or it might be the last thing you ever behold."

Yet, he, a mischievous trickster with mischief twinkling in his eyes, couldn't resist a jest even in the face of peril. Laughter wove its carefree dance through his voice as he quipped, "Ah, to meet my fate in the company of such a captivating spectacle." His grin broadened, stoking the emerald fires that smoldered within her verdant gaze. "A swift temper, it appears, is your steadfast companion."

Her glare deepened, her determination unshaken. "What else would you expect?"

Partaking in the playful exchange, his laughter slipped between their words, "My dear, if you keep this up, our charming stranger might just find himself yearning for more of your fiery eloquence."

Her frustration deepened, her patience teetering on the brink. "And you, warrior, should be on my side."

But he merely winked, his countenance unrepentant. "Ah, where's the amusement in that? I've always relished a spirited spectacle."

In the heart of the forest, it seemed, nature had become the audience for this playful skirmish of wits and resolve, observing with curious eyes.

He ventured a daring proposal, mischief dancing in his gaze. His words presented as an irresistible challenge. "Here's a wager, my dear Eladrin. I shall avert my gaze, granting you the privacy you seek to attire yourself, but with one condition—afterward, you must share your name and bestow upon me a reward for my impeccable conduct."

She bristled with anger at the audacious proposition, yet the weight of her predicament draped over her like a heavy mantle. "Agreed," she grudgingly assented.

He pivoted, his back to her, while the forest leaves rustled, their whispers carrying the secrets of the woods. She emerged from the stream's embrace, her form ensconced in silken garments that clung gracefully to her lithe frame. Swiftly, she garbed herself in attire befitting a woodland archer elf woven with the verdant hues of the forest itself. Retrieving her longbow, her movements flowed with an elegance imbued with purpose.

Drawing nearer, her presence carried the regal air of the ancient arboreal sentinels surrounding them. Her voice bore a note of caution and pride as she finally spoke, "I am Keisha, an Eladrin of E'vahona."

He turned back to face her, his eyes widening in genuine surprise. "Keisha," he repeated, savoring the name like a rare ambrosia. "A name as enchanting as the forest's melody."

Ong Swifthammer, who had observed their exchange with amusement, couldn't resist teasing her again. "Well done, Keisha. You've managed to keep your name a treasure well-guarded."

With the wager fulfilled and the forest's secrets woven into their encounter, the dark-haired warrior pivoted again to meet Keisha's gaze. A boyish grin played upon his lips as he introduced himself, his voice carrying the weight of newfound camaraderie. "I am Ong Swifthammer, a warrior of a distant city, now a humble wanderer of these woods."

Keisha acknowledged his introduction with a nod, her eyes reflecting a newfound warmth. "It is a pleasure to make your acquaintance, Ong Swifthammer."

Ong Swifthammer, adorned in armor that seamlessly blended black, silver, and green hues, bore the indelible marks of his odyssey through these bewitched woods. Having observed their banter and exchanged introductions, the forest seemed to emanate a serene benediction as they pressed onward together. The enigmatic woods whispered their hidden truths, promising uncharted adventures, while the bonds of friendship and shared tales burgeoned with each passing heartbeat.

Like a siren's call amid an enchanted forest, Keisha's voice beckoned Ong as he guided Thunder to the tranquil stream's crystalline edge. Like custodians of ancient lore, the waters carried their voices away, allowing their words to drift like leaves on a calm river. "Why have you ventured into Purplefire Woods?" she inquired, her tone imbued with genuine curiosity.

Within the tranquil arboreal haven, Ong turned to face her, his countenance earnest beneath the dappling sunlight that filtered through the verdant canopy. "I traverse these sacred woods on a mission of utmost importance," he began, his words flowing with the unyielding currents of duty. "The very lives of Goldmoor's sovereigns, King Alex and Queen Jeanne, hang in perilous balance, threatened by a sinister coalition of Druchii and an ominous warlock. I am bound by an oath to shield them from this impending darkness."

Their discourse unfolded like an intricate tapestry, woven with threads of destiny, each utterance adding a vivid hue to their shared purpose. In the heart of E'vahona, where the symphony of nature's rhythms played in harmonious concert, the convergence of Ong and Keisha felt like a poetic opus of determination and courage.

In the forest's heart, where the air thrummed with the age-old woodland secrets, Keisha's emerald eyes gleamed with thoughtful concern. Her presence, reminiscent of a guardian spirit of the woods, bore witness to the unfolding drama of destiny.

Her understanding unfurled with a quiet resolve that echoed the rustling leaves overhead. "I comprehend the gravity of the situation," she replied, words akin to a gentle breeze weaving through the forest's boughs.

"It may indeed be time for me to lend my bow to the defense of Goldmoor against these menacing Druchii."

However, as unyielding as the mightiest oak, Ong met her determination with a gaze that bore the weight of heartfelt concern. He shook his head, a protective aura enveloping him, a sentiment only a trusted friend could elicit. "Nay, Keisha," he cautioned, his voice a subdued murmur in the tranquil sanctuary of the woods. "The path leading to Goldmoor is fraught with peril, and the darkness that descends upon it is no ordinary shadow. It is a journey not to be undertaken lightly."

A spark of defiance, as searing as a lightning bolt, momentarily flared within her emerald eyes. Yet, beneath the surface, a steady determination simmered like an unseen current coursing through the forest's heart. Her lips curled into a fleeting, disdainful sneer—an unspoken rejoinder to his words.

Despite the fierce thoughts within her, Keisha opted for the pragmatic path of silence. She had always been a creature of deeds rather than words, her resolve unyielding and her spirit as untamed as the woodland itself. With a reluctant nod, she yielded to the wisdom of the moment, recognizing the futility of a fruitless debate. "Very well, Ong," she conceded, her voice akin to a soft breeze whispering through the leaves.

Ong's countenance blossomed with a warm, almost paternal smile as he redirected his attention to the ever-faithful Pumpkin, the shadowy panther who had silently witnessed their exchange. He retrieved a piece of tender deer meat from his horse's saddlebag, a token of gratitude for the vigilant guardian. With a deft flick of his wrist, he cast the succulent morsel towards Pumpkin, who responded with a low, resonant growl of appreciation. The sleek and graceful panther lunged with feline agility to claim its prize before retreating to a secluded nook in the clearing.

Keisha observed the silent interaction between man and beast, her eyes gleaming with an understanding that hinted at her comprehension of the unspoken bond that united them. "It appears you have forged a profound connection," she remarked, her voice carrying the weight of acknowledgment.

Ong nodded in agreement, his gaze remaining affixed to Pumpkin. "Indeed," he affirmed, his words resonating like the hushed rustle of leaves in a sacred grove. "A connection destined to burgeon with each passing day, for loyalty and companionship are the most precious treasures of our journey."

A fleeting smile graced Ong's lips as he shifted his attention back to Keisha, his emerald eyes shimmering with a mischievous spark. "But, Keisha," he began, his voice akin to the whispers of leaves in a secret forest, "since I have conducted myself with the utmost decorum, it appears you owe me a reward."

Keisha couldn't help but emit a soft, musical chuckle in response to his playful overture. Her tone bore the gentle cadence of a forest stream as she inquired, "And pray tell, what form should this coveted reward take?"

Ong's grin took on a sly and enigmatic quality as he extended his arm, his strong fingers gently enveloping her waist. With a purposeful yet graceful motion, he drew her closer into his embrace, his warm breath a caress upon her earlobe as he whispered against her lips. His voice was akin to the soft breeze rustling through the leaves of an ancient tree, "A kiss."

Keisha's fair cheeks adorned themselves with a delicate shade of pink, her gaze trapped by the cerulean depths of his eyes. Her instinct urged her to refuse and step back from this tender precipice. However, within the azure pools of his gaze, she discovered an unspoken promise that beckoned her to place her trust in him. Slowly, she yielded to the implied invitation and nodded, her emerald eyes reflecting a newfound vulnerability.

With an air of reverence, he leaned closer, his lips as soft as petals brushing against the ethereal curve of her neck. A delicate tremor coursed through her being as if the very roots of her existence had awakened beneath the gentle caress of his affection. They found themselves embraced by a tapestry of blossoming wildflowers, their fragrant perfumes mingling with the intoxicating allure of the moment.

As if guided by the unseen hand of the forest itself, he lowered her down onto the verdant tapestry below. Their shared laughter danced through the air, a harmonious duet that echoed amidst the leaves and blooming petals, a melody sung by nature's hidden heart.

When their lips finally melded in a tender, heartfelt kiss, it was as though a floodgate had swung open within them, unleashing a cascade of emotions akin to a symphony of heartbeats resonating in the tranquil hush of the forest. Keisha's breath caught a soft gasp that harmonized with his own. As their kiss deepened, they surrendered to the timeless embrace of the wilderness, their love a fragile yet potent force interwoven into the very fabric of nature.

Yet, as their enchanting union unfolded like a tapestry of dreams, the world around them seemed to stir as if the forest's whispers summoned them to its secret heart. The presence of Pumpkin, their vigilant guardian, returned with a graceful demeanor, intruding upon the lovers' intimate interlude. With a tinge of reluctance, Ong assisted Keisha to her feet, their gazes locked in a shared understanding that transcended the limitations of spoken language.

With a parting kiss that lingered, he released her, his fingers tracing a tender path from the nape of her neck to the fiery cascade of her hair. As he teased, a playful smirk played upon his lips, his voice a low, melodic refrain, "It seems our feline friend possesses impeccable timing, my dear. Thanks to Pumpkin, the symphony of our stolen moments must yield to the eternal serenade of the forest."

Keisha's lips curved into a knowing smile, their connection unbreakable. "Ong," she murmured his name, her voice as soft as the whispering leaves in the forest's embrace. "It appears you are a harbinger of adventure."

His smirk deepened, and his sapphire eyes shimmered with a playful promise that resonated with the very heartbeat of the woods. "Ah, Keisha, rest assured, this is but the overture. You may return to your path for now, but remember this forest and me. I pledge that the threads of destiny have woven our fates together, and our dance has only just begun."

In this enchanting forest clearing, bathed in the sun's warm embrace, Ong and Keisha reluctantly parted ways. Now bound by an inexplicable connection, their souls pulsed with an ethereal energy that transcended the mundane world. As they bid each other farewell, a sense of longing lingered in the air, akin to the fading notes of a half-remembered melody.

Ong stepped back into reality, his heart reverberating with the memory of their encounter. He couldn't help but feel the weight of his solitude as he tended to his noble steed, Thunder. The horse, a steadfast companion, embodied a silent understanding of the complexities of the human heart.

Its ebony coat shimmered like the night sky, starkly contrasting the vibrant emotions that swirled within Ong.

Mounted upon Thunder, Ong guided his loyal steed onto the familiar forest path, but the world around him had transformed. The dense foliage shrouded them, and the symphony of nature's orchestra filled the air—a gentle rustling of leaves, the melodious song of unseen birds, and the distant murmur of a hidden stream. The forest seemed to echo the profound connection he had forged on this fateful day.

Yet, beneath the serene surface of the forest's tranquility, Ong's thoughts roiled like a storm in the depths of his mind. He couldn't escape the enigma that was Keisha, a captivating presence that had penetrated his defenses like no other. "She has unlocked chambers within me that lay dormant," he reflected, his words carried away by the winds that whispered secrets to the ancient trees. "There is an aura of uniqueness, an uncharted territory in her presence. Why does she affect me so profoundly? I must seek her out again to uncover the answers."

With renewed determination, he gathered the reins again, his gaze fixed upon the path ahead, veiled in intrigue. The enigmatic Keisha had etched her presence upon his heart, and he knew their journey was commencing—a tapestry of mysteries and desires waiting to be unraveled. As he turned Thunder toward the distant horizon and the looming city of Goldmoor, the promise of adventure and discovery beckoned him forward like a siren's call that could not be denied.

On the other hand, Keisha found herself entangled in a web of emotions, her heart still racing from the encounter that had left her both irritated and irresistibly intrigued. Her slender fingers deftly smoothed the forest-green fabric of her attire, the vibrant hue matching the depths of her emerald eyes that shimmered with a captivating blend of irritation and fascination.

As she watched Ong, his silhouette melding with the lush embrace of the forest, she couldn't help but ponder the enigma he represented. "He will linger in my thoughts," she admitted, a sigh escaping her lips and a wistfulness softening her features. "And I'm left bewildered by the profound impact of his kiss. Such a sensation has never touched me before."

Amid her contemplations, a bittersweet memory surged like a haunting specter from the depths of her past. She was transported back to her childhood when her parents' love had been an unbreakable bond, an invincible fortress in her young eyes. Back then, she believed nothing could harm them, that their love would shield them from any harm that might befall them.

But life had a way of teaching harsh lessons. The memory of their untimely demise, their love extinguished by cruel fate, resurfaced, bringing a wave of sorrow. She couldn't hold back the tears that welled up, each drop a testament to the scars still lingering deep within her soul.

Keisha questioned whether she should dare to open her heart to Ong to embrace this newfound connection, knowing the heartache that love could bring. Her tears fell like silent rain, a poignant reminder of her parents' tragic end. She cried not only for their loss but for the uncertainty of what lay ahead with Ong, the fear of risking her heart once more in the face of a love that might be as fragile as it was profound.

Summoning her feline companion with a commanding gesture, she beckoned Pumpkin, the ebony panther materializing from the inky shadows like a specter from the night. "Pumpkin, heed my call!" With her unwavering protector, she fixed her gaze toward the distant city of Goldmoor, her resolve unyielding. "Our path leads us to Goldmoor. He shall soon realize that challenging my determination only strengthens my resolve. Moreover, if the Druchii are entangled in this intricate web of intrigue, the Eladrin must be made aware."

Pumpkin, a vigilant and loyal presence, fell into graceful stride beside her. They ventured deeper into the forest in unity, their footsteps blending harmoniously with the symphony of rustling leaves and the distant murmur of life. They followed the invisible threads of destiny that wove their fate toward the city where the enigmatic tapestry of the future awaited, a city brimming with secrets and challenges yet to be unveiled.

Chapter 2

Shadowfall Over Goldmoor: Phoenix and the Druchii's Conquest

Amidst an opalescent sky painted with strokes of twilight, Phoenix Shadowwalker sat majestically, every inch the evil sorcerer, upon his awe-inspiring mount, Zylron. The dragon was a monstrous marvel; his scales sparkled with the fiery glow of a dying sun and the raw power of a volcano on the cusp of eruption. Each flap of Zylron's titanic wings sent shivers through the canopy below, causing even the eldest of the emerald trees to shudder and whisper timeworn tales to the mischievous winds that pirouetted gracefully around them.

Far beyond the immediate verdure, the majestic city of Goldmoor stretched across the horizon. Like a crown jewel set against the backdrop of the world's end, Goldmoor, the Realm of Vacari's heart and soul, glittered with an ethereal luminosity, seemingly unaware of the tempest brewing above.

A chilling glee played on Phoenix's lips, his eyes, deep and blazing like the heart of an inferno, unwaveringly focused on the luminous city beneath. When he spoke, his voice was a melody of menace, intertwining with the symphony of the dragon's rhythmic wingbeats. "Zylron, my unwavering sentinel of the skies," he whispered with evil delight, "soon we shall plummet upon Goldmoor, consuming it like the relentless storm we are. Should the accursed Druchii dare to weave himself from the tapestries of legend as the prophecies have forewarned, the throne of Vacari will not elude my grasp. Soon, an eclipse of unparalleled darkness will trap the world, and all will tremble beneath our shadow."

Zylron, a colossal beast whose majestic form defied the bounds of reality, lowered his titanic head, casting a profound gaze from his luminescent eyes. Those radiant orbs held a deep intelligence that clashed starkly with the terrifying countenance he wore. A cavernous, sonorous rumble, akin to a symphony of purr and growl woven together, resonated from the very core of the dragon's throat, affirming an unbreakable bond that transcended mere mortal comprehension.

Above, in the boundless expanse of the heavens, Phoenix, the precursor of audacious ambition, let loose a chilling laughter that reverberated through the sky. Like an unholy overture, his mirth heralded the impending storm that would soon unfurl its dark wings. "Fret not, Zylron," he declared, his words carried away by the whimsical winds that danced around them. "For you shall have your choice of those brave enough to defy our dominion, and their fates shall be irrevocably sealed within the fiery embrace of your breath."

The city of Goldmoor, a shining jewel in the heart of the horizon, drew ever nearer. Its gleaming spires pierced the heavens with audacious pride, and its towering walls, standing resolute against the encroaching wilderness, emerged with increasing clarity. Goldmoor was a beacon of civilization amidst the untamed wilderness that sprawled beyond, a testament to humanity's tenacity. Phoenix and Zylron, two enigmatic figures, descended upon the city with a foreboding presence akin to harbingers of doom. Their destinies wove together in a dark, intricate ballet, an impending drama of power and conquest. Before them, the kingdom lay in tantalizing promise, and the world teetered on the precipice of a profound change that would forever reshape the annals of history.

Zylron, the colossal crimson dragon, lowered his massive head with a sense of impending destiny. His eyes blazed with an anticipatory fervor as they drew nearer to the heart of their audacious ambitions. The vast panorama of Goldmoor unfurled before them, its architectural marvels standing as monuments to a time long past. Shrouded in a billowing cloak that framed him like a harbinger of shadows, Phoenix leaned closer to his draconic companion. "Not just yet, Zylron," he murmured, a sly smile playing upon his lips like an unspoken prophecy. "Before we unveil our grand design, we must ensure the Druchii are precisely where we need them."

With the grace of an artist, Zylron descended upon an emerald clearing nestled beyond the city's imposing walls. The venerable trees of the ancient forest, their gnarled branches intertwined like elders in council, seemed to rustle in agreement, acknowledging the gravity of this momentous occasion. As they touched down, Phoenix's calculating gaze shifted to the waiting Druchii—a shadowy assembly, their armor as black as the abyss's deepest depths.

Standing with regal poise, Phoenix commanded attention, his presence an irresistible force. "Are we ready to proceed?" he inquired, his voice a velvety decree laced with unwavering authority.

From the depths of the shadows emerged Qellaun Deadcrusher, Phoenix's loyal lieutenant. His eyes gleamed with the predatory hunger of a faithful hound, poised to strike on the scent of his master's desire. "Yes, my lord, we stand poised to act upon your command," he affirmed with a respectful bow, his voice a chorus of unwavering allegiance that echoed through the ancient trees as if sealing their pact with the very essence of the forest itself.

A solemn nod from Phoenix forged the sinister covenant, sealing their unholy alliance. "Bear this in mind," he cautioned, his voice resonating like a malevolent chant, "We must ensnare the King and Queen in the living flesh. Their existence shall serve as the vise gripping the hearts of the people. So long as they draw breath, none shall dare to challenge the supremacy we wield."

"Crystal clear," Qellaun intoned, his soul pulsating with imminent conquest's electric thrill.

Phoenix reunited with Zylron, his fingers intertwined with the dragon's fiery mane, a crimson coronet merging seamlessly with the molten hues of the twilight sky. He cast one final, ominous glance towards his loyal Druchii, a wicked grin on his lips. "Let the tapestry of fate unfurl its shadows," he declared, his voice a cryptic whisper, its echoes resounding with the ominous pledge of absolute dominion. "The hour has come to grasp them by the threads and deliver this city into my outstretched palm."

The Druchii, cloaked in obsidian armor that gleamed with an eerie allure, fell into formation, a procession as stealthy as serpents slithering through the veins of Goldmoor's labyrinthine streets. As they infiltrated the cobblestone arteries of the city, the ancient stones bore mute witness to their silent, predatory advance.

Perched upon the colossal crimson dragon Zylron, Phoenix ascended above the city's time-worn spires, his eyes ablaze with the feverish anticipation of impending cataclysm, like a sorcerer surveying the city of his dominion.

The sorcerer of unparalleled might, Phoenix unleashed the storm of his arcane magic with a mere flick of his outstretched hand. A searing inferno burst forth from his fingertips, melding seamlessly with the fiery breath of his draconic ally. The once-impregnable archers perched atop the towering battlements, trapped within an all-consuming conflagration. Their anguished screams split the heavens as they were cast into the relentless embrace of the earth below, their fates irrevocably bound to the rigorous fusion of sorcery and draconic power.

Simultaneously, amidst the convoluted maze of alleys and boulevards that crisscrossed the city, the Druchii embarked upon a sinister dance of death. Dark magic crackled like malevolent lightning, manifesting as ominous energy bolts that seared through the ranks of guards audacious enough to obstruct their relentless advance. The resounding clash of steel and the cacophonous wails of agony resonated through the air as the Druchii, masters of the martial arts, engaged their foes in a gruesome ballet of brutality. Lifeless bodies descended like raindrops within a cyclone, forming a haunting testament to the unyielding resolve of Phoenix's malevolent comrades.

The once-pristine thoroughfares of Goldmoor, now besmirched with the gruesome tableau of their passage, bore witness to the chilling march of death and chaos. With every unrelenting stride, they etched a harrowing tapestry of devastation and carnage upon the city's canvas—a vivid testament to their unwavering pursuit of dominion and the sinister aspirations that shrouded their evil cause.

As the veil of impending night descended upon the outer terrace, it shrouded the royal guards of Goldmoor in ethereal shadows. Bedecked in armor that glittered like molten defiance, they unsheathed their gleaming swords, catching the last fading rays of sunlight. The blades ignited with a radiant blaze, casting an incandescent gleam upon the time-worn cobblestones. With their unwavering resolve, these stalwart defenders formed an impenetrable phalanx around their sovereigns—King Alex and Queen Jeanne—forging an indomitable bulwark against the encroaching storm of hostility.

Qellaun, the living embodiment of audacity among the Druchii, strode forth with a sinister air of confidence. His obsidian armor, etched with arcane runes that whispered of dark enchantments, seemed to narrate tales of maleficence with every echoing footfall. Tension hung thick in the air as he locked eyes with King Alex, a sarcastic smirk curving his lips. His audacious challenge resonated like a sinister symphony, an ominous prelude to the impending trials. "If death were our sole pursuit," Qellaun taunted, his voice a chilling refrain, "your men would now be but ashes. Worry not, King Alex, for Phoenix's designs transcend mortal comprehension."

King Alex, a figure of regal stature whose resolve rivaled the formidable walls of his citadel, cast an unwavering gaze upon his beloved Queen Jeanne. Their hands intertwined in a silent testament to their unyielding unity. His attention shifted to the Druchii, his voice resounding with a steely determination. "It would be prudent for you to retreat, for we are a kingdom that bows to no one," he declared, his words a defiant clarion. "Even in the face of death, our legacy shall shine as a beacon of hope, while your rule shall remain a fleeting specter in the annals of history."

An electrifying anticipation hung thick in the night air, pregnant with the promise of destiny, as an immense shadow descended upon the outer terrace of the palace. With a roar and a fierce rush of wind, a dragon, its scales shimmering like obsidian under the moon's otherworldly glow, descended with earth-shaking authority. It was a wondrous and fearsome creature, a living incarnation of ancient power.

A figure draped in the profound darkness emerged from the dragon's formidable back, a silhouette bearing an aura of enigmatic sovereignty. His silver hair cascaded like a radiant waterfall of liquid moonlight, a stark contrast to the unfathomable depths of his eyes, which appeared to harbor the secrets of eternity itself. With an imperious gesture, he compelled the royal guards to yield, their armor yielding begrudgingly to his will, as he advanced towards King Alex.

Intrigue and trepidation danced on the breath of the night as the enigmatic figure addressed the beleaguered monarch. His voice, as velvety as it was resolute, cut through the tension like a blade through the veil of darkness. "You possess keen insight, King Alex," he declared, his words dripping with a calculated menace. "The unwavering loyalty of your people to you is irrefutable. Therefore, I shall not claim your lives this night. Instead, I shall entrust them to the guardianship of these Druchii."

A shiver of chilling murmurs coursed through the assembled guards and courtiers, akin to the ghostly caress of a winter wind. The weight of the enigmatic man's pronouncement bore upon their shoulders, and the atmosphere crackled with palpable, eerie tension. King Alex and Queen Jeanne, once rulers of a thriving city, now teetered precariously on the brink of an abyss, mere pawns in a grand and malevolent scheme.

Beneath the boundless expanse of the cerulean sky, the titanic form of Zylron, the resplendent crimson dragon, descended upon a vast, undulating field. His arrival reverberated with earth-shattering solemnity, the very ground quivering beneath the awe-inspiring weight of his presence. As his colossal frame contacted the earth, the winds, now imbued with ancient wisdom, whispered their secrets in hushed reverence. Their playful dances took on the quality of an ode to the majestic creature that had graced their kingdom.

The day's taxing flight had exacted its toll on the mighty dragon. His wings, once unfurled like banners of unparalleled power, now rested gently against his massive body. Zylron had sought refuge in this secluded haven, a sanctuary untouched by the chaos of battle and the intrigues of rulers, where he could find solace and regain his strength. His fiery exhalations, once raging torrents of flame, now flowed in a steady, soothing cadence reminiscent of a dragon's lullaby.

This field, embraced by the nurturing arms of nature, had become his sanctuary. Here, amidst the whispering leaves and the rustling grasses, Zylron surrendered to the exhaustion that had enveloped his formidable frame. As the stars unveiled themselves in the velvety tapestry above, the dragon's colossal eyes finally drifted shut, and the dreams of an ancient and eternal being whisked him away to uncharted forests.

As time flowed on, a subtle transformation coursed through Zylron. His monumental chest's rhythmic rise and fall gradually slowed, and the radiant fire in his eyes began to dim, bearing the weight of the day's toils. It was a dragon's slumber, a mystical spectacle where a creature of boundless might yielded to the tender embrace of dreams. His massive form settled upon the field like a guardian titan, his scaly hide absorbing the warmth of the land as he held vigil over the earth's enigmatic secrets.

Time flowed on, and the world lay enshrouded in an eerie stillness, where even the breeze held its breath, allowing only the gentle rustling of the field's grasses to break the silence. Zylron, the indomitable sentinel, had surrendered to the realm of dreams, and his measured, unhurried breaths became the pulse of a world steeped in the tapestry of antiquity and fantasy.

In the delicate caress of twilight's dim glow, Phoenix, the enigmatic Warlock, executed a subtle pivot upon his heel. His eyes, twin orbs of unfathomable abyss, danced with an unsettling amalgamation of power and joy. In the presence of this enigmatic figure, an aura of mystique and whispered malevolence clung like a shroud as if he were a living embodiment of the world's concealed enigmas. Before him stood the King and Queen, adorned in regal splendor, their attire resplendent with the noble sigils of Goldmoor, defiant pillars amidst a storm, their guards brandishing weapons in a futile display of resistance.

Phoenix's voice, a lyrical symphony tinged with the chill of ominous intent, draped the air in a haunting melody. "I would extend," he continued, his words lingering like the ghostly echoes of a sinister song, "the counsel that your guardians lay down their arms unless they harbor a genuine desire to witness the untimely snuffing out of their own lives. You find yourselves at a numerical disadvantage, and I would prefer to avoid the unnecessary staining of these cobbles with crimson."

King Alex, an unyielding sovereign whose heart rivaled the kingdom he ruled, cast a tender, reassuring glance toward his cherished Queen Jeanne. With a reluctant nod, he redirected his gaze to the loyal sentinels who had pledged their unwavering allegiance to his service. "Lower your weapons," he intoned with the solemnity of a painful decision, "not for my sake, but for the sake of my beloved Queen. We yield, not out of frailty, but out of wisdom."

A sarcastic laugh escaped Phoenix's lips, its eerie resonance lingering like the phantom of a sinister melody. "Ah, the fervor of love," he mused, his gaze shifting to the captive Queen Jeanne, "a potent and capricious force." In his words, there simmered a nebulous pledge.

Phoenix's focus shifted toward Qellaun, his unwavering lieutenant, a figure enshrouded in shadow amidst the ranks of the Druchii. "You," he commanded, his voice heavy with unquestioned dominion, "shall ensure their separation in captivity. We cannot entertain the notion of King Alex hatching an escape, for it would imperil the life of his beloved Queen Jeanne."

With a solemn bow, Qellaun acknowledged his unwavering loyalty to the Warlock's directives. "As you decree," he affirmed, loyalty woven into every syllable.

Phoenix's laughter, a jarring counterpoint to the King's self-sacrifice, rippled through the taut, nocturnal atmosphere. "Take her away," he pronounced, sealing Queen Jeanne's fate. Darkness and destiny converged in this city, where love and intrigue twined in a fragile dance.

King Alex, a noble spirit aflame with a sincere devotion for Queen Jeanne, surged like a radiant guardian. A bastion of regal resolve, he stood unwavering between his cherished consort and the encroaching Druchii, a vigilant sentinel sworn to defy the looming shadows.

The sinister forces against King Alex were as evil as the very shroud of night itself. With a malefic grace, one of the Druchii, propelled by a hostility that oozed like venom, struck King Alex with a vicious blow. The impact sent him sprawling, a cry of torment escaping his lips as he was ruthlessly flung aside. Queen Jeanne, her wrists trapped with eerie elegance, became the captive of this lurking malevolence.

The Druchii, akin to phantoms of darkness, moved with an unsettling precision to claim their coveted prize. In that fleeting moment, Queen Jeanne's gaze locked onto King Alex's, and an unspoken exchange of love and despair unfolded. Torn from his side, she vanished into the abyss of shadow, leaving the King's anguished cry to resonate through the city. "I shall find you and set you free, my love," he vowed, his voice quivering under the weight of his boundless love and unwavering resolve. "Do not succumb to despair."

Qellaun, the embodiment of ruthless cruelty, allowed a cruel smirk to curl upon his lips as he redirected his attention to the stricken King Alex. His voice, steeped in malice, slithered through the night like a serpent's sinister hiss. "King Alex," he taunted, his words a dire omen, "divert your concerns less toward her and more toward your fate, for should you falter, envision the relentless horrors that will befall your beloved Queen." In this realm of dark magic and ceaseless ambition, love stood as a fragile ember amidst the encroaching shadows, and the stage was set for an explosive battle where hope and despair waged an unending war.

Keisha's odyssey through the enchanting depths of the Forest resembled a mystical pilgrimage of sorts. Ancient trees, their branches adorned with vibrant foliage, had taken on the role of her silent guides as she ventured beyond the confines of Goldmoor. With a subtle and graceful gesture, she beckoned forth her loyal companion, Pumpkin, a lithe and sleek panther whose eyes burned like emerald flames. In mere moments, Keisha and her feline ally found their perch atop the city's imposing walls. Their presence exuded an aura of unwavering determination.

Below them, a somber tableau unfolded. King Alex and Queen Jeanne, regal figures ensnared within an evil web, confronted their captor, the nefarious Warlock known as Phoenix. Above, a colossal red dragon, a living specter of dread, ascended into the boundless expanse of the heavens, its fiery breath dissipating into the distant skies. Keisha's heart quickened as she pondered her options, her discerning gaze firmly fixed upon the plight of the imprisoned monarchs.

At this dire crossroads, Ong, an eruptive force of nature, thundered onto the scene astride his ebony stallion. Druchii's adversaries were sent tumbling in his wake, his sword gleaming with righteous fury as he demanded the immediate release of the royal captives. Keisha's brow furrowed in vexation at his impetuous arrival, an unpredictable element woven into the intricate tapestry of their carefully crafted plans.

Turning to Pumpkin, her voice a gentle yet commanding cadence, she instructed, "Guard him with unwavering vigilance until my return. I must swiftly concoct a stratagem to thwart the dragon's impending assault upon the city." With that, she descended the gnarled branches of the towering oak, leaving Pumpkin to maintain a steadfast watch upon the precipice of the fortified wall.

As Keisha pressed on toward the presumed landing site of the dragon, her thoughts spilled forth in whispered frustration, each word pregnant with exasperation. "Stubborn man," she grumbled beneath her breath, the weight of her vexation hanging heavy in the air she breathed. Could he not grasp the dire consequences borne of his impulsive actions? With the city's fate teetering on the precipice of chaos, Keisha's mission to subdue the dragon evolved into a harrowing race against the relentless march of time and the impending specter of disorder that loomed ominously on the horizon.

Amid the tumultuous maelstrom swirling like a fierce storm, Ong Swifthammer, a warrior whose very name carried the weight of ancient legends, cleaved his path through the nefarious Druchii who dared to stand in his way. His blade, an extension of his soul, gleamed with fervent righteousness as it sundered the wicked foes who sought to obstruct his advance. The metallic symphony of clashing swords reverberated through the tumultuous air, an anthem of unyielding defiance.

"Clear my path!" Ong's voice, a thunderous battle cry, surged through the atmosphere, an unyielding force that left no room for doubt. His determination blazed like an unquenchable inferno, propelling him ever forward. Druchii warriors, whose hostility was challenged by the warrior's indomitable spirit, fell before his blade in a frenzied combat ballet, their dark ambitions shattered by his unstoppable resolve.

Phoenix, the enigmatic Warlock who held King Alex captive, pivoted with an air of otherworldly authority to confront the intrusion. His visage, chiseled from the harshest depths of resolve, contorted into a scowl as he addressed the audacious monarch. "Who dares to challenge me?" he demanded, his voice a frigid undercurrent slicing through the din of battle.

King Alex, a wise ruler well-versed in the gravity of the moment, bore a defiant smirk that mirrored the unyielding spirit of his people. "Ong Swifthammer," he declared, a note of pride woven into his words. "A warrior hailing from Crystal Vale possessed unwavering determination and boundless ferocity."

Phoenix's authority remained unshaken as he turned his piercing gaze upon Ong Swifthammer, his voice heavy with ominous power. "I command you to withdraw," he decreed, his words resonating like the mournful toll of a death knell. "Or face your inevitable demise." In this climactic confrontation, where the unwavering warrior clashed with the enigmatic Warlock, the kingdom's destiny teetered precariously on edge, a battle where valor fought head-on with otherworldly might.

Amidst the explosive clash of martial prowess and arcane sorcery, Ong Swifthammer, an unyielding and fearless presence, bore a smirk that defied the very forces of fate. His unwavering confidence radiated like a luminous beacon, a testament to his indomitable spirit. "I adhere to one rule," he declared, his eyes gleaming with defiance, "never to heed the commands of a deranged warlock. Now, indulge me and speak your name."

Phoenix, the enigmatic Warlock, locked eyes with Ong in a fusion of disdain and world-weary exasperation. He shook his head with a slow lament as though mourning the stubbornness of a man perched on the precipice of doom. "Swifthammer," Phoenix mused, his voice a harbinger of impending catastrophe, "do you not grasp that your existence hangs by the thinnest thread, ready to be severed in mere moments?" He paused; his tone bore the weight of inescapable authority. "But I shall indulge your curiosity, just this once. My name is Phoenix Shadowwalker, and I hail from the depths of Flameford. Now, heed my words and withdraw."

Ong's sneer, a testament to his unwavering resolve, felt like a blade poised to pierce the turbulent fabric of the chaotic tableau. "I could have guessed," he retorted with biting sarcasm, "that one who bears your visage hails from the accursed Flameford." Ong attempted to approach the captive King with measured strides, but the looming Druchii warriors, like incarnate shadows, obstructed his path.

"Why not," Ong's voice, firm and unwavering, defied the Warlock, "dismiss your lackeys? Release the King, liberate the Queen, and return to your wretched hamlet of Flameford. Stay your hand and avert the impending doom that draws ever nearer." In this dangerous standoff between an invincible warrior and an enigmatic sorcerer, the scales of power swayed precariously, the weight of an impending choice hanging heavily in the air.

The atmosphere grew taut as Ong's unyielding defiance lingered, a spark of audacity in the face of Phoenix's smoldering ire. With an explosive rage, Phoenix glared at the defiant warrior before him. "Enough," he roared, his voice resonating with malevolence. "End him!"

The Druchii, beings woven from the very fabric of shadow and darkness, obediently followed their master's command. They closed in on Ong with unnatural celerity, their weapons poised for the fatal strike. It seemed as though the unyielding warrior's fate had been irrevocably sealed, and the atmosphere crackled with the anticipation of impending doom.

Yet, as if emerging from the abyss of shadows, a streak of obsidian surged from the periphery. It struck with the silent swiftness of darkness, and the air resounded with the eerie symphony of demise. Two Druchii lay lifeless in its wake, their eyes forever sealed to the mortal world.

As the dust of this unexpected clash settled, a magnificent black panther, familiar to Keisha as Pumpkin, stood resolute at Ong's side. Recognition dawned in Ong's eyes as he beheld the majestic creature, a loyal companion who had rushed to his aid. He tenderly caressed Pumpkin's sleek head, and a gratitude and admiration-filled smile graced his lips. Amid this tumultuous and uncertain moment, a profound bond was forged between a warrior and a mystical ally, and the enigmatic tapestry of the fantasy world unfurled in all its captivating splendor.

Amidst the swirling maelstrom of this fantastical showdown, Phoenix's gaze, once ablaze with wrath, now held a glint of morbid curiosity as he regarded the warrior before him. "This is a peculiar occurrence," he confessed with enigmatic intrigue, "the first time I have encountered a warrior of such prowess accompanied by a magnificent feline companion."

Ong responded with a nonchalant shrug, his demeanor calm yet shrouded in the enigma of his connection with the majestic beast. "Perhaps," he quipped, his eyes scanning the tumultuous scene in search of Keisha, his steadfast comrade. Leaning closer to Pumpkin, his voice dropped to a hushed murmur. "Where is Keisha?" he inquired urgently, their predicament fueling his concern. Pumpkin, vigilant and fiercely protective, stared back at him, poised to defend against any who dared approach.

Phoenix, however, needed more patience for inquiries or the mysteries of fate. His piercing gaze shifted to the Druchii, his authority unwavering. "Extract the King from this place," he ordered, his voice heavy with the urgency of imminent departure. "I care not for the method but execute it now. Detain that warrior just long enough to ensure the King's imprisonment."

Ong, his indomitable spirit untarnished, couldn't help but wear a sardonic grin as he detected a subtle undercurrent of desperation in Phoenix's demeanor. "It seems," he retorted with a taunting smirk, "that the formidable warlock trembles at the prospect of defeat." His fingers brushed tenderly against Pumpkin's head in acknowledgment, silently conveying gratitude for Keisha's cryptic intervention. As he continued his quest to locate Keisha amidst the chaos, he focused on the encroaching Druchii, prepared for the impending confrontation.

Qellaun, the courageous commander of the Druchii, seized King Alex and directed him toward the towering parapet, his voice a resounding decree that reverberated through the battleground. "Maintain that warrior and his formidable panther's engagement," he ordered, his gaze ablaze with unyielding resolve. "Our primary directive is to secure the King's presence in the dungeons and assert our dominion over this treacherous domain." In this realm of fantasy and intricate stratagems, alliances shifted like tides, and the ceaseless struggle for supremacy unfolded with each heartbeat.

The battlefield, suspended between the ethereal and the mortal, quivered as tension reached its zenith. Ong, the unyielding warrior hailing from Crystal Vale, stood undaunted in the face of the impending Druchii onslaught. With every encroaching step of his adversaries, his grip on his gleaming sword tightened—a silent testament to his unwavering commitment.

As the Druchii surged forward, Ong's blade mastery unfolded like a hypnotic dance of death. His weapon, an extension of his very essence, cleaved through their malevolent ranks with graceful and meticulous precision. The metallic symphony of steel against steel resonated through the air—an orchestration of conflict narrating tales of bravery and unwavering spirit.

In the heart of this fantastical clash, Ong's unwavering determination carved a path through the Druchii, each strike a symphony of skill and resilience. His blade cut through his foes' malevolent enchantments and dark intentions as if they were illusions. He moved with the grace of a seasoned warrior, his attacks precise and relentless, a force of nature that seemed to defy the essence of darkness itself.

Pumpkin, the sleek and raven-black panther, mirrored her master's indomitable spirit in her defense. Her lithe form became a streak of shadow, a dance of deadly elegance as she pounced upon any Druchii who dared approach. Her fangs gleamed like moonlight as she engaged her adversaries, her guttural growls a primal warning to those who crossed her path. She was a fierce guardian, unwavering in her loyalty and commitment to protect her master.

Amidst the chaos of battle, Ong's unwavering resolve and unparalleled swordsmanship were a beacon of hope for the city. With every foe he dispatched, he carved a path toward victory, a living testament to the enduring strength of the mortal spirit. In this epic confrontation between light and darkness, heroes and villains, the kingdom's fate hung in the balance, a world where bravery and skill converged in a breathtaking spectacle.

As Ong battled, his thoughts briefly turned to his loyal companion, Pumpkin. He knew that her safety was of paramount importance to Keisha, and any harm that befell her would unleash Keisha's fury. With this knowledge, his determination burned even brighter, his commitment to protect his friend and fulfill his noble duty unshaken.

With unwavering resolve, Ong surged forward, drawing nearer to the enigmatic Warlock, Phoenix. His sword held high, and he proclaimed his readiness to confront the encroaching shadows and defend the city. At his side, Pumpkin stood as a loyal sentinel, her emerald eyes blazing with a fierce determination to protect her master and stand against the darkness.

Ong's unwavering determination and demand for answers pierced through the chaos of battle, his voice a thunderous call for justice. His words resonated with the righteous indignation of a hero determined to rescue the King and Queen from the clutches of darkness. "Where have you secreted away the King and Queen?" he bellowed, the unwavering strength of his spirit echoing through the charged air. "I demand answers now!" In this pivotal moment of destiny, Ong's bravery and resolve were the sparks that ignited the storm—a hero's quest to free those imprisoned by the machinations of darkness.

Meanwhile, amid the chaotic battlefield, Keisha, the cunning and relentless archer, moved with the grace and precision of a dancer. Her eyes spotted a hidden trap, an evil device designed to snare the unwary. A shiver of dread coursed through her as she observed the haunting display of bones scattered across the blood-soaked ground—a grim testament to those who had dared to confront the fiery wrath of the slumbering red dragon. Despite the horrors surrounding her, Keisha steeled herself against the encroaching darkness, her mind a resolute beacon amidst the chaos.

With supernatural precision, Keisha manipulated the net, her movements a testament to her unwavering determination. She carefully draped the entangling fabric over the massive form of the dragon, crafting a makeshift prison with a delicate yet dangerous dance of skill. Deep within her heart, she knew that this fragile web of captivity was but a feeble barrier between the world and the boundless power of the dragon, a storm waiting to be unleashed.

Turning away from the fearsome creature, Keisha's heart churned with a tumultuous sea of emotions. Ong consumed her thoughts, the brave warrior whose actions had stirred a complex blend of admiration and concern within her. She couldn't help but feel a deep apprehension about his reckless charge into danger, a courageous act that seemed to disregard the overwhelming odds stacked against them. Soft and laden with worry, her voice whispered on the breeze as she addressed the slumbering behemoth.

"That is not going to hold for long," Keisha murmured, her words carrying the weight of her uneasy resolve. "But hopefully, I can get Ong out of there before that dragon awakens." In the depths of her heart, a tangled web of emotions tugged at her spirit, torn between the fear for Ong's safety and the budding feelings that had begun to take root. She couldn't help but wonder, "What was he thinking, charging in without help?"

Her sparkling eyes shimmered with determination as they shifted from the colossal dragon to the city of Goldmoor, its towering walls a steadfast sentinel against the encroaching darkness. Her mission was far from over, and it beckoned like an uncharted path in a world where heroes and allies forged their destinies amidst the unrelenting tide of adversity and peril.

In the wake of the tumultuous battle, the air seemed to tremble with the intensity of Phoenix's seething fury. His anger, a tempest harnessed with chilling precision, surged like an evil force aimed at the Druchii, who had faltered in their mission but partially succeeded in securing the King's escape.

"What kind of imbeciles are you, Druchii?" His voice, dripping with disdain, reverberated through the atmosphere like the judgment of a merciless deity. "You can't even handle a lone warrior and his foolish panther?"

His incendiary gaze, fiery and unyielding, fell upon the gleaming sword, a symbol of defiance laid before him. With a mocking, evil, and disdainful laugh, he regarded the weapon with a casual wave of dismissal. "Do you truly believe that this measly sword poses a threat to me?" he taunted, his arrogance an impenetrable fortress. Yet, like a sinister tide, his attention inexorably shifted toward Ong, and his voice dripped with malice as he uttered the warrior's name. "Swifthammer, your time has come."

Phoenix raised his hands with an ominous inevitability, invoking the elements to heed his sinister bidding. Fire, the embodiment of destruction, descended from the heavens like a vengeful cascade, targeting Ong and his steadfast companion, Pumpkin. Phoenix's lips curled into an evil smirk, a reflection of cruel satisfaction, as the warrior's agonized cry pierced the air, the flames voraciously licking at his resolute form. In this dire moment, the stage was set for an explosive showdown between unyielding resolve and the relentless onslaught of elemental fury.

However, an unexpected tableau unfolded amidst the raging fire, and the air shimmered with Ong's unwavering valor. Ong, a towering monument of unyielding resolve, leaned protectively over the sleek panther, shielding Pumpkin from the relentless onslaught of flames with his mortal form. Phoenix could only shake his head in disdain, a maestro of hostility, his words dripping with the acerbic venom of contempt.

Keisha's conflicted yet unwavering heartbeat is in rhythm with the turbulent events below. Her respect for Ong, the courageous warrior whose fearless charge had drawn her worry and admiration, had grown with each passing moment. She had heard his scream of anguish and defiance, a clarion call that echoed with the resonance of unwavering courage.

The enigmatic Warlock, Phoenix, stood like a dark sentinel amidst the smoldering chaos. His aura, a shroud of malevolence, radiated with power and disdain. Keisha's keen ears caught his cruel comment about Ong's selfless act of protecting Pumpkin, the sleek panther.

Phoenix's voice, a chilling reminder of the hostility that lurked in the world, whispered through the tumultuous air. "Ong," he taunted with a sinister grin, his words an eerie echo of his wicked amusement, "you are a fool for squandering your valor to protect a panther that isn't worth the trouble."

Keisha's fingers tightened around her longbow, and her brows knitted in determination. In this realm of fantasy and peril, where heroes and allies stood against the encroaching darkness, she knew the time had come to lend her skill to the unfolding drama. Her arrows would sing a song of resilience, and her aim would be true as she stepped into the fray, her presence a symbol of unwavering solidarity with those who dared to defy the shadows.

Perched atop the fortified wall, Keisha embodied the essence of a guardian spirit, her bow an extension of her will. Her fingers caressed the polished wood with the intimacy of an artist, pulling the string with the grace of a masterful musician coaxing a haunting melody from a violin. The bowstring sang with a mournful whisper, a serenade to the fates that danced upon the precipice.

Like a harbinger of justice, her arrow quivered in readiness, its silver-tipped head shimmering with a deadly promise. The air seemed still as if the heavens held their breath in anticipation of the impending release.

Her resolute and unwavering voice cut through the charged atmosphere, her words like a clarion call of defiance. "Excuse me, ugly," she declared with the weight of impending judgment, "but that Pumpkin you are talking about..." Her sentence hung in the air like a verdict, her gaze locked onto the Warlock's throat, a mark of death's design. The line between life and death had been drawn with a single breath.

Ong, the stalwart warrior, turned toward her voice, his eyes alight with relief and admiration. Her arrival was a beacon of hope amidst the chaos, a reminder of their unyielding bond. "Well, there you are," he greeted with a grin, his voice a testament to the camaraderie they shared. "I was wondering where you were."

Keisha shook her head, her fiery spirit undiminished. "Do I have to do everything?" she quipped, her words tinged with the exasperation of a friend who had arrived in the nick of time. "He has a stupid dragon that had to be subdued before he called that thing back here. I am not sure about you, but I damn sure do not want to deal with a fire-breathing dragon, not to mention what he could do to this beautiful golden city or its people."

In this critical juncture, where the city's fate teetered on the precipice of chaos, Keisha's unwavering aim and unyielding determination were a testament to her resolve. Her arrow, a harbinger of salvation, was poised to pierce the heart of darkness and protect all she held dear in this realm of fantasy and peril.

In the tumultuous theater of this otherworldly confrontation, Phoenix, the enigmatic Warlock, seethed with an explosive blend of confusion and anger. Like daggers forged from obsidian, his piercing gaze settled upon Keisha, the intrepid elf who dared to defy him. His evil voice cut through the charged atmosphere like a scythe reaping the harvest of his disdain.

"You are an elf," he declared, his words carrying the weight of unwavering certainty, "and all Druchii follow me."

The air crackled with tension as Keisha, a lone figure in this battle of wills, stood her ground. Her presence was a testament to her unyielding spirit, a guardian of her people's legacy in a kingdom tainted by darkness. The clash of her resolve against Phoenix's malevolence painted the scene with vivid strokes of defiance and uncertainty, where allegiances wavered like a flickering flame in a storm.

Keisha's response rippled through the charged air like a sigh of exasperation amidst the storm of conflict. Like pools of wisdom gleaming beneath the emerald canopy of her presence, her eyes held a patient mockery that cut through the heavy atmosphere.

"Stupid Warlock," she rejoined, her voice carrying the resonance of ages past, "I am not a Druchii. I am an Eladrin, and we are creatures of the light, bound by the luminous tapestry of our heritage. We would never follow one such as you into the abyss." Her words, a cascade of truth, washed through the darkened space like a cleansing river, dispelling the doubts and misconceptions clouding the Warlock's understanding.

A subtle shift in the dynamics of power unfurled as Keisha, the keeper of knowledge and wisdom, stood steadfast, a sentinel against the encroaching shadows of ignorance. In this exchange, the boundaries of perception were redrawn, and the lines between light and dark, truth and deceit, grew more apparent, etching their significance upon the annals of this fantastical realm.

Keisha, an ethereal sentinel armed with her deadly longbow, poised like an arrow in mid-flight, her presence the embodiment of lethal precision. Her eyes, keen as falcon's talons, remained locked onto Phoenix, the enigmatic Warlock ensnared within her unfaltering crosshairs.

She shattered the tension-laden atmosphere in a voice that resonated with the weight of ancient oaths. "Now silence your twisted incantations and unbind Pumpkin and Ong," Her command cut through the air like a razor-sharp blade, unwavering conviction. "And before you doubt my marksmanship, know this: I am an adept of unparalleled skill, and I squander neither arrow nor patience, so heed my words and free them."

Like a shimmering blade suspended in the void, her words hung there, the implicit threat heavier than the sharpest edge. A stark warning is carved into the very fabric of reality, daring Phoenix to defy her and face the inevitable consequences. In this charged moment, Keisha's gaze, a beacon of unwavering determination, bore into the Warlock, her will as unyielding as the ancient roots of the world's mightiest oaks.

As the present collided with the echoes of the past, the tension in the battlefield reached its zenith. Qellaun, the Druchii commander, moved with a swiftness and determination that defied the confines of mere mortals. His loyalty to Phoenix, born from that fateful day when he intervened to save the young Warlock's life, surged like an unstoppable torrent.

With a grace that belied his armored form, Qellaun placed himself between Keisha's deadly arrow and the enigmatic Warlock. His movements were a testament to the complex tapestry of allegiances and loyalties woven in the realm of Vacari. At that moment, the past and the present converged, forging a path towards an uncertain future.

Keisha's arrow, once aimed with deadly intent, now found itself diverted from its target. The air seemed to hold its breath as Qellaun's intervention shifted the course of destiny. His eyes, a reflection of his unwavering dedication, met Keisha's gaze, conveying a silent message of determination.

"You will not harm him," Qellaun declared, his voice a stern proclamation. "The past has bound us, and I will not allow harm to befall Phoenix. There are debts to be repaid, and a future yet unwritten."

In this moment of confrontation, the battlefield transformed into a stage where past actions and present choices held the power to reshape the course of Vacari's history. The intricate dance of fate continued, its steps guided by the complex threads of loyalty, duty, and the interplay of light and shadow in a realm where nothing was as it seemed.

In this moment of tense confrontation, the city of Goldmoor stood at the crossroads of destiny, its fate hanging in the balance. The citizens who had once observed the events from a distance were now drawn into the heart of the unfolding drama. Fear and uncertainty gripped the onlookers as they were caught between the enigmatic Warlock, Phoenix, and the imposing Druchii enforcers.

The atmosphere crackled with apprehension as the citizens of Goldmoor watched the standoff, their lives intertwined with the complex tapestry of alliances and loyalties that had brought this moment to fruition. The once-golden city, now cast in the shadows of uncertainty, held its breath, awaiting the resolution of the looming conflict.

The Druchii enforcers, formidable in their obsidian armor and predatory demeanor, formed an imposing barrier that added a layer of tension to the already charged atmosphere. Their presence reminded them that the forces of darkness were ever watchful, and their allegiance to Phoenix added a complex dimension to the unfolding drama.

Amidst this fragile balance, Keisha's bow remained steady, her arrow poised, and Ong's unwavering spirit stood as a beacon of hope. The destiny of Goldmoor, Vacari, and all its inhabitants hung in the balance, waiting for the next move in this intricate dance of light and shadow, loyalty and power.

As Ong, Keisha, and Pumpkin made their way toward the city's towering gates, their departure from Goldmoor signaled the beginning of a new and dangerous chapter in their quest to rescue the captured King and Queen. The moon, a spectral sentinel in the night sky, cast its silvery glow upon them, bearing witness to the unbreakable bond that had solidified amidst the chaos.

Ong, the unwavering warrior, led the way with his majestic horse, Thunder, carrying him and Keisha on their noble steed. His chivalrous gesture, lifting Keisha into his strong arms, spoke volumes of their alliance and the shared determination to fulfill their mission. Their journey was fraught with trials that would test the very core of their mettle, a forging of destinies in a world filled with enchantment and treacherous landscapes.

Pumpkin, the ever-faithful panther, trailed behind them like a shadowy guardian, her emerald eyes watchful in the moon's ethereal light. The world of fantasy and peril unfolded its captivating tapestry before them, each step forward a testament to their unyielding resolve and the enduring strength of their alliance.

As they rode toward the unknown, the echoes of their recent encounter with the enigmatic Warlock, Phoenix, still reverberated in their minds. Their paths would undoubtedly cross with his once more, and the dance of fate continued to weave its intricate patterns. In a world where courage and defiance held the power to shape destinies, Ong and Keisha ventured forth with a shared purpose, ready to face the challenges ahead and save their realm from the clutches of darkness.

Chapter 3

The King's Dilemma: Phoenix's Reign of Threat

Amidst the opulent halls of Goldmoor Palace, where the air bore witness to centuries of affluence and might, a symphony of regal extravagance played its mellifluous notes upon the senses. Gilded archways, glorious and majestic, soared heavenward, their surfaces agleam with the lustrous sheen of purest gold, beckoning forth all who dared to cross their threshold. These were no mere entrances but portals to a realm where excess knew no boundaries.

Every facet of the palace bore the mantle of splendor. Walls draped in rich tapestries, woven with threads of royal blue and emerald green, whispered tales of bravery and forgotten heroes in hushed tones. As if imbued with the memory of monarchs and conquerors, the polished marble floors echoed with the resonance of history. Like celestial constellations brought down to earth, Chandeliers hung suspended from lofty heights, casting cascades of ethereal light that shimmered and pirouetted, giving birth to an ever-evolving sea of brilliance.

Goldmoor's palace was not merely a structure but a testament to a city's inexhaustible wealth and power that had defied the ravages of time. It radiated an aura of grandeur and majesty, a realm where dreams and aspirations transcended the confines of mortal imagination.

Within this opulent realm, Phoenix Shadowwalker, the enigmatic Warlock, held court upon a throne hewn from the very heart of obsidian. It was a seat wreathed in shadows, a physical manifestation of his mysterious presence. Twin orbs of malevolence gleamed from the depths of his shadowy countenance as they surveyed the opulent chamber. On his fingers, dark rings bore witness to his mastery over arcane arts, each a testament to the dark power he wielded as they tapped out a rhythm of dominance upon the armrest.

Summoning a voice as deep and resonant as the abyss, Phoenix uttered commands that could bend both wills and destinies. "Qellaun, step forth."

Moments, like fleeting shadows in a realm of perpetual twilight, passed before Qellaun, the unwavering commander of the Druchii, entered the chamber with profound deference. His eyes, reflecting his unwavering loyalty for Phoenix, locked onto the Warlock's piercing gaze as he knelt, a symbol of steadfast devotion. "You summoned me, Lord Phoenix?" he inquired, his voice a mere whisper in the grand tapestry of the palace's history, a tale of obedience echoing with the weight of power that enveloped them.

Phoenix leaned forward, his countenance a canvas for the eerie tapestry woven by the flickering shadows. In that dimly lit chamber, his features appeared as if carved from the very marble of night, his voice as cold and calculating as a moonless winter's night, slicing through the air like a blade forged in the fires of disenchantment. "Qellaun," he began, his words a symphony of icy precision, "I demand your justifications for the audacious interference involving the Eladrin archer and Ong Swifthammer. Such bold actions tread upon treacherous ground."

Qellaun, his figure shrouded in an aura of somber determination, inclined his head with a solemnity that resonated with the gravity of the situation. He poised himself to elucidate the intricate threads of his actions. "My lord," he commenced, his voice a measured cadence that carried the weight of his words, "it is a tale that traces its roots to a haunting memory. In the days when your father, an Eladrin archer, was anointing your nascent powers, clandestinely infiltrated our sacred gathering. Her arrow was poised to claim your father's life, and I swiftly shielded him in the crucible of that difficult moment."

Phoenix's piercing eyes narrowed, a portal to the past opening within them. It was a memory etched from the annals of his history, a moment where destiny had hung by a gossamer thread. "Continue," he commanded, curiosity surging like a storm.

With the finesse of a master storyteller, Qellaun unfurled the tale. "As the archer's arrow sought your father's heart, it found me instead, for I had moved you beyond its dangerous trajectory. The Druchii pursued her in the chaos, yet she eluded our grasp and vanished like a wisp of moonlight."

Phoenix nodded, understanding dawning like a waning crescent on the horizon. "A vendetta," he surmised, "born from the peril she posed to your life."

Qellaun nodded in solemn agreement, his loyalty to Phoenix akin to the unyielding roots of an ancient oak. "Indeed, my lord. I perceived her presence as a looming specter, a threat to your existence, and I could not allow that shadow to persist."

Phoenix reclined in his shadow-draped throne, the gravity of revelation settling upon him like a heavy shroud. After a pregnant silence that seemed to stretch beyond mortal reckoning, he issued his final decree. "Very well, Qellaun. Mobilize our Druchii. Seek out the Eladrin archer and Ong Swifthammer. Bring them before me. This tale conceals deeper secrets, and I am determined to unearth them."

Qellaun bowed deeply, his unwavering commitment to his lord manifesting in the profound dip of his obeisance. "As you command, Lord Phoenix," he affirmed, his footsteps resonating through the chamber like a promise etched in the annals of destiny as he embarked on his quest to fulfill his master's enigmatic desires.

As the days unfurled like ancient scrolls and the atmosphere grew pregnant with anticipation, the citizens of Goldmoor flowed into the resplendent palace like a river of diverse emotions. Each face bore the weight of hope, trepidation, and curiosity, like masks concealing the secrets of their souls. Phoenix stood at the heart of this swirling sea of humanity, a monarch-in-waiting, his demeanor a masterstroke of undeniable arrogance. His penetrating gaze swept over the crowd, a lordly smirk playing on his lips as if the air had consented to his command. With a calm gesture, he summoned Qellaun, his staunchest Druchii loyalist, back to his side, a chess piece strategically placed on the board of impending royalty.

"Yes, my Lord?" Qellaun's voice, a harmonious chord of obedience, resonated through the opulent chamber, an accompaniment to the unfolding spectacle.

Phoenix's voice dripped with condescension as he issued his decree, his words a cascade of icy disdain. "Ensure that your Druchii patrol the perimeters diligently, poised to quell any disturbances that may dare to mar this grand occasion."

"At your command, My Lord." Qellaun bowed with the utmost obeisance, a sentinel in dark armor, and dispatched his Druchii to weave their silent watch over the palace's opulent tapestry.

The Druchii moved with an eerie grace, their presence akin to phantoms amidst the lavish surroundings. They scoured the assembly with hawk-like vigilance, seeking any flicker of dissent or rebellion that might tarnish the forthcoming ceremony. When it came, their report was like the hushed whisper of a secret shared only with their master, a shadowy narrative woven into the very fabric of Goldmoor Palace.

"The ceremony stands on the edge of commencement, My Lord," Qellaun reported, his tone tinged with the electric anticipation that pervaded the palace's grandeur. It was a momentous occasion that would sculpt the destiny of Goldmoor and its people.

Phoenix's smirk, a wicked curve etched in the ink of his lips, underscored his satisfaction with the unfolding tableau. Like twin obsidian shards, his dark eyes gleamed with a sinister delight. Leaning closer to Qellaun, he wove his words like a thread of conspiracy in the grand tapestry of the palace. "Excellent. Now, where has King Alex been spirited away?"

The question hung in the air like a dagger poised for the fatal plunge, and in the heart of Goldmoor's opulent palace, a plot thickened, shrouded in shadows, and illuminated by the evil gleam in Phoenix's eyes.

Qellaun's laughter, a haunting reverberation in the exalted chamber, pirouetted through the air like the flickering flames of evil sorcery. "We've ensconced him within the depths of the nethermost dungeon," he disclosed, his voice a macabre sonata laced with sardonic amusement, "for we were uncertain of your preferred level of confinement." His words bore a melancholy cadence, a grim reminder of the abyss into which their wickedness plunged. "In the dungeon's heart, we've arranged his chains amidst twin stone pillars." The utterance of 'dungeon' conjured spectral tendrils that seemed to snake through the air. "He is securely ensnared, and once the traps are set, his captivity will become an impenetrable fortress."

Phoenix's smirk deepened, an embodiment of his nefarious machinations. "Excellent," he purred, his words oozing with cruel gratification. "Naturally, if the populace remains compliant, he shall languish there for the foreseeable future." His stratagems, cloaked in shadows, hinged upon the obedience of the masses. "Tend to his comfort personally and ensure that his wife and the citizenry adhere to my every command."

Qellaun's smirk, an unholy mirror of his master's malevolence, attested to their shared maleficence. "You are the very incarnation of malevolence, My Lord," he murmured, sealing their unholy pact, forging a path through treachery and darkness within the immersive realm of fantasy and tyranny.

The council members, their expressions a mélange of trepidation and resolve, approached the grand dais with measured steps. Each footfall resonated through the opulent chamber like an echo of history, a reminder of the weight of their decisions. Their robes, adorned with intricate sigils and symbols of authority, billowed like banners of ancient houses in a ceremonial procession.

Phoenix, a dark lord amidst the splendor, watched their approach with calculated indifference, his eyes akin to twin embers of malevolence smoldering within the cavernous recesses of his visage. The throne, a throne of shadows and secrets, cradled him like a maleficent monarch, and the council's presence merely added to the tapestry of impending doom.

As they reached the base of the dais, the council members arranged themselves in a semicircle, their collective presence a mosaic of political intricacies and veiled agendas. Like spectral echoes of conspiracy, their hushed whispers fluttered through the chamber, barely audible amidst the grandeur.

Phoenix, the master puppeteer in this macabre theater, raised a hand adorned with rings of arcane power, commanding silence with a gesture. The chamber obeyed, and a heavy pall of stillness settled over the assembly like the shroud of fate.

"Now," he intoned, his voice a wellspring of dark authority, "the ceremony shall commence, and with it, the destiny of Goldmoor shall be irrevocably altered."

The palace, a silent sentinel to the unfolding drama, bore witness to this momentous occasion. Its walls, resplendent in gilded opulence, seemed to lean closer, as if straining to capture every whispered word, every furtive glance, in the ever-evolving saga of power and betrayal. The air, charged with tension, held its breath, aware that this was a pivotal juncture in the immersive saga that unfolded within these hallowed halls.

Phoenix, a master manipulator reveling in the chaos he had sown, watched the council's dilemma unfold with an unmistakable dark delight in his evil countenance. His smirk persisted, a smug assurance of his dominance over their fate.

The council members, caught in uncertainty, exchanged furtive glances and whispered amongst themselves, their voices a tempest of calm deliberation. Their inquiries, like breadcrumbs in a labyrinth of intrigue, danced through the air, seeking answers amidst the shadows that enshrouded the enigmatic Warlock.

Finally, the council's spokesperson, a figure of unwavering authority, stepped forward with an air of solemnity. "We shall negotiate," they declared, their voice bearing the weight of the council's collective will. "Release King Alex from his captivity, and we shall consider your claim to the throne."

Phoenix's eyes gleamed with avaricious triumph as he perceived the council's capitulation to his demands. He nodded, a nod that held the promise of an impending accord. "Very well," he acquiesced, his voice dripping with deceit, "but the negotiations shall transpire in the depths of the palace's most hidden chambers, away from prying eyes."

With a sense of foreboding, the council agreed, their pact with the devil sealed at that moment. The palace's opulent walls, steeped in history and secrets, bore witness to the unfolding conspiracy, as the immersive tale of power and intrigue plunged further into the abyss of uncertainty.

With the council's reluctant surrender, the atmosphere in the grand chamber shifted as if the air had become denser with the weight of their decision. Phoenix, the puppeteer of their destiny, accepted their proclamation with a haughty satisfaction. His dark eyes gleamed with evil triumph as he approached the council, ready to claim the throne that had eluded him for so long.

As the council anointed him as King, the echoes of their voices reverberated through the opulent chamber, leaving a lingering sense of solemnity in their wake. The queen, though imprisoned, remained a symbol of unwavering defiance, a testament to the indomitable spirit that would continue to flicker in the kingdom's heart.

The council's choice, driven by pragmatism and the fear of dire consequences, marked a turning point in the immersive tale of power and intrigue. The fate of Goldmoor hung in the balance, poised between the oppressive shadow of their new monarch and the flicker of hope embodied by their captive queen.

In the grand chamber, the tableau of this dramatic saga reached its zenith, and the palace's ornate walls, adorned with glistening tapestries and ancient symbols, bore witness to a moment that would be etched into the annals of their city's history.

Queen Jeanne's heart ached with despair and defiance in the chamber where malevolence and cruelty danced like shadowy specters. Her beloved King Alex remained imprisoned, his fate hanging by the thinnest thread, while she was trapped in a web of darkness. Phoenix, the puppeteer of their torment, reveled in his sinister game.

As the queen's pleas for her husband's release were ignored, she was forced to witness an illusion of his torment. It was a vision that pierced her soul, a cruel reminder of the powerlessness she now faced. Her voice, a poignant cry for his freedom, was met with only the harsh grip of the Druchii, a cruel reminder of her captivity.

Phoenix's satisfaction at her suffering was palpable, and he asserted his dominance with a heartless smirk. The queen's fate hung in the balance, her destiny at the mercy of this evil king.

The council and subjects, once proud and noble, now knelt before their new ruler, their voices silenced by the relentless force of fate. The grand chamber, once a place of noble deliberations, now witnessed their submission, and the people were ushered out of the palace like a river flowing along the path of destiny.

Queen Jeanne remained a thorn in Phoenix's side, her defiance unwavering. His command to convey her to the tower and seal her fate only fueled her resistance. With a swift and defiant kick, she struck one of her captors, a Druchii, earning herself an evil glare in return.

Qellaun, the Druchii tasked with handling the queen, hoisted her over his shoulder, asserting his dominance over her. But Phoenix, the mastermind behind this dark drama, stayed his henchman's course with a chilling command.

The evil king cruelly took a heart-shaped necklace from the queen's neck, a token of their love, and tore a sliver of fabric from her bodice as a sadistic keepsake of her captivity. With that, he signaled for Qellaun to proceed, his thoughts turning to the captive King Alex.

The stage was set for a reign of unrelenting terror, and the elements of this dark tableau aligned seamlessly in the tapestry of power and cruelty.

Chapter 4

The King's Descent: Phoenix's Dungeon of Betrayal

In the heart of Goldmoor, an eerie and foreboding ambiance has enveloped those who dared to venture into its depths. This hidden sanctuary lay concealed within the shadowy bowels of the underground dungeon, a place of ancient and foreboding beauty.

Two imposing pillars, hewn from the very stones of the underworld itself, stood sentinel-like, rising tall and imposing like grim guardians of a long-forgotten secret. Iron shackles, wrought with evil intent, hung ominously from their cold and unforgiving surfaces, poised to ensnare any unfortunate soul who dared to step onto this desolate ground.

The air bore a weighty musk, heavy with the ghosts of centuries-old captivity, and a palpable chill seeped into one's very bones. Dampness clung to every surface like a shroud of sorrow, as if the stones themselves wept for the tormented souls condemned to this forsaken place. The ground beneath the pillars, a mosaic of fractured and weathered cement, bore the scars of an eternity of suffering.

Yet, amid the oppressive atmosphere, the water was the most haunting aspect of this underground prison. It was not ordinary water but an abyss of profound darkness that encircled the area, its inky depths plunging into unfathomable obscurity. The enclosed walls of this dreadful domain seemed to tremble in fear of what lay beyond, for the sound that emanated from the watery expanse was a mournful speech akin to the anguished whispers of a gloomy river from some forgotten, accursed realm.

As one drew closer to the water's edge, its surface, a mirror to the depths of despair, glistened with an unnatural luminescence, resembling the ghostly shimmer of forgotten dreams. It beckoned with an unsettling allure as though it held secrets that could drive a mortal mind to the precipice of madness.

Within this forsaken chamber of incarceration, the boundary separating reality from the arcane realms blurred. It was a place where the very earth conspired against the unfortunate souls cast into its embrace—a place where walls wept, water whispered, and pillars stood as solemn sentinels to a desolation that knew no end.

Descending into the subterranean depths of the accursed dungeon, Phoenix traversed the cold stone steps, each echoing with a sinister resonance that seemed to welcome his evil presence. An evil grin curled upon his lips, a wicked reflection of the darkness that consumed his soul as he approached the heart of dread in this wretched place. The fallen monarch, King Alex, languished in captivity in the shadowy depths.

In the dim recesses of the fetid chamber, an unholy sanctuary of despair, Phoenix's eyes were drawn to the twin guardians of torment — two towering stone pillars, their ancient surfaces etched with the scars of innumerable souls who had met their gruesome fate here. They loomed like mournful sentinels, bearing witness to the countless horrors that had unfolded within these cursed walls, silent and persistent as if awaiting their next victim with grim anticipation.

Phoenix laid a malevolent hand upon the iron-bound door to King Alex's cell, swinging it open wide to reveal the imprisoned sovereign. The heavy door creaked with an ominous finality as if sealing the fate of those who dared to enter this accursed domain. He seized the king's arm in one twisted and cruel motion, raising it high in a gesture of evil dominion. The heavy shackles affixed to the pillars resounded ominously, their cold iron links clinking with a macabre melody as Phoenix compelled Alex's hands into their unyielding grasp.

A sardonic smile twisted Phoenix's lips as he ensured the chains bit deep into flesh, a cruel testament to his mastery over the captive king.

Bending low, his countenance bathed in shifting shadows cast by the flickering torchlight, he secured King Alex's feet within the unrelenting embrace of the restraints. The foundations of the dungeon seemed to shiver in response, as though the venom of this unholy act sent shivers through the soul of this forsaken place. In this chamber of despair, where cruelty reigned supreme, Phoenix held dominion over the fallen monarch, and the dark echoes of his evil laughter mingled with the tormented whispers of the dungeon's tragic past.

Leering at King Alex with a disdain born of dark ambition, Phoenix taunted his erstwhile ruler, his eyes ablaze with a sinister delight that seemed to draw power from the dungeon's depths. "See how the mighty have plummeted from their lofty heights," he hissed, his voice a venomous serpent's whisper that echoed through the chamber. "Your dominion now lies in my grasp."

With a triumphant flourish, Phoenix circled the imprisoned king, his fingertips aglow with otherworldly fire, the ethereal flames dancing with spectral beauty. They cast eerie, shifting shadows upon the damp stone walls. "It would be the simplest of tasks to extinguish your feeble existence right here," he mused aloud, his voice dripping with ominous menace like the waters of Serpent's Lagoon.

Yet, unbroken by the chains that bound his body, King Alex met Phoenix's gaze with an unwavering resolve that mirrored the indomitable spirit of Goldmoor's citizens. "Beware, warlock," he cautioned, his voice a threat as sharp as a forged blade. "The kingdom's loyalty to you is but a fragile facade. They tolerate your rule out of respect for my queen and me. Harm either of us, and you shall kindle the embers of rebellion."

Phoenix's smirk widened as he reveled in the cruel ballet of power. "You underestimate me, King Alex," he replied, his voice a sinister purr, resonating with the arcane mysteries. "I am a maestro of the arcane arts, and magic is my realm. I could fool your subjects, making them believe you still draw breath while languishing in death's icy clutches. They would remain oblivious to the charade, and your kingdom would remain none the wiser."

In that dark and solitary chamber, the battle of wills between warlock and king raged on, their destinies woven together by the cruel hand of fate and the enchantment of sorcery. Alex's eyes blazed with righteous fury as he fixed a withering gaze upon Phoenix, whose malevolent visage appeared untouched by the specter of morality. "Where is my beloved wife?" he thundered, a clarion call of defiance that echoed through the stones of Goldmoor's underground prison. "You shall not lay a treacherous hand upon her, lest you beckon divine retribution!"

In Goldmoor, a city shrouded in shadows and secrets, the fate of King Alex and his city hung in the balance, like a delicate thread in the hands of fate, waiting to be woven into a new chapter of this dark and twisted tale.

Phoenix's laughter, a chilling reverberation within the dungeon's somber chamber, rippled through the oppressive air. It was a sinister and discordant symphony of dark amusement that grated upon the very souls of those condemned to witness it. "Your queen," he sneered, "shall find solace within the lofty embrace of a forsaken tower, where the shadows whisper secrets, and her despair shall be the only echo that answers her cries."

Alex's plea for mercy fell upon deaf ears, yet he remained undaunted, his resolve unyielding. "Release her from your nefarious clutches!" he demanded, his voice a rallying cry of hope amid the engulfing despair, like a beacon of light in the heart of Goldmoor's darkest hour.

The warlock's laughter, devoid of mercy, only fueled the king's indomitable spirit. Phoenix approached Alex with measured steps, malevolent intent dancing like spectral flames in his eyes. With an eerie flourish, he cast the queen's ornate necklace upon the cold, unfeeling post to which the sovereign was bound, the golden trinket now a haunting reminder of her captive plight.

Yet, Phoenix's malevolence knew no bounds as he seized a strip of silken fabric torn from the bodice of Alex's beloved queen. It hung like a tattered banner of despair from the iron bar, a sinister emblem of her vulnerability within the clutches of the warlock.

A sinister chuckle rippled from Phoenix's lips, an evil symphony that echoed through the desolate dungeon like a haunting refrain. His voice, tinged with dark amusement, sliced through the oppressive atmosphere. "Ah, Alex," he intoned with treacherous intent. "Your queen, a mere pawn in this grand game of shadows, holds little allure for me, save for the leverage she provides to quell your defiance and that of your steadfast subjects. Her fate, like yours, is a thread in the tapestry of my ambition, a tapestry that weaves darkness and despair throughout the city of Goldmoor."

Alex, his gaze a blazing ember of wrath, fixed upon Phoenix like an avenging deity of old, his very presence a testament to an unyielding determination that echoed through the confines of Goldmoor's forlorn dungeon. "I shall not abide any harm befalling her," he declared, his thunderous war cry reverberating like a solemn oath. He strained against the implacable chains that bound him to the forlorn pillar, every sinew of his being yearning for liberation, for the opportunity to confront his evil captor.

The king's resolve surged like a tempestuous tide, and he heaved on the chains with a Herculean effort, his muscles straining with the sincere desire for freedom. At that moment, his actions transcended the mortal realm, embodying a genuine thirst for justice and retribution, an unquenchable fire that burned brighter than the darkest sorceries of Phoenix.

The warlock's laughter, a haunting counterpoint to the king's defiance, reverberated through the chamber, for it was within this dismal realm of shadows and chains that the destinies of kingdoms and the souls of men teetered on a precarious precipice, like the fragile balance of power within the realm of Vacari itself.

In the dim-lit recesses of the dungeon's grim abyss, Phoenix's eyes, akin to gleaming embers of malevolence, flickered with a cruel intent. He cast a brief, disdainful glance upon the captive King, whose regal bearing was now stripped of all but defiant pride. In this moment of peril and defiance, the stage was set for a clash that would echo through the annals of Goldmoor's history—a battle of wills where the flames of hope burned fiercely against the encroaching darkness of tyranny and sorcery.

The stone floor beneath their feet bore witness to a surreal tableau, where scattered pools of water glistened like forsaken jewels amidst the encroaching shadows, their ethereal luminescence casting an eerie glow upon the grim surroundings. Phoenix's lips curled into a wicked smirk as he contemplated the dangerous game he was about to play.

"Perhaps," he mused, his voice a honeyed blend of malice and intrigue, "a gentle reminder of the peril you find yourself in is in order." With measured steps, he began to encircle King Alex, the whispered incantations of forgotten sorcery dancing like spectral fireflies around him.

As Phoenix's muttered invocations swirled, a luminous barrier, woven from the fabric of arcane forces, materialized. It encased the king and the eerie puddles in a shimmering cocoon of enchantment, a prison within the prison, sealing the monarch's fate.

Having erected his mystical fortress, Phoenix retreated to a distant precipice, where the cavern's stony maw seemed to meet the abyssal ocean itself. In his grasp, an ancient staff thrummed with arcane power, a conduit between worlds.

With a flourish of malevolent majesty, Phoenix thrust his staff into the solid rock, causing the very earth to shudder in response. The stone groaned and parted, revealing the fathomless depths of the abyss, where the relentless ocean tides roared with a cruel hunger.

As the seawater surged like a colossal leviathan, Phoenix's smirk deepened into a malefic grin. "A precarious situation you find yourself in," he purred with chilling satisfaction, his words echoing through the chamber like a dark prophecy. "Should this aqueous deluge persist, and you dare to venture beyond my ensnaring magic, your fate shall be sealed, and the relentless ocean shall become your eternal tomb."

In this macabre theater of magic and menace, the king's fate hung in the balance, and the shadows of Goldmoor's dungeon seemed to close in, bearing witness to a battle that transcended the mortal realm. In this battle, sorcery and defiance clashed in a symphony of despair and hope.

Indeed, the aqueous flood halted, yet a sinister undercurrent shattered the stillness. In the depths of the now-submerged cavern, a dark presence stirred. From the abyssal void emerged serpentine specters, devious and deadly, their malevolence unleashed upon the magic barrier with a relentless hunger.

Phoenix's laughter, a symphony of wicked glee, filled the cavern as he taunted his captive prey. "Should these serpents breach my ward, King Alex," he sneered, "your demise shall be a torment befitting legend, an agonizing descent into the abyss itself."

Phoenix, his dark sorcerous visage veiled in sinister purpose, pivoted towards the cavern's nethermost reaches, where the tenebrous depths concealed secrets untold. With a will forged from the darkest corners of his essence, he summoned forth an abomination of the abyss—an eldritch sea monstrosity, a creature born from the very nightmares of ancient mariners.

This monstrous colossus, its scales glistening with the malevolent sheen of primordial darkness, emerged from the abyssal maw like an infernal leviathan, a harbinger of doom. It inched ever closer, each ponderous movement evoking the relentless march of fate until its grotesque form loomed within the problematic view of King Alex.

With a malefic twinkle in his eyes, Phoenix redirected his attention to the captive monarch, who stood trapped in the sorcerous web of a magic barrier. "Fear not," he intoned, his voice dripping with sadistic reassurance, "for this grotesque behemoth cannot breach the bounds of this mystical cage. It hungers, it thirsts, but it is forever barred from your trembling form."

The warlock's wicked gaze bore into Alex's soul, his words a cruel, lingering promise of malevolence. "Know this," he continued a sibilant echo in the shadowy chamber, "while you remain ensconced within my enchantment, you are shielded from the wrath of this monstrous abyss. But should the barrier ever shatter at the hands of an intruder, the very heart of this cavern shall transform into an inescapable sepulcher—a churning abyss of certain death, where none shall emerge unscathed."

The ominous undercurrent of Phoenix's declaration hung heavy in the air, casting a shroud of inexorable dread over the captive king and the abyssal horrors that lurked beyond.

"I shall leave you," Phoenix declared with an evil grin, his voice like a venomous whisper, "with guardians born of chaos and nightmares, creatures to keep you company in this lonely abyss." His laughter, a cacophony of sinister mirth, reverberated through the chamber, a cruel reminder of the relentless venom that enveloped King Alex in the heart of Goldmoor's darkest hour.

With a glance, Phoenix summoned the grotesque chimeras, beings of grotesque fusion, amalgamations of the surreal and the disgusting. These unnatural sentinels, their forms a cruel mockery of the natural world, stood at the threshold of King Alex's imprisonment, their eyes aflame with an otherworldly malevolence.

These chimeras bore the forms of lion heads and serpentine coils, their bodies a nightmarish blend of regal ferocity and serpentine cunning. Their wings, unfurled like those of majestic eagles, added an unsettling grandeur to their monstrous visage. These grotesque amalgamations of creatures from both heaven and hell seemed to defy the very laws of nature, standing as horrifying guardians of the warlock's sinister domain.

As Phoenix turned his back on the captive king, his every step was imbued with the weight of impending doom. The heavy door, fashioned from the cold, unfeeling metal of a cursed realm, groaned as it swung shut, sealing Alex's fate within the underground abyss.

Outside the door, the warlock gestured with a flourish, and the chimeras assumed their vigilant posts, their grotesque forms serving as a testament to the horrors that lurked within this forsaken realm. Their roars, a symphony of discord, filled the chamber like a haunting lament, a haunting melody of despair and dread that echoed through the stones of Goldmoor's underground labyrinth.

King Alex's grim determination remained unwavering within the confines of the chamber itself. Yet, a new challenge was hidden in the stones that bound him. The stone walls of his prison bore the cryptic etchings of an intricate labyrinth, its maze-like design both a marvel of ancient craftsmanship and a testament to the warlock's evil cunning.

As King Alex surveyed the labyrinthine passages, his keen eyes discerned the deceptive trap doors, cunningly concealed within the cold, unforgiving floor. Though camouflaged beneath the labyrinth's intricate design, these treacherous portals promised the unwary traveler a descent into the abyss.

When unwittingly triggered, some trap doors would lead to dangerous subterranean chambers inhabited by monstrous creatures, the warlock's sinister pets lurking in the shadows. Even more ominous, others concealed darker secrets, abyssal depths that echoed with the whispers of long-forgotten horrors—a testament to the evil genius of Phoenix, who had woven a tapestry of suffering and despair within the stones of Goldmoor's dungeon.

The grotesque chimeras, guardians of the abyss, were harbingers of terror, their very presence a ghastly omen that cast a shadow over the labyrinth's twisted passages. Like the convoluted corridors of a twisted mind, the labyrinthine passages bore witness to the warlock's treacherous intellect, where every winding path seemed designed to confound and entrap. The ominous and foreboding trap doors added unpredictability and danger to a difficult journey, like hidden jaws waiting to snap shut on the unwary.

Resolute in his quest to rescue his beloved queen, King Alex understood that the path ahead was fraught with known and hidden peril, a treacherous odyssey through a realm of evil design. Every step he took required unwavering courage and cunning, for the labyrinth was a physical challenge and a reflection of the warlock's malefic mind.

King Alex, a beacon of indomitable spirit amidst the encroaching shadows, fixed his steely gaze upon the retreating form of Phoenix. His voice, a thunderous declaration of unyielding resolve, resounded through the cavernous abyss like a solemn oath, a vow etched in the very stones of the underground world. "Though you may hold sway in this bleak moment, warlock," he proclaimed with a voice that echoed through the labyrinth, "the relentless tide of destiny shall yet turn, and you shall reap the whirlwind for the torment you have wrought upon my beloved queen. I pledge this to you with every fiber of my being, and the echoes of my determination shall be your constant companion in this shadowed realm."

In the heart of Goldmoor's abyssal dungeon, the battle of wills raged on—a struggle that transcended the boundaries of magic and despair, a war where a king's love and determination burned as brightly as the most brilliant of stars, a beacon of hope in the darkest of hours.

His regal countenance, a mask of defiance carved from the most robust stone, turned toward the eldritch sea monster that loomed beyond the confines of his magical prison. A scowl etched upon his visage, he issued a silent challenge to the grotesque leviathan, his eyes aflame with a glimmer of relentless determination. He was a lone warrior against the abyssal horrors, his heart a steadfast anchor amidst the storm of hostility, a beacon of hope in the shadows of the abyss.

In the calm confines of his solitary captivity, King Alex's voice, tinged with the gravity of undying love and unwavering courage, whispered a vow to the stones that bore witness to his anguish. "Brave, my Queen," he murmured, his words a fragile benediction in the face of darkness. "I swear upon the fall of that malevolent warlock, I shall traverse the realms of shadow and retrieve you, bringing you safely back to our city's sanctuary."

With these solemn words, King Alex's promise hung in the air like a luminous hope amidst the encroaching abyss, a testament to his indomitable spirit and the enduring power of love in the face of unspeakable adversity. It was a promise that transcended the boundaries of the labyrinth, echoing through the shadows and the heart of Goldmoor itself. This vow would guide him through the treacherous depths of Vacari and beyond to rescue his beloved queen from the clutches of darkness.

Chapter 5

Locked in Regal Chains: The Queen's Imprisonment

Qellaun's grip on the Queen's arm was as unyielding as the implacable march of time itself, each step through Goldmoor's shadowy tower a relentless passage toward an uncertain destiny. The foreboding door to the chamber creaked open, revealing a room shrouded in darkness, a crypt of secrets entwined with the murmurs of long-forgotten legends. The Queen's wrists, long imprisoned by the cruel bite of restraints, were finally set free, the binding cords relinquishing their grasp with a sigh carrying the weight of countless sorrows.

Within the dim-lit chamber, Qellaun's eyes briefly met Queen Jeanne's, a meeting of glances akin to smoldering embers amidst the abyss. They were the unspoken overture to the storm, a brewing maelstrom known as "Phoenix." Like the first defiant gust of wind before a storm, her words were a whisper of rebellion in the face of impending chaos.

"Release me, you wretched fiend!" Her voice, though quivering, resonated with the regal authority that still clung to her even in this dire moment. Her words were a challenge thrown at the very shadows that enshrouded them.

But Qellaun, the sentinel of Phoenix's dark will, displayed no sign of faltering. He advanced upon the Queen, his presence casting a looming, foreboding shadow that stretched like a sinister omen across the room's farthest reaches. "Hush now," he hissed, his voice a venomous serpent's warning, "Your days of command have withered like leaves in the icy grip of winter."

Defiance blazed within Queen Jeanne, a hunger that even the deepest dungeons could not extinguish. She rose from her seat like a phoenix, her movement a rebirth of unwavering determination. Guided by the storm within, her hand met Qellaun's cheek with a resounding crack that reverberated through the chamber like a thunderbolt strike.

"Never presume to address me in such a manner," she declared, her words ringing like a clarion call, demanding respect in the face of tyranny.

In the heart of Goldmoor, where shadows clung like a cloak of uncertainty, Qellaun's patience hung by a fraying thread, like a delicate strand of spider silk. He captured the Queen's wrist with a swiftness that spoke of his dark, practiced mastery, compelling her back into the accursed chair. His grip was an iron vice that could crush flesh and hope, much like this shadowy tower's relentless grip of despair.

"This is your final warning," he intoned, his voice a chilling zephyr amidst the room's oppressive stillness. The air was thick with tension, much like the brooding atmosphere of Goldmoor itself. "Your orders are no more than dust scattered by the winds of fate, and you are fortunate that the harbinger of your reckoning has yet to descend upon you."

Phoenix, the enigmatic puppeteer of this dark drama, came to an abrupt halt before the door, his presence akin to a shroud of impenetrable darkness. The low murmurs from beyond the door sent ripples of amusement through his cold, calculating eyes, their depths concealing the enigmatic wisdom of countless ages. A sarcastic smirk played at the corners of his lips as he contemplated Qellaun's handling of the Queen.

"I must, in fairness, commend his restraint in dealing with that tempestuous woman," he mused, his voice akin to a serpent's hushed whisper. He deliberately pushed the door open, unveiling a tense scene.

Qellaun, a silhouette of unwavering loyalty, met Phoenix's gaze with a knowing look. The dim, flickering candlelight cast a spectral dance upon his countenance, rendering his features both foreboding and enigmatic, much like the eerie atmosphere of Goldmoor. "Indeed, My Lord," he acknowledged, his voice a low, gravelly rumble akin to distant thunder. "I have managed her according to your desires."

Phoenix's smirk deepened, mirroring the evil grin of a crescent moon. "Ah, naturally, Qellaun," he responded, his voice smoother than the darkest midnight, as he advanced into the chamber, his presence an eclipse descending upon the room. "It appears our Queen has wrestled with the tempestuous nature of her spirit."

Phoenix approached Queen Jeanne with measured grace, whose defiance still burned like a beacon of light in the dimly lit chamber. He leaned in, his eyes akin to twin orbs of smoldering coal, each word measured and deliberate. "Never again shall your voice be raised against any of my loyal subjects, dear Queen," he admonished his words, a chilling zephyr that promised frost to the very core. "Or you may discover that not all possess the admirable restraint of Qellaun."

Like a faltering star, Jeanne's gaze briefly flickered toward Phoenix before she turned her head away, her silence an emblem of unyielding defiance akin to a lone beacon of resistance in the dark.

Like the distant echoes of thunder, Phoenix's laughter resonated through the room as he pivoted to face Qellaun again. "Is Zylron prepared, Qellaun?" he inquired, his voice heavy with the weight of destiny's decree, like a proclamation echoing through Goldmoor's grand halls. "It is time to accompany our dear Queen to her new residence—the illustrious Serpent's Lagoon."

At Phoenix's imperious command, the trio, now accompanied by Zylron, the formidable red dragon, embarked on their journey toward the infamous Serpent's Lagoon. They ascended into the velvety night sky, perched atop the colossal dragon's back, their forms silhouetted against the vast expanse of stars. The wind whistled through their hair, like the plaintive cry of a mournful spirit, as the world below dwindled into insignificance, much like the distant cities of Vacari.

Serpent's Lagoon sprawled beneath them, a winding waterway weaving its treacherous path through a labyrinthine network of mangrove forests. The moon, a spectral lantern in the inky heavens, bestowed its eerie luminescence upon the lagoon's surface, casting silvery ripples that shimmered like the scales of a slumbering leviathan, much like the reflections in the waters of a hidden sub-realm. The atmosphere hung heavy with a foreboding stillness, punctuated only by the sporadic hisses of lurking malice, like the eerie whispers of long-forgotten legends.

Beneath the lagoon's opaque depths, serpents with eyes like gleaming emeralds slithered, their sinister intent a palpable presence in the watery abyss. Like polished armor, their scales glinted with a seductive allure, masking their treacherous nature. Their presence was an ominous undercurrent, their lithe forms intertwining in a sinister aquatic ballet, much like the dark intrigues of a kingdom.

As the trio descended toward Serpent's Lagoon, the resounding whoosh of Zylron's wings cleaved the air like the thunderous clap of an impending storm, echoing through the night. It was a clarion call not lost upon the vigilant denizens of the lagoon, for the grotesque heads of hydras began to surface from the depths. These nightmarish monstrosities, their gnarled reptilian bodies adorned with multiple serpentine heads, stood as the lagoon's formidable guardians, protectors of its enigmatic secrets, much like the ancient guardians of these treacherous waters.

The lagoon sprawled beneath them, a winding waterway weaving its treacherous path through a labyrinthine network of mangrove forests. The moon, a spectral lantern in the inky heavens, bestowed its eerie luminescence upon the lagoon's surface, casting silvery ripples that shimmered like the scales of a slumbering leviathan. The atmosphere hung heavy with a foreboding stillness, punctuated only by the sporadic hisses of lurking malice, like the eerie whispers of long-forgotten legends haunting the very essence of this watery realm.

Jeanne, once a queen, now a captive, gazed upon the lagoon's eerie beauty, her defiance still smoldering deep within her. She knew that her fate was intricately woven into the tapestry of this enigmatic place, like a prisoner of Serpent's Lagoon itself, caught in its serpentine coils.

In the celestial realm above, dragons, beings of both awe and terror, circled like vigilant sentinels of the night. Their iridescent scales shimmered with otherworldly colors as if painted by the hand of the cosmos itself. With wings that stretched like the canvases of cosmic artists, they ruled the skies with an imperious gaze, ever-ready to defend their dominion. Each resounding roar reverberated through the very fabric of existence, a symphony of power that echoed through the realms.

Meanwhile, on the tangled ground below, the winding roots of the mangroves seemed to writhe with a life all their own, as if imbued with a sentience that mirrored the lagoon's mysterious aura. Beneath the gnarled canopy, creatures of the nocturnal world lurked, their eyes glowing with ravenous hunger. They skittered and slithered amidst the underbrush, their movements a dance of primal instincts, like the shadows that crept within the heart of a dark forest.

As the colossal form of Zylron made contact with the lagoon's rugged shores, the party stood on the precipice of a realm brimming with perilous marvels. Here, they would navigate with cautious steps amidst the looming presence of dragons, serpents, hydras, and an ever-present shroud of the enigmatic. Serpent's Lagoon was where the boundary separating dreams from nightmares dissolved, merging into a surreal, treacherous reality, as if stepping into a realm woven from the fabric of the most haunting dreams.

Upon their arrival at this enigmatic destination, Queen Jeanne's eyes widened in sheer terror as she beheld the nightmarish spectacle unfurling before her. The moon's pallid luminescence unveiled the ominous ballet of hydras emerging from the lagoon's inky depths, their gnarled reptilian forms and serpentine heads casting grotesque, writhing shadows upon the world. Sinister serpents, emissaries of the aquatic abyss, slithered forth with eyes gleaming wickedly like evil spirits materializing from despair. In the face of this grotesque panorama, Queen Jeanne's terror surged into a piercing scream, a symphony of fear reverberating through the haunting night, a scream that echoed like a haunting melody in the eerie silence.

Phoenix, his evil grin a cruel crescent moon in the inky darkness, cast an appraising glance at her, his amusement a macabre jest. "Now, my dear," he purred, his voice a serpent's sibilant whisper that slithered through the air like a venomous snake, "let us seek a more suitable sanctuary. The great outdoors does not quite meet your refined expectations." His words hung in the air, dripping with dark irony, mocking the notion of sanctuary in this treacherous lagoon.

Guiding the Queen along, they embarked upon a journey through a labyrinth of winding corridors, each twist and turn to conceal the secrets of bygone eras. At the same time, the very walls seemed to bear the weight of untold chronicles, like the passages of a forgotten library in a timeless realm. Ultimately, they arrived at a towering skyscraper, a somber sentinel of obsidian nestled within the labyrinth's heart, its enigmatic door a portal to her impending captivity.

The heavy, ancient door groaned open, revealing a chamber shrouded in the impenetrable darkness of a predator's lair, waiting hungrily for its prey. Phoenix gestured inward, his smirk a sinister invitation into the abyss. "This, my dear, is your new residence," he declared, his voice chilling as the lagoon's inky depths. "As long as your dear husband conducts himself with utmost restraint, you shall remain untouched. However, should he dare to embark upon a quest to find you, the evil creatures that haunt our doorstep will inevitably find their sinister paths leading into this very tower."

With a solemn gesture, he extended his hand, invoking ancient enchantments that sealed the door behind them with an aura resonating with ancient, arcane power. "This seal," he intoned, his voice a mournful dirge for her impending isolation, "shall be your shield against the perils lurking without, yet it shall also stand as an unyielding sentinel against any would-be saviors."

With the utterance of this final decree, Queen Jeanne's destiny was irrevocably bound to the labyrinthine tower, a captive within a cryptic fortress where the threads of fate wove a dark tapestry of despair and shadow, like the intricate patterns of a cosmic loom.

Her gaze, a storm of apprehension and desperation, remained fixed upon Phoenix, her eyes like a tumultuous storm brewing on the horizon. "What have you done to my beloved husband?" she implored, her voice laden with her deepest fears, like a mournful lament carried on a haunted wind.

A chilling echo of Phoenix's laughter in the chamber filled the air like the ominous rumblings of an evil deity. "Fear not, my dear Queen," he replied, his tone saturated with icy amusement. "Your husband's safety resides firmly within his own choices. Should he heed my counsel, he shall emerge from this ordeal unscathed. However, should he decide to cast aside the restraints I have placed upon him, the dungeon's enigmatic secrets will become his difficult companions, and his path shall be fraught with darkness and uncertainty."

With a gesture as passive as a death knell, Phoenix beckoned Qellaun to his side, and together, they embarked on a grim mission to further fortify the labyrinth with a labyrinth of cunning traps, designed to dissuade and ensnare any potential rescuers. The maze, a phantasmal nightmare of twisting passages, whispered prophecies of doom to those who dared to enter like a siren's call to an uncharted abyss.

Within the confines of the Queen's chamber, the ominous guardians stood sentinel statues animated with an evil presence, their stony eyes concealing a deadly secret. They were like petrified sentinels, their very existence hinting at the treacherous journey that awaited any who dared to breach the Queen's prison. These stone figures, once perhaps sculpted with noble intentions, now exuded an aura of malice, their presence a foreboding omen.

Poisonous flora, wicked tendrils of green malevolence, slithered along the labyrinth's walls, their noxious scent cloaked in the sickly-sweet fragrance of deception. Each step through this botanical nightmare was a gamble with one's very existence, as these insidious plants lay in patient wait, eager to trap intruders in their lethal embrace. Their vines moved with a sinister grace, like serpents ready to strike, making the labyrinth a treacherous thicket of danger.

Venturing deeper into the labyrinth became an exercise in deciphering a malevolent riddle, a twisted dance of misdirection designed to confuse and trap. It was a macabre ballet where every turn led to a spiraling abyss of uncertainty, leaving those brave enough to navigate its winding passages lost and vulnerable, like prey in a trap, ensnared by the enigma of the labyrinth itself.

With each trap meticulously set, the labyrinth transformed into a realm of ever-escalating peril, a cryptic enigma that awaited anyone daring to challenge it. Within its sinister depths lay Queen Jeanne's uncertain destiny, her prison a web of treacherous designs, while the looming specter of doom cast its long shadow over her sanctuary.

After their meticulous work weaving the labyrinth's perilous tapestry was complete, Qellaun and Phoenix emerged into the enigmatic embrace of the night. Their sinuous shadows danced ominously as they made their way toward Zylron, the colossal red dragon who awaited them like an ancient sentinel of the skies. His presence was as majestic as a myth come to life, his wings like the embodiment of freedom.

As Zylron's mighty wings unfurled, they seemed to command the wild winds themselves. He soared through the heavens, his wingtips gently brushing against the velvety canopy of stars, drawing near the looming tower where Queen Jeanne's fate hung in precarious balance. The moon's pale luminescence painted an eerie, surreal portrait, casting inky shadows upon the tower's stony facade, like a haunting backdrop to a dark drama.

Phoenix's smile, more enigmatic than ever, played upon his lips as he spoke. "The labyrinth is now an enigmatic fortress, my dear Queen," he purred, his voice a dark serenade that echoed through the night, like the haunting melody of a forbidden song, "and rest assured, Qellaun and I shall be your shadowy sentinels, unwavering in our vigilant watch over your fate." His words were like a sinister promise, binding her to the fate woven for her in this labyrinth of darkness.

With a graceful turn, Zylron's wings sliced through the night air, a symphony of shadows and moonlight, as he embarked on his journey back to Goldmoor, carrying with him the secrets of the labyrinth, the fate of the Queen, and the lingering echoes of a cryptic, scary night. His departure was like the closing act of a dark opera, leaving behind a stage set for solitude and uncertainty.

Queen Jeanne's gaze followed the dragon's majestic departure, her heart a heavy burden, bearing the weight of her dire predicament. Her voice, a fragile whisper upon the night's ethereal breath, carried her hopes and longings into the boundless expanse of the heavens. "Please," she implored the stars, her silent plea like a fleeting comet's trail, "find me, my beloved husband, and guide me back to our cherished home." Her words were like a lament carried on in the winds of hope.

As she turned away from the moonlit window, the solitary chair awaited her like an ancient throne of isolation. She lowered herself onto it, becoming a lone figure in the very heart of her labyrinthine prison. The tapestry of her thoughts was woven with threads of despair. Yet, within its intricate design, a glimmer of hope sparkled like the distant radiance of a solitary star amidst the unfathomable abyss, a beacon of resilience in the face of darkness.

Queen Jeanne settled into the chair, an eerie sense of solitude and vulnerability enveloping her like an ominous shroud. Despite herself, her gaze was inexorably drawn back to the window, where the outside world unfolded in a haunting tableau.

The moonlight bathed the night in a silvery, ghostly glow, unveiling a chilling panorama. Serpents, their scales glistening with a beguiling, malevolent allure, slithered through the lagoon's waters like spectral denizens of the deep, their movements like a sinister aquatic ballet. Hydra heads breached the inky surface, their multifaceted eyes gleaming with a wicked, conscious intelligence, embodying the role of guardians in this labyrinthine prison.

Above, against the inky canvas of the night sky, dragons soared, their scales catching the lunar radiance and reflecting it like celestial jewels. Their roars reverberated like thunderclaps, and their mighty wings sliced through the air, casting eerie, undulating shadows upon the lagoon's tranquil surface. They were colossal titans, undisputed masters of the skies, their presence a testament to the otherworldly power of this realm.

Around the tower, the tangled roots of the mangroves seemed to writhe with a life of their own, concealing nocturnal creatures that skittered and slithered in the underbrush. Their eyes gleamed with the ruthless hunger of the night, unseen but an ever-present, evil presence in the enigmatic labyrinth surrounding the forsaken tower, like evil spirits lurking in the heart of a dark forest.

A tremor of trepidation coursed through Queen Jeanne as she beheld this eerie symphony of peril and obscurity. The sinister denizens that slithered and soared beyond her moonlit window were haunting embodiments of the dangers lurking within Serpent's Lagoon. Within the confines of her solitary fortress, surrounded by these evil specters, she was left to ponder her destiny, each fragile exhalation resembling a feeble whisper lost amidst the boundless chasm of the night, like a lost soul in the vast expanse of a nightmarish landscape.

Chapter 6

The Hunt Begins: In Search of Keisha and Ong

Qellaun, having returned to the transformed palace of Goldmoor, embarked on a journey that transcended the mundane. Every step he took reverberated through the glorious halls like the hallowed footfalls of a devout congregation in the sanctified aisles of a cathedral. The opulence of Goldmoor's palace, once a beacon of regal splendor, now seemed to shimmer with an eerie undercurrent of foreboding. The shadows, akin to an all-encompassing shroud of an enigma, clung to the edges of this gilded opulence, their inky tendrils weaving intricate narratives upon the walls as if ancient secrets, long ensnared, now sought emancipation.

With the poised grace of a seasoned diplomat threading through treacherous diplomatic waters, he finally arrived at the grand throne room, where Phoenix, the newly anointed sovereign, held his court. The air in the chamber felt heavy with the weight of destiny, as though the room held its breath in anticipation.

Upon crossing the threshold into this hallowed chamber, Qellaun couldn't help but be awed by the luxury surrounding him. Once a canvas adorned with images of prosperity and benevolent rule, the throne room had undergone a profound transmutation. Once graced with symbols of benevolent rule, the walls now bore the weight of clandestine conspiracies and veiled intrigues. Like a serpent coiled amidst a bed of gleaming jewels, the gilded embellishments shimmered with latent peril, their beauty concealing the treacherous nature of the court that unfolded within these walls.

Phoenix, radiant in his newfound authority, occupied the imposing throne. His presence was like a dark star at the center of a celestial court, a force to be reckoned with. His gaze, a vortex of unbridled power and unquenchable ambition, remained fixed upon Qellaun, who stood before him with unswerving loyalty, akin to a knight sworn to a mysterious liege, a pawn in a complex game of power and intrigue.

In a voice that reverberated through the chamber like the rolling thunder on the distant horizon, Phoenix finally spoke, his words laden with the profound gravity of a world forever altered. "Yes, My Lord?" Qellaun inquired, his voice a musical ode to unwavering loyalty, a melody of obedience in the presence of an enigmatic conductor orchestrating a symphony of darkness.

Phoenix's pronouncement lingered in the air, a decree that cast a looming shadow over the future of Goldmoor. It heralded the inception of a reign shrouded in obscurity, an era marked by unyielding dominion. As his words reverberated through the chamber like the tolling of a foreboding bell, they became an unforgettable testament to transforming a once-beloved city into a city of uncertainty and discontent.

"I must assume the mantle of governance over this city," he declared, his voice a solemn proclamation that resonated with the weight of destiny, "and our subjects must recognize that my rule starkly contrasts with that of their benevolent former king. From this day forth, I shall levy double taxation upon every citizen." His words were like a dark covenant, binding the city to a future fraught with economic hardship and unrest.

The citizens of Goldmoor, their ears attentive to the King's proclamation, experienced a turbulent cascade of astonishment and disquiet. The news of double taxation rippled through the chamber like wildfire, setting ablaze sentiments of discontent and unrest within their hearts. The once-revered monarch had yielded his throne to a ruler who seemed prepared to assert his sovereignty without hesitation, and the consequences were dire.

Beyond the gilded gates of the palace, the bustling thoroughfares of Goldmoor, once a vibrant tapestry resounding with laughter and animated discourse, now reverberated with the somber sonata of unrest and trepidation. The city's erstwhile lustrous golden hues, symbols of prosperity, had dimmed into the murky shades of anxiety. Like magic spoken in portentous verses, the metamorphosis had etched its indelible mark upon Goldmoor, once a beacon of hope, now a city enveloped in the shrouds of uncertainty and foreboding.

In the heart of Goldmoor, its denizens grappled with a newfound reality: their cherished city had undergone a profound transformation, and the decrees of their new King had irrevocably reshaped their lives. The specter of uncertainty loomed overhead, casting its evil shadow upon their once-thriving existence. With bated breath, they bore witness as the winds of change swept relentlessly through their beloved city like a fierce storm rending the fabric of their lives, leaving behind a tapestry of unrest and fear.

Within the opulent chamber, Phoenix's eyes blazed with an intensity akin to smoldering embers, their fiery gaze unyielding as it fixated upon Qellaun. The grandeur of the room, once a haven of luxury and grace, now seemed to bow in deference to the newfound regal authority of the King. Its once-immaculate decor bore subtle hints of encroaching shadows, akin to ancient tapestries murmuring of concealed perils, as though the very walls of the palace whispered secrets of a city in turmoil.

Qellaun," Phoenix intoned, his voice a clarion call demanding immediate attention, "it is time to unleash the Druchii. Send them forth, as ethereal phantoms shrouded in darkness, to pursue Swifthammer and the enigmatic Eladrin who dares to walk by his side. Swifthammer hails from the elusive Crystal Vale, a city we must mark as the genesis of their enigmatic trail. And," his voice assumed the serpentine hiss of intrigue, "I demand answers concerning this enigmatic Eladrin—her name, origins, and the purpose she serves at Swifthammer's side."

Qellaun, the embodiment of unwavering loyalty, bowed before the King's will. "Yes, My Lord, with utmost haste."

With a solemn nod, Qellaun retreated from the throne room, the weight of the King's command resting heavily upon his shoulders. The Druchii, akin to shadows conjured from the very abyss, poised themselves to embark on a journey of dark revelation, relentlessly tracking the enigmatic figures who had dared to trespass within their realm. As the grand chamber's doors closed behind him, the echoes of Phoenix's mandates lingered in the air, warnings of the impending darkness that would soon descend upon Swifthammer, the mysterious Eladrin, and their enigmatic secrets.

As Ong and Keisha entered the serene sanctuary of Purplefire Woods, the verdant canopy above stretched like the benevolent arms of a guardian, its emerald leaves offering solace to their weary souls. Thunder, their steadfast steed, bore the weight of their odyssey with stoic grace, pausing beside the babbling stream to seek respite.

Ong dismounted first with the graceful bearing of a gallant knight, his countenance adorned with a playful grin. He extended his hand toward Keisha, a flicker of active fire dancing in his eyes, denying her the descent to solid ground without his chivalrous assistance. "Allow me, my lady," he chuckled, his voice akin to the musical whispers of leaves exchanging secrets.

As Keisha stepped onto the terrain, Ong retained the tender hold of her hand, his tone adopting a more solemn cadence. "Keisha," he began, his voice a gentle rustling, akin to leaves stirred by a caressing breeze, "Goldmoor is no trifling city. It is shadowed by the dominion's specter, an ever-present haunting. My heart aches with concern for your safety."

His anxiety transformed into exasperation, and he gestured toward the ancient arboreal sentinels that surrounded them, guardians of their intimate conversation. "You are a treasure beyond measure to me, yet you persist in placing yourself in the path of peril. I cannot fathom why you would court such danger."

Keisha turned to Ong, her eyes radiant with curiosity as though they held the luminosity of a myriad of celestial galaxies. She posed her question with the delicacy of a petal carried on a gentle, lingering breeze. "Ong, what would your course have been if fate had not guided me to your side? Would you find yourself... adrift?"

Ong's unwavering and resolute gaze locked onto Keisha's, and his response resonated with the wisdom of time itself, each word a thread intricately woven into the tapestry of their conversation. "I would have forged a path, Keisha. My years as a seasoned warrior have given me the knowledge to confront perils, even as formidable as the warlock Phoenix."

His words carried the weight of conviction, a declaration of his unyielding determination to navigate the treacherous currents of fate, with or without her by his side.

A profound hush descended, thick as the night's velvet shroud, as if Ong's words were etched in unyielding stone, each syllable a weighty testament to the gravity of his sentiments. He continued his voice a gentle, moonlit caress upon the tranquil sea of their discourse. "Yet, Keisha, it does not alter the undeniable truth that you willingly ventured into the abyss of peril, a treacherous path fraught with dangers that could have exacted the price of your life. While I am eternally indebted for your selfless act in rescuing me, I implore you to pledge never to undertake such life-threatening risks lightly. Your well-being, Keisha, is more precious to me than the rarest gem, the brightest star, or the deepest enigma of the cosmos."

Keisha nodded, her cheeks aglow with a blush reminiscent of the dawn's unfolding hues, a bloom of warmth mirrored the colors of an awakening sunrise. She briefly averted her gaze, thoughts gathering like thunderheads on the horizon. Then, her eyes returned to Ong's, a constellation of determination gleaming within them. "I shall only say this, Ong: I shall endeavor, but I cannot forsake adversity if a chance exists to bring about change."

She turned toward Ong, her eyes filled with a genuine sense of wonder, as though she peered deep into the mystical heart of an uncharted forest. "Ong, how is it that we have woven such an enduring bond when the threads of our connection have only begun to unravel?"

Ong's gaze softened even further, his eyes resembling tranquil pools of contemplation, and he responded with a sincerity that flowed like an endless river through the corridors of time. "Keisha, sometimes destiny introduces you to another soul, and it feels as if the pages of your lives have been intricately woven together since the dawn of existence. I cannot articulate it precisely, but from the moment our paths converged, I sensed an unbreakable connection, a magnetic pull that drew me toward you. You are precious to me because you've already etched your essence upon the parchment of my heart, and I shall not permit any harm to befall you. It is because, within your actions and your spirit, I recognize someone worth defending, safeguarding, and cherishing, regardless of the briefness of our acquaintance."

Keisha's eyes, akin to twin lanterns burning in the depths of an enchanted forest, shimmered with an insatiable curiosity as she delved into the enigmatic forces that had drawn her inexorably toward Ong. "Do you suppose," she mused, a hushed whisper of intrigue, "that this is what my parents experienced when they first met? That intangible connection, the threads of fate weaving the tapestry of their lives?"

As the words danced upon her lips, a fleeting shadow of apprehension swept across her countenance, a passing cloud casting a transient chill upon the verdant landscape of her emotions. The memory of her parents, cruelly stolen from her at a tender age, lingered like a phantom at the fringes of her consciousness, and she couldn't help but wonder if their connection had been as profound before their untimely departure.

Ong contemplated her question with a furrowed brow, his features bathed in thoughtful contemplation. "Perhaps, one day, we may seek the answers from them," he proposed, oblivious to the tragic fate that had befallen her parents.

However, Keisha's reply was fraught with sorrow, her eyes brimming with unshed tears as she shared a painful truth. "Ong, my parents... they are no longer with us."

His eyes widened in sudden realization, regret flooding his features as he tenderly reached out to her. "Oh, Keisha, I did not know of your loss."

In a gesture imbued with tenderness, Ong drew her close, his touch akin to a comforting breeze on a frigid night, his thumb delicately wiping away her tears.

"Thank you," Keisha whispered, her voice trembling with gratitude. "Perhaps, in time, I shall share their story with you, but not just yet."

As laughter filled the forest, Ong, Keisha, and Pumpkin shared a fleeting moment of joy amidst the uncertainty of their situation. The infectious joy of their playful companion lifted their spirits, reminding them of life's simple pleasures even in the face of danger.

Ong's eyes sparkled with warmth as he looked at Keisha and whispered, "It seems Pumpkin has the gift of bringing light to even the darkest moments."

Keisha's smile radiated with affection as she nodded. "Indeed, he does. It's a reminder that we should cherish every moment, especially in times like these."

Pumpkin, tail wagging with enthusiasm, continued to frolic around them, his boundless energy a testament to the resilience of joy in adversity.

As the echoes of laughter waned, a serene hush draped over them, and Keisha's keen ears, attuned to the secrets of the forest, detected a distant susurrus—a whisper of voices that danced amidst the sylvan murmurs. Her eyes narrowed, picking up on the elusive source of this ethereal symphony. On the fringes of the forest, the voices crystallized, and she discerned the ominous, otherworldly cadence of Druchii, the language of the Dark Elves.

She turned to Ong, her countenance etched with gravity, and urgently confided, "Ong, it's the Druchii. I understand their dialect. They are drawing near."

Ong wasted no time. With enthusiasm, he made his way to Thunder, his loyal steed. Gathering Keisha into his protective embrace, he cradled her close, his body forming a shield against potential peril. "Hold fast," he instructed, his voice a low, soothing murmur to both Keisha and Pumpkin.

Amidst the embrace of Purplefire Woods, Ong guided Thunder into the heart of the forest. Yet, here, they ventured too deep; Keisha arrested him with a gentle touch upon his arm. She whispered in his ear, "There lies a concealed enclave not far from this point, where we may clandestinely eavesdrop upon them. Follow me."

Ong nodded, a flicker of gratitude in his eyes for Keisha's intimate knowledge of the forest. He entrusted her instincts as they discreetly altered their course, delving deeper into the woods towards their hidden vantage point, where they could secretly eavesdrop on the encroaching Druchii without unveiling their presence.

As Ong and Keisha crouched in their clandestine vantage point, nestled within the forest's very bosom, the Druchii soldiers' hushed voices wafted through the air like spectral whispers. Ong's brow furrowed as he exchanged a silent glance with Keisha, urging her to translate their dialect.

With a nod, Keisha leaned closer to Ong and murmured, "They've received orders to locate us and return us to Goldmoor. Their destination is Emeraldwoods, where they believe they may uncover clues. They have been ordered to capture us before we enter Crystal Vale." She paused, her countenance growing graver. "Phoenix seeks information about me—my name and further details concerning the Eldarin and the Eladrin's home."

Ong's jaw set, absorbing this critical intelligence. The situation had veered into treacherous territory. To elude capture and shield Keisha's identity and origins, they would need to outmaneuver the relentless pursuit of the Druchii. Ong nodded to Keisha with an unwavering gaze, silently expressing his gratitude for her decrypting the adversary's designs.

A soft, almost impish laugh escaped Keisha's lips as she leaned closer to Ong, her voice a conspiratorial whisper. "They will find no information about E'vahona," she confided, a glint of confidence gleaming in her eyes. "A concealed entrance and a potent magical barrier have guarded our homeland for centuries. Only those whom we trust may enter."

Ong couldn't help but be impressed by the layers of protection enveloping Keisha's ancestral realm. It infused hope into their quest to evade capture and unearth the truths hidden within the labyrinth of intrigue. "That is reassuring," he replied with a nod, a semblance of relief gracing his features. Their endeavor to evade capture had just received an unexpected boon.

In the heart of the ancient forest, their alliance solidified as though the very trees bore witness to the unspoken vows they exchanged. The whispers of leaves and the gentle sway of branches seemed to echo their determination, amplifying their resolve in the face of adversity. With its timeless wisdom, the forest held its secrets close, a sanctuary against the encroaching storm.

Ong fixed his gaze upon Keisha, a reflection of unwavering sincerity in his eyes as he posed a profound question laden with implications. "Keisha," he began, his voice carrying the weight of an ancient oath, "am I, in the depths of your heart, the guardian deserving of the secrets of your city's sanctuary?"

Keisha locked her gaze onto Ong's, her eyes like polished emeralds gleaming with wisdom and purpose. Her voice, soft yet carrying the weight of ages, unfolded like a parchment inscribed with the secrets of her people. "There are four sacred stipulations, Ong, carved into the very roots of our heritage.

First, you must seek an audience with Lord Karrenen, the vigilant sentinel of our realm, his wisdom a beacon guiding our way. Second, you must lay bare the purpose that fuels your desire to tread the hallowed ground of the Eladrin's ancestral sanctuary.

But it is in the latter two conditions that the deeper bonds between individuals and our Eldarin kin come to bear. The council has decreed that only those who share a profound connection with an Eladrin may step into E'vahano, for they alone will safeguard the sanctity of our culture.

These tenets have been venerable pillars in our heritage, upheld with unwavering devotion through the annals of time."

Ong's resolute nod conveyed his unwavering commitment, an unspoken pledge etched in the steely resolve of his features. He addressed Keisha with steadfast determination, eager to unravel the remaining mysteries. "I shall take the necessary steps to meet Lord Karrenen and lay bare the purpose that burns within my heart. Yet, Keisha, if there are additional conditions, I pray you reveal them. I wish to grasp the full scope of what it takes to earn your trust and, with it, the privilege of entering your ancestral realm."

Keisha sighed softly, her eyes veiled in a dance of uncertainty and contemplation. She weighed her words carefully, acknowledging the gravity of their burgeoning connection yet understanding the need for transparency. "Ong, these last two conditions delve into the deepest recesses of connections between individuals and our Eladrin kin," she began, her voice a soft lament. "But I am hesitant, caught between the traditions of my people and the bond we are forging."

Ong's gaze remained locked onto hers, his unwavering earnestness a steadfast anchor. "Keisha, I've chosen to walk this path with you, to delve into the enigmas of your world. Please trust that my resolve and commitment to understanding your culture are unwavering. Share these conditions with me; we shall navigate their intricacies."

The silence followed was pregnant with contemplation, the verdant embrace of the forest their only witness to this pivotal moment in their journey.

As Keisha unveiled the second condition, her voice quivered like a fragile leaf trembling in the breeze, and her gaze remained averted as though she feared Ong's reaction. "One of the conditions pertains to Lord Karrenen's curiosity about your sentiments towards me," she confessed, "especially if there is a romantic entanglement between us."

Ong absorbed this revelation with measured contemplation, his thoughts weaving intricate patterns of understanding and respect for the customs and inquiries of Keisha's people. He nodded thoughtfully and then, with gentle determination, inquired about the final condition, his voice a reassuring presence in the tranquil forest. "And what of the last condition?"

With her head still bowed, Keisha disclosed the most formidable conditions humans had rarely met. Her words bore the weight of tradition and the legacy of her father's example. "The ultimate condition," she revealed, "is the most formidable, one that most humans cannot fulfill—a condition my father upheld. Should someone we hold dear be trapped by an adversary, manipulated as a pawn to divulge E'vahona's location, that individual must steadfastly refuse, regardless of the circumstances."

A heavy sigh accompanied Keisha's admission, and she turned her head aside, unable to meet Ong's gaze, her heart heavy with the realization of the burden she had placed upon him. "I understand if you cannot accept these conditions, Ong," she confessed, her voice laced with vulnerability. "Discerning this before you become further entwined with me is best.

Ong's countenance bore the weight of their shared destiny, his eyes like twin pools of steadfast determination, reflecting the depths of his resolve. The stillness that enveloped them seemed to hold its breath as if nature paused to listen to his solemn pledge.

"Keisha," he began with a gentle reverence that hung in the air like magic, "I cannot foretell the future, nor can I divine the trials that may cross our path, but I can offer you this: a promise etched in the stone of my heart. I shall employ every fiber of my being to protect your homeland, unswayed by the whims of fate. Though I may never fully grasp your father's hardships, I shall uphold his legacy with unwavering devotion. I will meet Lord Karrenen and lay bare my intentions, and if our hearts find a common beat, I shall face the remaining conditions with unwavering resolve."

A soft breath of hope danced between them, like a whisper of wind rustling through the leaves of a sacred tree. Ong's countenance softened further, his eyes now adorned with a tender, reassuring smile. It was a smile that radiated warmth and an unshakable commitment.

"Keisha, your worth is beyond measure," he declared with a quiet intensity, "and I am not one to falter in the face of adversity. I stand by your side, unyielding, unflinching, through whatever trials may lie ahead."

With their hearts entwined in purpose and their destinies intertwined, Ong leaned in, closing the distance between them, and their lips met in a kiss that sealed their pact, a promise of unity and unwavering support.

The ancient forest, with its towering trees and whispering leaves, bore witness to their pledge, a promise woven into the very fabric of their shared adventure.

Keisha's voice wavered like a fragile flame caught in a gentle breeze. Her emotions laid bare as she unraveled a thread of her past for Ong. She embarked upon telling a tale that held the gravity of ancient legends, her words laden with sincerity, a precious gift shared with utmost trust.

"In preparation for your meeting with Lord Karrenen, you must first become acquainted with the story of my parents," she commenced with a hesitant yet resolute melody. "This narrative is intricately interwoven with the ultimate condition, a complex tapestry of love and sacrifice."

She paused briefly, allowing the weight of her words to sink in like the solemn hush before a pivotal moment in history. "Allow me to unveil but a portion of this chronicle. My mother, Serena, embodied the grace and skill of an elven archer, while my father, Eldric, was a human mage with fiery red hair and emerald eyes—hence the origin of my distinctive features." Her gaze seemed to transcend the present, traversing the corridors of time to a distant past.

"Their love, born amid our enchanted realm, flourished into a profound bond," she continued, her voice a vessel for memories long held. "When the shadows of destiny cast their ominous veil upon us, my father faced capture at the hands of the Druchii, the malevolent specters that haunt our history. Like the darkest forces of fate, his captors demanded my mother's ultimate loyalty—a betrayal of our sacred sanctuary in exchange for his release. It was a choice that ripped her heart asunder, for her love for him and her duty to our homeland were intertwined like roots deep within the earth."

Keisha's voice trembled under the weight of the memory, like a fragile leaf fluttering in the face of an oncoming storm. "And so, they parted ways," she whispered, the words carrying the bittersweet echoes of love and sacrifice. "Before their hearts were severed by the cruel hand of fate, my father's parting words to her were these: 'Serena, never forget I love you, and take care of Keisha. Farewell, my love.'"

As she concluded her tale, the air seemed to hum with the resonance of that profound moment. Ong, a silent witness to her history, offered a comforting touch upon her shoulder, his eyes reflecting the sorrow and determination within the narrative.

In the quiet moments following Keisha's revelation, Ong's voice, hushed and reverent, drifted like a whispered incantation amid the solemnity of the forest. "Keisha, I stand in awe of the trials your mother and father faced," he murmured, words bearing the weight of deep respect and admiration. "Their love, enduring and sacrificial, shines like a radiant star amidst the tapestry of their devotion to E'vahona. I am profoundly honored that you have chosen to share this poignant tale with me. Rest assured. I solemnly pledge to harness every resource to ensure their sacrifice was not in vain."

He paused momentarily, the intensity of his gaze locked onto hers like twin constellations converging in a cosmic embrace. "Though our companionship is still in its nascent stages, please understand this, Keisha: I already hold you in the highest regard, and the well-being of your homeland is a matter of profound significance to me. No matter what adversities lay ahead, we shall face them together, just as your parents did in their time."

Keisha acknowledged his words with a nod, her eyes reflecting a shared understanding of the prudence that must govern their actions, especially in the shadow of the relentless Druchii pursuit. "Your wisdom is undeniable, Ong," she concurred. "Prudence shall indeed guide our path, especially as we confront the relentless pursuit of the Druchii. I shall send word to Lord Karrenen, informing him of your intentions. While we await his response, our journey to Crystal Vale shall continue."

With a glance laden with gratitude, Ong's hand clasped hers, a touch both gentle and persistent, a silent testament to their unity in purpose.

"Thank you, Keisha," he said, his voice soothingly. "Together, we shall navigate this path, one measured stride at a time, ensuring our arrival at Crystal Vale, our beacon of hope, remains unscathed."

Having forged their alliance with unwavering determination, the two brave souls ventured forth, their resolve undiminished, their shared objective gleaming on the horizon like a radiant beacon, symbolizing their indomitable spirit.

Ong cast a contemplative glance over his shoulder at Keisha, his brow furrowing with a modicum of concern. "Keisha," he began, his voice a river winding through the valleys of his thoughts, "is there an alternate route, a clandestine trail leading to Emeraldwood Forest and the hidden sanctum of Crystal Vale, one that circumvents the perilous traverse of that narrow waterway?"

In response, Keisha's soft laughter wafted like a gentle breeze, her head swaying in a tender negation. "No, Ong," she replied, her words a whispering leaf rustling in the forest of their conversation, "that singular path, treacherous though it may be, stands as our sole conduit to their sanctuary. It was carefully crafted to remain concealed and safeguarded, offering no straightforward alternative for travelers like us."

Ong nodded thoughtfully, his mind a tapestry of stratagems, threads of contingency woven with care to navigate the formidable path ahead and ensure their unscathed passage through the treacherous terrain.

Keisha regarded Ong with tender admiration, her voice a murmur of wisdom as she shared her insight. "Not far from our current location, there lies a cavern—a hidden respite that could serve as our sanctuary for the night. Journeying through the forest after nightfall carries its perils, and it is prudent to seek refuge when the opportunity presents itself."

Ong considered her counsel, recognizing the sagacity in securing a haven for the night's reprieve. He nodded in agreement. "Very well," he assented, his voice a solemn vow, "lead the way to this cave. We shall take our rest there and resume our journey with the dawn. Our safety shall forever remain our paramount concern."

Guided by Keisha's unwavering guidance, they ventured deeper into the woods, their forms cast in elongated shadows as the waning daylight surrendered to the encroaching night, the forest embracing them in its enigmatic embrace.

As the radiant day descended into the embrace of twilight, Phoenix, a formidable figure, stood like an unyielding monolith at the epicenter of Goldmoor's gathering. His determination was an impervious fortress against the currents of doubt that swirled around him. His proclamation had sliced through the air, a trumpet blast demanding the citizens bear the unbearable weight of doubled taxes. Yet, like ripples on the surface of a serene pond, murmurs of discontent rippled through the crowd, and palpable hesitation hung in the air, a heavy cloud obscuring the sun of compliance.

Amidst this turbulent sea of doubt, a solitary torch of courage ignited—an audacious shopkeeper, Taldor, who strode forth, unswayed by the oppressive atmosphere. His voice, a clarion call of dissent, pierced the gathering's uneasy silence, "My lord, I implore you. The yoke of double taxes is too grievous for my modest establishment to bear."

The incarnation of unshakable authority, Phoenix turned his steely gaze upon Taldor, his countenance an unyielding citadel. Without uttering a word, he beckoned a Druchii enforcer, a harbinger of darkness, who advanced with grim determination. In a swift and heart-rending tableau of power, the enforcer laid claim to Taldor's cart of goods, sending it into disarray. With a resounding crash, the once-pristine merchandise lay strewn about, a poignant symbol of defiance crushed beneath the heel of authority.

The collective breath of the citizenry caught in their throats, and trepidation danced like phantom specters in their eyes as they beheld the stark consequence of dissent. Taldor, his visage drained of color, now comprehended the exorbitant price of his audacity.

Like a tempered blade slicing through the heavy silence, Phoenix's voice resounded across the square, his mandate as unyielding as forged iron, devoid of mercy. "Witness the fate that befalls those who dare to defy the dominion's edicts. The doubling of taxes is not a choice but an inevitable decree. You may choose submission and flourish or resistance and bear the weight of your transgressions."

A suffocating pall of disquiet blanketed the assembly, and, one by one, the citizens yielded to the relentless demand for doubled tributes. In his unwavering quest to maintain control at any cost, Phoenix had woven fear into the very tapestry of his rule, employing it as a weapon to quash the seeds of rebellion.

Chapter 7

In Shadows' Pursuit: Journey Through Purplefire Wood

Ong and Keisha stumbled upon a hidden sanctuary deep within the forest's bosom, a haven concealed beneath a lush canopy of emerald leaves and towering craggy sentinels. Nature herself had woven this refuge, a secret enclave, shielding them from the prying eyes that sought to trap them, especially the relentless pursuit of the Druchii.

The equestrian guardian, Thunder, received a gentle beckoning, his presence artfully nestled beneath a verdant tapestry of boughs, blending seamlessly with the forest's shadowy embrace. The ancient trees' branches intertwined like lovers' fingers cast dappled shadows upon the mossy ground, creating an intricate mosaic of light and shade. Meanwhile, Pumpkin, the ever-curious feline, moved with the grace of a curious spirit, her coat a shimmering veil of ebony and amber as she stalked through the sanctuary. The cave's entrance beckoned like a mysterious portal to another world.

Ong, a seasoned maestro of wilderness survival, approached his loyal steed, Thunder, with the practiced precision of a seasoned ranger. He retrieved their essential supplies from his well-organized pack, a meticulously curated ensemble of survival necessities that bore witness to his expertise. Within the sanctuary of the cave, he unrolled a bedding as if unfolding a cherished piece of art, placing it tenderly upon the rocky floor. The cave exhaled an earthy, ambrosial scent akin to the very breath of the land itself, mingling harmoniously with the woodland's fragrant symphony. Together, they composed a soothing lullaby for their senses, cradling the uneven terrain beneath the soft bedding.

Within this sanctuary, the ethereal echoes of leaves rustling in the breeze and the distant murmurs of an unseen stream melded into a tranquil backdrop, offering respite from the enigmatic perils of the forest. Here, they could steal a moment of serenity, a temporary break from their arduous journey.

Seated at the cave's entrance, Keisha's thoughts converged on a matter that lingered in her mind's recesses. Her gaze, as warm as a sunbeam, turned toward Ong, her eyes brimming with gratitude. "Ong," she began, her voice a melodious sonnet, "I wish to convey my deepest appreciation to you for safeguarding Pumpkin during our encounter with Phoenix. She holds a cherished place in my heart."

She paused momentarily, a shadow of concern briefly flickering across her eyes. "Are you injured from our confrontation with him? You went to great lengths to protect her."

Ong's nod carried a soft smile that seemed to infuse the air around them with tenderness. "Keisha, know that Pumpkin's safety is a promise etched in my heart."

He shifted his demeanor to address his condition, his tone reflecting a matter-of-fact resilience. "Regarding my injuries, they are but minor wounds, thanks to the swift actions of our spirited ally here." A nod toward the raven perched upon his shoulder signified his appreciation. "A minor burn marks my back, a remnant of my defense of Pumpkin from Phoenix's fiery assault. It poses no grave concern; time shall mend it."

In the cave's tranquil haven, where the evening's zephyrs whispered secrets through the leaves, Keisha gracefully rose from her seat, her intent an unspoken promise radiating from her eyes. "I shall return shortly," she declared, turning toward the cave's entrance.

Ong's brow furrowed with concern, his voice beginning a protest that was cut short, "Wait, Keisha, it's not safe to—" Yet, before he could finish his admonishment, she had disappeared, leaving him alone with his thoughts and the mysterious sanctuary of the cave.

Frustration welled within Ong, his exasperation echoing softly in the cave's confines. He couldn't comprehend why Keisha was so persistent in her defiance of the safe refuge offered by the cave, like a sanctuary amidst the treacherous wilderness.

A fleeting interlude passed before Keisha reemerged, her presence a whisper on the cave's earthy stage. She carried a humble bundle of herbs and a modest piece of clay in her delicate hands. Ong watched her return with an intrigued curiosity, pondering the enigma of her intentions.

With a determined undertone, Keisha turned toward Ong, her cheeks adorned with a subtle blush akin to the blush of dawn caressing the sky. Her request unfolded like a fragile bloom amidst the forest of her emotions, a gesture as delicate as leaves swaying in a gentle breeze. "Would you," she inquired softly, her voice a tender refrain, "mind removing your chest armor?"

Ong awakened to his playful spirit, yielded to the temptation to tease Keisha, his eyes alight with joy like twin stars illuminating the twilight of their shared amusement. "Is this," he playfully inquired, "an excuse to scrutinize me more closely, Keisha?"

Keisha's cheeks were adorned with a deeper blush, her throat clearing as she countered with a harmony of protest. "No, you are being silly," she retorted, her tone an echoing melody of mild embarrassment. "It's so I can apply the salve properly." The herbs and clay she held became instruments in her unspoken symphony.

With a mock sigh of theatrical disappointment, Ong acquiesced to her request. He peeled away his chest armor, unveiling the minor burn on his back, a canvas for Keisha's gentle ministrations. As her tender touch conveyed the healing salve, he found himself attuned to the exquisite softness of her hands against his skin as though they embodied a soothing lullaby.

Once the salve had been expertly applied, he turned to face her, his eyes resonating with a profound gratitude that welled within his soul. "Thank you, Keisha."

In response, Keisha's radiant smile illuminated the cavern's heart, a beacon of warmth that cut through the cave's shadows. With every passing moment, their bond deepened, an unspoken covenant forged in the crucible of their shared experiences, akin to the melding of kindred spirits within the tapestry of destiny.

The fire crackled within the sheltering sanctuary of the cave, sending forth a symphony of ephemeral sparks that danced through the cavern's depths. Like ancient spirits, Shadows wove their enigmatic tales upon the rocky walls, their movements silent poetry of darkness and light. In this ethereal interplay of illumination, Ong's gaze, akin to a flickering ember, found its way to Keisha. His lips curved into a tender smile, a silent expression of gratitude that welled within him like a rising tide. It was an unspoken ode to the whims of fate that had guided his steps to her side on that fateful day by the stream, where he had stumbled upon her, a vision of otherworldly beauty enshrouded amid her serene bath. A soft chuckle, a testament to the unpredictable hand of destiny, escaped his soul as he recalled the vivid memory of her fiery reaction to his unexpected intrusion.

Caught in the ripples of his amusement, Keisha turned her gaze upon him, her eyes shimmering like stars that had witnessed the secrets of the night. "What," she inquired with playful interest that mirrored the radiant moonlight, "is so funny?"

Ong's smirk, a knowing crescent of mirth, deepened as he settled against the rocky cave's embrace. "Ah," he answered, a mischievous spark glittering in his eyes, "just a fragment of our first encounter," alluding to that memorable day without revealing the full tapestry of their initial meeting.

Her brow momentarily furrowed, a constellation of inquiry etched across her features as she regarded him. "Very well," she conceded with an affectionate roll of her eyes, her irises mirroring the moonlight dance.

Their playful exchange, as delicate as the flutter of moth wings, yielded to the gravity of the approaching night. On the fading day, painted elongated shadows upon the cave's canvas, an artwork in constant flux, and Ong's vigilant gaze turned to Keisha. Concern cast its protective shadow upon his features. "The hour grows late," he noted, his voice a reverent whisper to the night's symphony. "We should seek slumber."

Keisha nodded in concurrence, her eyes tracing the fading twilight's descent as it gracefully yielded to the dominion of stars. Like tendrils of moonlight reaching out to entwine with his, her gaze followed Ong's movements as he meticulously prepared his bedding. Her demeanor was solemn, acknowledging their shared need for rest, as if they were both players in an age-old symphony, tuning their instruments before the night's grand performance.

A flicker of hesitation in her eyes, a fragment of doubt carefully concealed within the intricate tapestry of her expressions. Perplexed yet attuned to the nuances of her emotions, he furrowed his brow and gently inquired, "Where do you intend to rest?"

In response, she gestured gracefully to the rocky floor, the ground uneven and unforgiving, as if preparing to settle upon it with the grace of a woodland spirit. Like a brooding tempest brewing on the horizon, Ong's frown deepened, his concern etched upon his features like ancient runes of protection. His words carried the weight of caution and care, a gentle rebuke to her steadfast determination. "Rocks are no place for slumber; they court discomfort."

Yet, Keisha, unyielding as an ancient tree, remained steadfast and unswayed. Her spirit reflected the forest they found themselves in, resilient and unwavering in the face of adversity. "I'll manage," she asserted, her voice as steady as the roots that anchored the mightiest of trees, a testament to her inner strength and connection to the natural world surrounding them.

Like the steady flow of a river, Ong's well of patience had run dry. He intentionally closed the distance between them, his determination cutting through the uncertainty in the cave's cool air. In a surprising twist, he gathered Keisha into his arms, his strength an unwavering fortress around her. As he cradled her against his chest, his keen senses detected the chill of her skin, a shiver of vulnerability coursing through her like a hidden stream. Like the wind's lament, his exhale escaped in a sigh, his voice a blend of concern and affection, warm and soothing as a sunbeam breaking through a forest canopy. "You should have disclosed your discomfort," he chided gently, his breath a comforting breeze that brushed against the curve of her ear.

Enveloped within his protective cocoon, Keisha felt the reassuring warmth of his body against hers, a hearth's radiant glow offering solace. She leaned into his embrace, her voice a soft, grateful whisper, like the gentle rustle of leaves in a sacred grove. "I hadn't even noticed," she confessed, their hearts beating in synchrony, a rhythm that harmonized their souls within the heart of the cave's sanctuary.

In the sheltering arms of the cave's protective cradle, Ong carried Keisha as if she were a cherished relic from an ancient legend, his features etched with unwavering determination. The lines of his countenance mirrored the stalwart vigilance of a sentinel guarding his most precious treasure. His resolute declaration, delivered with the solemnity of a knight's oath, resonated throughout the cave's ethereal chamber. The enigmatic aura of the cave, steeped in the secrets of ages past, bore witness to this unspoken vow that transcended the limitations of mere words.

Within the quiet cocoon of the cave, Keisha released a gentle sigh, a testament to her yielding to Ong's unwavering insistence. She had traversed untamed forests and faced unyielding adversaries, yet she chose not to wage a battle of wills in the face of Ong's steadfast resolve. With a subtle gesture, she consented, making her way toward the edge of his bedroll. Like wisps of wind tracing ancient runes in the soil, her nimble fingers explored the rugged fabric beneath her, finding a patch of comfort amidst the unyielding terrain.

Yet, Ong's gallant spirit knew no bounds. A wry smile graced his lips as if painted by the playful brushstrokes of moonlight. He extended an invisible thread between them with fluid grace, a silent summons weaved into the very fabric of his intentions. The cave's sacred and timeless ambiance and the whispers of ancient echoes bore witness to this intricate dance, a weaving of destiny's design.

Keisha, in response, released a soft sigh, her surrender to Ong's unwavering will apparent. The corners of her lips curled with a playful defiance that mirrored the spirited rebellion of a forest brook against the rigid mountains. "If you insist," she quipped, her voice akin to a melodic stream of acknowledgment, much like the brook yielding to the mountain's enduring presence.

Ong's laughter, a cascade of joyous emotions, melded with the cave's echoes, resonating through the hallowed chamber. He was resolute in his desire to keep her close, their bond forged unbreakable by the anvil of circumstance. "You always seek a challenge, don't you?" he teased, his voice a gentle breeze that stirred the cave's slumbering secrets.

Like stars embedded in the velvet tapestry of night, their gazes remained locked in a dance of playful rebellion and tender affection. Keisha, her eyes aflame with the spirit of an untamed phoenix, retorted with a lively spark, "Well, it keeps life from growing dull."

Surrendering to the tranquil sanctuary of the cave's embrace, Ong enveloped her in the circle of his arm, a sentinel of the night wrapped in the mystical aura of the cavern. "Simply remain by my side," he implored, his heart harmonizing with an unsung melody of unspoken vows.

Keisha, in response, released a sigh of pure contentment. Her body yielded to his protective warmth, nestled beneath the celestial ballet of shadows that painted the cave's canvas. Within this ethereal stage, she surrendered to the gentle allure of slumber, her spirit finding respite within the cradle of Ong's unwavering embrace.

Ong, the vigilant sentinel, stood watch over her with eyes that mirrored the ageless wisdom of stars. He marveled at her unyielding spirit, a comet of determination streaking through the vast cosmos. Like an unsolved enigma, a question lingered in the recesses of his thoughts – what had forged her into such a fiercely independent lone star, even when the night sky offered the comforting tapestry of constellations?

He pondered the mysteries of her self-reliance, knowing well the communal bonds that typically bound the Eladrin. Yet, Keisha seemed to stand apart, a solitary figure amidst the celestial expanse of her people. She would extend her care to those in need, tending to the wounded and protecting them, yet she reserved her independence regarding her well-being. Ong felt an unwavering resolve growing within him to shield her and demonstrate that she need not be the solitary star in her constellation.

He sealed their intertwined destinies with a tranquil smile, his eyes gently closing as his protective embrace enveloped her, creating a haven of dreams. Together, they surrendered to the all-encompassing lullaby of the night, finding solace in the forest wilderness, where their shared journey unfolded like a mesmerizing tapestry under the starlit sky.

Within the grandeur of Goldmoor's regal throne room, Phoenix, a sovereign bedecked in the resplendent regalia of dominion, occupied his gilded seat. His visage, a meticulously chiseled embodiment of poise, masked the turbulent currents that surged beneath his facade. The tempestuous impatience emanating from him seemed to crackle through the air, a palpable storm brewing within the hallowed confines of the throne room.

With a regal bearing befitting his exalted rank, Phoenix summoned Qellaun, his venerable counselor. Qellaun, like a spectral guardian of arcane knowledge, advanced towards the throne, bearing a blend of reverence and vigilance akin to a falcon circling its elusive quarry.

"Qellaun," Phoenix called, his utterance laden with the urgency of impending storms, "draw near. We must delve deeper into this enigma."

Qellaun, his presence resonating with the serenity of celestial bodies, halted with measured precision. "As you command, My Lord."

Phoenix's gaze, twin orbs of incisive brilliance, bore into his counselor's very soul as if probing the labyrinthine recesses of uncertainty. "Speak, Qellaun. Please share with me your knowledge of the enigmatic Eladrin. Why does their city remain beyond our grasp?"

Qellaun's voice, reminiscent of the steadfast stones of ancient citadels, began to unfurl the intricate tapestry of history. "My Lord, E'vahona, the veiled city of the Eladrin, has stood as an enigmatic enigma, cocooned within the annals of time, its enigmatic secrets safeguarded with unparalleled vigilance."

Phoenix's patience danced with irregular rhythms like a flickering flame amidst the storm's heart. "A riddle spanning countless eras? Clarify."

With the eloquence of a timeless river's flow, Qellaun continued his words with an unrelenting current of revelations. "E'vahona," it is rumored, is an ancient citadel, its walls woven from the strands of potent enchantments. A celestial guardian, a Goddess of Light, encircles the city within her protective shroud, obscuring its whereabouts from mortal grasp."

Phoenix's ire, a conflagration stoked by the relentless storm, surged like molten lava. "Why, Qellaun, was my father ensnared by this hidden gem?"

In the pregnant silence between them, Qellaun wrestled with the gravity of divulgence. "My Lord, the allure of E'vahona lies in its fabled arcane treasures, a wealth beyond measure. Your father perceived its mystical might as the key to dominion over Vacari and all those that make Vacari their home."

Phoenix's hand tightened, the remnants of forgotten dreams crumbling. "Then, Qellaun," he declared with an imperious air, "it is imperative that you delve into our chronicles, engage our most erudite scholars, and decipher every enshrouded syllable about E'vahona, the Eladrin, and the deity that veils it from my reach. The treasures concealed within that hidden city shall be mine, for I shall not suffer defiance."

With a solemn bow, Qellaun embarked on a treacherous odyssey through the vast repository of Goldmoor's knowledge. Yet, as he ventured deeper into the labyrinth of wisdom, a shroud of foreboding descended upon him, for he intuited that the conquest of E'vahona and the unraveling of its mysteries would usher forth consequences even the indomitable Phoenix could scarcely fathom.

Phoenix, a storm of wrath barely contained by regal composure, surged through the labyrinthine passages of Goldmoor Castle. His strides echoed like rolling thunder, each step a proclamation of the turmoil raging within his heart. With its grim chambers steeped in the agonized echoes of past transgressors, the dungeon awaited him.

As Phoenix advanced, a humble citizen, their countenance etched with trepidation, inadvertently stepped into his path, unknowingly challenging the unbridled tempest of his fury. Without hesitation, Phoenix's hand crackled with scarlet lightning, arcs of energy cascading like vengeful serpents poised to strike.

As the lightning bolt rents the insolent soul, the air splits apart with an explosive, electric roar. The hapless citizen, writhing in agony, collapsed onto the frigid stone floor. Their voices drowned amidst the dungeon's relentless echoes.

Unyielding and unperturbed, Phoenix's steps resounded through the corridor, and the flickering torchlight cast menacing shadows as he advanced inexorably toward the dungeon. His next victim awaited there, and his thirst for knowledge and power remained insatiable.

Monolithic guardian statues, hewn from the heart of obsidian mines, stood as formidable sentinels at the entrance of Goldmoor Castle's dreaded dungeon. They loomed, each towering above a tall man, their eyes gleaming like incandescent sapphires. As he stormed towards the dungeon's depths in relentless fury, Phoenix beckoned, and these ancient sentinels stirred with a guttural groan.

Azure flames, ethereal and pulsating, encircled the statues, casting eerie, undulating shadows upon the cold, damp stone walls. Like captive spirits yearning for release, these flickering flames spiraled upward, imparting an almost malevolent glow to the age-old carvings on the walls. The statues' presence was ominous, an embodiment of the cruelty that awaited those who dared venture deeper.

Descending into the abyssal heart of the dungeon, Phoenix approached the portal, leading to the ultimate chasm where King Alex's grim captivity endured. With calculated malice, he marked the entrance with a sinister glyph, a pulsating sigil that throbbed with an otherworldly malevolence.

The door groaned open, revealing a yawning maw of darkness. In this lonely void, King Alex, emaciated and broken, awaited his tormentor. Phoenix's laughter, a wicked symphony, reverberated through the chamber's desolation as he taunted, "How the mighty have fallen, dear King Alex. Your kingdom lies in ruins, and your defiance has delivered you to this wretched abyss."

Phoenix stood before the imprisoned King Alex, his eyes like smoldering coals in the dimly lit chamber. The atmosphere was laden with foreboding, and the shadows seemed to draw near, eager to witness the unfolding confrontation.

With a commanding tone, Phoenix demanded, "Tell me, King Alex, the secrets of the Eladrin. Where is their hidden city, E'vahona?"

King Alex locked eyes with Phoenix. Though feeble and battered, a defiant spark ignited within his gaze. A sinister smile curled upon his lips, a glimmer of triumph amid the gloom. Then, much to Phoenix's bewilderment, he erupted into laughter—a resounding, mocking laughter reverberating through the dungeon's stone confines like a discordant symphony.

Phoenix's anger surged, his frustration manifesting in a blaze of sapphire flames that licked at the damp, moss-covered walls. Yet, King Alex's laughter persisted as if he found Phoenix's desperation amusing.

"Even if I possessed the knowledge of E'vahona," King Alex finally spoke, his voice dripping with scorn, "I would sooner see the world crumble than share its secrets with the likes of you, Phoenix."

With an imperious sweep of his hand, Phoenix summoned spectral phantasms to frolic within the confines of the cell, their forms contorted and eerie. They murmured twisted half-truths and taunted King Alex with surreal visions of despair.

However, the unyielding monarch merely arched an eyebrow and spoke unwaveringly, "Your illusions cannot shatter my spirit, Phoenix. I possess no knowledge of the whereabouts of their city. For centuries, they have safeguarded that enigma, and I now understand why."

Phoenix's wrath surged, his power crackling like frenzied lightning within the claustrophobic space. He stood as an ominous specter amidst the surreal phantasmagoria, poised to unleash his fury upon King Alex's unyielding defiance.

Within the dim and oppressive embrace of the dungeon, a palpable tension lingered, a weighty shroud that hung in the air. King Alex's unwavering silence had incited Phoenix, who, in his exasperation, had resorted to the dark allure of spectral illusions in a futile attempt to break the stubborn monarch.

Yet, King Alex, his spirit resolute as the bedrock of mountains, remained unwavering in his loyalty to the Eladrin. With steely determination, he shook his head, refusing to offer any further responses to Phoenix's relentless inquiries.

Phoenix's anger reignited, his eyes ablaze with an incendiary resolve. In a voice that resonated like the distant rumble of thunder, he intoned, "Very well, King Alex. If you persist in withholding the secrets of E'vahona, then perhaps your wife shall be the one to reveal them."

With these ominous words, Phoenix turned and exited the dungeon, his presence receding like a tempest retreating into the distance.

Alone within the oppressive hush of his cell, King Alex swallowed hard, his eyes locked onto the chamber's exit. He comprehended the peril that loomed over his cherished queen, a storm of fear and love churning within his chest. His voice quivered with a plea that carried through the darkness, "Please, my love, be safe."

In the heart of the forest, where ancient arboreal sentinels whispered their secrets to the winds and the forest's canopy above wove an intricate tapestry of shadows upon the verdant floor, Ong and Keisha discerned an unusual noise that cut through the evening's tranquility. It was a subtle disturbance, like the faint rustling of leaves on a still night, but it was enough to draw their attention.

As the dwindling embers of daylight clung tenaciously to the horizon, Ong's senses, finely tuned like a harpist's strings, discerned this ominous rustling beyond the sheltering embrace of their secluded cave. His gaze shifted to Keisha, who lay cradled within the rocky alcove, her eyes a blend of curiosity and concern. With a gentle and imperative gesture, he urged her to remain concealed, enfolding her form in a protective cocoon. A silent request escaped his lips, a sincere hope that she would remain undisturbed.

Ong inched towards the cave's entrance with his trusty blade unsheathed and gripped firmly in his hand. All his senses stood alert, heightened by the forest's murmurs and whispers. His movements were as silent as a wisp of moonlight, his silhouette merging seamlessly with the encroaching night, a shadow within shadows.

Emerging from the sanctuary of the cave, Ong's sharp eyes fell upon two sinister silhouettes that seemed to have materialized from the shadows of the twilight-draped woods. Druchii soldiers, their ebony armor an extension of the encroaching night, were trapped in a nefarious undertaking beneath the gnarled boughs of an ancient sentinel, their intentions shrouded as the forest's secrets.

Ong, a master of stealth and cunning, opted for discretion over reckless confrontation. He began a silent retreat, like a phantom fading into obscurity, careful not to awaken the Druchii's suspicions. His every motion exuded grace and skill that was the hallmark of his training and experience.

However, as he navigated the unforgiving terrain, a dry twig betrayed his presence with an abrupt snap, fracturing the silence like a brittle promise. The Druchii soldiers, attuned to the discordant note in the forest's symphony, pivoted with predatory swiftness, their malevolent gazes locking onto the intruder. The atmosphere hung heavy, charged with the imminent promise of violence.

In the blink of an eye, a vortex of action unfurled. Ong, swift as a forest-born predator, lunged at one of the Druchii with a blinding burst of agility. His blade cleaved through the air like the judgment of a vengeful spirit, catching the soldier unguarded and off balance.

The Druchii's response was a startled cry as he staggered, a fallen shadow cast adrift in the gathering gloom and ultimately succumbed to the earth's unforgiving embrace.

Meanwhile, the second soldier, unyielding in the face of chaos, retaliated with lightning speed, launching a relentless strike toward Ong. Blades clashed like the opposing forces of nature, each clash echoing through the ancient woods like a primal battle hymn. The dance of steel and fury raged unabated, combatants locked in a desperate struggle for supremacy.

Yet, Ong's indomitable resolve to safeguard Keisha and ensure his survival proved the more potent force. With a final, resolute stroke, he sent his adversary sprawling upon the forest floor, conquered and defeated.

Standing amidst the fallen foes, Ong's breath came in ragged gasps, his form bathed in the gentle caress of moonlight. The ancient forest bore witness to the tumultuous conflict, an impartial observer of the ceaseless cycle of destiny and the unwavering spirit of those who dared to defy the encroaching abyss.

Amidst the echoing symphony of steel and shadows, Ong paused to reclaim his breath, a lone sentinel amidst the fallen Druchii warriors. The ancient forest, serene yet vigilant, enfolded the aftermath of their deadly ballet in the enigmatic embrace of its time-honored boughs.

His gaze, a brief interlude in the tapestry of conflict, turned back to the secluded cave, a sanctum where Keisha remained concealed from the tumultuous dance beyond their rocky refuge. A silent covenant to protect her at any cost etched itself upon the tablet of his heart.

Retracing his steps with the grace of a forest spirit, Ong re-entered the cave, his presence a silhouette bathed in moonlight's tender, silvery kiss. Keisha, an embodiment of grace and vigilance, held her longbow like an elegant instrument, its arrow nocked and eager, ready to pierce the veils of darkness.

A tender smile played upon Ong's lips as he whispered, his voice a soft serenade to the night, "No need for that, Keisha. It's me."

Her sharp, discerning eyes held his figure in their piercing gaze, seeking the truth in his words. Slowly, she lowered her weapon, the tension in her slender frame yielding as she recognized the familiar form of her steadfast guardian.

"What transpired out there?" she inquired, her voice a gentle breeze, carrying the fragrance of concern.

Ong settled beside her, his armor a gentle murmur against the rocky floor of their sanctuary. With a sigh that seemed to stir the moonlight's play of shadows upon his countenance, he began to weave the tale of their encounter with the Druchii soldiers, each word a step along the path of their shared narrative.

"Rest shall be a scarce commodity," he continued, "and the relentless march of the Druchii continuing to dodge our every move. We must gather strength and embark on the treacherous road to Crystal Vale. It is a path lined with the thorns of peril, but together, we shall navigate its twists and turns."

Keisha nodded, her trust in Ong, an unwavering anchor. The cave, a tranquil sanctuary amidst the untamed wilderness, enfolded them as they settled onto a makeshift bedroll. The burdens of their shared destiny and the trials that lay ahead found momentary respite in the embrace of slumber, a haven nestled within the heart of the forest's enigma.

As Keisha reclined beside Ong, the silent symphony of the night enveloped them, a seamless tapestry woven from the threads of moonlight and shadow. His arm, a steadfast sentinel, encircled her, a guardian's embrace promising solace amid uncertainty. The rhythmic cadence of his breathing, like the gentle whisper of leaves rustling in the wind, provided a comforting lullaby.

For Keisha, trust had always been a rare jewel, a gem of the heart guarded with the utmost caution. Life's crucible had etched its lessons upon her soul from an early age, forging a steely resolve that kept her walls high. Yet, in the presence of Ong, a flicker of vulnerability danced within her like a lone ember amidst the darkest night. She dared to trust, for his character had proven itself worthy of the fragile gift she offered.

As the moonlight bathed them in its silvery glow, Keisha's gaze lingered upon Ong's slumbering form. She watched him, her heart a silent witness to the unspoken bond that had formed between them. It was a bond born of shared trials and the quiet understanding of transcending words.

Over time, the weight of their journey's demands began to wane, and like a weary traveler finding respite at an oasis, Keisha succumbed to the embrace of slumber. Her trust in Ong, an exquisite bloom that had unfurled amidst the wilderness of their adventures, cradled her as she ventured into the realm of dreams, where the boundaries of their world expanded beyond the tangible into the ethereal tapestry of their shared destiny.

Chapter 8

Veiled Agendas: Phoenix's Pursuit

As the celestial painter's brush stroked the dawn canvas, the heavens blushed, awash in a symphony of rosy pinks and molten golds. In this ethereal dawn's tender embrace, Ong stirred from his slumber, welcomed by the caressing fingers of the morning sun. Like dozing titans, his senses awakened from their nocturnal reprieve, stretching languidly to grasp the newborn day's promises. The cave, a sentinel in the heart of the enigmatic forest, had cradled them through the night, offering sanctuary from the enigma beneath the arboreal canopy.

With the grace of a maestro, Ong embarked on his morning ritual, collecting the bedding roll with the poise of an alchemist unveiling long-hidden secrets. Thunder, his stalwart confidant, stood regally nearby, embodying power and devotion. Each fold of the bedroll, meticulously and reverently repacked, found its place upon Thunder's saddle, a testament to the seasoned traveler's artistry.

While Ong tended to their equine companion, Keisha ventured into the woods. Like whispers on the breath of zephyrs, her steps scarcely disturbed the forest's delicate equilibrium. The woodland, rousing from its nightly slumber, confided its secrets to her keen ears. Hidden among the emerald foliage, the treasure she sought awaited her discovery — plump, succulent berries, their hues akin to miniature gemstones adorned with the morning's dewy diadem.

With the agility of a fairy, she plucked the ripest jewels, her fingers as gentle as a lover's caress, ensuring no dissonance marred the symphony of the woods. Each berry, a morsel of vibrant flavor and invigoration, nestled within her palm, their colors an ode to nature's palette.

Returning to the cave, Keisha's heart danced like a butterfly in the breeze, but her companion's brow bore the weight of concern. Ong's voice, gruff yet laced with tenderness, was a question unspoken, a sentinel posted at the gates of his apprehension. Keisha, the embodiment of empathy, unfurled her explanation like a healing poultice, soothing his furrowed brow with her words.

Ong's nod, a silent exhalation of gratitude, presaged a shift in their shared journey. With purposeful strides, he advanced, strong arms enveloping Keisha in a protective shroud. With the fluidity of a seasoned ritual, he raised her, her lithe form weightless as a wisp, and placed her upon Thunder's back. Thus, their odyssey through the forest, a voyage into the heart of enchantment, recommenced, two souls intertwined by destiny's invisible thread.

As they embarked on their journey, it was as though the very forest stirred from its slumber in harmonious resonance with their departure. Creatures of grandeur and minuscule wonders, united in a symphony of dawn's awakening, offered their voices to the burgeoning day. Their calls were like a siren's haunting melody, beckoning forth Pumpkin, the ever-playful feline, who, with lively grace, joined their procession, his feline enthusiasm a testament to the enchantment of the moment.

The trio embarked on their quest with the radiant sun casting long shadows at their backs and an uncharted trail unfolding. Ong and Keisha, their souls bound by a shared purpose and an unwavering spirit, ventured into the unknown. The narrow pathway, a ribbon of destiny suspended like a fragile thread over a glistening waterway, seemed to hold its breath in anticipation, drawing them inexorably toward the heart of Crystal Vale, where destination and destiny twined together like lovers in an eternal embrace.

The forest bore witness to the hushed murmur of leaves as Kelru Palvoh, a formidable Druchii Archer Captain, ventured deeper into the heart of the woods. His obsidian locks cascaded like a waterfall of shadows, a frame for a countenance as sharp as the gleaming edge of a blade. His eyes, as black as the abyss itself, glistened with an unwavering resolve, their depths concealing a relentless pursuit that knew no bounds.

Cloaked in garments of crimson and obsidian, his attire was a symphony of darkness, a testament to his unwavering allegiance to the enigmatic forces that governed his kind. His movements bore a predatory grace, a ghostly specter amidst the lush splendor of the woods.

As Kelru Palvoh approached the grim tableau of two fallen Druchii, his expression remained stoic. The lifeless bodies, cast aside like abandoned chess pieces, bore the unmistakable marks of brutality. His unspoken command hung heavy in the air, demanding retribution that could not be denied.

With a curt gesture, he beckoned his subordinates, and a squad of Druchii soldiers gathered, their forms blending seamlessly with the forest floor like shadows in the night. Each soldier, a living testament to their order's rigorous training and unyielding discipline, awaited orders with palpable tension.

The hunt commenced, an exacting exploration of the woods as they sought the elusive culprits responsible for the savage demise of their kin. The towering sentinels of the forest, beneath the emerald canopy, combed the terrain for any traces, their footfalls softer than the sigh of the wind.

Yet, as they pressed forward, the forest jealously guarded its secrets, revealing nothing but its enigmatic beauty. The tranquil rhythm of nature's heartbeat persisted, leaves swaying to an ancient song, and the mystical stillness of the woods embraced them, concealing the transient chaos of mortality.

In due time, the squad chanced upon the cave, its gaping maw offering no clue of concealed mysteries. It stood as a natural formation, bearing no immediate trace of recent events, betraying neither the presence of Ong and Keisha nor the cryptic nature of their quest.

Kelru Palvoh's lips curled in a silent snarl of vexation, his quarry eluding him for now. Reluctantly, he commanded his troops to move forward, for the hunt had only begun. The woods clung to its secrets like a mysterious lover, refusing to yield to the probing gaze of a relentless pursuer. The shadows whispered their riddles, promising answers that would remain veiled for the time being as the saga of pursuit and evasion unfolded.

Within the splendid halls of Goldmoor, where every whispered echo reverberated with echoes of grandeur and dominance, Qellaun returned, his measured footsteps carrying the burden of disheartening revelations. His scholarly odyssey had traversed the labyrinthine archives, where scrolls of ancient wisdom divulged their secrets in long-forgotten tongues.

Phoenix, the imperious sovereign of Goldmoor, awaited his trusted advisor with thinly veiled impatience. His obsidian robes, adorned with emblems that shimmered with the luminosity of his reign, seemed to imbibe the feeble light of the hall, casting shadows that waltzed like ethereal specters upon the polished marble floors.

Qellaun's countenance wore the weight of disillusionment as he approached the throne, the epicenter of Phoenix's dominion. His obeisance was profound, a mark of reverence that could scarcely veil the uneasiness etched into his demeanor. "My Lord, I have plumbed the depths of our boundless archives and scoured the archives of history, yet. Regrettably, the knowledge I have uncovered merely echoes what I have already conveyed."

Phoenix's gaze pierced Qellaun's like a blade's edge, his simmering frustration concealed beneath the veneer of regal composure. His voice, as resonant as thunder veiled in silk, carried the gravity of unfulfilled expectations. "Qellaun, the elusive secrets of E'vahona, the enigmatic Eladrin, and their patron goddess persist in their enigmatic shroud. However, I shall not be deterred."

With unwavering resolve, Phoenix issued a command reverberating throughout the palace, a summons tapping into the boundless might at his disposal. "Summon Zylron, my draconic ally. We shall journey to the Serpent's Lagoon to commune with Queen Jeanne. If King Alex's efforts prove fruitless, perhaps the queen shall unveil the answers we seek."

As the palace stirred with the promise of another quest, the halls seemed to resonate with Phoenix's unwavering determination. He was a ruler who would not yield, even if it meant venturing into the uncharted realms of the unknown and confronting a queen whose grace was as serpentine as her secrets. The world beyond beckoned, and within the heart of Goldmoor, the echoes of power swirled like an impending storm, foretelling the tumultuous path ahead.

Veiled in the arcane cloak of their dark arts, Phoenix and Qellaun materialized on Serpent Island with a presence that transcended the mortal realm. Their abrupt arrival sent a tremor coursing through the very foundations of the tower, and Queen Jeanne, trapped within her shadowed confines, momentarily faltered in the face of these enigmatic interlopers. Their intense, awe-inspiring might eclipse the dim prison that had long been her sanctuary.

Phoenix advanced with an aura of impending reckoning, his eyes aflame with a fiery intensity that sent a frigid shiver racing down Queen Jeanne's spine. He demanded revelations, his voice resonating like the ominous rumble of a thunderhead heralding an impending storm. "Speak of the Eladrin, specifically the one who graced your city. Unveil every fragment of knowledge."

Queen Jeanne's resolve, rekindled like tempered steel, met Phoenix's penetrating gaze with unyielding determination. "In our city, I have glimpsed no Eladrin," she replied, her voice resolute and unwavering. "I cannot proffer what lies beyond my grasp."

Beneath the surface of Phoenix's countenance, a tempestuous rage smoldered as he leaned closer, his breath a scalding reminder of the infernal power that coursed through his veins. "Do you fancy your husband's plight miserable now? Ponder your response, Queen Jeanne. Your obstinacy shall only summon further tribulations upon his tormented existence."

With a pivot, Phoenix withdrew, the ominous eddies of his cloak swirling in his wake. "Five days shall you have to reconsider," he declared, a lingering specter of dread trailing behind his departure. In a flourish of shadowed sorcery, they dissolved from Serpent Island, leaving it far behind as they returned to the heart of Goldmoor, their quest for knowledge and vengeance unabated.

In the heart of the forest, Ong and Keisha embarked on their shared odyssey, their connection deepening with each passing day. The world unfurled around them, vibrant and teeming with the marvels of nature. Purplefire Woods, a distant sanctuary from Keisha's home of E'vahona, held a place of profound affection in her heart, a love born from the purples that adorned the forest like royal vestments.

As they ventured further into the woodland's heart, Ong's instincts, honed to a razor's edge, guided them to a serene stream. Its waters glistened like molten silver, a liquid tapestry beneath the dappling sunlight wading through the verdant canopy above. Thunder, their steadfast companion, merited a moment of respite, prompting Ong to gently lower Keisha from the saddle, her feet finding purchase on the plush, mossy terrain.

Ong surveyed their surroundings with a contented exhalation, absorbing the beauty that enveloped them. The woods harmonized in a symphony of existence, the music of birdsong and the gentle murmuring of the stream composing a tranquil sonata. A smile graced his features as he embraced the serenity of this place, a stark contrast to the unforgiving crucible of their battles.

Keisha, her heart resonating with an affinity for the forest's enchantment, returned his smile and spoke in dulcet tones, her voice a vessel of warmth and wistfulness. "Indeed, Ong," she began, her gaze a tender caress upon the woodland, "these woods, though distant from my homeland, occupy a cherished niche in my soul. Their allure, unique and captivating, holds me in thrall."

In the embrace of their sylvan sanctuary, Ong and Keisha, have allowed themselves a moment of reverence for the forest's tranquility, an oasis of serenity before their journey would once again thrust them into the maw of the unknown. Amidst nature's splendors, they fortified the bonds sustaining them through the trials ahead.

Ong's inquisitiveness mirrored the boundless expanse of the surrounding forests, an insatiable hunger for knowledge, and a thirst for understanding. He could not resist the temptation to unravel the enigmatic tapestry of E'vahona, the realm that Keisha held close to her heart. He turned to her, his question a simple yet profound key to unlocking the lush secrets of her homeland.

"Keisha," he inquired, his voice a vessel of earnest curiosity, "pray, tell me of the woodlands that cradle E'vahona?"

Like a soft caress of ancient forest breezes, Keisha's response unveiled the essence of E'vahona. Her words wove a vivid tableau of her homeland as if the very trees whispered their secrets to her.

"Emeraldwood Forest and Emberwood Forest," she breathed, her tone a hymn of reverence for the enchanting realms that embraced her city.

Ong, his voice resonating like the hushed counsel of a seasoned wanderer, illuminated the path that would lead them to Crystal Vale.

"To reach the sacred Crystal Vale," he elucidated, his eyes ablaze with the stories of adventurers and explorers who had ventured through these lands, "we must traverse the very heart of the empyrean Emeraldwood Forest." His words lingered in the air, bearing the weight of the impending adventure.

Continuing, Ong shared his wisdom, words bearing the knowledge of one who had traversed these woods intimately. "You see," he began, "I originate from the very heart of Crystal Vale," a sense of homecoming tinged his voice. "It is a realm adorned with enchanting beauty, guarded by the resplendent sentinels of the Emeraldwood Forest. It stands as a testament to the mesmerizing wonders that our world holds."

Keisha's eyes ignited like twin embers at the mere mention of the sacred forests, and she turned to Ong, her countenance awash in an ethereal glow. "Emeraldwoods," she began, her voice a rhapsody of reverence, "is a realm of unparalleled beauty, where the very tapestries of green unfurl in the forest's heart. And just as Purplefire Woods dons a regal purple mantle, Emeraldwoods adorns itself in myriad shades of green. As for Emberwoods, though I have not ventured there often, it too possesses its unique hue."

Ong couldn't help but notice the love that resonated in her words when she spoke of the forests. He leaned in with a boundless curiosity as the wilderness they traversed. "Keisha," he inquired, his voice a vessel of genuine intrigue, "is this deep reverence for the forests a sentiment shared by all Eladrin, or is it a rare gift that resides solely within you?"

Keisha's eyes shimmered with a connection that transcended the ordinary as she entrusted her thoughts to Ong. "You see, Ong," she began, her voice a lyrical melody of hidden wisdom and ancient bonds, "most elves, especially the Eladrin, harbor a profound communion with nature. It courses through our veins, akin to the life force that pulses within the world. But in my case, it's as if the roots of these very forests have woven themselves into the essence of my being."

Ong turned his gaze toward Keisha, his eyes like deep pools of curiosity amid the verdant forest's splendor. "Did one of your parents possess this remarkable gift?" he inquired, his words a thread of intrigue woven into the tapestry of their conversation. "How you speak of it suggests it's a rarity even among Eladrin."

Keisha's nod was graceful, her head a gentle incline like the bowing of a blossom before a zephyr's kiss. "Indeed," she affirmed, her voice a whisper as if sharing a sacred secret with the rustling leaves, "it is a rare gift, and neither of my parents held such a connection. Lord Karrenen has conjectured that perhaps the convergence of their spirits bestowed this gift upon me, though even he remains uncertain. I know it is a rare and profound treasure entrusted to me."

As Keisha spoke, a gentle breeze swept through the forest, its caress delicate as a lover's touch, as if the elements leaned in to listen to her words. The trees, ancient sentinels, bowed to acknowledge her connection to the world around them.

"In moments," Keisha continued, her voice ethereal as a forest nymph's, "I can feel the forest's heartbeat, the very pulse of life that courses through its veins. And when a disturbance disrupts the delicate balance between life and death, the woods confide their secrets in me. It is a gift and a burden, Ong, one that has been my companion since childhood."

The forest seemed to hold its breath, as though recognizing the extraordinary nature of Keisha's bond with the natural realm. In the presence of such a unique connection, the woods itself fell into a hushed reverence, a silent witness to the profound communion between Keisha and the world around her.

Ong regarded Keisha with fascination and concern, his eyes like ancient scrolls, their pages filled with the wisdom of countless ages. "When the forest's equilibrium is disturbed," he probed, his voice a wellspring of rational inquiry, "does it manifest as physical discomfort, or does it resonate within your soul?"

Keisha paused, her gaze a respectful exploration of the rustling leaves and the fractured tapestry of sunlight filtering through the venerable trees. Her words flowed like a gentle stream, bearing the weight of her unique connection to nature. "Most often," she elucidated, her voice a meandering explanation, "it is akin to a delicate vibration, a sensation that ripples through my very being—an awareness that something has strayed from the harmonious symphony of life. It doesn't inflict pain, per se, but rather, it's a profound recognition, like a gentle pull at the threads of my essence."

A contemplative pause hung in the air, marked by the solemnity that marked Keisha's expression. Her voice, when she continued, bore the gravity of unspoken truths. "However," she confided, her words as soft as the whispering leaves, "I have been told that in the event of a grievous injury to the forest, a wound that strikes at its very heart, I may perceive it more intensely, perhaps even in a physical sense."

Ong's countenance wore a veil of concern as he cast his protective gaze over their verdant sanctuary. "It is difficult to fathom," he mused, his words tinged with sorrow. "The notion that anyone would willingly inflict harm upon these resplendent woods is a somber thought. But in these tumultuous times, we must remain vigilant, for even the most sanctified sanctuaries may succumb to the relentless ambitions of others."

As Ong gazed at Keisha, his thoughts meandered through the labyrinth of contemplation, focusing on her revelation that harm to the forests could inflict pain upon her. It was a notion that stirred a profound disquiet within him, an inexplicable unease that surged like an untamed river. He couldn't rationalize why, but the mere prospect of her suffering filled him with an ineffable sorrow.

The idea of Keisha in anguish was intolerable, and he felt an unyielding determination welling within him. He couldn't bear the notion of her pain, and he vowed to himself then that he would stand as her guardian, an unwavering sentinel, to ensure she would never be harmed.

Amidst the tranquil embrace of the forest, where rustling leaves played like the delicate strings of nature's orchestra and the harmonious chorus of birdsong orchestrated a symphony of serenity, Keisha's senses surged to life. A subtle shift in the forest's pulsating heartbeat reached her, a dissonant note disrupting the natural concerto. Her eyes dilated, pupils, capturing the essence of the woods, her instincts coiled like a predator ready to pounce.

Before she could voice her unease, a looming shadow cast its dark pall over them, and a harsh, discordant voice cleaved through the hallowed tranquility. "There she is! Seize the Eladrin!"

Keisha's heart thrummed with a frantic tempo as the formidable figure of Kelru Palvoh, the Druchii Archer Captain, materialized, leading a cohort of his warriors directly toward her. Panic threatened to engulf her, but Ong's unyielding resolve became a beacon of salvation. With a seamless and fluid motion, he hoisted her onto the back of their loyal Thunder, positioning himself behind her.

"Hold fast!" Ong's command rang out, his voice a steady lifeline amidst the storm of uncertainty. Thunder sprang into motion, its sinewy muscles propelling them through the woods with the swiftness of a fleeting breeze. The pursuit was underway, a high-stakes gambit where life and death hung in precarious balance.

As the thunderous hoofbeats of their pursuers closed in, Keisha's sharp eyes discerned a concealed grove, an oasis of emerald-green foliage and mossy-laden stones. She pointed with frantic urgency, and Ong steered Thunder toward the sanctuary with unwavering determination. They darted into the grove, slipping through a translucent veil of shadows like ethereal specters, leaving their relentless pursuers to thunder past, their malevolent designs thwarted by the beguiling charisma of the forest.

As twilight's brush painted the sky in dusky hues, the forest seemed to suspend its very breath, an ancient arboreal choir murmuring cryptic secrets of bygone eras. Keisha and Ong, pursued by the implacable Druchii, found themselves nestled within the very heart of this enigmatic woodland.

Above, the verdant canopy unfurled, an intricate tapestry of emerald leaves and silhouetted branches, bestowing upon them a sanctuary. A concealed grove, unsullied by the malevolent gaze of the Druchii, cradled them within its arboreal embrace. The atmosphere bore the heavy scent of moss and earth, a fragrant refuge from the relentless encroachment of danger.

Ong, an unyielding bastion of strength, enfolded Keisha tenderly against his chest. His heartbeat, a rhythmic cadence amidst the tumult, quickened as the cacophonous symphony of pursuit drew nearer. He held her close, akin to a guardian spirit shielding a delicate flame from the encroaching gales of adversity.

The Druchii, sleek and sinister as incarnate shadows, prowled the forest's bosom with a feline grace. Their eyes, glistening like shards of polished onyx within the waning light, darted in every direction. Branches seemed to sigh beneath their inquisitive touch, and leaves conspired to divulge secrets known only to the ancient forest.

Kelru Palvoh, the enigmatic commander of their relentless pursuers, finally issued a silent command to halt their relentless chase. The sun, sinking below the horizon, cast an eerie tableau of blood-red reflections upon the obsidian armor of the Druchii. It was a telltale sign that the time had come to release the relentless pursuit to the embrace of the encroaching night. Darkness, the Druchii's silent accomplice, would be their ally, and they would bide their time until the first rays of dawn.

With an abrupt, stoic gesture, he beckoned his retinue to gather by a babbling stream, its waters akin to liquid silver under the fading twilight. Here, they would make their camp, their restless spirits momentarily satiated, but the smoldering fires of determination still burned fiercely within them.

As the Druchii withdrew into the shrouded veil of the forest, Keisha and Ong remained ensconced in their tender embrace. The forest, once more, held its collective breath, and the night whispered secrets of both peril and promise. This realm, steeped in enchantment and danger, had trapped them, entwining their destinies with the enigmatic heart of the woods.

Ong, a master of the wilderness, guided Thunder, his steed, through the hidden grove with a preternatural finesse honed by years of traversing unforgiving landscapes. The noble beast, akin to a spirit of the wild, moved with fluid grace, a creature born of the terrain itself. Ong brought them to a halt beside a tranquil stream, its gentle murmurs a lullaby to their wearied souls.

Nevertheless, as Ong surveyed their makeshift sanctuary, a sigh of resigned acceptance escaped him. This was far from the ideal campsite, devoid of the comforting flicker of a campfire to ward off the encroaching darkness. Above, the dense canopy of leaves and branches conspired to conceal even the faintest glimmer of starlight.

With a gentleness reserved for precious moments of respite, Ong lowered Keisha by the stream's edge. His brow furrowed in contemplation as he surveyed their temporary refuge. Fingers traced the hilt of a hidden blade, a silent acknowledgment of the lurking dangers that refused to be forgotten. It was an austere place for a reprieve, lacking in the creature comforts of civilization, yet it would have to suffice.

He embarked on the humble task of preparing their camp, artfully arranging leaves and moss into a semblance of bedding that cradled them within nature's embrace. Like a vigilant sentinel, Keisha remained where she was, her wide eyes watchful in the dimly lit sanctuary. Ong's expression knitted with an unease born of their enforced separation. Unable to endure the distance any longer, he approached her with a relentless stride and, without a word, swept her into his arms.

Amidst the tranquil stillness of the grove, Ong's voice was a gentle murmur, a pledge forged in the sanctity of their bond. "We shall not endure such trials again," he vowed softly, his words a solemn covenant.

Keisha nestled against his chest, her trust in him an unshakable foundation. From his hidden cache, Ong retrieved a handful of berries, the fruits of Keisha's earlier foraging expedition, and offered them to her. Their flavors, a sweet testament to life's resilience amidst encroaching darkness, erupted in a burst of sensation upon their tongues.

The night enveloped them mysteriously as they settled beside the babbling stream. Ong held Keisha in a protective cocoon of his embrace, their shared warmth warding off the evening's chill. The forest, alive with its myriad secrets and concealed wonders, bore witness to their presence in its silent vigil.

In this fragile juncture, with the world held at bay and the future a realm of uncertainty, they sought solace in each other's presence. The tender allure of slumber beckoned, and together, they succumbed to its embrace, their journey continuing in the realm of dreams yet to be woven.

Chapter 9

Phoenix's Obsession: The Search for Eladrin Wisdom

Within the heart of the Druchii encampment, where malevolent shadows performed their sinister ballet, Kelru Palvoh stood as a sentinel of darkness. His very presence commanded unwavering obedience, and as the night's cloak descended upon the world, his words bore an authority that sent shivers coursing through the ranks of his warriors.

Amidst the campfires' crackling tongues, casting eerie and capricious light upon the armored figures gathered around their leader, each warrior bore the indelible mark of the Druchii—an emblem of their ruthless prowess and unwavering determination. It was as if they had conspired with the night to veil their treacherous designs.

Kelru Palvoh's voice, akin to a serpent's insidious whisper, slinked through the air, capturing their rapt attention. "We shall commence anew," he intoned, his words laden with a deadly resolve. "Once more, let the woods be scoured. Our elusive quarry remains beyond our grasp."

The Druchii warriors, like shadows given palpable form, melted into the inky abyss of night, their movements stealthy as the grave. Their eyes, cold and calculating, darted through the labyrinthine forest, akin to gleaming daggers, searching for any trace of their enigmatic prey.

Yet, the forest, a realm steeped in ancient sorcery and concealed enigmas, seemed to defy their relentless pursuit. No vestige of their quarry lingered, no sign to pierce the shroud of mystery that enshrouded their path.

As the night unfurled its dark tapestry, the Druchii begrudgingly returned to their leader, their frustration etched upon their otherwise stoic countenances. Kelru Palvoh's gaze bore into them, a chilling reprimand.

"We shall press on," he decreed, his voice resonating with unyielding determination. "To Crystal Vale, where the trail may yet unveil itself. Darkness is our confederate, and it shall reveal our quarry."

The Druchii warriors, akin to an implacable tempest, plunged deeper into the forest. Their relentless journey into the heart of obscurity continued, a pursuit fueled by malevolent ambition and an insatiable thirst for dominion. The mysteries of Crystal Vale beckoned—an enigmatic realm teeming with secrets that only the most sinister of souls would dare to unearth.

Under the shroud of night, Ong and Keisha found solace in the grove, a sanctuary woven from shadows. The forest, a vast tapestry of inky hues, surrounded them, every murmur of the night an ethereal thread in the weave of their refuge. The hours unfolded like elusive spirits, and with the deepening of night, an eerie serenity settled upon the grove.

In the profound stillness, Ong's senses, finely tuned by years of wilderness survival, detected a subtle dissonance in the nocturnal symphony. A distant rustle, a whisper in the darkness, pricked at his instincts. He held Keisha close, a steadfast bulwark against the unknown, resolute in his refusal to let even the faintest trace of danger breach their sanctuary.

As the pallid light of dawn gently bathed the grove, casting the forest in muted shades of gray and green, Ong and Keisha stirred from their restless slumber. The promise of a new day brought a rekindled sense of purpose and urgency.

With meticulous precision, Ong repacked Thunder, his motions deliberate and efficient. A trace of uncertainty flickered in Keisha's eyes as she suggested venturing beyond the grove to ascertain if their pursuers had relented. Ong's response was swift and resolute, an unspoken vow to safeguard her. It was a rare glimpse into his unwavering protectiveness, an emotion conveyed through actions rather than words.

Keisha met his gaze, her silent acknowledgment reflecting the gravity of their situation and the unspoken bond uniting them. With gentle determination, Ong gathered her into his arms, her presence fragile yet resolute against his chest. With practiced ease, he placed her upon Thunder, positioning himself behind her—a vigilant guardian in the face of uncertainty.

As they departed the grove, Thunder, unwavering in loyalty, heeded Ong's guidance. Beyond the protective veil of their sanctuary lay a world of enigmas and dangers, yet they would confront it together. In their wake, the grove stood abandoned, its sanctuary relinquished.

In the dappled light of dawn, as Ong and Keisha embarked on their journey beyond the grove's protective embrace, a subtle shift in the forest's symphony heralded the return of an old companion. Pumpkin, a paragon of loyalty and unwavering companionship, emerged from the shadows, her sleek form a testament to resilience in the face of adversity.

Pumpkin's ebony fur, a mesmerizing tapestry, glistened like the flickering embers of ancient fires, memories lost in time. For the night, the forest had been her refuge, a sanctuary of rustling leaves and the hushed confidences of ancient trees. Now, as she reunited with Ong and Keisha, her eyes, liquid emerald pools, held an unspoken communion with the path they tread.

Pumpkin's return bore the weight of whispered promises, an assurance that some bonds endured, unbroken by the capricious hand of fate. Alongside Thunder, she padded with a grace that mirrored the forest's silent watchfulness, embodying the profound connection between man and beast.

As they navigated the slender path leading to Crystal Vale, their journey evolved into a harmonious blend of determination and camaraderie. With its time-worn trees and concealed wonders, the forest stood sentinel over them, a benevolent guardian with untold secrets awaiting revelation.

Ong's unwavering hold on Keisha symbolized his relentless commitment to her safety. Thunder, guided by the firm hand of his master, bore them forward into the unknown with an air of quiet confidence. And Pumpkin, the forest's sentinel and guardian of its mysteries, walked by their side, her presence a silent testament to the understanding that they traversed this fantastical realm as a unified force.

Their journey persisted, each step bringing them nearer to the heart of Crystal Vale and the enigmatic destinies that lay beyond. The bonds they shared, visible and concealed, would be their wellspring of strength as they confronted the impending challenges lurking in the heart of the encroaching darkness.

In the hallowed sanctuary of Goldmoor's ancient library, where the flickering light of candles performed a mesmerizing ballet upon the timeworn scrolls and age-old tomes, Qellaun labored ceaselessly. His countenance, etched with the gravitas of his mission, bathed in the soft, golden radiance, cast long, ink-darkened shadows upon the parchment-laden tables.

The library, a repository of eons past, seemed to draw breath in reverence to Qellaun's solemn pursuit. Rows of shelves, each bearing the weight of centuries of knowledge, stood as silent witnesses to the enigmas they contained. The air was pregnant with the aroma of aged paper, carrying the profound weight of forgotten histories.

With the precision of a master craftsman, Qellaun meticulously unfurled scroll after scroll, his slender fingers tracing the intricate tapestry of ancient scripts. The Eladrin and their elusive citadel, E'vahona, remained the unavailable puzzle pieces he relentlessly pursued.

Every scroll held the allure of revelation, and Qellaun's eyes, a mirror of unwavering commitment, roved over the delicate calligraphy of aged texts. These words wove tales of the Eladrin, a race cloaked in mystique and drenched in magic, and whispered fables of E'vahona, buried within cryptic legends and shared in hushed, secretive tones.

The capricious dance of candlelight played tricks upon the parchment, casting eerie shadows that tantalizingly obscured as much as they unveiled. Qellaun's intellect, a labyrinthine repository of knowledge and curiosity, ventured through the meandering alleys of these ancient scriptures, questing for the concealed keys that might unlock the vaulted secrets that remained maddeningly just out of reach.

Yet, even in his relentless excavation of the scrolls, the ever-present shadow of Phoenix hung heavily over him. The dark lord's insatiable yearning for dominion and supremacy bore down upon Qellaun like an oppressive yoke. With every line he read, every word he deciphered, he drew nearer to unveiling the enigmatic revelations that Phoenix coveted with unbridled desperation.

In the heart of Goldmoor's library, a covert war of intellects and indomitable wills waged on. Qellaun sifted the sands of time through these sacred scrolls, striving for the elusive truths of the Eladrin and E'vahona. Simultaneously, the evil presence of Phoenix swelled, casting an ever-lengthening shadow over the city and its beleaguered inhabitants. Within the ancient walls of the library, these age-old adversaries clashed, embodying the ceaseless pursuit of knowledge and the looming darkness that sought to extinguish it.

Amidst the looming spires of Goldmoor, where shadows clung like tendrils of malevolence to every cobblestone, Phoenix's commands were whispered through the darkened alleyways. Like a shadowy decree, his will summoned the Druchii from the city's farthest reaches to carry out his insidious bidding.

The Druchii, clad in armor as dark as the night itself, moved with an eerie grace that seemed to defy the laws of sound. Like shards of onyx, their eyes gleamed with an unsettling hunger for knowledge. Each step was a quiet echo of impending doom, a reminder of their power.

In the heart of Goldmoor's labyrinthine streets, the citizens, burdened by the weight of their dark ruler's commands, were gathered like sheep before the wolves. Their faces, etched with fear and resignation, bore the marks of a city held hostage by its tyrant.

In Phoenix's orders, precision and ruthlessness converged. The Druchii were tasked with extracting information from the citizens about the Eladrin, those elusive beings who had woven their secrets into the fabric of E'vahona, a city hidden beyond the veil of reality. Their inquiries focused on the enigmatic Eladrin archer who had bravely stood by Swifthammer's side during the conquest of Goldmoor—a mysterious figure etched deeply into the dark annals of the city's history.

As the questions began, the air grew thick with trepidation, an oppressive weight that hung over the beleaguered citizens like a storm cloud on the verge of unleashing its fury. Their voices, trembling like leaves caught in a relentless gale, wavered as they spoke in hushed tones of the Eladrin's otherworldly grace and the elusive city of E'vahona. In the dimly lit alleys and squares of Goldmoor, they whispered tales of a city where reality wavered, dreams and nightmares melded into a surreal tapestry.

Yet these utterances, painted with the brush of integrity, were not offspring of candid disclosure. No, they emerged from a chasm of dread that clung like a shroud to the hearts of Goldmoor's besieged residents. The populace, their visages etched with the scars of subjugation, understood that honesty was a fleeting luxury in the presence of Phoenix and his enigmatic Druchii. Truth was a delicate and treacherous commodity.

With each syllable they articulated, they wove intricate tales crafted from the fragile strands of their imaginations, conjuring narratives of Eladrin sorcery and otherworldly allure. Every word served as a lifeline, a desperate effort to stave off the omnipresent specter of Phoenix and his vindictiveness. Their voices did not sing with knowledge but rather resonated with the primal instinct of survival. They resembled candles in a lightless room, their flames flickering in the dread of being extinguished.

In this intricate ballet of deception and despair, Goldmoor's denizens navigated treacherous seas of falsehoods and illusion. Their words were a bitter tribute to the oppressive shadow that engulfed their lives. The very soul of the city trembled in the face of its tormentor, and truth, as elusive as the enigmatic secrets of the Eladrin, lay concealed beneath layers of deceitful whispers.

Goldmoor, once a realm teeming with energy and strength, had been plunged into obscurity by Phoenix's insatiable hunger for knowledge and dominion. The Druchii, his shadowy enforcers, extracted confidences as if wringing drops of lifeblood from trembling victims, with each revelation adding a fragment to a puzzle that held the promise of revealing the riddles of the Eladrin and their hidden citadel.

In this intricate tapestry of fear and reluctance, the destiny of Goldmoor swung in a precarious balance, and its populace was trapped between the ruthless machinations of an evil lord and the timeless mysteries that resided beyond the grasp of mortal understanding.

In the heart of Goldmoor, beneath the very bedrock that had once upheld his majestic castle, King Alex languished in the unforgiving abyss of the dungeon. The air within was dense with the lingering echoes of despair and the crushing burden of his kingdom's agony, an intangible specter that mirrored the turmoil plaguing his city.

The dungeon's somber walls, slick with the moisture of anguish, hemmed him in like the relentless jaws of destiny. The ashen stones bore witness to the anguished souls who had trodden this cursed path before him, their tormented spirits lingering in the mortar and stone. It was a realm of desolation, where the feeble ember of hope flickered like a distant star in the infinite night.

Once the brave sovereign of a thriving realm, King Alex now wore chains forged from the alloy of regret and impotence. From the depths of his incarceration, he could hear the distant echoes of his people's suffering, their mournful cries forming a haunting chorus that resonated through the marrow of his being. He was acutely aware that the whispers that had reached his ears, tales of the enigmatic Eladrin and their concealed city of E'vahona, were spawned from the crucible of fear and desperation.

He begrudgingly acknowledged a painful truth in his prison's cold, unforgiving abyss. He, too, was ignorant of the elusive city's whereabouts. The Eladrin, with their time-honored sorcery and enigmatic customs, had veiled their city in impenetrable secrecy, a bastion of mystery that remained an enigma even to a king.

His heart ached for his subjects, for the trepidation that held their hearts captive and the shadows that obscured their destinies. Despite his incarceration and powerlessness, King Alex bore the ceaseless weight of their suffering as if it were a crown of thorns upon his regal brow, an enduring testament to his boundless love for his city.

In the dungeon's relentless hush, he forged a resolute covenant with himself—a vow to unearth the truths veiled in shadows, to liberate his beleaguered people from the clutches of the encroaching darkness that had ensnared Goldmoor. The air throbbed with the weight of unspoken sorrows, but King Alex's spirit blazed with unwavering determination. He yearned to reclaim his city from the abyss, silently grateful that the knowledge of E'vahona's whereabouts remained elusive.

Within the gloomy confines of his underground purgatory, King Alex's thoughts meandered like enigmatic riddles through the corridors of his mind. Amidst the oppressive gloom, he could not help but dwell upon the fate of his beloved Queen Jeanne. She, too, had been trapped in the relentless tendrils of this unfolding tragedy, and his heart pulsed with apprehension for her well-being. In the unfathomable depths of his despair, he clung tenaciously to the hope that somewhere, beyond these frigid and pitiless walls, she stood unbroken—a beacon of tenacity and resilience amidst the encircling shadows. His love for her was an unyielding flame, burning as an indomitable testament to the enduring strength of their bond.

As the guardian of hope in a city trapped by an evil warlock, Queen Jeanne fixed her gaze upon the deceptively calm waters just as she and King Alex were. The lagoon, a beguiling Eden, concealed beneath its surface secrets that mirrored the tumult within her heart. In those shimmering waters, Hydras, serpents of the abyss with vicious intent, and other eldritch inhabitants writhed and stirred, emerging from the deep to stalk the accursed isle.

The queen understood that rescue would require nothing short of a miracle. The isle of Serpent's Lagoon was a forsaken realm, a nightmarish enclave where her captor's evil influence held unchallenged dominion. Her isolation weighed her down like the relentless currents swirling beneath the serene surface. Yet, her thoughts remained steadfast with her people in Goldmoor, and the image of her husband, King Alex, imprisoned and burdened with the suffering of their kingdom, haunted her every waking moment.

As the memory of Phoenix's last visit clawed at the edges of her consciousness, she shivered. His evil presence had left an indelible scar upon her soul—a mark of fear and despair that she could not escape. With each passing day, the impending return of the dark lord loomed on the horizon like an approaching storm, a harbinger of further anguish for her people. In the depths of her despair, Queen Jeanne grappled with the knowledge that she, too, had become a prisoner, trapped by the relentless grasp of Phoenix's dark ambitions. She knew nothing about the Eladrin archer who had aided Ong Swifthammer on that fateful day when Goldmoor fell.

Her heart yearned for salvation like a fragile bird confined within a gilded cage. Whispers of the Eladrin had reached her ears—enigmatic beings who danced upon the precipice between light and shadow. Their legends spoke of warriors who fought for the dawn, and in the depths of her soul, she clung to the hope that these stories held a glimmer of truth, a spark of possibility that they might come to Goldmoor's aid.

With her head bowed, Queen Jeanne's thoughts spiraled into a prayer, whispered in the sacred silence of Serpent's Lagoon. Her prayers were for her people and her husband, the imprisoned king who bore the weight of their kingdom's suffering. Her faith, an unwavering beacon, ascended into the heavens—an emotional plea for deliverance and the safety of her beloved king.

Within the hallowed sanctuary of Goldmoor's labyrinthine library, Qellaun toiled with unyielding determination, a solitary beacon of hope amidst the kingdom's darkest hour. Each parchment he unfurled, each ancient symbol he deciphered, brought him a step closer to unraveling the enigma that had long eluded him—the elusive Eladrin and their hidden citadel, E'vahona.

Yet, in the profound stillness of the library's sacred solitude, his thoughts wandered to a weighty dilemma that gripped his heart. He knew that his sister, Lyra, a formidable Druchii sorceress in her own right, possessed the knowledge and arcane talents that could aid his quest. She stood as a potential ally in the face of Phoenix's menacing presence, a glimmer of hope within a realm where despair held dominion.

However, the price of involving Lyra was a heavy burden to bear. Like a storm poised to unleash its fury, Phoenix's wrath was a force to be reckoned with, and the repercussions of his anger were shrouded in perilous uncertainty. Qellaun paused, the gravity of his decision pressing upon him.

In the shadowed recesses of the library, he weighed the pros and cons of seeking his sister's assistance. The flickering candlelight cast intricate patterns of doubt upon his visage as he carefully considered the risks and potential rewards. The choice to introduce Lyra into the vortex of darkness that had consumed Goldmoor was meaningful, one that could irrevocably alter the trajectory of their intertwined destinies.

For now, he persisted in his solitary pursuit of enlightenment, the ancient scrolls murmuring their cryptic secrets to him in the profound stillness of the night. Yet, in his contemplation, the idea of seeking Fel Thalor's counsel and, with it, the involvement of his sister Lyra lingered like a haunting specter—a choice that held the power to shape the fate of the entire realm.

Chapter 10

Siblings of Sorcery - The Journey to Fel Thalor and the Recruitment of Lyra Deadcrusher

The sun descended low on the horizon, its molten rays stretching long, languid shadows across the cobbled courtyard of the splendid palace. As Qellaun ascended the marble steps, his cloak billowed behind him like the wings of a raven cloaked in shadows, a silent emissary of the arcane. Each step upon the cobbles whispered secrets of long-forgotten craftsmanship, and the palace itself stood as an opulent colossus, its towers reaching for the heavens like outstretched fingers yearning for divine touch.

Within the palace's chambers of opulence, Phoenix, a brooding figure of regal bearing, paced with the restless energy of a lion confined within a gilded cage. His eyes, blazing like the heart of a dragon's fiery maw, bore into the very soul of his realm. His dark robes clung to him like a shroud, emphasizing the tense sinews that held his form and the ebony cascade of hair cascading down his shoulders.

"Qellaun!" Phoenix's voice echoed through the room like a tempest unfurling, an elemental force. "You return empty-handed once more!"

Qellaun, his eyes heavy with the weight of worlds, exhaled a sigh, his shoulders yielding beneath the unseen burden of his failure. "I have plumbed the depths of ancient tomes and unraveled the secrets of hidden realms, my lord, yet the knowledge we seek eludes me like a phantom."

Phoenix's wrath erupted like a supernova, his words a conflagration of furious intensity. "You dare to return without answers, yet you dare not utter the one hope that hovers on the precipice of oblivion?"

The air grew dense with unspoken truths, the charged atmosphere between them pressing upon their souls like a relentless storm. Qellaun, his gaze a nexus of defiance and rueful acceptance, met Phoenix's fiery stare. "My lord, I harbored fears for her safety and hoped to discover an alternative. But now, I see no other recourse. My sister, Lyra, resides within the shadowed heart of Fel Thalor, the formidable Druchii fortress. She wields great sorcerous power and may hold the very key to the secrets we seek."

Phoenix's fury flared anew, a maelstrom of betrayal and vexation. "You withheld this knowledge from me? Do you deem me a fool, Qellaun?"

The room seemed to constrict around them, the palace's grandeur fading insignificance as their clash of wills took precedence. Yet, Qellaun, a bastion of calm amid the storm, held his ground. "No, my lord, not a fool. I wanted my sister to have different choices than I did. But now, it seems we have no choice. We must embark on a perilous journey to Fel Thalor and beseech Lyra for her aid."

Phoenix's wrath smoldered like the embers of a dying fire, but a spark of understanding ignited beneath its fiery surface. He released a protracted, weighty breath, the burden of Lyra's existence settling upon him like a cloak of inevitability. "Very well, Qellaun. We shall journey to Fel Thalor and beseech Lyra for her assistance. But do not stretch my patience further. The sands of time slip through the hourglass, and our world teeters at the edge of an abyss."

The palace, a living monument to forgotten epochs, stood witness to their solemn pact, the air pregnant with the gravitas of their decision. As they readied themselves for the dangerous quest ahead, an aura of destiny enshrouded them, as palpable as the arcane energies that coursed through the veins of their fantastical realm.

Deep within the heart of Fel Thalor, the ancient Druchii fortress, Lyra, a sorceress whose power was unmatched, practiced her arcane arts in a chamber bathed in an eerie, ethereal radiance. The atmosphere shimmered with mystical potency, and the room was adorned with tomes bound in shadowy leather, each a repository of secrets as profound and abyssal as the inky depths of the void. Candles cast eerie, twisted shadows upon the obsidian walls as Lyra delved deeper into the abyss of arcane mysteries.

Lyra herself was a beguiling enchantment-given form. Her obsidian hair cascaded like a long, twisted river of shadow, brushing against the floor as if spun from the very fabric of the night. Her eyes blazed like crimson supernovas, twin pools of smoldering intensity that unveiled the depths of her sorcerous prowess. Adorned in a gown that blended silver and crimson, she moved with a grace that transcended mortal limitations, each of her steps a seductive ballet of allure and peril.

As she summoned her spells, the chamber resounded with an ethereal symphony, the air charged with the essence of arcane might. Symbols and sigils wove intricate patterns around her, swirling in mesmerizing designs as she harnessed the forces of magic. Yet, even amid this profound sorcery, Lyra's thoughts strayed to distant horizons, an unspoken anticipation pulling at the strings of her heart.

Word of her brother's impending arrival had reached Lyra through the clandestine murmurs of shadowy allies. Her heart quickened, a mixture of joy and curiosity igniting within her. It had felt like an eternity since she had last laid eyes upon Qellaun, her brother, and now he approached, bearing with him a mysterious companion of great import. The prospect filled her with both eagerness and intrigue. Who was this enigmatic guest, and what mission had led them into the heart of Druchii darkness?

Lyra's eyes glittered with anticipation as she resumed her arcane endeavors, the enchantments coalescing around her like a storm of untold potential. She pondered the hidden truths on the cusp of revelation, the destiny that awaited their intertwined fates, and her unique role in the unfolding tapestry of their fantastical world. In that very moment, amidst the eldritch energies of her sorcerous craft, she became both a guardian of shadowy knowledge and an intrepid seeker of the enigmatic future that beckoned, ready to embrace both the veiled realms of darkness and the radiant light.

Deep within the shadowed heart of the Forest, Kelru Palvoh, a commander of cunning and malice, stood poised on the precipice of a narrow, winding path—this labyrinthine trail wound through the ancient woodland, a delicate thread weaving together disparate regions of Vacari. The sinister beauty of the woods enveloped him on all sides, a realm where twilight's eternal embrace held sway, and the very trees conspired in hushed, shadowy conversations.

Kelru, a spectral figure shrouded in obsidian armor that gleamed with a cruel and icy brilliance, surveyed the terrain with eyes resembling polished onyx, sharp and unfeeling. His entourage of Druchii, their dark armor bearing wickedly etched runes, moved through the forest with a mesmerizing, deadly grace. Amidst the forest's soft murmur, their presence felt like an ominous intrusion, an affront to the natural harmony of the woods.

With the meticulous calculations of a seasoned strategist, Kelru devised a sinister stratagem, a malevolent snare intended to capture any unsuspecting traveler who dared tread this difficult path. The Druchii, masters of deceit and ambush, orchestrated their movements like a deadly ballet. They meticulously concealed pitfalls, ensnaring traps, and hidden archers in strategic locations, their expertise in deception and surprise akin to a macabre symphony.

As the sun's last embers cast an eerie, blood-red pallor upon the forest, Kelru sensed the anticipation of impending darkness and evil designs. He knew that the Eladrin and their warrior companion were inexorably drawn into the sinister depths of the forest. With every passing moment, the forest's verdant embrace seemed to tighten, the tangled undergrowth conspiring to trap their prey further.

The air grew thick with an unspoken foreboding, and rustling leaves whispered grim tidings of impending calamity. Kelru Palvoh, the conductor of this malevolent ballet, awaited with bated breath, his eyes glittering like twin shards of obsidian. In the heart of this eldritch woodland, beauty and malevolence performed an eternal, haunting waltz, a sinister trap they had meticulously set. The fate of those who dared to tread this treacherous path now teetered on the edge like a fragile, fleeting dream.

Deep within the heart of the enigmatic forest, Ong bore the weight of unease like an impending storm pressing upon his broad shoulders. The palpable tension hung in the air, woven into the fabric of the shadows that clung to ancient trees and tangled undergrowth. Each step he took was a cautious dance with the unknown, a vigilant watch for the lurking specter of the Druchii, those sinister and elusive denizens who claimed this shadowy realm as their own. Yet, Ong, relentless in his protector's role, was determined to shield Keisha from the heavy burden of his concern.

Beside him, Keisha moved with a grace that defied the encroaching darkness. Like pools of emerald fire, her eyes remained locked on the path ahead, her determination unwavering as the towering sentinels of the forest loomed above them. Ong couldn't help but admire her steadfastness, a beacon of courage illuminating their path through the enigma of the woods.

However, Ong, grappling with the ever-present worry for their safety, yearned for a moment's respite. His searching gaze descended upon a small crystalline stream, its sinuous course weaving through the woods. The stream's waters glistened like liquid sapphires under the gentle caress of dappled sunlight. Recognizing the need to pause, gather their thoughts, and contemplate their choices in this labyrinth of uncertainty, he skillfully guided Thunder, his loyal steed, toward the stream's edge.

Thunder, a magnificent creature with sinews of steel rippling beneath a coat as dark as night, exuded a majestic presence. As they approached the tranquil oasis, his powerful hooves struck the earth like the resounding echoes of thunder, a testament to his untamed spirit. With a gentleness born of deep affection and his enduring concern for Keisha's well-being, Ong dismounted, sweeping the archer with hair aflame and eyes aflame like emerald jewels from Thunder's back. He set her down by the stream's edge, her form delicate yet resilient, like a wildflower in the heart of the forest's mysteries.

As Keisha's feet graced the velvety moss that lined the stream's edge, she turned to Ong, her emerald eyes locking onto his with a profound mixture of gratitude and understanding. Their unspoken connection, a labyrinthine weave of emotions too intricate to articulate, shimmered like a hidden spring in the heart of a mystical forest. Ong was acutely aware of the looming threat posed by the Druchii, yet equally aware that his feelings for Keisha had grown like the ancient trees of this enchanted land, their destinies now intricately entwined.

Amidst this momentary pause by the stream, bathed in the gentle caress of twilight, Ong and Keisha harnessed their inner resolve, preparing to confront the enigmatic challenges ahead. The woods themselves seemed to murmur cryptic secrets, and their unspoken connection held the promise of adventures yet untold, their hearts harmonizing like a melody that resonated through the very soul of the forest.

In the heart of this mystical woodland, where shadows pirouetted in eternal twilight, Keisha turned her gaze upon Ong. Like pools of verdant reflection, her eyes bore the gravity of unspoken worries, a multitude of thoughts suspended in the air like the delicate threads of an unsolved enigma.

"They lie in wait for us, do they not?" Her voice, a gentle lament, cascaded through the ancient trees, and her eyes, like twin emerald lanterns, searched Ong's countenance for elusive answers.

Ong, the keeper of hidden knowledge, felt his heart quicken with a tumultuous blend of emotions. The forest seemed to hold its breath, and the rustling leaves stilled as if anticipating his response. He was acutely aware of the Druchii's lurking presence in the shadowy depths, their evil intent a constant specter in this enchanted forest.

Ong's expression bore the complex fusion of protectiveness and unwavering resolve. "We must proceed cautiously, for this land is treacherous, and our adversaries are masters of deceit."

Keisha, her determination as unyielding as the ancient trees that encircled them, met Ong's eyes with a hint of audacity. "Then permit me to venture ahead to the crossing alone," she proposed, her words akin to an arrow released from a taut bowstring, a bold challenge to the lurking dangers. "I could lead them away, lure them from this place, thereby ensuring your safe passage to Crystal Vale."

Ong's emotions swirled a storm of concern and righteous anger. His care for Keisha ran deep, her well-being a weighty burden upon his heart. "No!" His retort carried an intensity bordering on wrath. "I shall not permit you to confront this peril in solitude. We shall traverse this terrain together, just as we have since our journey's inception."

In that moment, their bond, forged through countless trials and shared ordeals, shone like a radiant beacon amidst the shadowed woods. Their unspoken connection, more potent than any sorcery, bound them irrevocably as they stood at the precipice of the unknown. The forest bore witness, and destiny itself held its breath, recognizing that the fate of these two brave adventurers was intricately interwoven with the enigmatic secrets of the woods, a tale yet to be unveiled in its entirety.

Keisha directed her gaze toward Ong in the heart of the mystical Forest, where the air was imbued with enchantment and shadows clung to the ancient trees like echoes of time. Her emerald eyes possessed a profound depth, as though she sought answers hidden within the ever-shifting patterns of sunlight that wove through the forest's leafy canopy.

Keisha began with a sense of urgency that hung like a gathering storm, "Ong, you must comprehend. In these direst moments, I have always been the one to take that difficult step forward. I must place myself in harm's way to secure the safe return of the others."

Ong, emotions turbulent beneath his stoic exterior, could no longer contain his exasperation. He shook his head in frustration, his voice echoing with the resonance of his profound concern. "Keisha, I am not 'the others,' and I shall not passively stand aside, allowing you to thrust yourself into the maw of danger."

As Ong and Keisha's lips met in that passionate and profound kiss, time seemed to slow within the mystical forest. The world around them faded into the background, and all that existed at that moment was the intensity of their connection. It was a kiss that spoke of unspoken devotion, love that had weathered trials and tribulations, and a commitment to face whatever challenges lay ahead.

The forest, with its ancient trees and whispering leaves, bore witness to this profound moment. It was as though the very essence of the woods acknowledged their love and resolved to defy the looming peril. Their kiss, amidst the enchantment and uncertainty of their quest, became a symbol of unity and strength.

When they finally parted, their eyes met with a renewed sense of purpose and understanding. In that shared kiss, they had found the strength to face the dangers that awaited them, hand in hand. With its enigmatic secrets, the forest seemed to offer its silent blessings, and destiny continued to weave its intricate tapestry around them.

With hearts aflame and determination burning brightly, Ong and Keisha resumed their journey through the mystical Forest. They were ready to confront whatever challenges lay ahead, fortified by the unbreakable bond they had reaffirmed in that sacred kiss.

In the evil heart of Fel Thalor, Phoenix acknowledged the high priestess's reverence with a subtle nod, his piercing gaze unwavering. The air around them was heavy with the weight of ancient sorcery and dark machinations, and the very stones of the stronghold seemed to resonate with an eerie, aware presence.

"High Priestess," Phoenix replied his voice a chilling whisper that echoed through the crimson-hued corridors of Fel Thalor. "I have returned with a purpose that intertwines with the shadows that enshroud this place."

The high priestess rose from her bow, her eyes gleaming with a sincere devotion to the dark arts. She knew that Phoenix's presence heralded significant and dangerous endeavors. "How may the might of Fel Thalor serve your ambitions, Lord Phoenix? The secrets of this stronghold are yours to command."

Qellaun, standing beside Phoenix, watched the exchange with a calculating gaze. He understood the gravity of their mission, the necessity of unlocking the secrets concealed within Fel Thalor's depths. The high priestess, a guardian of arcane knowledge, was a key to their quest, and he awaited Phoenix's lead, ready to delve into the enigmatic heart of the stronghold.

Phoenix's crimson eyes flickered with an evil gleam as he addressed the high priestess. "We seek knowledge, High Priestess, knowledge of the Eladrin and their hidden citadel, E'vahona. We have come to unravel the mysteries that have eluded us for far too long."

The high priestess's lips curled into a dark smile, her devotion to the shadows mirroring their own. "The secrets of E'vahona are enigmatic and well-guarded, Lord Phoenix. But within Fel Thalor's depths, we shall uncover the answers you seek. Follow me, and we shall descend into the abyss of knowledge."

With that, she turned and led them deeper into the shadowed heart of Fel Thalor, where the ancient secrets of their world and the mysteries of the Eladrin awaited, shrouded in darkness and betrayal.

Within the eerie heart of Fel Thalor, a dread-soaked stronghold, Phoenix stood momentarily bewildered by the unexpected reverence shown by the high priestess. Her deferential demeanor, a stark departure from the evil atmosphere of the fortress, left him with an enigmatic puzzle to ponder.

Turning to Qellaun, his faithful companion in this arcane journey, Phoenix found reassurance in the intrigue glint dancing within his ally's eyes. Qellaun's calming hand rested upon Phoenix's shoulder, a silent promise that all would be revealed in time.

"Exercise patience, my friend," Qellaun advised in hushed tones, his words a soothing balm against the backdrop of enigma that enveloped them. "Our answers await within the library, where my sister, Lyra, holds dominion over the fathomless wellspring of knowledge we seek."

With a graceful withdrawal, the high priestess left them to navigate the labyrinthine corridors of Fel Thalor. In her wake, the secrets woven into the very stone and shadows of the stronghold whispered as ancient incantations and the covenant of unrevealed truths hung palpably in the air. It was an unspoken pact, poised to unfurl within the hallowed temple of knowledge, where Lyra, the sorceress of enigmatic power, awaited their arrival.

Within the sacred sanctuary of Fel Thalor's library, Phoenix and Qellaun stepped into a realm of forgotten wisdom and arcane mysteries. The hallowed space seemed to breathe with the whispers of knowledge that spanned centuries, bound within the pages of ancient tomes. Each step they took reverberated softly on the polished marble floor, echoing through the grand chamber.

The shelves, towering like monoliths of hidden truths, held countless volumes clad in dusty leather and bound with ornate runes. These tomes murmured in long-forgotten tongues, their voices a symphony of secrets. The air, heavy with the scent of aged parchment and tinged with the subtle aura of mystical energies, enveloped the duo like a shroud of anticipation.

Lyra, the sorceress of enigmatic power, stood like an ethereal guardian amid the labyrinthine shelves at the heart of this repository of esoteric wisdom. Her presence exuded an otherworldly grace and a profound connection to the arcane.

Qellaun, bearing the weight of ancient knowledge and reunited with his sister, approached Lyra with a fraternal embrace. Their connection transcended mere words, a bond forged through shared experiences and the unspoken understanding of their mission.

"Lyra," Qellaun greeted, his voice infused with affection and the long-awaited relief of their reunion. "Time has kept us apart for far too long."

Lyra's eyes, pools of fondness and curiosity, met her brother's gaze. Her voice, a musical resonance carrying the echoes of the arcane, responded, "Indeed, dear brother. But your arrival carries a sense of purpose beyond mere family reunion."

As Qellaun shared a moment of brotherly connection with Lyra, he unveiled a hidden truth, a fragment of Phoenix's past obscured by the sands of time. Shrouded in enigmatic significance, this revelation hung like a tantalizing riddle.

"Lyra," Qellaun continued in hushed tones, "within the labyrinth of our shared past, there exists a concealed truth, a fragment of history from Phoenix's childhood, obscured by the sands of time. It is a facet of his existence that he may not recall."

Lyra, a beacon of wisdom and insight, nodded in understanding, her gaze an unwavering beacon of perception. She seemed to have glimpsed a shard of recognition in Phoenix's depths, which had remained elusive to others. Her words resonated with purpose, casting a subtle enchantment over the library.

"Yes," she murmured, her voice carrying the weight of a sacred mission. "It is high time for him to reconnect with the wellspring of his power. Very well, dear brother. Accompany Phoenix to a place of respite, and I shall gather the scrolls and artifacts that may kindle the embers of his forgotten memories."

With a wordless acknowledgment of their unbreakable bond, Qellaun turned to Phoenix. Together, they would guide their enigmatic companion toward a sanctuary of reprieve and rediscovery, where the tapestry of a long-buried past would unravel like ancient runes, unveiling the mysterious secrets beneath the surface of his consciousness.

Chapter 11

Phoenix's Awakening: Secrets Unveiled in Fel Thalor

In the dim-lit, labyrinthine recesses of Fel Thalor's library, where the very air crackled with the murmurs of concealed knowledge, Lyra, the sorceress of enigmatic wisdom, dispatched a trusted messenger to call forth Phoenix and Qellaun from the shadows. The messenger's footfalls reverberated like a sacred chant as they echoed through the towering alcoves of arcane tomes.

Within moments, Phoenix and Qellaun emerged from the obscurity of the library's depths, drawn by the beckoning summons of their enigmatic host. Their inquisitiveness ignited by the sight of scrolls and mystical artifacts meticulously arrayed upon a sturdy oaken table, they approached with reverence.

Adorned with intricate symbols that danced like starlight on a moonless night, vellum scrolls lay open, their pages waiting to unveil the ancient secrets they guarded. Nearby, an otherworldly sphere emanated a soft, ethereal radiance, casting its enchantments into the far corners of the chamber.

Lyra's eyes, wellsprings of ageless knowledge, met Phoenix's gaze with a blend of solemn recognition and determined purpose. Her voice, a lilting invocation laden with the gravitas of secrets kept for generations, began to weave its enchantment.

"Phoenix, what you are on the cusp of discovering should have been unveiled to you long ago," she began, her words a soft symphony reverberating with the weight of ancient enigmas. "Your father, a paragon of wisdom and might, had harbored intentions to bequeath this knowledge unto you. Alas, his life met an untimely end."

Phoenix, his countenance painted with a mosaic of curiosity and sorrow, hung upon her words, yearning to unearth the buried legacies of his past.

Lyra continued her revelation, her voice an incantation of history's echoes. "Qellaun, your steadfast confidant, had sworn an oath of silence and a covenant of safeguarding to your father. It was a pact forged in the crucible of unwavering allegiance, binding him to defend you and uphold the sacred mysteries your father held close."

The revelations unfolded like chapters in an ancient tome, each word a brushstroke upon the canvas of destiny, as Phoenix and Qellaun stood poised to reclaim the legacy of knowledge and power that had long lain dormant within the shadowed corridors of their shared history.

Phoenix's eyes widened like twin orbs of revelation as the profound legacy of his father and the profoundness of Qellaun's devotion enveloped him. The room, imbued with the quiet aura of expectation, held its collective breath, the scrolls and the mystical sphere throbbing with latent potency, awaiting the revelations that would soon unfurl like the long-awaited pages of an ancient tome.

In the hallowed chamber of arcane knowledge and silent covenants, Phoenix stood poised on the precipice of his history, ready to unveil the secrets veiled in shadow for too many seasons. The legacy of his father, the unwavering fidelity of his companion, and the enigmas of his destiny converged like celestial constellations aligning in the sprawling tapestry of his existence.

Lyra's voice, a mellifluous incantation of esoteric wisdom, continued to weave its spell within the dim-lit enclave of Fel Thalor's library. Her eyes, reminiscent of smoldering coals, bore a profound melancholy tinged with a glimmer of optimism as she addressed Phoenix.

"Phoenix," she intoned, her words a gentle caress of the arcane, "your power is no mere luck, for your father was a warlock of unparalleled distinction. Within you resides an extraordinary gift, an inheritance of darkness, and the potential for transcendence."

With an air of anticipation that hung like a cloak of charisma, she tenderly presented him with a miniature, intricately wrought magical sphere. Its surface shimmered with an ethereal luminescence, reflecting the hidden revelations it safeguarded.

"Within this sphere," Lyra elucidated, her voice a beacon through the abyss of uncertainty, "rests a glimpse into the past—a ceremonial ode to dark enchantments, an unholy rite that unfurled in the very heart of Flameford. You, a mere child then, were anointed with your father's sinister birthright."

As Phoenix cradled the sphere within his palms, its pulsating energy coursed against his skin, resonating with the unfathomable depths of his warlock potency. Lyra's pronouncements reverberated within the chamber, and the sphere, like a keeper of ageless secrets, began to unveil its concealed truths.

The unfolding vision resembled a tapestry of twisted shadows, where flames pirouetted with an eerie luminescence, casting their haunting glow upon the tableau of the sinister ceremony. Phoenix beheld himself as a child, innocence surrounded by the evil silhouettes of his father's sinister cultists. The atmosphere hung heavy with malevolence, shadows intertwining like ethereal serpents, trapping the innocent youth in an unholy embrace.

The scene, illuminated by the crimson glow of the malevolent flames, bore witness to the dark legacy thrust upon him—a legacy that would forever shape the path of his destiny, intertwining his life with the threads of arcane secrets and sinister powers.

Yet, from the veils of darkness emerged a figure—a resolute Eladrin archer, her hair spun from the finest strands of gold, and her features exuded her kind's ethereal grace. With swift precision, she disrupted the ceremony, shattering the chains of darkness that bound young Phoenix. The malefic ritual recoiled, retreating into the very heart of Fel Thalor, seeking refuge in the most bottomless abyss.

In this moment of revelation, Phoenix bore the weight of his father's sinister legacy and the resilience of his spirit. The mystical sphere within his grasp pulsed with newfound potency, and the secrets once cloaked in darkness now basked in the luminous light of truth. He comprehended that his powers, a curse and a blessing intertwined, were not merely a mark of infamy but also a testament to his strength—a force that could be wielded for his dire purposes.

Lyra, the sorceress, watched with intent as Phoenix absorbed the truths of his lineage. The chamber itself seemed to resonate with echoes of bygone ages, and the promise of a new beginning for Phoenix—the warlock with a singular gift and a destiny interwoven with shadows—began to take shape, much like a dark phoenix rising from the ashes.

In this moment of awakening, Phoenix's purpose became clear. He was no longer a pawn of darkness but a force of balance—a harbinger of redemption and a guardian against the encroaching shadows. With newfound clarity and resolve, he embraced his heritage and the power that lay dormant within him, ready to forge a path that would shape the destiny of Fel Thalor and the enigmatic realm of Vacari itself.

In the dim-lit recesses of Fel Thalor's chamber, where malevolence lingered like a haunting melody, Phoenix's gaze remained unswerving upon the vision held within the arcane sphere. His curiosity, devoid of empathy or remorse, blazed like a relentless wildfire amid the shadows.

"Who was she?" he inquired, his voice a cold, calculating whisper infused with a morbid fascination.

Lyra's crimson eyes, mirroring the flickering images within the sphere, began to weave the enigmatic archer's tale. Her voice, reminiscent of a haunting lament, bore the weight of a gruesome narrative.

"She was Serena," Lyra commenced, her words a melancholy dirge, "an Eladrin archer—a guardian of her people and a relentless seeker of vengeance. Her husband, a human mage named Eldric, had been trapped by your father and the Druchii."

Phoenix's brow remained furrowed, though now it expressed a sense of grim satisfaction rather than empathy as the final pieces of this dark puzzle slotted into place with chilling clarity.

"Serena's husband harbored a secret," Lyra continued, her voice dripping with the dread of unspeakable truths. "He possessed knowledge of the whereabouts of E'vahona—a knowledge he clung to with unwavering resolve, even under the most excruciating torment. Ultimately, he paid the ultimate price for his steadfast silence."

Phoenix's comprehension deepened as the narrative unfolded, yet it lacked sympathy. He recognized the magnitude of suffering his father's actions had wrought, and an unsettling, twisted smile etched itself upon the contours of his lips. Serena's quest for vengeance had been born from heartbreak, an echo resonating through the annals of time, and Phoenix reveled in the sinister tapestry of it all.

Lyra's voice grew softer as she concluded the somber tale. "Serena's thirst for vengeance knew no bounds. She was willing to disrupt the sinister ceremony and thwart your father's evil designs, even at the peril of her own life."

In the chamber of secrets, where history bore a heavy mantle and echoes of a tragic past lingered Phoenix grasped the depths of his father's malevolence and the legacy of torment he had inherited. Like a specter from the abyss, Serena's presence in his life held the promise of both answers and repercussions. The strands of destiny continued to weave their intricate patterns in the tapestry of his enigmatic existence.

Qellaun's solemn and weighted, gravity voice carried the tale forward, piecing together the fragments of the dark puzzle that had been his father's life.

"Serena," he began, his words an ominous undertone, "driven by her unyielding determination, met her fitting end. After her initial attempt to thwart your father and the Druchii failed, she remained undeterred, making yet another audacious endeavor to disrupt their wicked machinations. However, it culminated in her demise."

As he listened, unmoved by the unfolding narrative, Phoenix's eyes, bereft of empathy or compassion, now held a perverse satisfaction.

"She crossed paths with the Druchii once more," Qellaun continued, his voice growing even graver, "in the ensuing confrontation, she met her demise. The same fateful event ultimately led to your father's downfall."

As the last vestiges of the story fell into place, Phoenix harbored a chilling sense of justice. He understood the extent of Serena's resolve and the price she had paid for her actions. In the dim-lit chamber of Fel Thalor, where past and present converged like winding rivers, Phoenix's heart remained untouched by the tendrils of empathy or remorse. The legacy of darkness enveloping him only reaffirmed the path of hostility he had chosen for himself.

Within the dim-lit confines of Fel Thalor's chamber, where ancient enigmas and veiled ambitions danced in an unholy embrace, Phoenix's gaze remained transfixed upon the phantasmal visions unfurling within the mystical sphere. He discerned the sinister cadence of his father's ambitions in the chilling tableau before him, weaving an ominous tapestry that resonated with his evil desires.

"My father," Phoenix murmured, his voice a wicked undertone that slithered through the air like a venomous serpent, "he too coveted E'vahona."

Qellaun, a steadfast presence beside him, nodded solemnly, his countenance an emblem of unwavering resolve. He served as a firm reminder of the revelations they had unraveled—the age-old Elven sanctuary, E'vahona, revered by the Eladrin, harbored a fount of arcane power that could magnify Phoenix's own, bestowing upon him an unfathomable wellspring of hostility and might.

"Indeed," Qellaun affirmed, his voice an unwavering resonance within the chamber's sacred hush, "E'vahona is a repository of primordial potency, an enshrined haven that has remained concealed for untold ages. It can amplify your dominion, endowing you with immeasurable power."

Now imbued with a sinister luminance, Phoenix's eyes turned towards Qellaun. His words dripped with ominous resolve, an oath of vengeance cast in stone.

"We shall seize this citadel," he declared, his voice reverberating with malice, "and the Eladrin shall lament the day they crossed paths with my father and me."

Phoenix's proclamation hung like a harbinger of doom within the chamber of arcane secrets and veiled truths. The destiny of E'vahona, an ancient wellspring of power, became irrevocably entwined with the maleficence coursing through his veins. Enshrouded by shadows, the future beckoned with the allure of conquest and retribution as Phoenix plunged further into the abyss, his aspirations taking on darker hues and the shades of his intent looming more formidable than ever.

Lyra, aglow with mingled admiration and caution, approached Phoenix, her robes of crimson silk whispering faintly in the chamber's pregnant stillness. In her outstretched hand, she cradled an ancient scroll, its labyrinthine glyphs etched with the abyssal secrets of the ages.

"Phoenix," she began, her voice a musical incantation woven with the wisdom of the ages, "this scroll bears the ancient sigils of a tongue steeped in abyssal power. Within its cryptic passages lie the keys to unlock further enigmatic darkness, drawn from the unfathomable depths of shadow." With a deliberate gesture, Lyra extended the scroll toward Phoenix.

His eyes, smoldering orbs of insatiable curiosity, seized the offering with a commanding resolve. As his fingertips brushed against the time-weathered parchment, the chamber itself seemed to quiver, a palpable weight of darkness descending upon him, tendrils of shadow coiling around his form like spectral serpents.

Qellaun and Lyra stood as witnesses, their breaths held in the presence of the arcane spectacle unfolding before them. Shadows conjoined and vanished in a fleeting heartbeat, leaving Phoenix drenched in an ominous aura—a testament to his newfound powers.

Once impenetrable to mortal comprehension, the scroll now harbored secrets privy only to Phoenix. A sinister satisfaction danced in his gaze as he addressed Lyra and Qellaun.

"The power has been transmitted to me," he proclaimed, his voice resonating with an eerie timbre. "The abyss has entrusted me with its mysteries."

In the chamber where arcane wisdom and shadow's embrace converged, Phoenix had delved deeper into the abyss. He emerged as a harbinger of newfound might, his journey into darkness now navigated by eldritch secrets whispered to him from the core of shadow itself.

With a demeanor of evil purpose, Phoenix pivoted his attention toward the magical sphere that had laid bare the mysteries of his lineage and bequeathed him boundless might. His digits, pulsating with eldritch energies, ensnared the globe.

Then, in a sudden and violent rupture, he crushed the crystalline vessel within his grasp. Shards of arcane essence erupted, malefic sparks scattering before dissolving into the ether. The chamber's eerie luminescence dimmed, and the cryptic enigmas it harbored were eternally extinguished.

Turning his piercing gaze upon Qellaun and Lyra, Phoenix's voice rang out, a chilling edict reverberating through the chamber's pregnant silence.

"The revelations bestowed upon me this day," he intoned, his voice resonating with the weight of newfound authority, "shall bind both of you by an unbreakable oath of silence, a covenant forged in the crucible of the abyss itself. Know that should this vow ever be transgressed, you shall each be consigned to the unholy servitude of the abyss, becoming its dreaded minions."

Qellaun and Lyra, their eyes twin mirrors reflecting fear and reluctant acceptance, nodded in somber concurrence. A pact sealed by silence required no spoken words, for it was now etched into the marrow of their existence, their shared destiny now intertwined with the shadowy forces that prowled the depths of their souls.

In the chamber where arcane secrets and newfound malevolence coalesced, the resonance of their vow lingered in the air, a haunting testament to the darkness that had bound them together—a night that had taken root in the very essence of their beings.

With his voice brimming with an eerie authority and a cold command, Phoenix turned his piercing crimson gaze upon Lyra. She stood before him, a figure poised between kinship and servitude.

"Prepare yourself for departure from Fel Thalor," he ordered, his words dripping with an unsettling potency. "From this moment forward, you shall serve me personally, just as your brother does."

Lyra, her genuine emotions hidden behind a mask of reluctant compliance, nodded, acknowledging her inescapable fate.

"Fel Thalor itself," Phoenix declared, his voice resonating with unnatural power, "shall continue to be a loyal servant, offering unwavering support in our relentless pursuit of Swifthammer and the enigmatic Eladrin archer."

With a chilling decree that hung in the air like a shadowy shroud, he issued a precise ultimatum: "You have but a solitary hour to make ready."

Phoenix executed a sharp about-face and strode forth from the chamber without deigning to await a response. His departure left behind the lingering aura of his newfound power and the heavy reverberations of his hostility—a grim presence that now bound them all. In Fel Thalor, where secrets and shadows converged like intersecting streams of darkness, the destiny of its inhabitants had taken a darker turn. The promise of servitude and conquest hung palpably in the air, an ominous cloud that foretold an uncertain future.

Qellaun, his gaze laden with the burden of remorse, shifted his attention to his sister, Lyra, the weight of their shifting fates settling upon his shoulders like an impossible load.

"I beg your forgiveness for the upheaval in your life," he whispered, his voice a lament infused with sorrow.

Lyra, her eyes aflame with a peculiar blend of empathy and hope, bestowed upon him a tender smile. "It's alright, dear Qellaun," she reassured him. "Surely Phoenix can't be as dreadful as the rumors suggest, can he?"

Qellaun's head shook slowly, his countenance clouding with a foreboding premonition. "Oh, Lyra, you underestimate him. He is every bit as evil as the tales convey and then some. Yet, there's no turning back now. Let us seek solace in the notion that you will serve someone of immense power."

Lyra's smile remained unwavering as she enveloped her brother in a heartfelt embrace, a silent pact of understanding passing between them. Then, with steadfast determination, she turned away and proceeded to prepare for her new life in servitude.

Qellaun observed his sister's departure, his heart laden with the solemn recognition that their world had irrevocably changed. With Phoenix's newfound dominion and his relentless pursuit of E'vahona, their future lay cloaked in uncertainty—a tapestry is woven with the threads of shadowy ambitions and sinister desires.

In the grand courtyard of Fel Thalor, Lyra approached Phoenix, her crimson robes billowing gently in the breeze. Her gaze, a mixture of curiosity and unwavering obedience, fixed upon the enigmatic warlock.

"Shall we embark on our journey to Goldmoor astride your formidable dragon?" Her voice bore a melodic lilt, carrying curiosity and acceptance of her newfound servitude.

In response, Phoenix issued a simple yet affirmative nod. "Indeed, we shall."

Ever vigilant and protective, Qellaun extended his hand, a gesture of polite care, to aid Lyra in mounting the colossal red dragon. With deliberate grace, she ascended the dragon's back, her elegant crimson and silver gown a striking contrast against the dragon's iridescent scales. Qellaun, unwavering in his commitment to her safety, took his place behind her, a guardian in the face of their impending journey.

As Phoenix issued the command, the mighty Zylron, the embodiment of draconic majesty, unfurled his wings with magnificent prowess. With one powerful beat, they were lifted skyward, ascending into the cerulean heavens, leaving the ominous silhouette of Fel Thalor behind.

The journey unfolded with swiftness and exhilaration, the wind whistling past them as they soared towards their destination, the city of Goldmoor. Upon their triumphant arrival, Phoenix pivoted towards Qellaun, his voice laced with a directive underscored by unwavering authority.

"Escort Lyra to the library," he ordered the subtle nuances of his tone affirming his mastery. "Her quest for knowledge regarding E'vahona begins there."

Qellaun's response was a regal nod, a silent acceptance of his charge, and with Lyra at his side, they embarked upon a journey to the formidable library. The library's architecture, a testament to the ancient lore and hidden truths it safeguarded, loomed imposingly before them, its dark stone walls resonating with the weight of knowledge.

The embodiment of power and unwavering determination, Phoenix strode purposefully in the opposite direction, each step echoing his steadfast purpose. The destiny of their quest, a tapestry woven from shadows and enigma, teetered on the precipice of uncertainty.

In the heart of Goldmoor, within the hallowed chambers adorned with countless tomes and scrolls, Lyra's quest would unfurl like the unfolding pages of a spellbound manuscript. The looming shadows of destiny, the threads of ambition, and the allure of E'vahona would continue to shape their narrative—a tale intricately interwoven with darkness and unfettered determination.

Chapter 12

The Tenuous Crossing

In the heart of the ancient forest, Kelru Palvoh, a cunning Druchii leader, stood like a dark sentinel amidst the lush, verdant gloom. The towering trees loomed overhead, their gnarled branches interlocking like ancient secrets, casting dappled shadows that played upon the forest floor. Here, nature seemed to conspire silently as if holding its breath in anticipation.

Kelru's voice, laden with the sinister authority that bound his minions together, cut through the calm stillness like a dagger forged in shadows. His words hung in the air, heavy with the hostility that permeated the woods. "Prepare yourselves," he commanded his voice a venomous hiss that slithered through the underbrush. "Their arrival is imminent."

The Druchii warriors, clad in ebony armor that seemed to absorb the light around them, appeared as spectral figures in the dim forest. Their eyes, gleaming with a predatory hostility, acknowledged their leader's orders with an enthusiasm that bordered on fanaticism. Their mission was unequivocal: capture the Eladrin alive, for Phoenix's insatiable thirst for knowledge teetered on the precipice, awaiting the secrets that only a living captive could reveal.

From among the ranks of the shadowy warriors, a voice dared to question, its tone a mere whisper in the looming darkness, as if fearing to disturb the ancient trees. "What of Swifthammer, the indomitable warrior?"

Kelru's cruel smile returned, his crimson eyes aflame with unyielding resolve. "Phoenix desires him for interrogation," he hissed, his voice a sinister promise, "but if the warrior proves too formidable, then we shall have no choice but to extinguish his life."

The forest, a timeless and enigmatic entity, seemed to shiver in response to Kelru's declaration. The weight of their ominous mission hung heavily in the air, like a storm gathering on the horizon. In this twilight realm, where secrets intertwined with shadows, the fates of the Eladrin and the warrior swung precariously, woven into the darkness of the Druchii and their unwavering pursuit of their sinister master's desires.

Meanwhile, Ong and Keisha ventured deeper into the heart of danger, their every footstep a dance on the precipice of peril. Keisha, her fiery hair cascading like molten lava, voiced her concerns in hushed tones, her words a whisper carried by the rustling leaves that seemed to conspire with her.

"Do you not think," she murmured, her voice barely audible above the forest's symphony of secrets, "that they may wait for us along the path? This seems the perfect setting for an ambush, a treacherous trap laid in the very heart of this dense and shadowed forest."

In the heart of the woods, Ong, his raven-black hair framing a face etched with resolve, cast a protective gaze upon Keisha. His azure eyes shimmered with concern and unyielding determination, his grip on Thunder's reins a tangible testament to the gravity of their situation.

Soft-spoken but brimming with unwavering determination, Keisha offered her suggestion, her words a delicate echo in the tranquil forest. "Allow me to proceed alone," she urged, her voice carrying the weight of sacrifice. "They seek to capture, not to kill. You could slip away while they focus their attention on me."

Ong, his resolve as unbreakable as the ancient trees surrounding them, halted Thunder's powerful stride, dismounted with care, and extended a steadying hand to assist Keisha from the saddle. Their eyes met in a moment of shared understanding, a silent exchange of emotions that resonated louder than words.

"Absolutely not," he declared, his voice infused with unswerving determination. "I will not allow you to face them alone. While I may not fully comprehend your penchant for safeguarding others, that changes here and now."

Like a gentle breeze rustling through the leaves, Ong's voice softened as he continued, his unwavering gaze a soothing anchor amid turmoil. "Keisha, you mean more to me than you could ever fathom. The thought of any harm befalling you is unbearable to me. My feelings for you run deeper than friendship, and I refuse to let you willingly place yourself in harm's way."

His heartfelt declaration resonated in the tranquil forest, his words embracing protection and care. Gently, Ong placed Keisha back into Thunder's saddle, his determination to shield her akin to an impenetrable shield. By their side, Pumpkin, their loyal companion, followed faithfully, a steadfast sentinel in their perilous journey. Together, they resumed their cautious path toward the forest's edge, their destinies entwined, newfound understanding blossoming amidst the looming shadows of impending danger.

As they rode, the weight of their situation pressed upon them. The ominous presence of the Druchii and the enigma of what lay ahead cast a profound shadow over their path. Yet, amidst the encroaching darkness, a shared moment of vulnerability lingered, their unspoken emotions woven into the very fabric of the ancient forest, their hearts entangled in an intricate dance of fate.

Within the forest's verdant embrace, Ong and Keisha embarked on their perilous journey toward the ominous path awaited them. Their newly kindled connection grew stronger with every step, a bond forged in the crucible of danger and vulnerability. As they ventured deeper into the heart of the woods, their hearts beat in unison, and the treacherous path ahead, though shrouded in uncertainty, felt slightly less daunting with the assurance of their shared strength and the blossoming understanding between them.

Their passage through the forest continued, a wordless communion of emotions conveyed through the rustling leaves and the enigmatic shadows surrounding them. Keisha's heart swelled with the profound realization that she couldn't recall a time when someone had cared for her so deeply. Their unspoken sentiments resonated within her, touching her with heartfelt sincerity.

Ong, attuned to the unspoken emotions coursing through her, discerned the soft fall of her tears. Without hesitation, he leaned her gently against his protective form, enveloping her warmly as they rode onward. His presence conveyed a reassurance that transcended mere words.

"Keisha," he whispered, his breath a comforting warmth against her ear. "Fear not. We shall conquer this path together."

In that fleeting moment, amidst the rustling leaves and the ever-present shadows, their unspoken connection deepened, a bond solidified in the crucible of danger and vulnerability. Together, they pressed onward, hearts entwined, and the challenging path ahead, while still difficult, seemed a little less foreboding with the strength they derived from each other and the burgeoning understanding that bound their souls.

The forest, a realm of ancient and majestic beauty, wrapped Ong and Keisha in its verdant embrace, a sanctuary where secrets whispered amidst the rustling leaves and the distant murmurs of the natural world. Their conversation unfolded in hushed tones, like the softest notes of an elusive melody, barely audible above the chorus of nature's voices. Here, amidst the tranquil embrace of the woods, Keisha unveiled the source of her tears, not born of worry but stirred by the profound emotions of Ong's heartfelt declaration.

In response to her unspoken resolve, Keisha's nimble fingers embraced her longbow, its polished wood gleaming with an understated luster. With an elegant fluidity, she notched an arrow, her movements a testament to her unwavering determination. Sharp and vigilant, her gaze scanned the looming forest canopy, the guardian of their shared journey.

Ong, his heart a wellspring of tenderness and admiration, regarded the resilient archer at his side. Her spirit was a force of nature, a captivating blend of strength and vulnerability that he admired and cherished. He leaned to tenderly kiss her head tenderly, silently acknowledging their unspoken connection. Their shared resolve propelled them forward, their thoughts and discussions reserved for a safer time, their focus unwavering on the treacherous path ahead.

Their loyal companion, Pumpkin, moved gracefully at Ong's urging. Lush and unforgiving forest encroached upon their path, its depths concealing beauty and peril. But with newfound determination and watchful eyes, they ventured toward the ominous way, their unity a beacon of hope in the encroaching shadows of the forest.

Deeper within the woods, Kelru Palvoh, the cunning Druchii leader, remained enigmatic, his figure melding seamlessly with the shifting silhouettes of the trees. His presence was as cold as the depths of winter, and his crimson eyes surveyed the forest's edge with a predatory intensity, seeking the subtlest signs of their quarry.

The air was pregnant with anticipation, a tension gripping the forest's heart. Kelru's Druchii warriors, swathed in ebony cloaks, were poised like coiled serpents, their faces concealed beneath eldritch helmets. Their ashen complexions bore the mark of a dark purpose, a living testament to their allegiance to their ruthless leader and the malevolent quest they pursued.

In the heart of the forest's labyrinthine depths, Kelru Palvoh, the wily Druchii commander, raised his gloved hand with a silent signal that cut through the stillness like a phantom's whisper. His fingers, shrouded in obsidian gloves, coiled with a silent intent while his voice, as sibilant as a serpent's hiss, slithered through the ancient trees.

"Any moment now," he muttered, his gaze a predator's fix on the dense foliage. His crimson eyes, akin to the predatory eyes of a lurking shadow, scoured the wilderness. "They should soon emerge from the depths of the forest, step into the open clearing, and then unwittingly tread the path of their doom."

The Druchii warriors under Kelru's command, poised like lurking panthers, responded in unison, their voices a collective whisper of malevolence. "Yes, Commander," they murmured unwavering loyalty, a sinister chorus echoing through the shadowy canopy.

Kelru's nefarious designs had been set into relentless motion, and the fate of their elusive quarry hung in the balance, a delicate thread upon which destiny wavered. With grim determination, they awaited the precise moment when Ong and Keisha would unwittingly dance into the treacherous snare concealed along the path, their capture an impending inevitability as the encroaching shadows of pursuit closed in like inexorable fate.

As Ong and Keisha, their senses finely tuned to the ever-present threats, emerged from the forest's shrouded embrace into the open clearing, the path before them remained an enigma, a treacherous labyrinth of perilous uncertainties. Each step was a delicate traverse along the precipice of danger, where the wrong move might plunge them into the abyss.

Yet, just as they approached the dangerous threshold of the path, a low, menacing growl resonated from the depths of Pumpkin, the ebony panther who shared their journey. Her sleek, obsidian form bristled with primal instincts, her muscles coiled with an unspoken warning. Ong, casting a puzzled gaze at Keisha, furrowed his brow in curious concern.

"What is she sensing?" he whispered, his voice a murmur of intrigue.

Her emerald eyes were wide with bewildered wonder. Keisha shrugged, her usual confidence momentarily giving way to an unknown enigma. "I have no idea," she admitted, her words a fleeting echo in the forest's labyrinthine silence.

Realization bloomed like a fragile, rare flower in the labyrinth of Ong's keen intellect. Thunder's robust frame quivered as Ong dismounted with fluid grace, his boots making a soft, purposeful crunch on the forest's mossy floor. A nearby rock, rugged and unassuming, found itself lifted into Ong's grip. With the grace of a true marksman, he sent the stone sailing through the air, its trajectory guided by his uncanny precision. The rock landed with a muffled thud, striking the unseen target in the direction that had ensnared Pumpkin's keen instincts.

The forest's sacred silence shattered in the echoing aftermath of Ong's clever ruse. A discordant symphony of snapping branches and clanging metal reverberated through the woods, announcing the activation of a concealed trap. This surprise sent a shiver dancing down their collective spines.

Between them, laughter swirled like a secret shared amidst the lurking peril, a testament to their unwavering camaraderie in the face of danger. Their gazes, touched with gratitude, converged upon Pumpkin, who stood as a vigilant sentinel, her obsidian form a stark contrast to the surrounding shadows. "Well done, girl," Ong praised her, his voice a soft, warm caress of appreciation.

With the immediate threat expertly averted, Ong remounted Thunder with the lithe grace of a warrior in command. "Hold your ground, Keisha," he instructed, his words an unspoken vow of protection. He then turned his attention to Pumpkin, his blue eyes conveying unwavering trust. "Lead the way."

Guided by Pumpkin's feline instincts, they ventured along the treacherous path, their laughter lingering like a radiant beacon amidst the forest's shadowy embrace.

A heavy silence in the forest's heart settled over the Druchii warriors like a palpable shroud, their crimson eyes, akin to predatory stars, slicing through the gathering darkness. The eerie stillness that had descended upon the forest was broken only by the whispering leaves and the distant calls of enigmatic creatures, their ghostly cadence forming a spectral backdrop to the warriors' contemplation.

Before them, the path stretched like a riddle waiting to be unraveled, an enigmatic puzzle poised at the intersection of destiny and danger. The cacophony of traps had sprung with a thunderous flourish, leaving the Druchii bewildered, their curiosity piqued by the peculiar absence of the usual screams and agonized cries accompanying such incidents.

Uncertainty clung to the air like a lingering mist, a nebulous veil enshrouding the Druchii warriors in a cocoon of doubt. Their voices wove a tapestry of cautious dissent in the hushed interplay of nervous glances and murmured deliberations. Some among them yearned to draw closer to the enigmatic path, the siren call of curiosity vying with the tendrils of caution that tightened around their resolve. Meanwhile, others hung back, hesitating at the precipice of the unknown, wariness etched in the lines of their faces.

Amid this gathering storm of uncertainty, Kelru Palvoh, their commanding presence, remained unwavering in his determination. His tactical mind knew the perils of hasty action and understood that the premature reveal of their existence could irrevocably compromise their intricate mission. His voice, dripping with authority, cut through the discord like a blade forged of dark purpose.

"Hold your positions," he commanded, his words bearing the weight of irrevocable purpose. "Patience is our most potent ally. We shall observe and strike when the time is ripe."

The Druchii warriors, with heavy hearts but acquiescent spirits, heeded their leader's strategic wisdom. Their gaze remained fixated upon the enigmatic path, tantalizing and shrouded in an uncharted enigma. Kelru, too, grappled with unanswered questions, his mind a labyrinthine maze of schemes and inquiries, while the forest itself seemed to conceal secrets beneath its leafy tapestry. Like the shadows that clung to their forms, their pursuit would persist, veiled in mysteries and uncertainty.

As Ong and Keisha, accompanied by Thunder and Pumpkin, emerged from the treacherous path and confronted the lurking Druchii, the forest exhaled a tense breath, awaiting the impending clash of opposing forces.

Ong vaulted back onto Thunder's saddle in an orchestrated dance of seamless precision. At the same time, Pumpkin, her feline instincts sensing danger, emitted an ominous growl, her obsidian eyes locked onto the concealed adversaries. Ong's voice, low and charged with urgency, reached Keisha's ears as he imparted a solemn directive, the gravity of the situation etched in his tone.

"Exercise caution. We take no unwarranted risks."

Keisha, her longbow poised like a harp string drawn taut, surveyed the forest with keen eyes, her fingers poised like a maestro's, ready to release a storm of arrows upon the lurking Druchii. The tension that gripped the forest was a palpable overture to the imminent conflict, like the gathering tempo of an ominous symphony.

The once tranquil forest, now transformed into a stage of turmoil and fury, bore witness to a tumultuous clash between Ong, Keisha, and their loyal companions and the Druchii who had sought to trap them. The cacophony of battle, the clash of weapons, and the agonized cries of the wounded reverberated through the ancient trees, as if the very forest had awoken in response to the confrontation.

Amidst the chaos, Keisha's arrows continued to sing their lethal tune, each shot finding its target with uncanny precision. Her skill with the bow was like poetry in motion, a deadly ballet that left Druchii warriors in her wake, their enigmatic figures felled by her relentless accuracy. Her resolve was unyielding, her determination unwavering as she defended herself and her allies with deadly grace.

Pumpkin, their loyal companion, was a force of nature unto herself. Her sleek, obsidian form moved with predatory grace, and her claws and fangs struck ruthlessly. She was a whirlwind of dark fury amidst the

Druchii ranks, a relentless guardian who left chaos and confusion in her wake.

Ong, the brave protector, was a vision of controlled power. His sword, an extension of his soul, moved with a fluidity that defied mortal limitations. He parried attacks with grace and struck with precision, his movements a testament to his unwavering determination to protect Keisha and ensure their survival.

In the heart of the forest, amidst the swirling maelstrom of battle, Ong, Keisha, Pumpkin, and their adversaries clashed like titans, the outcome of their deadly dance hanging in the balance, and the ancient trees themselves seemed to hold their breath, bearing witness to a struggle born of shadows and destiny.

The forest seemed to respond to the tumultuous clash as if the trees whispered ancient incantations of support and protection to their defenders. The leaves rustled in harmony with the battle's rhythm, and the branches reached out like spectral hands, offering their blessings to those who fought in their sacred realm.

Thunder's powerful hooves pounded the earth with a relentless determination, each stride a thunderclap that echoed through the forest. He was a steadfast beacon of hope, carrying Ong and Keisha ever closer to the sanctuary of Emeraldwood Forest, where the shadows that pursued them dared not tread.

Ong and Keisha were a formidable duo in the heart of the ancient woods, and their resolve was unwavering in the face of adversity. Their movements were a dance of deadly precision, a testament to their unyielding bond and shared purpose. Each strike and parry was a step closer to victory, and their hearts beat in harmony with the primal rhythm of battle.

Pumpkin, their loyal companion, was a force of nature, her ebony form a whirlwind of fury amidst the Druchii ranks. Her growls and snarls filled the air, a haunting chorus that struck fear into the hearts of their adversaries. She was a guardian of the forest, a protector of her allies, and a living embodiment of the wild spirit that dwelled within the ancient woods.

The forest watched and listened as the battle raged on, its ancient wisdom bearing witness to the clash of mortal wills. The outcome of this deadly dance hung in the balance, and the forest seemed to hold its breath, awaiting the resolution of the fateful confrontation.

In the heart of the ancient woods, a cacophony of chaos erupted as a storm unleashed. Kelru's voice, a seething storm of fury, reverberated through the old trees, shattering the eerie silence that had enveloped the forest moments before. It was as if the air crackled with his anger, and the forest seemed to recoil.

Some of the Druchii, their faces etched with panic, attempted to scatter like leaves caught in a violent gale. Their ebony-clad figures quivered with fear as they beheld the approaching maelstrom of battle, a black storm racing toward them with relentless determination.

"Get back here!" Kelru's voice, like a primal roar, boomed through the woods. His words were a thunderclap of command that echoed through the ancient trees. His crimson eyes blazed with wrath that mirrored the inferno of the battle below, a relentless fire that consumed all reason.

With a fury born of Kelru's command, the Druchii warriors transformed into an evil tempest. Their ebony-clad forms became a blur as they raced through the narrowing gap between the treacherous path and the looming sanctuary of the Emeraldwoods. They moved like shadows given life, driven by an insatiable hunger for the elusive quarry that slipped through their fingers like elusive mist.

The forest, a realm of ancient power and enigmatic beauty, stood as a silent witness to the unfolding drama. Its ancient oaks and gnarled branches seemed to reach out, their spectral forms forming a barrier between the pursuing Druchii and the sanctuary of the Emeraldwoods. The very leaves whispered secrets of protection and defiance, urging Ong and Keisha onward in their desperate flight.

The battle between light and darkness continued to rage in the heart of the woods, and the outcome hung in the balance. The sanctuary of the Emeraldwoods beckoned like a distant promise, a glimmer of hope amidst the encroaching shadows.

Pumpkin, their mysterious guardian, became an impromptu leader in their desperate flight, her instincts keenly attuned to the urgency of their situation. With a primal speed born of peril, she urged Ong and Keisha forward, her ebony form a shadowy sentinel directing their escape.

Amidst the frantic rush, Ong's laughter echoed through the chaos, a defiant note in the face of danger. His eyes, alight with exhilaration, held a spark of irreverence that matched the infectious thrill of their escape. "It appears Pumpkin just earned herself a promotion to boss," he quipped, his humor a testament to their shared camaraderie and the exhilaration of their flight.

Keisha's laughter joined his, a melodic counterpoint to the discord of the chase. In that fleeting moment, they found solace and laughed amidst their hearts pounding. Together, they sprinted toward the beckoning sanctuary of the Emeraldwoods. The towering trees, ancient sentinels of the forest, drew ever nearer, their canopy a promise of safety that seemed to embrace them with open arms.

As Ong and Keisha plunged deeper into the lush heart of the forest, leaving behind the fading echoes of their pursuers, Kelru's voice hung in the air like a haunting specter of authority. His distant commands whispered through the trees, a futile reminder of their former tormentors.

Kelru himself, burdened by the weight of failure, felt the tension in his shoulders relent as he witnessed his quarry slipping through his grasp. A heavy sigh escaped his lips, and his crimson eyes gazed into the depths of the verdant wilderness, acknowledging the futility of pursuing them further.

Resigned to their misfortune, he turned to his loyal cadre of Druchii warriors, a collective realization of their inadequacy weighing heavily in the air. "Head to Crystal Vale," he commanded, his voice a weary reflection of the resignation brought on by defeat.

However, one of his warriors, driven by ambition or perhaps foolishness, dared to question the decision, suggesting a return to Goldmoor. Kelru's gaze, sharp and cutting as a serrated blade, fixed upon the daring Druchii. Low and filled with dangerous ire, his voice sliced through the air like a vengeful curse. "Do you wish to be the one to deliver the news of our failure to Phoenix?"

The warrior's countenance drained of color, like the fading hues of a sunset, as he recoiled from the dreadful notion of facing Phoenix's wrath.

It was a fate so nightmarish that no Druchii dared entertain the thought. With a collective understanding, they averted their gaze from the path leading back to Goldmoor, resigning themselves to a journey toward Crystal Vale. Heavy were their hearts, burdened by the knowledge of their defeat in the heart of the Purplefire Woods.

Under the indigo shroud of the evening, Ong and Keisha ventured deeper into the heart of the Emeraldwoods Forest. The towering trees, their branches twisted like ancient sages in meditation, stretched heavenward as if seeking to commune with the celestial realms. Like pages of an untold saga, leaves rustled in muted conversation with the ever-watchful moon. The forest floor, where moss and dew-kissed ferns conspired, pulsed with its vitality, each footfall a heartbeat in the living symphony of nature.

The night air was an alchemical blend of scents, an elixir of earthiness, pine zest, and wildflowers' faintest brush. Like celestial couriers, fireflies pirouetted in ethereal constellations, sketching ephemeral runes of light amidst the swaying foliage. Above, the canopy crafted an intricate tapestry of ebony and silver, where stars pierced through the leafy veils like celestial diamonds, a stellar parade in the grand theater of the night.

After an eternity of cautious progress, they discovered a serene meadow basking in the gentle caress of silvery moonlight. At its heart lay the promise of reprieve: their bedrolls, meticulously arranged like sanctuaries amidst the forest's embrace. The clearing was an oasis of tranquility, untouched by the encroaching tides of shadows—a sacred sanctuary where the tumultuous world beyond seemed to dissolve into oblivion.

Keisha, her russet hair aglow like molten copper beneath the moon's tender touch, cast a pensive gaze upon the inviting bedrolls. Ong, with a soft smile that hinted at reverence, couldn't help but appreciate the transformation he observed in her. It was as though the crucible of their journey had imbued her with a serene wisdom—a newfound appreciation for life's simple luxuries.

While Ong chuckled affectionately, noting her graceful approach to her bedroll and growing proficiency in making a wilderness bed, Keisha couldn't help but ponder silently. Did she need to tell him that, as an Eladrin, she was accustomed to sleeping in trees or hidden in the foliage when she traveled? It was a subtle difference in their ways, and she cherished the moments when Ong's world and hers converged, like now, under the moonlit canopy of the Emeraldwoods.

As they readied themselves to surrender to slumber beneath the verdant embrace of the Emeraldwoods Forest, the world around them seemed to hold its breath—an enchanting tableau of nature and magic interwoven in the heart of the night. The forest, a sentry in silence, whispered its age-old lullaby, and Keisha and Ong, kindred spirits amidst a world of marvels, sought solace in the tranquil sanctuary they had discovered.

The moon watched over them, its silver gaze an unspoken witness to their shared moments of vulnerability and strength. In the heart of the Emeraldwoods, surrounded by the nocturnal symphony of nature, they prepared to rest, knowing that their dreams would be woven with the ethereal threads of the forest's enigmatic secrets, and their journey would continue with the first light of dawn.

Chapter 13

Powers Unveiled

In the heart of the Goldmoor library, a sanctum where time itself whispered through the hallowed halls, Qellaun and his sister Lyra embarked upon a reverent pilgrimage through the depths of antiquity. Here, amidst the towering shelves that stretched like ancient sentinels, their fingers brushed the vellum pages of age-old tomes and the delicate parchment of scrolls, all enigmatic keys to unlock the enshrouded fables of the mythical city, E'vahona.

The library, an awe-inspiring knowledge labyrinth, bore witness to their noble quest, each step taken like a delicate dance across the pages of history. The shelves rose high, their wooden spines adorned with dust and reverence, like the columns of a forgotten temple. The air was thick with the scent of aged parchment, which spoke of countless generations seeking wisdom within these walls.

Lyra, her eyes aglow with the ethereal dance of candlelight, turned towards Qellaun, her voice a dulcet sonnet amid the profound silence of this literary labyrinth. Her words, like whispers of ancient spirits, hung in the air, adding to the mystique of their surroundings. "Qellaun," she whispered, her voice as soft as the breath of a gentle breeze in the Purplefire Woods, "we must tread with the grace of moonlight, for the Eladrin have been the silent guardians of E'vahona's mysteries, and the path to its enlightenment may be as veiled as the city itself."

Qellaun, his resolve carved in unyielding stone, nodded in concordance with his sister. The library's ambiance was a benediction, a testament to the solemnity of their mission. E'vahona was more than mere bricks and stone; it was an enigma, a puzzle that beckoned them to decipher its cryptic riddles.

As they continued to immerse themselves in the age-old texts and arcane scrolls, their journey for E'vahona metamorphosed into a sacred odyssey, a pilgrimage through the annals of history in search of elusive verities. Each page turned was a step deeper into the shadows of time, each inscription a whispered secret from the past. Together, within the sanctuary of knowledge, they strove to unveil the esoteric enigmas that veiled the city's existence and its enigmatic legacy. The library itself seemed to come alive, its essence resonating with their purpose, as if the spirits of long-gone scholars were guiding their quest through the annals of Vacari's history.

Amidst the towering monoliths of ancient wisdom, where the tomes held the echoes of tales long eclipsed by the sands of time, Qellaun's voice reverberated like a haunting aria. His eyes, alight with the incandescence of cherished memories, found solace in the depths of his sister's gaze as he discussed the past with her.

"I remember," he began, his voice a serenade of nostalgia, "the human mage Eldric, whose wisdom was coveted by the Druchii with the zeal of infernos. Eldric was a flame in the darkness, a beacon of knowledge in a world shrouded in shadow. The Druchii, their grasp relentless, trapped him, yet his spirit remained unbroken, a tempest refusing to be tamed. He harbored the coveted secrets of E'vahona, secrets he guarded with an indomitable spirit."

With an unwavering intent that cut through the very fabric of reality, Lyra stood as a sentinel, her senses attuned to the narrative woven by her brother. The library, a cathedral of forgotten wisdom, seemed to bow in silent reverence, its ancient walls privy to the unfolding drama. Shadows danced like spectral performers on the walls, adding an eerie, otherworldly ambiance to their shared recollection.

"In the deepest recesses of his heart," Qellaun continued, his voice an elegy sung by a somber bard, "Eldric cradled a love that transcended the confines of existence itself. His heart was irrevocably bound to Serena, the valiant Eladrin archer whose loyalty knew no surrender. Her spirit was like a guardian of the Purplefire Woods, unwavering and fierce. Even in the face of torment, she shielded the sanctum of her people, refusing to unveil its coveted secrets. The Druchii, their treacherous tongues dripping with promises and threats, implored her to reveal E'vahona's elusive whereabouts. Yet, even though the price of her silence meant the sacrifice of her beloved and possibly her own life, she remained steadfast."

As they recounted this tale, the air in the library seemed to thicken with the weight of history, and the presence of Eldric and Serena, though long gone, lingered like wraiths among the tomes. The Goldmoor Library, a sacred repository of knowledge, continued to witness the enduring saga of E'vahona and those who had sacrificed everything to protect its mysteries.

Like the capricious whims of fate, the flickering candlelight danced upon the contours of their faces, casting intricate and shifting shadows that mirrored the labyrinthine complexities of their tale. The library, an elegy etched in ancient tomes and whispered tragedies, held its very breath as the narrative unfurled. It was as if the walls had ears, and the tomes were eager participants in this enchanting recollection.

With its silent scrolls and solemn echoes, the library had become the witness to a saga of love and defiance, a tapestry woven from threads of destiny and the enduring spirit of those who dared to defy the darkness. The shelves seemed to bow in reverence, and the air hummed with anticipation as if the past itself were listening.

As if draped in the very tapestries of history itself, the weight of ancient ages settled upon Qellaun and Lyra, their voices reverberating through the dimly lit chamber of wisdom. In each uttered phrase, they unearthed shards of a narrative buried deep within the unforgiving sands of time—a narrative that held the elusive key to E'vahona's enigmatic mysteries and the intricate shadows that clung to Phoenix's destiny. The Goldmoor library had transformed into a living chronicle of Vacari's past, where the past and the present intertwined in a storytelling dance that transcended time.

Like the ethereal fingers of destiny, the flickering candlelight caressed the contours of their faces, weaving intricate shadows that mirrored the convoluted twists of their tale. The library, a solemn repository of knowledge and sorrow, seemed to draw an anticipatory breath as the narrative unfurled. The very essence of the library, with its ancient tomes and whispered sorrows, hung in the air, waiting to absorb every word of this poignant saga.

An evil specter loomed in the shadowed corners of memory—a sinister silhouette of oppressive authority, the visage of Phoenix's father. Qellaun's voice bore the weight of sorrow and injustice as he recounted the cruel edict that had sprung from the lips of the Druchii sovereign. "In the tempest of his wrath," he intoned, each word a solemn dirge, "Phoenix's father commanded the dark Druchii priestess to extinguish their lives, a grim order meant to silence the voices that guarded E'vahona's secrets. The very air seemed to shudder at the retelling of this dark decree. Yet, like a specter weaving through the ancient forest, Serena eluded her captors, slipping away through the embrace of the ancient trees, vanishing into the sanctuary of the woods."

Once more, like an impenetrable shroud, the burdens of the past descended upon Qellaun and Lyra. Their voices resonated with echoes of love, sacrifice, and the relentless pursuit of power within the somber confines of the chamber of wisdom. With each uttered word, they chiseled away at the stone of history, revealing the hidden facets of a tale bound by threads that transcended time.

In the heart of the sprawling library, beneath the watchful gaze of towering shelves, Qellaun and Lyra exchanged a knowing glance, a silent exchange of shared thoughts and unspoken truths. The weight of their personal and ancestral history lingered like the fragile scent of ancient parchment.

Lyra, her red eyes imbued with the wisdom of their dark Druchii lineage, confessed a shadow of uncertainty. "I don't recall that," she admitted, her voice a gentle breeze stirring the dormant pages of memory.

Qellaun's laughter, akin to a fleeting ripple of obsidian on the tranquil surface of their conversation, shattered the stillness that hung like an ethereal veil within the sacred sanctum of the library. "You were but a fledgling then," he mused, his tone dripping with a fondness that transcended the bounds of time. "No wonder those memories have eluded your grasp." The library seemed to join in their shared moment of fun, its silence broken by the delight of siblings bound by the weight of history and the enduring strength of their connection.

In that fleeting moment, they morphed from mere siblings into custodians of a shared past, stewards of secrets woven intricately into the very tapestry of their lineage. Qellaun's words hinted at the inevitable passage of years, the relentless sculptor of their intertwined destinies.

Lyra acknowledged the integrity of her brother's assessment with a solemn nod. Yet, despite the gaps in her memory, her resolve stood unyielding. "Perhaps," she ventured, "deep within the labyrinthine recesses of Fel Thalor's library, there exists a scroll, forgotten by time, that might breathe life into the shadows that obscure our history."

As the siblings traversed the labyrinthine corridors of knowledge, the air hung heavy with the intoxicating aroma of age-old tomes, and the faint echoes of history whispered their secrets. The library, a veritable tomb of wisdom, enfolded their quest within its venerable embrace. Each step they took was a reverent journey through the annals of time, guided by the flickering candlelight and the timeless knowledge contained within these hallowed walls.

However, even as they plunged deeper into the annals of time, Lyra voiced her lingering doubts. "Discovering the tale of Eldric and Serena may not lay bare the secrets of E'vahona," she conceded, "but perhaps, within the very parchment of these pages, we shall unearth threads that will illuminate our path through the labyrinth of our elusive quest."

Qellaun, ever the pragmatist, nodded in solemn agreement. "Our dark yearnings," he intoned with a subtle undercurrent of trepidation, "mirror Phoenix's insatiable lust for power. We must grasp at anything that might sate his unquenchable thirst." The weight of their mission pressed upon them, and the library seemed to echo their determination with every turn of its age-worn pages.

Within the shadowed recesses of the library's aisles, the weight of their mission bore down upon them, akin to the importance of an ancient tome filled with the enigmas of E'vahona and the mysterious power that remained tantalizingly just beyond their grasp. The winds of destiny whispered their secrets in the hidden corners of their thoughts and driven by an indomitable determination, they continued their relentless search, knowing that the answers they sought lay concealed amidst the boundless volumes of arcane lore. Each page they turned was like a step deeper into the heart of a mystery that had eluded them for centuries.

In the dim, subterranean depths of Goldmoor's dungeon, an ominous hush draped the atmosphere like a somber shroud. The labyrinthine passages bore witness to the weight of ages, their cold, stone walls echoing the kingdom's clandestine enigmas and the hushed chronicles of torment endured. It was a place where secrets festered, and the very stones seemed to carry the weight of the city's darkest histories.

Phoenix, the enigmatic harbinger of Goldmoor's ominous destiny, descended the winding stone stairwell with deliberate, unhurried steps. His cloak, the hue of abyssal depths, billowed ominously around him, a living embodiment of his malice. The flickering torches that lined the dank walls cast elongated shadows, and the feeble glimmers of light danced like ethereal wraiths upon the periphery of his vision, painting a macabre, foreboding scene.

Arriving at the dungeon's very core, Phoenix's eyes, as crimson as the embers of a cursed fire, locked onto the figure of King Alex. Even in chains, the monarch's regal bearing remained unvanquished. His eyes, glacial and steeped in defiance, met Phoenix's gaze with a smirk that bespoke unwavering resolve. It was a clash of wills, a battle of unyielding determination between two opposing forces.

"You shall discover naught in this abyss," King Alex proclaimed, his voice unwavering, his words a fortress against Phoenix's relentless quest for knowledge. "Even if I held the very secrets you covet, I would sooner witness you wither in the stygian depths than grant you the satisfaction you crave."

A malicious grin curled upon Phoenix's lips, his countenance an embodiment of the darkness that consumed him. Power crackled around him, akin to a storm amassing its fury. He spoke not with mere words but with the arcane might coursing through his veins. The air seemed hostile as the confrontation between these two forces reached its crescendo.

With a raised hand, Phoenix summoned the depths of his newfound sorcery, dark tendrils of evil energy spiraling around him like maleficent serpents. The dungeon quivered as his wrath took shape, and King Alex's defiant smirk wavered. The ancient stones themselves seemed to hold their breath, aware of the impending clash of powers that would shape the destiny of Vacari itself.

Agony surged through King Alex's form, his indomitable spirit momentarily quelled by the infernal torment wrought upon him. He gasped, his kingly determination unraveling before the ruthless onslaught of Phoenix's dark sorcery. It was a harrowing sight, the once-proud monarch brought low by the venom of his captor, a reminder of the unforgiving cruelty that dwelled within Phoenix's heart.

Yet, as swiftly as the storm of torment had arisen, Phoenix withdrew his unholy powers, leaving King Alex trembling and fractured. With one final, chilling glance, he turned and retreated from the dungeon, his malevolent presence dissipating like the fading remnants of a haunting nightmare. The air seemed to heave a sigh of relief at his departure, but the scars of his visit lingered, etched into the very stones of Goldmoor's darkest depths.

In the aftermath of his departure, the dungeon was submerged in spectral silence, with King Alex's labored breaths and the mournful clinking of chains reverberating through the frigid stone corridors. The dungeon's clandestine secrets remained veiled, and the spirit of its captive king endured, unbroken, even as Phoenix's malevolent intent seeped into the very bedrock of Goldmoor.

As the last vestiges of Phoenix's malevolence retreated from the dungeon's depths, King Alex remained ensnared but undefeated. His labored exhalations persisted, entwining with the haunting silence of the dungeon, a testament to the enduring fortitude of a sovereign unjustly imprisoned.

A glimmer of curiosity ignited within King Alex's eyes, an ember of intrigue that flickered despite the torment that trapped him. His gaze remained steadfast upon the retreating form of Phoenix, who appeared to command newfound powers that defied rational explanation. In a voice of disbelief and fascination, the king murmured, "New powers... How?"

The question hung in the air, a riddle cloaked in an enigma, hinting at secrets not yet unveiled. The mystery of Phoenix's ascension lingered within the dungeon's heart, where shadows concealed more than they revealed, biding their time until the day the answers would emerge from their obsidian depths. The dungeon seemed to hold its secrets close as if guarding the enigma of Phoenix's dark transformation until it was right to unravel.

Phoenix traversed the hallowed library corridors with a regal bearing that seemed to mold the shadows in his wake. Towering shelves laden with the ancient scrolls of forgotten lore stood like sentinel giants, their silence echoing the profound knowledge they harbored. Yet, as he ventured into the heart of this sanctuary of wisdom, a scene awaited him, a sight that fanned the ember of his fury into a roaring inferno.

Amidst a secluded nook, Qellaun and Lyra, his trusted Druchii confidants, stood in harmonious camaraderie, their laughter a rare and unexpected symphony. Dark eyes sparkled with shared amusement, their mirth contrasting with the typically oppressive atmosphere that clung to the library's air. It was like a momentary respite from the darkness that had crept into this sacred space.

Phoenix's scowl deepened, his ire simmering beneath the surface like molten magma as he beheld this paradoxical tableau. He strode toward them with relentless purpose, each footfall resonating with an ominous intensity.

"What sorcery is this?" he thundered, his voice a forceful storm that shattered the fragile laughter like brittle glass. "Did my command to seek knowledge of E'vahona escape your comprehension?"

Qellaun and Lyra recoiled as though caught in the sudden onslaught of a storm, the carefree joy that had danced between them mere moments ago dissolving into the bone-chilling reality of their dark master's ire. Phoenix's eyes, aglow with an unholy conflagration, pierced through them like twin daggers, and the air thickened with unbearable tension.

Before they could summon a response, Phoenix unleashed the formidable wellspring of power that coursed within him. Sinister tendrils of malevolent energy surged forth, ensnaring Qellaun and Lyra in their cruel embrace, their anguished cries a haunting dirge reverberating through the library. The room appeared to quiver in empathy with their torment, its silent walls compelled to witness the relentless retribution upon those who dared defy Phoenix.

With a final flourish of his newfound might, Phoenix released his hold on them, leaving them gasping for breath and trembling, their bodies aflame with searing pain. He pivoted on his heel and stormed away from the library, wrath still fuming as he left Qellaun and Lyra to tend to their physical and emotional wounds. Once a sanctuary of knowledge and a rare respite from darkness, the library was again plunged into the abyss of fear and despair.

As the menacing specter of Phoenix receded, Qellaun and Lyra exchanged a glance fraught with unspoken truths. The once-glimmering delight that had danced upon their lips was now a fading memory, eclipsed by the chilling reality of their servitude. Lyra conveyed her silent contrition through her eyes, an apologetic gaze that spoke volumes about her earlier innocence.

Before they could address the lingering pain, Qellaun turned to his sister with a deep concern etched into his features. "Are you alright?" he asked, his voice laced with worry and sympathy.

Although wounded in both flesh and spirit, Lyra summoned a wry smile that held the bitterness of revelation. "You were right," she murmured to her brother, her voice tinged with the sour taste of acceptance. "He is far worse."

The cost of defiance and the abyssal depths of Phoenix's hostility had been laid bare in the library, where the pursuit of knowledge and the erratic dance of shadows intertwined. Their shared ordeal illuminated their servitude's harsh realities, leaving them to grapple with the profound darkness that permeated their world.

As the first delicate rays of dawn filtered through the verdant canopy of the time-worn forest, Ong and Keisha found themselves in the tranquil interlude preceding the resumption of their journey. The forest stirred, awakening to a chorus of melodic bird songs, and the air seemed to hold its breath, pregnant with the promise of a new day. Yet, beneath this veneer of hope, an impending and profound conversation weighed upon them like a dormant tempest.

Ong turned to Keisha, his eyes brimming with concern and profound curiosity. "Keisha," he began, his voice a gentle murmur intermingled with the forest's awakening, "regarding what you shared earlier, about feeling as though no one truly cared for you... I cannot help but ponder."

Keisha met his gaze with a gaze of her own, her eyes baring the weight of untold years of concealed sorrow. "It is an undeniable truth," she admitted, her voice a soft confession. "After losing my parents, I traversed a path of solitude. The Eladrin, in their kindness, took me in as was expected, yet without my parents, I never truly felt like I belonged."

The forest that enveloped them appeared to eavesdrop, its ancient arboreal sentinels standing as silent witnesses to Keisha's heartfelt revelation. The profound solitude she had grappled with, her relentless struggle to carve out her niche in a world that often appeared indifferent to her existence, seemed to hang heavy in the air. But in the presence of Ong, who had become her steadfast companion and confidant, she had unearthed a connection that defied the loneliness that had defined her past.

With the forest as their audience and the dawn as their backdrop, Ong and Keisha found themselves poised on the precipice of a deeper understanding, ready to embark on a journey of shared introspection and companionship that would transcend the confines of the wilderness.

Ong tenderly clasped her hand in his, an unspoken assurance of their shared journey ahead. The bonds of friendship and empathy they had woven through trials and tribulations had evolved into a wellspring of strength. Together, they would navigate the enigmatic challenges that lay ahead, each drawing solace from the unwavering presence of the other. In the forest's heart, their silent accord deepened, much like the age-old roots of the towering trees that enveloped them.

In the tranquil moments of dawn, as the forest stirred in hushed reverence, Keisha turned her gaze toward Ong, her eyes harboring a question wrapped in the gossamer threads of curiosity and vulnerability. "Ong," she whispered, her voice as soft as the caress of a morning breeze, "have you ever known the depths of love?"

Ong met her gaze, his eyes, as deep and cerulean as the boundless ocean, tinged with a contemplative air. But before he could reply, Keisha pressed on, her words carrying the weight of ages and the wisdom of her elven heritage. "You see," she began, her tone laden with solemnity, "love, for elves, is not a fleeting sentiment. It is a sacred and profound bond that transcends the temporal realm. Even when losing a beloved, we do not seek another. It is a connection that spans the boundaries of time and space."

Ong considered her words for a moment, his encounters with love, or what he had mistaken for love, flickering like distant stars in his memory. He shook his head slowly, a rueful smile gracing his lips. "I have walked a path of fleeting passions," he conceded, "but love, in its truest sense, has eluded me."

With a tender and knowing smile, he scooped Keisha into his arms, a gesture imbued with effortless strength and graceful elegance. As he placed her upon Thunder's saddle, he leaned closer to her, his voice a breathy whisper, scarcely audible above the rustling foliage. "However," he confessed, his cobalt gaze locking onto hers like twin stars in the predawn sky, "that may be changing now."

In the soft, halcyon interlude, Ong couldn't resist the inexorable pull that drew him toward Keisha. He gently cupped her face with a touch as tender and lingering as a lover's caress, and their lips met in a gentle, sweet kiss. It was a kiss that spoke of unspoken vows and an indomitable connection that seemed to defy the trials and tribulations of their journey.

The forest, its ancient arboreal sentinels standing sentinel in silent witness, appeared to hold its breath as if nature itself recognized the profound significance of this burgeoning bond. In the tender embrace of their kiss, Ong and Keisha's hearts murmured in silent harmony, and their path forward, though veiled in uncertainty, seemed to shimmer with the radiant light of their shared emotions.

Ong and Keisha, their budding connection still tingling in the air, grasped the gravity of their predicament with unwavering clarity. The verdant, age-old canopy of emerald-hued trees surrounding them seemed to exhale ancient secrets of danger and adventure as they mounted Thunder, their loyal and steadfast steed. Ong's sturdy, protective arms enveloped Keisha, wrapping her in a sanctuary of safety and cherished belonging amidst the inevitable uncertainty. "Stay close," Ong whispered to Keisha, his voice a lulling refrain amidst the serene, arboreal symphony. "We must move with alacrity to outpace the pursuing Druchii."

Ong urged Thunder onward, charting their course along the path that led to the fabled Crystal Vale. With its towering arboreal sentinels and enigmatic shadows, the forest seemed to enfold them within its mystic embrace as if it, too, had assumed the mantle of their guardian.

Their journey through the forest bore witness to their indomitable strength and unyielding resolve. Every step taken, every rustle of leaves, and every avian serenade served as a reminder of the untamed splendor and concealed dangers of this enchanted realm. With the ominous specter of the Druchii trailing close behind, their quest assumed an urgency that propelled them deeper into the very heart of the forest.

As the day unfurled around them, Ong and Keisha rode in unison, their hearts harmonizing with the cadence of Thunder's steadfast hoofbeats. The forest seemed to murmur its age-old secrets while the gentle zephyrs bore their aspirations and anxieties, carrying them toward the distant Crystal Vale.

Amid the viridescent wilderness, their love story is interwoven with the fabric of their adventurous odyssey, a narrative of two souls who found solace and fortitude within the sanctuary of each other's presence. They journeyed onward, their destination shrouded in enigma, but their spirits unwavering, their love an unwavering beacon that guided them through the unfathomable riddles of the boundless Emeraldwood Forest.

Chapter 14

Unyielding Pursuit and Enduring Love

In the tranquil heart of the Emeraldwood, a sacred grove untouched by the relentless march of time, Ong and Keisha had ventured for hours beneath the glorious canopy of ancient arboreal giants. Verdant leaves wove a lush tapestry overhead like stained glass, casting a celestial mosaic of ethereal light upon the forest floor. It was a realm of emerald hues and whispered enigmas, a sanctuary amidst the crucible of their arduous odyssey.

As their sojourn through this enchanting wilderness wore on, Ong's vigilant gaze scoured their surroundings, a sentinel for peril and sanctuary. He sensed the inexorable tendrils of weariness weaving through his sinews, the burden of their quest weighing upon him like the armor of destiny. His loyal steed, Thunder, perceived his master's silent plea and bore him with unwavering elegance.

Then, as if summoned by fate itself, a crystal-clear stream materialized from the depths of the forest, its gentle murmur a mellifluous sonata in the tranquil woods. Ong recognized the moment of divine respite, the need to rest his tired form and honor his steadfast companion.

Guiding Thunder to the stream's edge, Ong descended from his saddle with the grace of a seasoned nomad. His outstretched hand, firm yet gentle, assisted Keisha as she descended from the noble steed. Grateful for the reprieve, Keisha settled by the stream's edge, her gaze trapped by the iridescent waterway as it wove through the woods like a liquid serenade of existence.

While Thunder sated his thirst with the elixir of calm, revitalizing waters, Ong's unwavering focus centered solely on Keisha. The memory of their earlier discourse lingered, an ephemeral mist lingering in the verdant air, the vulnerability in Keisha's eyes etched into his soul. He recalled the instant she had queried him about love, her voice quivering like a delicate leaf in a gentle breeze.

As he observed her, Ong couldn't help but reflect upon her life before they blended their paths. She had bared her heart, divulging a solitary journey akin to a lone star amidst the vast celestial tapestry. Ong's eyes traced the details of her face, a canvas adorned with the brushstrokes of a life known only to her.

In the heart of the Emeraldwood, encircled by the ancient sentinels of the woodland, Ong and Keisha found themselves ensconced in a fleeting moment of solace—a pause in the grand tapestry of their epic quest. The forest, a repository of enigmatic whispers, wove its secrets through the air. The stream's melodious cadence persisted, and their connection deepened, entwining their destinies like the gnarled branches of the ancient arboreal giants overhead.

Within this tranquil oasis nestled amidst the heart of the Emeraldwood, Ong narrowed the distance separating him from Keisha. With a tender touch, he gently redirected her gaze toward him, and it appeared as though the very world surrounding them held its collective breath as if in eager anticipation of the revelation soon to unfurl.

His eyes, profound pools brimming with insight and compassion, locked onto Keisha's, and in that singular moment, the intricate tapestry of their shared odyssey unfurled before them, a masterpiece of emotion and purpose. He commenced, his voice a mellifluous refrain harmonizing with the symphony of nature that enveloped them. "Keisha," he began, "what occurred to your mother? I yearn to comprehend, to assemble the fragments of the indomitable and resolute woman standing before me."

As fleeting as a spectral whisper, Keisha's gaze grazed the verdant carpet of grass beneath them, her thoughts akin to an explosive maelstrom held in check. The burden of her past descended upon her like an ancient, gnarled tree, its roots penetrating the very depths of her soul. When her voice finally emerged from the depths of her being, it carried the weight of myriad years gone by. "Serena, my mother," she began, "was cruelly wrested from my grasp by a marauding band of remorseless Druchii."

As Ong's protective arms enveloped her, providing solace and unwavering support, he murmured his heartfelt condolences, his spirit weighed down by the profound sorrow on her countenance. "I am deeply sorry, Keisha," he whispered, his words a tender caress against the canvas of her ear.

In that solemn moment, he couldn't help but ponder the tender age at which she had been forcibly severed from her mother's embrace. With the utmost gentleness, he inquired, "Keisha, how many years had you seen pass when the cruel hand of fate snatched her away from you?"

Keisha, her turbulent emotions hidden beneath a veneer of composure, bowed her head again, her gaze an unwavering fixation upon the lush tapestry of verdant grass as if seeking solace in its intricate patterns. Her voice, a fragile melody, cascaded forth like leaves carried away by a gentle breeze. "I was but a tender bud in the garden of life. Just two fleeting moons after my father met his grim fate," she confided. "My mother harbored a ravenous thirst for vengeance, Ong. She yearned to avenge my father's cruel demise, and so she departed, bearing with her a promise of return." She shifted her gaze towards Ong, permitting the tears, like raindrops upon a fragile petal, to fall unhindered. "There's a secret known only to me and now, to you," she continued, her voice shaky. "As she was leaving, I implored her not to go, but despite my pleas, she departed. I carried the weight of guilt, thinking it was my fault."

Ong's heart resonated with empathy for the girl left empty, the anguish of abandonment etched deeply into the very core of her being. Without uttering a word, he drew her close, enfolding her within the sanctuary of his embrace. In that sylvan haven, where the ancient arboreal witnesses stood sentinel, Ong cradled Keisha, binding their destinies with an unspoken vow that she would never retread the path of solitude.

As Ong's arms enfolded her and his whispered vow of steadfast support hung like an indelible oath, Keisha felt emotions welling within her. Yet, amidst the cocoon of his embrace, a glimmer of fragility still lingered in her eyes. She turned her gaze toward him, a questing intensity in her eyes, and with a trembling quiver in her voice, she uttered softly, "Ong, I implore you not to make pledges that might wane with the shifting winds of the future. The tides of destiny are erratic, and you may uncover a life beyond this tumult devoid of my presence."

Ong, his heart aching in resonance with her pain, held her even closer as though to shield her from the fickle uncertainties of the world. His voice, a gentle cadence laced with a poignant touch of sorrow yet brimming with unwavering resolve, commenced, "Keisha," he began, "I shan't feign knowledge of the enigma that tomorrow may unveil. Nevertheless, I want you to apprehend that in this very moment, within this sylvan realm, and in every moment to come, I stand beside you. It is not a duty that binds me but an ardor born of choice. My promise articulates my dedication to you, to the tapestry of 'us' that we weave together."

He tenderly pressed his lips against her forehead and a kiss imbued with silent reassurances that transcended the confines of spoken language. "Let our journey unfurl in its enigmatic way, Keisha, and may we confront each nascent day in unison, our support and care intertwined. Irrespective of the meandering course of the path, I yearn for you to be an integral part of it."

Keisha's voice quivered with uncertainty as she voiced the haunting question that had besieged her thoughts. "Ong, do you truly desire my presence in your existence? What if fate guides you to another soul?"

Ong's reply emanated with unswerving conviction, a testament to his deep sentiments as he held her in an embrace of unwavering devotion. "Keisha," he commenced, his voice a bastion of steadiness and sincerity, "what we share, the sentiments I harbor for you, are not easily supplanted. My life's journey has traversed countless paths, yet I have never encountered a spirit like yours. You are a paragon of strength, independence, and a heart that radiates even in the darkest hours."

A brief pause followed, their gazes locked in an unbreakable communion, his words carrying the weight of his zeal. "I crave your presence in my life, Keisha, not solely for this fleeting moment but for whatever the future bestows. Love is a voyage fraught with unpredictable twists and turns, and I cannot predict what lies ahead. But within the bounds of the present, you are the one I keenly wish to walk alongside at this very instant."

Ong's voice bore the resonance of profound sincerity. His heart laid bare before her. "I have never encountered someone who understands me as you do, someone who makes me feel complete. If you are persuaded to tread this path with me, Keisha, I will choose you consistently."

Keisha's eyes shimmered with teardrops as she gazed upon Ong, her voice a tender murmur steeped in emotion. "I had never imagined intending a future entwined with another, Ong. But since our paths converged, everything has undergone a profound transformation. I cannot envision my life devoid of your presence despite the brevity of our shared journey thus far."

Ong's smile, radiant with profound warmth and deep affection, drew Keisha close, their lips converging in a gentle kiss. At that moment, the world dissolved into insignificance, leaving behind only the two souls intertwined within the cocoon of their newfound connection. Their love had burgeoned amid the crucible of trials and tribulations, a love that had now solidified into an indomitable bond, weaving their destinies into the intricate tapestry of fate.

As Ong and Keisha found solace in their intimate moment amidst the sylvan beauty, the forest's tranquility shattered like fragile glass under the ominous footfalls of Druchii warriors. Ong's voice barely rose above a murmur as he addressed her, "These warriors certainly possess a knack for spoiling the mood."

Despite the imminent peril, a soft giggle escaped Keisha's lips. Swiftly, Ong scooped her up and settled her atop Thunder, mounting the faithful steed himself. With an unwavering resolve gleaming in his eyes, he redirected Thunder and steered them deeper into the forest, their destination now set for the sanctuary of Crystal Vale. The relentless pursuit of the Druchii warriors served as a crucible, forging an unbreakable bond between them as they confronted the trials of their shared odyssey.

Kelru Palvoh, a figure of dread and authority among the Druchii, seethed with mounting frustration as his relentless pursuit of Keisha proved futile. His stern visage, marred by the darkened pallor of anger, betrayed the torment brewing within. He barked imperious orders to his Druchii acolytes, their cloaked forms melting into the forest's shadows as they fanned out to scour the stream where Keisha's ephemeral presence had recently graced.

His muttered utterances, a cascade of venomous words slithered through the air, revealed the burgeoning ire festering within him. "I will not return to Lord Phoenix empty-handed," he grumbled, his voice trembling with trepidation at the prospect of enduring their master's relentless wrath. The specter of failure, the chance of returning without at least Keisha in his clutches, was a fate he could scarcely bear to contemplate.

The Druchii warriors, their eyes aflame with determination, combed the area around the stream like vipers seeking elusive prey. An eerie silence marked their efforts, the forest holding its breath in anticipation. Kelru Palvoh, a brooding figure amidst the somber woods, watched their every move with a hawk-like vigilance. The gnawing sense of urgency intensified a relentless drumbeat in his veins. He couldn't afford to let Keisha slip through his fingers, not when she was so tantalizingly close to crossing into the safety of Crystal Vale. His only hope was to apprehend her before she reached Swifthammer's sanctuary, for he knew that time was running out and the stakes had never been higher.

As Qellaun and Lyra ventured toward Phoenix, the weight of newfound knowledge pressed upon them like an impenetrable tome. Qellaun's thoughts echoed Eldric's last words, and he couldn't help but wonder about the significance of the name he had spoken.

Lyra's curiosity couldn't be contained any longer. "Do you recall the name he mentioned, brother?"

Qellaun paused, his mind a labyrinth of memories. A faint, wistful smile danced upon the precipice of his lips. "Indeed," he responded, his voice imbued with a subtle tenderness. "The name 'Keisha' did grace his lips," his words akin to the distant echo of a heartfelt melody. "In his final moments, as he surrendered his breath to the cosmos, he also confessed an undying love for his wife."

Ever the cynic, Lyra smirked with an air of skepticism that draped her words like a shroud. "And yet, Serena met her inexorable end, a poignant testament to Keisha's orphaned state."

Qellaun nodded his acquiescence, a graceful acknowledgment of the factual verity within her utterance. "You speak the truth," he conceded, his tone tinged with the weight of that somber reality. "However, we mustn't discount the possibility that the benevolent Eladrin, in their celestial benevolence, might have enfolded her into their nurturing embrace, rearing her as one of their own."

With newfound purpose and a torrent of unanswered questions, they hastened towards Phoenix's presence in the palace, eager to seek clarification and perhaps uncover the enigmatic truth behind Eldric's final words.

Within the glorious bosom of the palace, Phoenix's demeanor mirrored the tempestuous heavens that occasionally blanketed their shadowy realm. Frustration, akin to the gathering tempest clouds, brooded within him, for the strands of knowledge he had cast into the boundless abyss of inquiry had yielded meager gleanings. His thirst for enlightenment concerning the enigmatic Eladrin, the arcane enigmas of E'vahona, and the mysterious figure accompanying Swifthammer remained an insatiable yearning, as vibrant as a lightning strike in the darkest of nights.

As Qellaun and Lyra traversed the threshold, Phoenix's ire manifested with the intensity of a lightning bolt. His resonant voice, akin to the lashings of a storm, assailed them, commanding the presentation of tidings of profound import and beseeching the elixir of knowledge to quench his insatiable thirst. And present it, they did.

Qellaun's voice, reminiscent of a tranquil lull after the storm's fury, unfurled, weaving the threads of their discoveries into an intricate verbal tapestry. He unveiled the name that had fluttered from Eldric's lips in his final moments - Keisha - and the profound avowal of love for his wife.

A storm of contemplations churned within Phoenix's mind, akin to tempestuous currents vying for dominance. He spoke, his voice still emitting tension, seeking illumination amidst shadows. Could they dare entertain that the Eladrin accompanying Swifthammer might indeed be this Keisha?

Qellaun responded to Phoenix's query with a measured tone, "I cannot assert with absolute certainty that this Keisha is identical to the Eladrin who journeyed with Swifthammer. However, her father bore red hair, a rarity among elves, and Keisha also possessed crimson locks. The possibility that they are the same is undeniably plausible."

A glimmer of comprehension ignited within the enigmatic abyss of Phoenix's contemplations, akin to a distant star twinkling in the vast night sky. The puzzle pieces were aligning, and he could discern the nascent path forward, a trail of shadows that hinted at revelations yet concealed.

A crooked smile, as cryptic as an obscured passage deep within the labyrinthine recesses of the darkest dungeons, etched itself upon Phoenix's lips. The revelation of Keisha's lineage, an amalgamation of humanity and Eladrin, had kindled a curiosity within his shadowed heart. Why had she, the progeny of an improbable union, ventured into the company of Swifthammer? The puzzle remained incomplete, but an intriguing fragment had found its place.

He assented with a begrudging nod, bestowing upon them a reluctant approbation as he acknowledged the fruits of their tenacity. "You have, by sheer determination, unearthed but a morsel of knowledge from the abyss," he observed, a subtle undercurrent of satisfaction interlacing his words. "Return to your endeavors. Plunge deeper, for we are tasked with revealing the tapestry that enshrouds Keisha's enigmatic narrative. This marks the inception of our odyssey into the obscurities of the past."

With this pronouncement, he dismissed them, his gaze already tracing arcane pathways to other shadowy realms of inquiry as they withdrew, retreating into the labyrinthine corridors of the library. Their resolve was unwavering, determined to chase the wisps of knowledge wherever they might lead.

Within the dimly lit chamber of his palace, Phoenix presided, encircled by an array of eerie, otherworldly artifacts culled from the farthest reaches of realms unknown. His frustration, akin to a simmering storm cloud, had amassed a tempest of impatience and wrath within him. He had implored answers from his subordinates and spies alike, yet the elusive nature of the Eladrin and the veiled enigmas of E'vahona continued to elude his grasp. With a scowl, he extended his hand toward a communication device. This magical artifact enabled him to contact his trusted commander, Kelru Palvoh, who remained entrenched in the field, a steadfast sentinel in their ceaseless pursuit of knowledge and power.

Phoenix: (activates the communication device) Kelru, report immediately.

Kelru: (responding through the device) Lord Phoenix, we have embarked upon an exhaustive expedition, scouring the expanse for any vestige of the Eladrin who accompanies... (pauses, the words hanging in the air like a lingering mist) Swifthammer.

Phoenix: (impatiently) What tidings have you brought me thus far?

Kelru: (nervously) Alas, my lord, the shroud of ambiguity enshrouds the Eladrin's identity. Our efforts persist, yet the definitive answer eludes our grasp.

Phoenix: (harshly) Be mindful, Kelru, that my tolerance wanes. The Eladrin bears the name Keisha. You shall retrieve her, whatever the cost may be.

Kelru: (resigned) As you command, my lord.

Phoenix: (severs the connection)

Kelru: (turns to his assembled troops) You've all witnessed our lord's decree. We shall not return empty-handed. The pursuit of Keisha shall continue, ceaseless and unrelenting, until she is within our grasp.

In the dimly lit expanse of his throne room, Phoenix, an embodiment of dark authority, brooded over his next strategic move. The relentless passage of time had woven a web of impatience around him, the shortage of information regarding Keisha and the enigmatic E'vahona gnawing at him like an insistent itch, and five long days had elapsed since his last visit to his other captive, Queen Jeanne, entangled within the foreboding confines of the Serpent Lagoon tower.

With a sinister, feral grin, he relinquished his grip on the obsidian throne, his footfalls resonating ominously as he embarked upon the ascent of the tower's spiraling staircase. Upon reaching its apex, the beleaguered gaze of Queen Jeanne met his, and she instinctively recoiled, her regal bearing fractured in the face of his palpable malevolence.

Phoenix emitted an evil chuckle, savoring the essence of her fear. "Ah, Queen Jeanne," he intoned, a mocking sneer curling upon his lips, his crimson eyes ablaze with sadistic glee.

The queen's voice trembled as she implored, "Please, Lord Phoenix, I beseech you once more. I remain ignorant of the knowledge you seek."

The amusement in Phoenix's countenance dissipated, replaced by an iciness that emanated an unyielding resolve. He strode across the chamber, a solitary figure in silence. Finally, he redirected his attention to her, his presence a suffocating weight in the room. "Your tenacity is commendable," he observed, his voice dripping with ominous menace. "Yet, be assured, Queen Jeanne, I possess means to extract truths from even the most obdurate captives."

As the queen's dread enshrouded her, he stood as a looming specter, his presence inescapable. The room seemed to contract, and the atmosphere grew leaden with her reticence.

As he drew nearer to Queen Jeanne, Phoenix luxuriated in the trepidation that danced within her eyes. Her quivering form bore witness to the mastery he held over her. He relished the tension, savoring her fear, before initiating his questioning line.

"Queen Jeanne," he hissed, a malevolent murmur that sent shivers coursing down her spine, "what secrets do you harbor regarding the Eladrin and their realm, E'vahona? And what of the red-haired Eladrin, an archer known as Keisha? Speak now, or your torment shall be unending."

Queen Jeanne's voice quivered like a fragile reed in the storm as she protested, "I do not know what you seek. I pledge it on my life."

Phoenix, an evil puppeteer of pain, lingered momentarily, contemplating her response like a conductor poised before a symphony of suffering. He savored the intoxicating bouquet of her fear, recognizing that breaking her would necessitate more than mere threats. With a maleficent smile that mirrored the waning moon's sinister crescent, he invoked a perverse strain of sorcery, unleashing a torrent of searing agony that coursed through her very being. The tower's forsaken chambers bore witness to Queen Jeanne's anguished cries, a mournful aria of torment that clawed at the soul.

As the relentless waves of torment subsided, Phoenix withdrew his sinister magic, leaving Queen Jeanne gasping for the breath of respite, her visage marred by the rivulets of tears that traced her anguished countenance. "I grow weary of this dance," he declared with a cruel smile akin to an evil jester in his dark carnival. "Though you may be devoid of the knowledge I seek, I shall bestow upon you some company."

With a flick of his hand, he conjured spectral denizens, eerie apparitions that stalked the shrouded recesses of the tower's labyrinthine shadows, their eldritch presence exacerbating the queen's paralyzing terror. Without another word, Phoenix departed the tower, leaving behind the haunting symphony of her pleas, an ominous refrain that reverberated in his wake like a spectral song.

Beneath the argent caress of the moon's silvery light, Kelru Palvoh, an indomitable force, commandeered his unyielding cadre of Druchii warriors in their ceaseless chase of Ong and Keisha. Their footfalls, executed with a spectral grace, were as noiseless as the phantoms haunting the night's darkest corners. The atmosphere quivered with a palpable tension that hung like an oppressive shroud, a testament to their unwavering resolve.

One among Kelru's Druchii, a sinister presence shrouded in a veil of inky shadow, his voice dripping with malice, murmured, "Keisha, dear Eladrin, emerge from your concealment and embrace the inevitable."

Laced with nefarious intent, the chant hovered in the night air, settling like a curse upon the forest's hallowed ground. Within the inky recesses of the woods, Keisha and Ong, nestled amidst the verdant tapestry, exchanged a furtive glance infused with trepidation. Ong's visage hardened his resolve into an unyielding bulwark as he drew Keisha close, enfolding her within his protective haven. In hushed tones, he vowed, "I shall not permit their clutches to ensnare you."

Within the foreboding depths of the forest, beneath the unblinking gaze of the Druchii, Ong steered Thunder onto a concealed, less-trodden path. It meandered toward the heart of Crystal Vale, a sanctuary nestled in the embrace of the natural world, a respite from the relentless hunt orchestrated by their implacable pursuers.

Chapter 15

Reaching Crystal Vale

As Ong and Keisha ventured deeper into the fringes of Crystal Vale, the arboreal majesty of the ancient forest gracefully yielded telltale signs of civilization. Towering, dignified trees parted their verdant curtains to grant passage to quaint cottages nestled beneath their boughs, while a concealed brook, its waters crystalline and pure, breathed whispered secrets of this tranquil sanctuary. Sunlight filtered through the leaves above, dappling the path with a play of shadows and light, creating a serene, almost ethereal atmosphere.

Their sojourn, however, encountered an abrupt interlude—a discordant note in the symphony of their journey. An arrow, an embodiment of grace and lethality, cleaved the air with a haunting whistle, its final destination a gnarled sentinel of the woods, where it settled with a soft thud. The air grew taut with tension as Ong, guided by instinct, reached for the hilt of his sword, ready to confront any looming menace.

Yet, as the contours of Keisha's lips curled into the gentle arc of a knowing smile, an ineffable serenity overcame her. She shook her head with a delicate motion, forestalling Ong's reflex to impel Thunder into a thunderous gallop. "No rash action is warranted, Ong," she murmured, her gaze unwaveringly affixed upon the arrow embedded within the aged tree's sturdy trunk.

Ong's countenance melded confusion with a tinge of curiosity. "How do you discern this arrow's origin, Keisha?" he inquired, his voice a canvas painted with both wariness and curiosity.

Delivered with poise and unwavering certainty, her response resounded through the sylvan enclave. "This is not a harbinger of peril but rather a vessel of communication," she elucidated. "The mark upon this arrow is the emblem of Lord Karrenen, signifying his authorship. You, Ong, had sought an audience with him, and this is his cryptic confirmation of his willingness to engage."

The forest around them seemed to hold its breath, as if awaiting the next act in this enigmatic drama, a testament to the mystique that veiled Crystal Vale and its residents.

As Keisha's wise words took root within Ong's consciousness, his initial skepticism gradually ebbed away like the receding tide, leaving a burgeoning trust in her wisdom. With measured resolve, they guided Thunder toward the venerable arboreal sentinel that had been the arrow's final destination. Ong, acting with the precision of a skilled artisan, carefully extricated the arrowhead, unveiling a tightly bound scroll affixed to its sturdy shaft.

The moonlight filtering through the leaves cast a silver sheen upon the parchment as Ong unfurled it with deliberate gentleness. The message, an embodiment of elegant brevity, pronounced, "Yes, I will meet with him," followed by the specified rendezvous location and a directive to arrive within a week.

Upon absorbing the message's contents, Ong's countenance transformed, transcending the shroud of uncertainty to embrace unwavering determination. He tenderly secured the parchment within the sanctum of his vestments, his gaze converging with Keisha's in a silent communion of shared purpose. The path to the anticipated meeting with Lord Karrenen lay unobstructed before them, and they recognized the gravity of this summons, vowing to honor it with the reverence it merited.

Like a conscious witness, the forest enveloping them seemed to hold its breath as if poised on the precipice of destiny's revelation. With newfound determination coursing through their veins, they resumed their journey, each step a resolute testament to the inevitable fate that awaited them in the heart of Crystal Vale. The ancient trees stood sentinel, their whispers of encouragement echoing through the tranquil night.

Kelru Palvoh, the enigmatic Druchii commander, abruptly halted his retinue of sinister warriors with a commanding flourish of his hand, his crimson eyes, like blood moons, scrutinizing the perilous threshold that marked the boundary of Crystal Vale. The roots of Ong's existence lay within the heart of this seemingly benign human enclave. A vicious grin, akin to a serpent's sly ruse, danced at the corners of his lips as he whispered his nefarious stratagem to his loyal acolytes.

"We shall tarry here," he decreed, his voice dripping with the malefic wisdom of a seasoned predator. "Let them wade deeper into the sanctuary of Crystal Vale, where the deceiving shroud of safety will unfurl its treacherous web."

One among his impatient followers dared to challenge their leader's tactics, and his voice was tinged with impertinence. "Why not strike swiftly, Commander? Why linger in the shadows?"

Kelru's cruel smile, a harbinger of doom, stretched more comprehensively, and he pivoted to confront the impudent Druchii, his gaze ablaze with withering disdain. "Simpleton," he hissed, his words sharp as ice shards. "Crystal Vale masquerades as a human settlement but conceals alliances, warriors, and fortifications. To rush in recklessly is to beckon annihilation. We shall bide our time."

With a sweeping gesture, Kelru beckoned toward the concealing sanctuary of the Emeraldwoods, an emblem of their asylum within the shadowy abyss. "We shall wait," he proclaimed, his resolve unyielding. "Patience, my brethren, is our ally, and Crystal Vale, the birthplace of Warrior Swifthammer, shall unknowingly become the crucible of their demise."

The Druchii, though begrudging in their surrender, acknowledged their commander's grim wisdom. They enshrouded themselves amidst the twisted branches and murmuring leaves of the Emeraldwoods, their malevolent presence woven into the tapestry of the forest, an implacable tempest of darkness concealed within the tranquil periphery of Crystal Vale.

As Ong and Keisha ventured forth from the verdant embrace of the emerald woods, they found themselves immersed in the heart of Crystal Vale. This captivating human city sprawled gracefully by the tranquil shores of a sprawling lake. The city's beauty, an exquisite fusion of artifice and nature, unfolded before them like a masterpiece.

Majestic waterfalls cascaded like crystalline lace, descending from towering cliffs that enveloped the city. As the waters plummeted, they birthed fleeting rainbows that pirouetted through the air, their colors intermingling in a mesmerizing dance. Like ancient storytellers, these waterfalls whispered enchanting secrets to the land below, their melodious serenade an everlasting gift to the city's residents.

The architecture of Crystal Vale stood as a testament to human ingenuity and artistry. Graceful edifices adorned the streets, each one a unique masterpiece. Elaborate facades bore intricate carvings and vibrant mosaics, imbuing the cityscape with character and allure.

The thoroughfare of the city thrummed with vitality. Inhabitants, going about their daily routines, filled the air with laughter and conversation, harmonizing with the urban symphony. Along the cobbled pathways, street vendors beckoned with their stalls, a kaleidoscope of colors and fragrances that tantalized the senses.

Lanterns, exquisite in their wrought iron craftsmanship and adorned with stained glass, hung like luminous jewels suspended above the streets. Their soft radiance bathed the thoroughfares in a warm, inviting glow, offering guidance and solace to Ong and Keisha as they journeyed through the city's intricate labyrinth.

With each step, they were drawn deeper into the vibrant tapestry of Crystal Vale, their presence in this enchanting city marking a significant juncture in their quest.

In Crystal Vale, Ong was not an enigmatic traveler but a cherished community member who had introduced an exotic guest to their fair city.

Among the passing townsfolk, nods and greetings were directed at him, their eyes recognizing Ong as one of their own. The warmth of belonging stirred within him, a reminder that amid their arduous journey and enigmatic quests, there were places where he transcended the status of a stranger, finding solace as a cherished member of a close-knit community. This comforting notion added an extra layer of comfort to their adventurous odyssey.

"As Keisha gracefully crossed the threshold into the city's heart alongside Ong, her Eladrin heritage, a blend of ethereal grace and mystique, stood in stark contrast to the predominantly human canvas of Crystal Vale. With each step through the cobblestone streets, her presence became a focal point, drawing the heightened attention of passersby. While Ong was a cherished member of their community, known for his solitary nature and not one for traveling with companions, Keisha's presence was a source of genuine curiosity. Her very existence cast ripples of hushed awe and intrigue through the crowd. Ever the vigilant protector, Ong remained close by, a silent sentinel guarding against prying gazes that lingered too long. Together, they ventured deeper into the heart of Crystal Vale, their synchronized footsteps becoming a part of the city's vibrant rhythm. Here, human civilization's artistry wove seamlessly with nature's marvels, creating a harmonious fusion untouched by discord and emanating a welcoming warmth that enveloped them. Keisha, attuned to the city's subtle nuances, felt herself embraced by its open-hearted ambiance, a testament to Crystal Vale's spirit of unity and acceptance."

As Ong and Keisha ventured deeper into the bustling heart of Crystal Vale, the lively streets continued to weave the vibrant tapestry of life before them. Brimming with vitality, the city stood in stark contrast to the dangers they had faced in the untamed wilderness.

Their journey veered down an unforeseen path when an abrupt commotion disrupted the harmonious hum of the crowd. A creature of ebony elegance dashed toward them in a streak of midnight grace. Pumpkin, the sleek black panther, embodied untamed beauty against the city's ordered existence.

A collective gasp escaped the lips of the onlookers as they bore witness to this unexpected apparition. People instinctively retreated, a symphony of gasps and hushed murmurs echoing through the crowd. Uncertainty and awe danced in their widened eyes, their minds aflutter with questions regarding the intentions of this wild presence.

Keisha's heart quickened, her concern for Pumpkin's safety etched across her features like an intricate tapestry of worry. She turned to Ong, who mirrored her apprehension while wearing the mask of composure that only a seasoned traveler could master.

With a gesture of measured authority, Ong and Keisha came to an elegant pause in their journey. Ong raised his hand with a grace that commanded attention, and his voice, resonating with a note of unwavering assurance, pierced the tension-laden air. "Hold! Everyone, I beseech you, remain tranquil," he implored.

Like a sea held at bay by a steadfast lighthouse, the crowd fixed their collective gaze upon him, their initial trepidation momentarily eclipsed by a thirst for understanding. Ong, recognizing the need to quell their fears and dispel their uncertainties, continued his soothing oratory. "This magnificent creature is Pumpkin, a loyal companion to Keisha. Rest assured, as long as no harm befalls us, Pumpkin poses no threat."

In his words, Ong wove a cloak of reassurance, attempting to mend the fabric of their disrupted tranquility. Amidst the vibrant tapestry of Crystal Vale's life, this moment was a testament to their unpredictable and captivating journey.

Standing as a steadfast companion beside Ong, Keisha nodded in graceful agreement. Her voice, though as gentle as a breeze rustling through the leaves, carried a subtle undertone of caution. "Pumpkin is not only our loyal protector but also a dear friend. She bears no ill will toward anyone in your splendid city. Rest assured that her presence holds no menace to your peace."

Like a choir awaiting the conductor's lead, Crystal Vale's inhabitants focused on Ong and Keisha. The joint tension that had hung like a heavy shroud in the air began to dissipate. A silent exchange of glances between the city's residents marked the shift from apprehension to cautious acceptance. With each measured step forward, the rhythm of daily life in Crystal Vale resumed its harmonious cadence. The initial shock of Pumpkin's appearance gradually waned, leaving behind whispers of curiosity and wonder.

Once again bustling with activity, the cobbled streets of Crystal Vale became a living tapestry woven with threads of intrigue. Pumpkin, a shadowy sentinel, moved silently behind Ong and Keisha as they continued their journey through the enchanting city. She symbolized their unbreakable bond and was a testament to how the extraordinary was seamlessly interwoven with the ordinary in a world where the boundaries blurred into a mesmerizing dance.

As they ventured deeper into the heart of Crystal Vale, Ong couldn't escape the looming weight of responsibility, which clung to them like a storm cloud heavy with rain. Their duty was clear: to report the events that had transpired in Goldmoor to King Manard and to alert him to the looming threat posed by Phoenix and the Druchii. He cast a sidelong glance at Keisha, noting the subtle traces of nervous tension that had etched into her features.

Bending slightly to bring his voice closer to her, Ong whispered reassurance with words as tender as a lover's caress against the backdrop of the bustling city. "Worry not, my dear. I do not doubt that the King will find you utterly charming."

Ong's words flowed like a soothing river, carrying a genuine warmth to calm the ripples of Keisha's apprehension in the face of their impending royal encounter. With his unwavering support and encouraging tone, they pressed on, their journey leading them ever closer to the heart of Crystal Vale. Here, the tapestry of their destiny would be woven into the intricate fabric of the realm, forever intertwining their fate with its future.

As whispers of the exotic lady brought to Crystal Vale's gates by Lord Ong began to trickle through the palace, an undercurrent of intrigue swept through the courtiers like a clandestine breeze. The sensation was uncommon, and the air hummed with the delicate murmurs of curiosity. One of the vigilant palace attendants, always swift to bring matters of note to the king's attention, approached King Manard with a furrowed brow and a respectful bow.

"Your Majesty," the attendant began, his voice a reverent whisper, "there is a beautiful, exotic lady at the city gates, accompanied by Lord Ong. It is an uncommon sight. The lady also has an exotic black panther as a protector."

His regal demeanor was undisturbed, and King Manard regarded the attendant with a thoughtful nod. He was deeply familiar with Lord Ong and recognized that this departure from his usual reticence was significant. With a calm yet decisive gesture, the king issued his instructions.

"Inform the guards stationed at the city gates that the moment Lord Ong and his exotic guest, along with the enigmatic panther, set foot in the palace, they are to be escorted directly to the throne room," the king ordered.

The attendant, his eyes reflecting the gravity of the situation, nodded with deference and promptly carried out the king's mandate. As he departed, King Manard remained in a state of quiet anticipation. It was evident that fate had unfurled an unusual twist in the otherwise serene tapestry of Crystal Vale, and the king was determined to unravel the enigmas that lay before him, ready to confront whatever destiny had laid at his feet.

Approaching the grand palace gate of Crystal Vale, Ong and Keisha found themselves confronted by an imposing duo of guards. These sentinels, adorned in gleaming armor that bore the city's emblem, exchanged a meaningful look as they beheld the exotic couple, with the sleek black panther, Pumpkin, in tow, her presence adding a striking contrast to the scene.

One of the guards couldn't resist a jest, nudging his companion and inclining his head toward Keisha. "Well, Ong, you certainly bring a sight for sore eyes today. Who's this enchanting, exotic lady accompanying you?"

Keisha's cheeks tinged with a delicate blush at the compliment, and she momentarily lowered her gaze in modesty. Ever the protective guardian, Ong responded with a warm smile. "This is Keisha, and she is indeed quite extraordinary."

Intrigued, the guard shifted his attention to the magnificent creature, Pumpkin, who had observed the exchange with alert eyes. "And what of this majestic beast? May I have the privilege of petting her?"

Ong, displaying his characteristic grace, nodded in agreement. His eyes met Keisha's, and an unspoken understanding passed between them in that shared moment. "Certainly," he consented, allowing the guard to approach Pumpkin with cautious reverence.

As the guard extended his hand toward Pumpkin, the enchantment of Crystal Vale continued to work its magic, wrapping itself around them like a silken shroud. The grand palace stood as a regal sentinel in the backdrop, ready to embrace its exotic visitors.

With the assurance of their guards, Ong and Keisha made their way into the palace's grand entrance, where the splendor of the royal court awaited them. As they crossed the threshold, the guards announced their arrival with a flourish, their voices resonating through the opulent halls. "Lord Ong and his exotic companion, Keisha."

A touch of surprise danced in Keisha's eyes, briefly reflecting on the unusual situation. However, before they could delve further into it, King Manard, a regal presence seated upon his ornate throne, extended a gracious gesture, beckoning them to approach.

Ong and Keisha stood as paragons of humility before the regal presence of King Manard, who observed them with an astute gaze that seemed to reach into the depths of their souls. Ong, the embodiment of modesty, turned towards the king, a faint yet respectful smile gracing his features, and gently reminded him, "Your Majesty, you are well aware that the title is a mere honorary distinction. I bear no lordly rank."

In response, King Manard's eyes held a glint of amusement, a spark of knowing wisdom that danced within their depths. "Indeed, Lord Ong," he replied with a playful lilt to his tone, "we all understand that it is but a token of appreciation for your immeasurable contributions to Crystal Vale. However, with the exotic Lady Keisha in our midst today, it felt only fitting to employ it."

Ong acquiesced with a nod, acknowledging the king's perspective while subtly conveying his sentiments. "Your Majesty, you know my views on this matter."

The king's laughter, a rich and melodic resonance, filled the grand chamber like the harmonious chime of distant bells. "Ah, Ong," he exclaimed, his joy a testament to the warmth of the moment, "forever the embodiment of humility. Your unwavering dedication to our city is a living testament to your character. However, for the present, let us set aside such minor distinctions. Weightier matters require our attention."

King Manard's gaze shifted to Keisha, his eyes an artist's palette, mixing curiosity with respect as they studied her every facet. "Lady Keisha," he began, "your markings signify that you are an Eladrin, at least by my knowledge. Yet, your remarkable red hair and emerald eyes are not traits commonly associated with the Eladrin."

Keisha met the king's curious gaze with unwavering composure. "Your initial observation is indeed correct, Your Majesty. I am an Eladrin, but my lineage is exceptional. My father, Eldric, was a human mage possessing a rare combination of red hair and green eyes."

An unspoken understanding passed between King Manard and Ong in the quiet following moments. The king noted Ong's protective stance, an unspoken vow to shield Keisha from harm. For now, King Manard chose to absorb the presence of the enigmatic Lady Keisha and her intriguing lineage, allowing her story to unfurl at its own pace within the hallowed halls of Crystal Vale.

Ong redirected his focus to King Manard, his eyes alight with unwavering resolve. "Your Majesty, we bear tidings of great gravity concerning Goldmoor and the malevolent warlock, Phoenix, who has ruthlessly seized control of the city."

King Manard, his regal countenance undisturbed by the news, nodded with solemn gravity, understanding the weight of the words conveyed by his loyal subjects. Yet, as he observed the palpable weariness etched upon the faces of both Ong and Keisha, he discerned the wisdom of granting them respite. "Lord Ong, Lady Keisha," he began, his voice a river of empathy, "I can discern the trials you have endured on your arduous journey. Let us defer our discussions until the morrow."

King Manard summoned a court attendant with an effortless wave, whose presence seemed almost ethereal amidst the palace's grandeur. "Escort our esteemed guests to chambers within the palace, where they may find solace and restoration."

The court attendant bowed gracefully, his movements fluid as he gestured for Ong and Keisha to follow. Leading them up a majestic spiral staircase adorned with tapestries that whispered tales of a bygone era, he halted before a pair of shining doors, each a masterpiece in its own right. Speaking with a voice like the rustling of leaves in a serene forest, he offered gentle guidance, "These chambers have been prepared for your stay. May you find tranquility within, and we shall reconvene on the morrow."

As the court attendant departed, leaving Ong and Keisha to the embrace of their respective chambers, Ong ushered Keisha into her abode with a reassuring smile. His parting words lingered like a promise, carrying the hope of refreshing reprieve in the heart of the palace while Keisha was left to her contemplations within the sanctuary of her chamber.

Within the confines of her opulent chamber, Keisha gravitated toward an inviting chair strategically positioned by the window. There, with an air of pensive gravity, she directed her gaze toward the sprawling canvas of Crystal Vale that lay illuminated beneath the tapestry of the night sky. The celestial luminaries above sparkled with ethereal grace, akin to distant gems set against the black velvet expanse.

As her thoughts meandered through the labyrinth of their mission and the enigmatic secrets she held close to her heart, the city below enveloped her in a symphony of serenity. Like ageless guardians, the stars cast their silvery radiance upon her, bestowing a quiet wisdom that seemed to seep into her soul. The city's gentle nocturnal murmurs provided a lulling serenade, a harmonious backdrop to her contemplative reverie.

Tomorrow loomed on the horizon, heralding both revelations and tribulations, yet, for this fleeting moment, she found refuge in the palace's embrace, where even the most burdened hearts could discover solace.

Meanwhile, Ong, attired in fresh and gleaming armor, had found his sanctuary within the confines of his chamber. Having sated his appetite with the palace's provisions, he yielded to the call of companionship, the invisible thread that bound him to Keisha.

He approached the connecting door with measured steps, a bridge between their rooms. His heart danced between hope and concern as he recognized her absence from the bed. A shadow of apprehension brushed across his countenance, swiftly dispelled by the tender understanding that washed over him when he beheld her.

Nestled in slumber's tender embrace, Keisha occupied a chair in the room, her visage serene and unburdened.

Without disturbing her tranquil repose, he carefully lifted her, a feather-light presence, and arranged her form upon the inviting sanctuary of the bed. Ensuring she was warm, he lingered for a moment, captivated by the grace of her repose.

"I never envisioned finding someone like you," his soft and reverent words were offered to the hushed room. "Especially not within the confines of a forest. But I shall be your guardian, your champion. I shall safeguard you and find a treasure beyond measure in your presence."

With that whispered declaration, he withdrew, leaving her to the tender embrace of dreams, his heart unwavering in its commitment to her protection and devotion.

Before retiring to his chamber to seek solace in slumber, Ong found himself pausing in the hallowed corridor outside Keisha's chamber. An unexpected tableau awaited him, stirring his heart with surprise and deep affection.

In the dimly lit passageway, a scene transcended the ordinary boundaries of human-animal interaction. A sentinel of ebony grace stood– Pumpkin, the sleek black panther, guardian, and confidant, waiting with infinite patience. Her fur, an inky veil, seemed to absorb the ambient shadows, making her appear as if she were woven from the very night itself.

Ong's eyes, tender and appreciative, descended upon this magnificent creature, and with a gesture akin to a silent, unspoken pact, he invited her to enter. Pumpkin, an embodiment of regal serenity, flowed gracefully into the chamber, her presence a sentinel's vow to protect and watch over her charge.

As the door closed behind Ong, sealing them within the sanctuary of Keisha's chamber, the trinity – Ong, Keisha, and Pumpkin –ensconced in a cocoon of trust and companionship. Ong knew that with Pumpkin standing vigil, their respite would be guarded, even within the familiar walls of the palace.

A last, lingering glance was cast upon Keisha, whose slumber was overseen by her loyal protector. Then, the door closed, and Ong ventured to his chamber, enveloped by a profound sense of comfort; though laden with its mysteries and uncertainties, the night cradled them within its embrace, a testament to the enduring bonds that transcended the realm of mere mortals.

Chapter 16

Tales of Treachery and Triumph: Unraveling Goldmoor's Secrets

As Ong's day began in the embrace of Crystal Vale's opulent palace, the first tendrils of dawn painted the chamber with a palette of soft gold and amber. It was a scene that whispered enchantment, as if the world had been bathed in tranquility. The room, a tapestry woven with grandeur, seemed to hold its breath in the tender moments of dawn as if time itself paused to savor the beauty of the morning.

With a slow and graceful motion, Ong emerged from his slumber, casting aside the blankets surrounding him through the night. His bare feet met the cool caress of polished stone floors, a tactile reminder of the palace's enduring luxury. Beyond the chamber's windows, the faint chirping of birds orchestrated a harmonious symphony, announcing the arrival of a new day with a triumphant chorus as if the world itself rejoiced in its awakening.

Ong, dressed in garments befitting a nobleman, moved with a poise that spoke of both regality and purpose. In a small kitchenette nestled within the chamber's alcove, the aroma of freshly baked bread mingled with the fragrant herbs, weaving a tapestry of scents that enveloped his senses. With the skilled hands of an artisan, he assembled a breakfast of simple elegance, arranging slices of warm, golden-brown bread and artisanal cheese upon a porcelain plate.

Balancing the breakfast on a tray, Ong approached the adjoining door that led to Keisha's chambers. As he entered, he found her in the embrace of slumber. Bathed in the soft, golden light of morning, she appeared as a slumbering goddess, every contour of her form an ode to grace. Pumpkin, their loyal feline companion, stood vigil by her side, a silent sentinel guarding her dreams.

In this tender tableau, Ong's heart swelled with a love that knew no boundaries. Keisha, the radiant sun of his world, lay before him, a testament to the enduring power of their love. Trials and tribulations had marked their journey, but those challenges had only strengthened the unbreakable bond that now united them, much like the palace's splendid crystal walls.

Leaning against the cool, age-weathered stone wall, Ong was adrift in a sea of memories. Within his thoughts, he conjured the echoes of Keisha's laughter, the unyielding determination that had first ensnared his heart, and the unwavering resolve that defined her. As he watched her slumber, a profound appreciation washed over him. Their shared journey was a testament to their indomitable spirit, their love a radiant torch amidst the relentless shadows encroaching upon their world.

Ong's surroundings in the peaceful embrace of the Crystal Vale palace's corridor mirrored the luxury that enveloped him. The walls, adorned with tapestries of unparalleled artistry, wove together ancient legends in vibrant threads, each narrating a tale that spanned the annals of centuries. The polished marble floor beneath his feet bore a lustrous patina, reflecting the city's resplendence as if the ground whispered grandeur stories.

The tender morning light, akin to liquid gold, streamed through the graceful arches of the windows, casting kaleidoscopic patterns of luminance upon the corridor's marble expanse. Every stride carried a solemn burden of purpose, an understanding of the weight that pressed upon the shoulders of those who trod these hallowed halls.

In this city of luxury and nobility, Ong was approached by one of King Manard's loyal attendants. Draped in regal attire that bore the marks of years of unwavering service to the monarchy, the attendant moved with dignified grace, a living testament to the kingdom's enduring traditions. With a profound bow that bespoke reverence, the attendant addressed

Ong, their words laden with the gravity of an impending audience with the sovereign.

"Lord Ong," the attendant began, their voice a tranquil river of authority, "King Manard requests your esteemed presence at your earliest convenience to discuss the recent unfolding events at Goldmoor and the looming specter of the Phoenix threat."

Ong nodded, his mind a tapestry woven with the harrowing threads of recent days. The relentless pursuit by the Druchii, driven by their insatiable hunger for Keisha's capture, had pushed them to the precipice of their endurance. The prospect of an audience with the king weighed upon him like a leaden cloak, its burden palpable in the air.

"We shall present ourselves once Lady Keisha awakens," Ong declared, his voice a clarion call of stubborn determination. "These trying days have tempered our resolve, and our foremost concern is safeguarding our realm."

The attendant, bearing the solemnity of unwavering loyalty to their monarch, nodded in understanding. With a parting bow, he withdrew, leaving Ong alone in the corridor. The echoes of their discourse lingered, a prologue to the pivotal deliberations that awaited them.

Amidst the corridor's grandeur, time-honored traditions and regal opulence conspired to cast an aura of solemnity. The palace itself, a living tome of history, enveloped them in an ambiance that whispered secrets of centuries past.

Keisha stirred within her adjoining sanctuary in the subdued embrace of dawn's tender rays. The initial kiss of sunlight painted her features with a gentle, ethereal luminosity as she rose from slumber. Her movements were a symphony of grace, unfolding like the petals of a fragile blossom at the break of day.

With tender fingers, she combed through her lustrous mane, a cascade of fiery red that shimmered like flames flowing over her shoulders. The act of self-grooming was both a presentation ritual and a silent pledge—an affirmation of her inner fortitude and unyielding spirit.

Her eyes, still touched by the ethereal hues of dreams she had ventured through in the realm of sleep, gleamed like twin stars rekindling in the night sky. Even in the solitude of her chamber, Keisha exuded a quiet but unshakable determination, a living testament to her enduring resilience.

Unbeknownst to her, Ong's discourse with the royal attendant continued in the corridor, weaving a tapestry of impending choices and weighty responsibilities. As he prepared for their imminent audience with the king, Keisha's emergence heralded a subtle shift in the tides of destiny, her presence a reminder that in the face of adversity, the indomitable spirit of the Guardian endured.

When Keisha stepped into the corridor, her presence breathed life into the grandeur of Crystal Vale Palace. Accompanied by Pumpkin, their feline guardian, the creature's fur gleamed like a polished amber jewel beneath the palace's opulent chandeliers, casting a radiant glow that mirrored the resilience of those who walked these hallowed halls.

Amidst the opulence and the grandeur of Crystal Vale Palace, Keisha's vibrant spirit radiated like the sun's rays piercing through a verdant canopy of emerald leaves. With each step, she embodied a symphony of grace and unyielding determination, a living testament to her arduous journey and unwavering resilience.

In the distance, Keisha espied Ong, locked in conversation with the royal attendant, a figure of regal authority, their exchange akin to a dance of carefully chosen words. Her emerald eyes, akin to precious gemstones, sparkled with quiet curiosity as she approached, her footsteps reverberating softly upon the marbled corridor like the footfalls of a curious forest nymph.

"Ong," she inquired, her voice a soothing cadence akin to the musical whisper of a forest brook, "has the royal attendant bore tidings from King Manard? Is he prepared to grant us an audience?"

Ong's gaze locked onto hers, forging an unspoken connection between them. His reply, tinged with unwavering resolve, marked their readiness to confront the looming challenges. Side by side, they ventured toward the throne room, their footsteps resounding with an unshakable purpose amidst the hallowed halls of Crystal Vale Palace.

In the dimly lit confines of Goldmoor's castle dungeon, King Alex languished in his dank cell, his once-proud bearing reduced to a mere shadow of its former glory. He bore the weight of his captivity with stoic resignation, the stillness punctuated only by the occasional water drip from the damp, gloomy walls.

It was within this desolate abyss that Phoenix, the sinister sorcerer, made his malevolent presence known. As he crossed the threshold into the dungeon, his arrival seemed to taint the air, casting an eerie pall that clung to the room like an evil spirit. His eyes, aglow with wicked intent, bore into the captive king like twin orbs of malice, a harbinger of impending doom.

"Ah, King Alex," Phoenix sneered, his voice a venomous melody that dripped with dark amusement. "I trust your accommodations have been to your liking. The shadows I left behind in your tower, alongside your beloved Queen Jeanne, must have woven quite a haunting tapestry in your dreams, wouldn't you say?"

King Alex's eyes, two blazing orbs of simmering fury, bore into Phoenix. His fists clenched involuntarily, the very air pulsating with his pent-up rage. "You wretched fiend! Release my wife from the cursed torment you've inflicted upon her!"

Phoenix's laughter, a wicked sonata, reverberated through the frigid stone chamber like an evil echo. "I found Queen Jeanne's conversation with our shadowy companions most delightful. She pleaded for their mercy, a pitiful symphony of desperation. But alas, mercy is a language foreign to their dark hearts."

The king's visage contorted with unbridled rage, his voice a fierce declaration of defiance. "Mark my words, Phoenix! You shall pay for your atrocities!"

Phoenix's twisted smirk widened as he drew nearer to the cell bars, his predatory gaze locked onto King Alex's. "Speaking of payment, my dear king, I come bearing tidings. We have unveiled the identity of the Eladrin who accompanies the human warrior Swifthammer. Her name is Keisha."

King Alex's fury reached a searing crescendo, his voice a thunderous proclamation. "And what sinister designs do you harbor with this knowledge? Be wary, for her people and Swifthammer himself will guard her with unyielding resolve."

Phoenix's grin remained malevolent as he raised a sable hand, dark energies crackling in his fingertips like malevolent lightning. "I have a multitude of intentions, King Alex. But first, would you care for another taste of my formidable power?" He unleashed a storm of arcane force with a cruel flourish, ensnaring King Alex in a maelstrom of unbearable torment.

As the king gasped for breath, Phoenix turned to depart, his final words dripping with ominous promise. "I shall oversee the progress of Qellaun and Lyra in the library. Rest assured, King Alex, our scheming is advancing, and the full extent of our dominion shall soon become apparent."

With that grim proclamation, Phoenix vanished from sight, leaving King Alex to grapple with the encompassing darkness that had trapped his world, literally and figuratively.

Alone in his cell's dimly lit and forlorn confines, King Alex's thoughts churned like tempestuous currents in a tumultuous sea. He sat ensconced within the looming shadows, the weight of his powerlessness pressing upon him like a leaden shroud. Phoenix's malevolent laughter still lingered, an ever-present specter haunting his senses, a stark testament to the hostility that had fractured his once-peaceful realm.

In his contemplations, as he sought to fathom the whereabouts of his beloved Queen Jeanne, an insidious despair clawed at his spirit. The cruel reality that any escape attempt hinged upon first unveiling her concealed location felt like an unrelenting manacle, chaining his soul to this forsaken place.

Amidst the oppressive darkness, a flicker of hope pierced through the gloom. King Alex clung tenaciously to the glimmer of possibility that Ong, the brave warrior from Crystal Vale, might be on a quest to beseech aid from his homeland. Within the chronicles of the time, Crystal Vale had been known as the bastion of light, the steadfast guardian of hope itself. Perhaps they would rise gallantly to confront the encroaching abyss that now gripped Goldmoor.

And then, there was Keisha, the enigmatic Eladrin who journeyed in the company of the human warrior Swifthammer. The Eladrin, ethereal beings of grace and unbounded power, held the embodiment of luminescence within their essence. Deep within the chambers of his heart, King Alex nurtured a slender ember of hope—that Keisha might extend her hand to beckon her kindred spirits, rallying them in a harmonious chorus of strength and resilience, a symphony of light against the encroaching tide of darkness.

As each moment flowed by, King Alex's resolve crystallized. Despite the cruel confines of his cell, he remained steadfast, an unwavering beacon of defiance against the encroaching despair. He clung to the hope that his allies, Ong and Keisha, would rise like valiant defenders of light, allying to push back the looming darkness. In the dungeon's oppressive depths, a glimmer of his unwavering resolve burned like a distant star, a testament to his unyielding determination to defy the ever-encroaching shadows that threatened to devour his world.

The throne room within the heart of Crystal Vale's splendor was a testament to the city's luxury, its majesty echoing through the intricate tapestries that adorned the walls and the radiant crystal chandeliers, casting a celestial glow. King Manard, a figure of regal authority and wisdom, occupied the throne, embodying the strength and sagacity of the realm.

Before the sovereign, Ong, Keisha, and their devoted companion Pumpkin stood as if bathed in the gentle, diffused radiance of the chamber's crystal-infused aura. King Manard's perceptive gaze, sharp as a honed blade, remained riveted upon Ong, his words carrying the weight of an unspoken question, hanging in the air like a heavy tapestry, pregnant with curiosity.

"Intriguing travelers," King Manard commenced his voice, a resonant testament to his regency, "before we delve into the weighty matters concerning Goldmoor and the looming shadow of Phoenix, I am compelled by a burning curiosity. Ong, recount the tale of your encounter with this exotic soul, our Eladrin companion. What twist of fate has brought her to your side in this difficult journey?"

Ong met the king's gaze without hesitation, bearing an aura of profound respect and unwavering earnestness. "Your Majesty," he began, his words steeped in the moment's gravitas, "my first encounter with Keisha transpired amidst the sacred groves of Purplefire Woods, where I sought solace and respite for my faithful steed, Thunder. The threads of fate interwove our destinies further when she arrived in Goldmoor, despite my counsel to steer clear of that beleaguered city." A subtle glance toward Keisha carried a wellspring of warmth, an unspoken testament to the shared odyssey they had embarked upon.

King Manard, his eyes pools of contemplation, nodded in a manner that bespoke his deep understanding. "A meeting forged by destiny's hand, it would appear," he mused, his curiosity temporarily set aside. "For now, let us direct our attention to the pressing concerns that lay before us—the shadow that looms over Goldmoor and the menacing presence of Phoenix."

Ong, his voice an unwavering current, embarked on the harrowing narrative that had befallen Goldmoor. His words flowed with a storyteller's grace, sketching a vivid tableau of the chaos that had wrested control of the once-thriving city.

"A malevolent warlock by the name of Phoenix has seized dominion over Goldmoor," Ong revealed, his words a heavy tapestry of impending doom. "Within his grasp, he holds King Alex, though the depths of his captivity remain a veiled enigma. Yet, the darkness deepens, for he has also trapped King Alex's beloved Queen Jeanne. Her whereabouts shroud us in uncertainty, and it is believed that King Alex will not move to free Goldmoor or permit others to do so until she is safely returned to his side."

King Manard, his countenance a portrait of regal contemplation, absorbed Ong's words with empathy and unwavering determination. He comprehended the profound gravity of the situation and the personal bonds that ensnared King Alex. Yet, urgency tinged his voice as he spoke.

"A distressing revelation, indeed," King Manard replied, his tone a reflection of the immense weight of the crisis. "Whispers of this warlock, Phoenix, and the ominous escalation of his power have reached my ears since the fall of Goldmoor. Our adversary has strengthened, and his evil intentions cast a looming shadow. We must proceed cautiously, for this darkness threatens not solely Goldmoor but the equilibrium of our entire realm."

A tableau of gravity and understanding unfurled in the heart of Crystal Vale's glorious throne room. The formidable challenge of confronting the enigmatic warlock and quelling the rising tide of his malevolence now loomed large, casting an imposing shadow over the path ahead.

Like a serpentine river winding its way through the chamber, Ong's words flowed with a current of profound concern and the relentless pursuit that had dogged their every step since their departure from Goldmoor. The presence of the Druchii, those nefarious dark elves, lingered like a lingering wraith, an ominous specter etched indelibly into the very fabric of their journey.

"King Manard," Ong began, his voice a resolute pillar of unwavering determination, "from the moment Keisha and I departed Goldmoor, we found ourselves relentlessly pursued by the Druchii, who serve as agents in Phoenix's sinister design. But what troubles us more, my liege is that this malefactor has unveiled Keisha's name. It has become evident that he covets her capture above all else, driven by an insidious fascination with her Eladrin lineage."

Keisha's gentle yet unwavering voice interjected with a revelation of her own, a crucial piece to the intricate puzzle. "It is not solely because I bear the mantle of an Eladrin," she expounded, her eyes shimmering with the depth of her knowledge. "Phoenix's desire to capture me is intimately tied to our hidden sanctuary, E'vahona. The knowledge of its existence is a dangerous secret that must remain veiled at any cost."

This revelation hung in the air like a gathering storm, casting a shadow over their aspirations of restoring tranquility to the realm. King Manard, his countenance a tapestry of contemplation, nodded thoughtfully, fully grasping the gravity of the situation and the labyrinthine layers of intrigue that enshrouded them.

King Manard's gaze, a beacon of curiosity and respect, gravitated toward Keisha. The Eladrin, a subject of fascination throughout the realm, had been steeped in legend and lore, their renown as champions of light echoing down the annals of time. Yet, the enigma surrounding E'vahona had endured, a riddle composed of scattered fragments.

"I have heard the whispers of the Eladrin," King Manard commenced, his voice bearing the weight of age-old legends. "The tales sing of your kind as sentinels of luminance, protectors of realms, and wisdom seekers. But regarding this enigmatic realm of E'vahona, the chronicles are as diverse as the night sky's constellations. Keisha, would you, in your wisdom, shed light upon the significance of this elusive realm in the eyes of one like Phoenix?"

The question, a fragile tapestry of curiosity, hung suspended in the air, awaiting Keisha's delicate hands to weave the intricate threads of understanding and unveil the profound significance of E'vahona.

As Keisha embarked on unraveling the enigma that was E'vahona, her words unfurled like an ancient scroll, carrying with them the weight of centuries gone by. Within the grandeur of the palace's throne room, it seemed like the very stones trembled in reverence to the ancient power she narrated.

"E'vahona," Keisha's voice resonated with sacred reverence, "is not merely a concealed realm; it is a timeless font of magic, steeped in the essence of ages long past. Within its hallowed confines, the very fabric of reality intertwines with the threads of arcane might. It is where the convergence of mystic energies has birthed a symphony of unparalleled magic."

King Manard and the assembled court listened with rapt attention, their fascination a palpable presence that seemed to reverberate.

"Furthermore," Keisha continued, her words akin to incantations, "E'vahona shares a unique communion with the Goddess of Light herself. Her divine presence imbues the air within its walls, rendering it a sanctuary of unrivaled potency. And hidden within this realm lie sanctified sites, where the boundaries of mortal existence and divine realms intersect, forging bonds of power that defy mortal comprehension."

The room was charged with an aura of wonder, as though the very atmosphere had become infused with the charisma of E'vahona.

Keisha's voice, laden with the solemnity of an ancient oath, continued to peel back the layers of E'vahona's enigma, her words akin to the unfurling of long-guarded scrolls, revealing secrets that had been passed down through countless generations.

"E'vahona," she intoned with the reverence of a devotee, "is a divine endowment from the Goddess herself, entrusted to the Eladrin with the gravest of charges. We were selected as its stewards and sentinels, and this honor was coupled with the most solemn of vows. An oath binds us, a covenant that enshrouds the whereabouts of E'vahona in an impenetrable veil, shared only with those deemed worthy."

The chamber appeared to hold its breath as Keisha unveiled the price exacted by this sacred commitment.

"According to the terms of this hallowed covenant," she continued, her words a solemn echo in the room, "we, the Eladrin, swore an irrevocable pledge that, even in the direst of circumstances—be it capture, torture, or the specter of death—we would not divulge the secret of E'vahona, not even to safeguard our own lives or those dearest to our hearts."

Once tethered to the present, Keisha's gaze turned distant as she added a heart-rending note. "My father, a human mage who cherished my mother with profound love, paid the ultimate toll for this vow, sealing the sanctity of E'vahona with his life."

Her words hung in the air like a melancholy requiem, an ode to the profound commitment of the Eladrin to their hidden realm.

King Manard's eyes bore into Keisha, his regard a fusion of reverence and comprehension as he absorbed the gravity of her revelation. The immense burden of the Eladrin's solemn oath pervaded the atmosphere, embodying their unwavering resolve.

"I now perceive," King Manard spoke in hushed tones, his voice a vessel of empathy, "why the location of E'vahona is shrouded in such profound secrecy. The price your people pay to safeguard it is an exorbitant one."

His gaze briefly traversed to Ong, who stood steadfast, offering Keisha the comforting embrace of his presence—a silent refuge amid the tumultuous sea of her memories. King Manard, a keen observer, discerned their profound connection, an unspoken alliance birthed in the crucible of trials and united by an unwavering purpose.

"In these turbulent times," the sovereign continued, his voice unwavering, "we must pay homage to the sacrifices that preserve these sanctified realms. I am grateful for your unreserved candor, Lady Keisha, and for entrusting us with this sacred knowledge."

With those words, King Manard made it clear that he was poised to act guided by this newfound enlightenment, his resolve fortified by the comprehension of the Eladrin's unparalleled devotion.

Within the hallowed halls of Crystal Vale's throne room, Ong, radiating a profound inner strength, advanced toward King Manard, his presence imbued with a sense of purpose as weighty as the very world itself. His words, chosen with meticulous care and carrying a subtle undercurrent of expectation, bore the gravity of a significant petition.

"Your Majesty," Ong commenced, his voice an orchestra within the room's luxury, "Lady Keisha and I shall embark on a journey of profound consequence in the coming day or two. The destination it shrouds in veiled secrecy, for I am to engage in a clandestine rendezvous with Lord Karrenen, a venerable luminary within the Eladrin Council. The matter we shall discuss demands the utmost discretion." Ong's unwavering beacon gaze held the weight of unwritten history as he continued, "This meeting is of monumental importance, marking the inaugural encounter between Lord Karrenen and myself."

It was a mission meaningful with implications, for King Alex's liberation and the liberation of Goldmoor rested in their hands. The quest to locate Queen Jeanne ensnared within Phoenix's evil grasp cast an ominous shadow over their purpose. Ong's request lingered in the chamber like a solemn vow, underscoring the gravity of their mission.

Within the bounds of Crystal Vale," Ong's voice resounded like a clarion call, "we must undertake a discreet investigation to unveil the wretched place where King Alex's cherished Queen Jeanne languishes unjustly. Her freedom, held in captivity, serves as the cornerstone upon which the edifice of Goldmoor's salvation is founded, a fragile and uncertain foundation. Should any clues emerge, I beseech Your Majesty to impart them unto me, for the release of the Queen stands as our paramount endeavor."

King Manard, a sensible and solemn sovereign, nodded in solemn concord, his determination harmonizing with Ong's. "We shall leave no stone unturned in our quest to ascertain the whereabouts of Queen Jeanne. Her freedom is an invincible cornerstone of our cause, and we shall not withhold any intelligence we gather from you."

Keisha's utterance carried a somber undertone; a dark symphony of concern played out in her eyes as they turned to Ong. Her delicate yet resolute voice quivered under the weight of impending perils.

"You see," she commenced, her words a whispered prayer, "the Druchii, those shadowy sentinels, lie in wait beyond the confines of Crystal Vale. And your imminent rendezvous with Lord Karrenen... I cannot bear to be the spark for misfortune."

Before the thread of her worry could unravel further, Ong's response cleaved through the air, a proclamation as unwavering as the northern star, every syllable a testament to the love that bound them.

"Hold," he commanded, his voice possessing an imperious edge. "You shall tread no further along that treacherous path. I have etched my devotion to you in indelible ink and shall not allow any harm to befall you. Together, we shall confront the looming specters of danger."

King Manard, a monarch whose wisdom bore the weight of epochs, interjected with an affectionate smile. "Desist in your endeavors to sway him, my dear. When Ong has set his course, it bends only in the face of an adamant heart. I may be taking liberties with my words, but even a cursory glance reveals the sincere love within him."

In that moment, King Manard's gaze shifted briefly, a subtle gesture that allowed the tender emotions of the present to linger, much like the echo of a haunting melody.

With a grace born of wisdom, the monarch poured a glass of water, an act as soothing as the gentle caress of a healing spell—a silent testimony to his unspoken support and profound comprehension.

Keisha's gaze, a testament to her affection and good-natured concession, alighted fondly upon Ong. Like twin pools of reflection, her eyes held a playful resignation, a warmth radiating from her lips as a modest smile tugged at their corners.

"Very well," she acquiesced, her surrender marked by a soft chuckle, "you claim victory this time." Like musical notes in a serenade, her words carried an undertone of affection.

Ong, his laughter a sonorous symphony, resounded with tenderness and love. "This time?" he echoed, his voice a playful melody, "Ah, my dearest, be assured that when it comes to ensuring your safety, I plan to emerge victorious every time."

With their playful exchange tenderly sealed, Ong's countenance shifted to one of solemnity as he addressed King Manard. "Our departure draws nigh," he began, his words a weighty refrain. "And I pray that the next encounter graces us with cause for jubilation—the liberation of Goldmoor."

King Manard, his regal nod carrying the gravity of their mission, acknowledged the mantle of responsibility they bore. Ong and Keisha departed the palace, their path leading them toward the stables where Thunder awaited, their journey a canvas painted with uncertainty and an unwavering resolve to confront destiny head-on.

Chapter 17

Prelude to Shadows: Meeting with Lord Karrenen

As Ong and Keisha ventured forth from the enchanting embrace of Crystal Vale, they embarked upon a profound journey deep into the heart of the Emeraldwoods. Under the grand canopy of ancient arboreal guardians, they found themselves cradled in a world of glorious greenery, where dappled sunlight performed a glamorous, golden ballet on the forest floor. Thunder, Ong's steadfast steed, carried them forward with a grace that seemed to emanate from the serene surroundings.

However, amid the tranquil beauty enveloping them, an ominous undercurrent pulsed through the woods. Unseen and unfelt by the travelers, the Druchii, sinister beings with an unrelenting thirst for Keisha's capture, had keenly detected their intrusion. Like specters cloaked in the undergrowth, they observed and patiently awaited their moment, their eyes flickering with malevolence.

In an abrupt rupture of the sylvan hush, the forest resonated with harsh, guttural voices as the Druchii sensed the presence of their prey. Their leader, Kelru, issued sharp commands, spurring his minions into a frantic pursuit. With unyielding resolve, they relentlessly chased the unsuspecting pair.

Keisha's heart quickened as she glanced back at Ong, her anxiety etching delicate lines upon her features. His steady voice echoed in her ears, encouraging her to grasp Thunder's reins with unwavering determination as they delved deeper into the woods. Pumpkin, their tireless feline companion, followed their lead.

The relentless pursuit of the Druchii swelled in volume, their ominous presence drawing nearer. Panic threatened to overwhelm them until Keisha's discerning gaze discerned a hidden refuge between two colossal forest titans. Ong, placing his trust in her instincts, deftly steered Thunder toward this concealed sanctuary.

With the thundering rhythm of hoofbeats, the Druchii raced past their covert haven, the din of their chase fading like a dissipating tempest. Ong held Keisha gently, his instincts honed by years of traversing untamed landscapes, silently instructing her to remain perfectly still.

In the tranquil sanctuary of their concealment, tension hung thick in the air, a tangible reminder of the imminent peril they faced. The emerald foliage formed a protective shield, granting them a fleeting respite before they resumed their difficult journey toward their rendezvous with Lord Karrenen.

Deep within the heart of the shadow-draped woods, Kelru, the unwavering leader of the relentless Druchii hunters, seethed with frustration. His countenance contorted, a canvas of wrath and impatience, as he commanded his men to cease their relentless pursuit. In this ancient arboreal realm, gnarled branches appeared to entwine and close ranks around the vexed Druchii, silently bearing witness to the storm of their leader's rage.

His harsh voice, grating like stones against bone, bore the weight of their collective vexation. "Where in the abyss have they vanished to? It's as if they possess some accursed enchantment that allows them to elude our grasp every time we draw near." His comrades exchanged glances filled with wary dissatisfaction, and their inner turmoil mirrored in the haunted depths of their eyes.

One among Kelru's loyal subordinates, a Druchii tempered by unwavering loyalty but now tinged with exasperation, dared to voice a question born of desperation. "Do we possess even the faintest inkling of their intended destination, Kelru?" His voice quivered with urgency as he sought a glimmer of hope.

With a vehement shake of his head, Kelru set the air ablaze with the zeal of his frustration. "No, they could be making their way to any conceivable location—perhaps returning to Goldmoor in an audacious attempt to rescue King Alex or attempting to find Queen Jeanne." His thoughts raced through a labyrinth of sinister possibilities. "We cannot persist in this futile pursuit, yet facing Phoenix's wrath with empty hands is an equally untenable fate."

Surveying the dense woodland that enshrouded them, Kelru reluctantly conceded to a decision forged from the crucible of circumstance. "We shall retrace our steps to Goldmoor, but we must proceed cautiously. I would rather endure the tedium of a return journey than provoke the unbridled fury of Phoenix with nothing to show for our efforts." His vigilant gaze swept their surroundings, unaware of the concealed presence that lingered just beyond the periphery of their senses.

Unbeknownst to the relentless Druchii hunters, Ong and Keisha lay concealed beneath the verdant canopy, steps away from the unfolding conversation. Ong suppressed a burgeoning wave of laughter, savoring the irony of their predicament. He offered a gentle tug on Thunder's reins, urging the noble steed to remain patient as a sentinel until the imminent threat had safely passed.

As the Druchii riders dwindled into mere shadows on the horizon, a profound sense of relief cascaded upon Ong and Keisha like a soothing breeze on a languid summer's day. Ong could no longer restrain his joy, and his laughter bubbled forth like a jubilant stream, dispelling the tension that had gripped their hearts during their evasive maneuvers.

Keisha turned her gaze toward Ong, her eyes dancing with amusement and gratitude, a spark of shared triumph. "It appears," she remarked with a knowing smile, "that we may have the rare opportunity to traverse this forest without the harried pace of fugitives."

Ong nodded in agreement, his eyes tender as they locked onto hers. "Indeed, my beloved. While the thrill of the chase can be exhilarating, a more tranquil journey would be a welcomed respite. Nevertheless," he added sternly, "I would endure any hardship to ensure your safety."

Their lips met in a tender kiss, a testament to their shared affection amidst the labyrinthine uncertainties of their quest. Returning to their map, Ong's fingers traced intricate paths on the parchment's surface. "According to Lord Karrenen's instructions, there is yet another woodland in this vicinity," he pondered aloud. "The Emberwoods Forest, it is named. Curiously, it is advised that we steer clear of its confines."

Keisha nodded in concurrence, her voice carrying the weight of wisdom. "The Emberwoods are indeed a realm of enchanting beauty, yet they reside perilously close to the territories of Fel Thalor and Flameford," she elucidated, caution lacing her words.

Ong's eyes locked onto Keisha's, a silent understanding passing between them as the name "Flameford" resonated like a foreboding bell tolling in the depths of his memory. It was a place he had heard of before, a word spoken with both trepidation and awe. "Flameford," he murmured, the syllables weighed with the knowledge of the sorcerer they sought to thwart. "That's where Phoenix claims as his origin, the heart of the fire from which he draws his power. We should try to avoid Flameford."

With renewed resolve and a clear path, they embarked on their journey again, leaving behind the shadows of uncertainty to embrace the promise of their shared adventure. They trod cautiously, ever mindful of the problematic territories nearby, their steps a cadence of determination echoing through the lush forest.

In the radiant splendor of Crystal Vale, where the city's walls gleamed like the facets of precious gemstones, King Manard summoned his loyal soldiers into the grandeur of the throne room. The chamber was a living testament to the kingdom's enduring glory, adorned with intricate tapestries and golden accents that symbolized its regal heritage. Yet, a shadow had fallen upon this opulent setting, and it was within that shadow that the king addressed his brave warriors.

With the regality befitting the highest peaks of the realm, King Manard stood before his assembled troops and began to recount the grim tidings from Goldmoor. His voice, a harmonious blend of authority and deep concern resonated through the ornate hall as he unveiled the distressing narrative of the captive monarchs.

As he spoke of King Alex's likely imprisonment in the foreboding depths of the Goldmoor Dungeon, the king's words hung in the air like a heavy fog, each soldier acutely aware of the ominous fate that awaited their sovereign. Yet, the mention of Queen Jeanne's enigmatic disappearance cast the darkest shadow over the gathering. The uncertainty surrounding her whereabouts weighed heavily on their hearts, a looming specter of unease that veiled the room in an aura of foreboding.

King Manard, a paragon of wisdom and compassion, marshaled his troops with an unwavering command that stirred their souls. His impassioned plea urged them to scatter across the land, to probe every hidden crevice and obscure corner where the sinister sorcerer, Phoenix Shadowwalker, might have concealed their beloved queen. The mandate was as crystal clear as the kingdom's grandest chandelier: they must leave no stone unturned, no shadow unexplored. Their adversary would not concern himself with the treacherous nature of Queen Jeanne's captivity; his only concern was that it remained veiled in obscurity.

His soldiers, a bastion of unwavering loyalty, nodded with resolve. Determination etched upon their faces like intricate runes, they readied themselves to embark on this harrowing quest. With a unified sense of purpose, they dispersed throughout the land, their footsteps echoing against the marbled floors—a poignant testament to their devotion to their sovereign and homeland.

Once the grand chamber had emptied of its valiant occupants, King Manard lingered in the throne room. His shoulders, usually bearing the weight of a kingdom's hopes, sagged ever so slightly beneath the burden of his profound worry. His voice, reduced to a mere whisper, conveyed his apprehension. "May we find her," he murmured, his thoughts dwelling on the unimaginable trials Queen Jeanne might be enduring in the clutches of darkness.

Above, the emerald leaves rustled in harmony with the gentle breeze, casting dappled shadows upon the forest floor below. As Ong guided Thunder through the lush expanse of the Emeraldwood Forest, the air was redolent with the fragrant embrace of wildflowers and the earthy scent of ancient trees. It was a tranquil oasis amid the turbulent events of their journey—a place where the very heart of nature whispered secrets to Ong as he rode, and the ancient arboreal sentinels bore witness to his unwavering determination.

As Ong's steady gaze fell upon Keisha, nestled against his chest, her delicate countenance softened by the gentle embrace of slumber, a warm smile played upon his lips. Her unwavering trust in him, a thin thread that bound them together, found solace in this fleeting moment of respite. In the quiet of the forest, he cherished the profound peace that enshrouded them, a sanctuary amidst the tumultuous currents of their journey.

With whispered words of solace and tenderness, Ong continued his steady march, a vigilant guardian on a mission to safeguard their shared future. The path ahead remained veiled in mysteries yet to be unveiled, and with each passing mile, they drew nearer to the enigmatic meeting place destined to weave the tapestry of their fate.

In the heart of the forest, a figure of ethereal grace awaited their arrival, standing in a sunlit clearing where the golden beams filtered through the verdant canopy. Lord Karrenen, an elf of striking presence, bore a mane of silver hair that flowed like a cascading waterfall down his shoulders. His eyes, deep and ancient as the very roots of the world, held the wisdom etched into the annals of countless years. As Ong and Keisha approached, the aura of a seasoned mage enveloped him, an embodiment of arcane mastery.

Acknowledging their presence with a subtle nod, Lord Karrenen's gaze lingered on Keisha for a moment, tracing the echoes of an ancient prophecy. Then, it returned to Ong. The air around them seemed charged with anticipation, setting the stage where destinies converged.

Ong guided Thunder to a graceful halt, his eyes momentarily resting on Keisha, who had drifted into slumber during their journey. With a gentle whisper, he roused her, and as her eyes fluttered open, she glimpsed Lord Karrenen, her demeanor instantly shifting to an alert vigilance. Ong assisted her in dismounting, and Lord Karrenen acknowledged her with an insightful nod.

The tremor of apology infused Keisha's voice as she glanced at Ong, her concern for dozing off during this critical moment palpable. However, his reassuring gesture quelled her worries. With a measured nod from Lord Karrenen, Ong introduced the purpose that had brought them to this enigmatic rendezvous. His words carried the weight of solemn intent, their resonance echoing through the forest's serene confines. In response, Lord

Karrenen inquired if Ong comprehended the stipulations of their pact, and Ong's confident affirmation resonated with the elder elf's approval.

In the tranquil embrace of the ancient forest, Lord Karrenen motioned for them to follow, seeking a private audience with Ong before their dialogue could fully unfold. As they distanced themselves from Keisha, Ong turned to offer her a comforting smile. His whispered reassurance carried on the wings of the wind, "Do not worry." Left to her own devices in the tranquil clearing, Keisha awaited the unfolding of Ong's fate, wrapped within the murmured secrets of the forest.

Beneath the leafy canopy of the serene forest clearing, Lord Karrenen extended his invitation with a regal nod, a wordless beckoning for Ong to take a seat. This was the pivotal moment they had been summoned for, a juncture where destinies hung in the balance, awaiting the stroke of their choices.

With deliberate words, Lord Karrenen delved into the heart of the matter. Ong's request for this meeting bore the weight of his desire to access E'vahona, the elusive hidden realm of the Eladrin. Lord Karrenen, ever astute, recognized the gravity of Ong's intent, the profound significance of the knowledge he sought.

In his soft-spoken manner, Lord Karrenen alluded to the four stringent rules, well-known to Keisha and now shared with Ong. The first rule had been met through Ong's formal request, but beyond this initial step lay a labyrinth of uncertainty.

Lord Karrenen's gaze held a searching depth as he ventured deeper into the heart of the matter. His question was not mere words but a litmus test of Ong's trustworthiness, a gauge of his character. Could Ong prove himself worthy of the sacred trust required to be entrusted with the well-guarded secret of E'vahona? Before their dialogue could advance further, this pivotal query dangled in the balance, awaiting Ong's response.

In the sacred enclave of the forest, Ong met Lord Karrenen's question with the solemnity it deserved. His eyes locked onto Lord Karrenen's, and within their depths gleamed the earnestness of his intentions.

"Lord Karrenen," Ong began, his voice imbued with a weight that mirrored the moment's gravity. "I understand the profound importance of the trust one must earn to access E'vahona. It extends beyond mere words; it encompasses the essence of one's character and convictions."

His declaration unfolded like an intricate tapestry, each word woven with sincerity and purpose. "My purpose stands twofold. Firstly, I seek the knowledge and power hidden within E'vahona to bolster our ongoing battle against the encroaching darkness that threatens our world. I believe the unique connection the Eladrin hold to the light and ancient magic can shine as a beacon of hope in these trying times."

Ong allowed a moment of quiet reflection before continuing. "Secondly, my aspiration extends to forging a profound alliance that transcends mere convenience and mutual gain. I yearn for a lasting bond between our peoples, a union that will stand as a testament to our shared values and aspirations. I am fully aware of the significance of the trust I seek, and I solemnly pledge to uphold it with unwavering dedication and unwavering respect."

His unwavering gaze held steady, a reflection of his relentless determination. Ong stood before Lord Karrenen, aware that the path ahead remained obscured by shadows, but he remained steadfast in his resolve to tread it, no matter the challenges that lay in wait.

Lord Karrenen acknowledged Ong's responses with a dignified nod. "Your answers, Ong Swifthammer, display both wisdom and steadfastness. Yet, before we proceed, I must pose one more pivotal question: Can you solemnly pledge to safeguard our secrets—the sacred bond that tethers us to our concealed realm, preserving them untarnished and inviolate? These secrets encompass the most intimate knowledge of our people, history, magic, and the essence of our existence. Will you bear this burden with unwavering dedication, even in the face of profound temptation or dire circumstances?"

Ong's gaze remained unwavering as he met Lord Karrenen's eyes, his determination as unshakable as the mountains themselves. "Lord Karrenen, I comprehend the profound weight of the secret you entrust to me. I swear upon my honor and the lives of those dearest to me that I shall safeguard the location of E'vahona with the utmost diligence. I shall unveil it solely to those who have earned your trust and the trust of your people.

My commitment to preserving the sanctity of your hidden realm is unwavering, even in the most trying of circumstances."

His solemn oath hung in the air, binding his fate to the enigmatic destiny before him.

Lord Karrenen regarded Ong with a measured gaze, his silver eyes piercing into the depths of Ong's sincerity. After a contemplative pause, he nodded, conveying approval and cautious optimism. "Very well, Ong Swifthammer. Your words bear the weight of authenticity, and I sense your profound commitment to our shared cause. Now, let us direct our attention to the final two rules."

The intensity in Lord Karrenen's gaze remained unwavering as he continued, his voice solemn and probing. "Now, Ong Swifthammer, I must pose a question that delves into the deeply personal, yet it is a matter of utmost significance to us. What, in your heart, is the true nature of your relationship with Keisha? How would you define the bond that ties you, and what significance does she hold in the tapestry of your life and heart?"

Ong Swifthammer met Lord Karrenen's penetrating gaze with unwavering sincerity that radiated from his very being. He responded earnestly, his words imbued with the depth of his feelings. "Lord Karrenen, Keisha is more to me than words can encapsulate. She is the guiding star that lights my path in this dark and tumultuous world, my steadfast anchor when the storms of life threaten to overwhelm me. She is not just a companion; she is the solace of my heart, its protector, and its enduring love. Keisha carries a radiant light that has illuminated my life in ways I never dared to dream of. Her presence fills my days with purpose and meaning. I pledge to protect her with the entirety of my strength and to stand firmly by her side through all trials. She is a dear friend, my heart, partner, and life's cherished love."

His words hung in the air like a solemn vow, binding his fate to the unfolding destiny before them.

Lord Karrenen's unwavering gaze remained fixed upon Ong Swifthammer, his silver eyes like twin beacons of scrutiny, delving into the essence of Ong's character and steadfast devotion.

Then came the weighty, final question, delivered with a solemnity that echoed through the serene forest clearing, an inquiry that cut to the core of loyalty and resolve.

"If Keisha were to fall into the clutches of our adversaries," Lord Karrenen's voice resonated like a haunting refrain, "and they were to propose her release on the condition that you reveal the secret location of E'vahona, how would you respond?"

Like a poised sword, the question hung in the air, a test of trust but the unbreakable bond Ong shared with Keisha and his unyielding commitment to safeguarding E'vahona.

Ong Swifthammer's unwavering gaze met Lord Karrenen's as he contemplated this ultimate, most arduous question. A profound solemnity settled over him as he carefully crafted his response.

"In the gravest of circumstances," Ong began, his voice steady and relentless, "where Keisha's very life hangs in the balance, and the price demanded is the revelation of E'vahona's location, I would bear the burden of that choice with a heavy heart. Yet, I would remain steadfast in my commitment to shield our hidden realm. I would reject the demand, fully aware of the potentially dire consequences. However, I would tirelessly seek alternative avenues to secure Keisha's freedom, exploring every conceivable path that does not compromise the safety of E'vahona. Within my heart, I would yearn for a resolution that spares her life and our secret's sanctity. Nevertheless, I fully grasp the solemnity of the oath I aspire to uphold and the sacrifices it may demand."

As Ong concluded his response, he bore the weight of the unspoken sacrifices that might loom on the horizon, his devotion to Keisha and the preservation of E'vahona unwavering in the face of the most agonizing choice.

With the weight of Lord Karrenen's scrutinizing gaze finally lifted, Ong Swifthammer felt a profound sense of accomplishment and relief wash over him. His measured responses had secured the trust he so ardently sought, and in this pivotal moment, he comprehended the immense significance of his achievement.

Lord Karrenen, his silver eyes gleaming with approval, nodded solemnly, acknowledging Ong's unwavering sincerity. "You have passed, Ong Swifthammer."

With that definitive pronouncement, Lord Karrenen extended a beckoning hand to Keisha, who approached with cautious anticipation. The Eladrin lord directed his attention to her directly, his gaze bearing the weight of centuries of wisdom and discernment. "I have heard all that he has spoken and believe in his words. Ong Swifthammer is granted entry into E'vahona."

A swell of excitement and anticipation coursed through Ong's being as they prepared to follow Lord Karrenen deeper into the hidden realm. Keisha, her hand firmly grasping Ong's, followed closely behind the Eladrin lord. Their path led them through a captivating grove adorned with vibrant, otherworldly flora, each step carrying them further into the heart of enchantment.

Ong moved with deliberate steps, his trust in Lord Karrenen unwavering as they navigated a labyrinthine maze. The twists and turns seemed like a dance of destiny, guiding them toward an unknown revelation.

Their journey eventually brought them to the precipice of a breathtaking waterfall, where cascading waters shimmered like liquid silver. Lord Karrenen, an aura of serene authority enveloping him, approached the rocky edge. With a simple touch, the magical barrier dissipated, unveiling the hidden realm of E'vahona, a place of ancient secrets and untold wonders.

Stepping into the hidden realm of E'vahona, Ong and Keisha were engulfed by an overwhelming sense of wonder. It was a world where magic flowed like an ever-present river, and mysteries waited in the shadows, concealed from the prying eyes of the outside world.

As Keisha, a proud guardian of this mystical realm, led Ong deeper into E'vahona, his heart swelled with a profound sense of awe. The ethereal beauty enveloped them was a living tapestry of vibrant colors and shimmering enchantments. The air itself seemed to dance with the subtle melodies of arcane energies.

Turning to Ong, Keisha's eyes gleamed with affection and a deep sense of belonging. "Welcome to my home, Ong, and now, yours as well."

In those words, Ong felt a surge of warmth and connection. This hidden realm wasn't merely a place; it was a fragment of Keisha's heart, a precious gift she willingly shared.

Guided by Keisha, they ventured through the verdant gardens of E'vahona, winding their way through a fragrant maze of exotic blooms. With each step, they delved further into the heart of this enchanting realm, where secrets lay waiting to be unveiled. Their journey led them to a tranquil and intimate clearing, where the ambiance exuded tranquility.

Nestled within this idyllic setting stood a charming, modest house. Keisha spoke with a touch of apology in her voice, "I apologize for its size, Ong. It was my solitary abode, but now, it's our sanctuary. We can seek another dwelling if you prefer."

However, Ong was enchanted not by the dwelling size but by the love and care radiating from every corner. He looked at Keisha with genuine warmth, realizing that perfection was not defined by grandeur but by the bonds that thrived within. With a heartfelt smile, he replied, "It's more than perfect, Keisha. I would be honored to share this space with you."

Keisha gracefully guided Ong through the enchanting abode, where the air carried a gentle scent of lavender and sweet herbal fragrances. The walls were adorned with tapestries that depicted scenes of vibrant forests and glistening waterfalls, each stroke of the artist's brush capturing ethereal beauty. It was a dwelling that bore a quaint charm, and within its walls, the heart of the house pulsed with life, echoing the very soul of its inhabitant.

As they strolled through this magical retreat, Ong's gaze was irresistibly drawn to an array of crystals, their varied hues glinting with an otherworldly radiance. Purple amethysts dangled like dewdrops, their multifaceted surfaces refracting the faintest beams of light and casting a mesmerizing, almost supernatural glow upon the room. Each crystal seemed to whisper secrets of ancient magic, tales of Eladrin wisdom, and the unbreakable bond between the realm and its cherished inhabitants.

In the tranquil heart of this hidden sanctuary, Keisha led Ong to a charming garden, a verdant oasis within E'vahona. Lush foliage and vibrant flowers coexisted in harmonious splendor, their colors an awe-inspiring palette that defied imagination. A flash of bounding orange caught the eye among the blossoms and leaves, a furry form filled with playful exuberance.

Pumpkin, Keisha's ever-faithful feline companion, chased after imaginary prey with wild abandon, a whimsical spectacle that brought a heartwarming smile to Ong's lips. The garden was not merely a collection of plants but a realm of tranquility and wonder, a testament to Keisha's innate connection to the natural world.

As Ong marveled at his surroundings, Keisha's words brought him back to the present moment. She mentioned Lord Karrenen's impending visit, a reminder of the responsibilities and the profound journey ahead. The thought of meeting the Eladrin council and the other residents of E'vahona filled him with a sense of anticipation and reverence. It was an exploration into an unfamiliar yet enticing world, and Ong couldn't help but feel a profound warmth and belonging within the embrace of this charming abode. It was a world he eagerly embraced, ready to become an integral part of its enchanting tapestry.

Chapter 18

E'vahona's Secrets: Delving into Goldmoor's Knowledge

In the heart of Goldmoor, within the majestic confines of the library, Phoenix Shadowwalker embarked on a journey through aisles brimming with tomes of timeless wisdom. The very atmosphere weighed heavy with the fragrant embrace of centuries-old parchment, and the soft rustle of pages turning reverberated through the chamber like a sacred melody, a chorus celebrating forgotten truths. The library stood as a sacred sanctuary of history and concealed mysteries, its towering shelves ascending like an obelisk to the unquenchable thirst for enlightenment.

Qellaun and his sister, Lyra, lingered in the embrace of the ancient scrolls and leather-bound volumes, their visages etched with unwavering resolve as they combed through the chronicles of ages past in pursuit of elusive revelations. The flickering candlelight cast shadows stretching into eternity upon the shelves, where countless sagas, fables, and myths lay dormant, waiting to be awakened.

Their quest had become an unyielding odyssey, a relentless pursuit of untangling the enigma that shrouded E'vahona and its enigmatic inhabitants, the Eladrin. Text after text, scroll upon scroll, they plunged headlong into the annals of time, tracing the winding path of knowledge that might lead them to the legendary hidden realm. Yet, their toil had, thus far, yielded naught but fragments of enigmatic wisdom, tantalizing crumbs of lore that pirouetted at the very edge of comprehension.

The texts wove tales of E'vahona as a realm enshrouded in mystique, its existence veiled within the murky mists of time. Accounts, silvery with the weight of centuries, merely whispered of its presence, yet none dared breach the impenetrable fortress of its secrecy. The Eladrin, appointed as the vigilant sentinels of this enigmatic realm, bore the sacred mantle entrusted to them by the Goddess of Light. It was an unyielding covenant, a divine pledge etched into the very essence of their being – the solemn duty to safeguard E'vahona from the relentless encroachments of darkness.

In the dimly illuminated confines of the Goldmoor library, Phoenix Shadowwalker's inquiry lingered like a haunting echo. His voice, laden with intrigue, pierced through the somber silence that enshrouded the chamber. Cloaked in an aura of insatiable ambition, his very presence bore witness to an insatiable hunger for the enigmas of E'vahona. This hidden realm tantalizingly danced just beyond their grasp.

Qellaun and Lyra, their countenances bathed in the soft, wavering radiance of flickering candles, regarded him with the fatigue of indefatigable seekers. Their relentless pursuit of knowledge had yielded naught but meager fragments of enigmatic lore, akin to breadcrumbs leading them ever deeper into the winding labyrinth of E'vahona's mysteries. The ancient scrolls and time-worn tomes bore inscriptions that whispered of a realm beyond compare—a timeless font of magic where the very tapestry of reality intermingled with the potent strands of arcane might.

In the hallowed sanctuary of knowledge, Lyra's voice, a mere whisper, responded with a measured wariness. "Phoenix, we have unearthed precious little, but we have glimpsed the singular nature of E'vahona. It is rumored to be a wellspring of primordial magic, where the warp and weft of existence entwine with the pulsating threads of arcane prowess. A confluence of energies, a nexus of inscrutable and potent forces."

Phoenix absorbed her words with an avaricious spark in his eyes. The allure of boundless power, an untapped reservoir of magic that could reshape the course of his destiny, beckoned him from the distant veil of E'vahona. It was a temptation nearly impossible to resist, an obsession that seized hold of his heart and soul.

"If I could stake my claim upon E'vahona," Phoenix mused, his voice echoing through the cavernous corridors of the library, "the realm itself would prostrate before me, and my dominion would know no limits. Press on in your pursuit. Each scroll, each parchment, every word may be a fragment of the puzzle, a key to unlocking the portal to that coveted realm."

As Qellaun and Lyra continued their pursuit of knowledge within the library's dimly lit chambers, their quest for answers seemed to grow more complex and enigmatic with each passing moment. The flickering candlelight cast long, twisted shadows that danced upon the pages of ancient tomes, as if teasing them with the hidden truths they sought.

"I wonder," Lyra began, her voice a reverent murmur that reverberated amidst the ancient manuscripts and the musty aroma of erudition, "if our library in Fel Thalor might yield further insights. Given the centuries-old animosity between the Druchii and the Eladrin, it might prove prudent for us to explore our archives there. The question remains whether Phoenix would consent to our journey."

Qellaun, his knowledgeable expression bathed in the soft, ethereal radiance of candlelight, met Lyra's gaze with an expression mirroring the profound contemplation of their shared intellect. Her proposition bore the weight of wisdom, for Fel Thalor, their ancestral stronghold, safeguarded secrets and enigmas woven into the fabric of history itself.

It was a place steeped in the ancient enmity between the Eladrin and the Druchii, a repository of wisdom where the threads of the past wove intricate tales of power and peril. Qellaun nodded sagely, his eyes reflecting the faint shimmer of arcane symbols etched into the library's time-worn stones. "You may be onto something, Lyra. Our library in Fel Thalor may harbor darker truths concealed beneath layers of silence due to the longstanding feud between our peoples. As for Phoenix, his consent to our expedition is conceivable, but his insatiable thirst for knowledge knows no bounds. I would not be surprised if he chooses to accompany us, seeking updates at every twist and turn of our quest."

With a shared determination, they resolved to approach Phoenix, their enigmatic and ambitious ruler, and discuss the possibility of relocating their quest to the heart of Druchii territory—Fel Thalor, where the echoes of history whispered secrets long cloaked in shadow. The pursuit of

E'vahona's mysteries continued, their path fraught with uncertainty and intrigue.

As Kelru advanced toward the heart of Goldmoor, the city's grandeur and complexity seemed to loom larger with each step. The twilight painted a somber backdrop to his journey, and the unease in the air was palpable, a reflection of the ominous circumstances that had befallen the kingdom. His resolve, however, remained unwavering.

Before the imposing royal palace, with its intricate architecture and stately presence, Kelru paused for a moment to gather his thoughts. He knew the encounter awaiting him inside those regal halls was profoundly significant for himself and the entire kingdom.

With each stride he took toward the palace's entrance, Kelru carried the weight of responsibility and the unanswered questions that had led him to this moment. His determination to confront Phoenix and seek answers for the kingdom's plight burned like a beacon in the encroaching darkness.

The massive and ornate palace doors stood as a threshold to the unknown, symbolizing the challenges and uncertainties ahead. Kelru steeled himself, ready to face the enigmatic ruler and demand accountability for the troubling events in Goldmoor. His resolve remained unyielding, a testament to his loyalty and duty to his kingdom and its people.

In the opulent chambers of the palace, where grandeur and power intermingled, Kelru's presence and submission to Phoenix were but a fleeting moment in the chronicles of the ruler's dominion. The throne, an emblem of Phoenix's authority, loomed above like an immovable sentinel, casting a shadow upon the very essence of the kingdom.

Kelru's graceful and deliberate bow was a testament to his reverence for the ruler of Goldmoor. Yet, despite his outward display of respect, an underlying tension lingered in the air, like the calm before a storm.

Sitting upon the throne like an enigmatic sorcerer, Phoenix exuded an aura of menacing authority. His obsidian eyes bore into Kelru's soul, as if seeking to extract the truth from the depths of his being. In that gaze, there was an unspoken demand for answers, an expectation of success that weighed heavily upon Kelru's shoulders.

As Kelru began recounting the mission's outcome, his voice quivered, and his words hung like a fragile thread. His failure bore down upon him, and he struggled to find the right words to convey the dire news. His apprehension was evident, and he could feel the growing impatience in Phoenix's gaze.

Phoenix's swift and merciless reprimand cut through Kelru's faltering words like a blade. The ruler's wrath, infused with evil magic, hung like a storm ready to break. Kelru's plea for mercy was ignored as the ruler's dark power ignited, instantly sealing his fate.

In the wake of Kelru's untimely demise, the palace bore witness to the cruelty of Phoenix's reign. The attendant, a mere witness to the ruler's wrath, was tasked with erasing all traces of failure, leaving behind only the echoes of a swift and unforgiving punishment.

Within the opulent chambers of the palace, the cycle of power and consequence continued as a testament to the unforgiving nature of the ruler who held dominion over Goldmoor.

In the shadowy and foreboding presence of Phoenix, the mastermind behind the kingdom's dark machinations, Qellaun and Lyra, the Druchii siblings, stepped into the palace's ominous chamber. The throne symbolized power and treachery and beckoned them closer to the heart of Phoenix's nefarious plans.

Within this palace, where arcane energy crackled in the air, Phoenix Shadowwalker occupied his onyx throne, a twisted symbol of his sinister ambitions. His eyes, like smoldering embers, burned with the thirst for dominion, casting an oppressive aura over the once-peaceful realm of Vacari.

Qellaun and Lyra, bearers of Druchii lineage and centuries of accumulated knowledge stood before the enigmatic ruler. Their expressions reflected their unwavering determination, their purpose resonating within the chamber—a quest to unearth the mysteries that had long eluded them.

With a subtle gesture, Phoenix invited them to state their purpose. Qellaun, his voice like velvety darkness, answered the unspoken question, hinting at their true intentions beneath the guise of scholarly curiosity.

Lyra, radiant in intellect, echoed the proposal, framing it as a request to return to Fel Thalor and delve into their library. The undercurrent of tension hung in the air as they presented their plea, seeking permission to explore the depths of their ancestral knowledge.

In the weighted silence that followed, Phoenix considered the implications of their request. Finally, he spoke, his words heavy with ominous agreement, granting their wish to be prepared within the hour with a foreboding command.

As the siblings left the oppressive atmosphere of the throne room, Lyra leaned close to her brother, her words a barely audible whisper, "Your intuition served us well. He will accompany us." In a realm where trust was as elusive as a fleeting wisp of smoke, their forthcoming journey to Fel Thalor would unveil secrets that had the potential to shift the balance of power, all under the watchful eye of their evil master.

Fel Thalor, the ancient stronghold of the Druchii, loomed ominously on the horizon, a testament to the enduring dominance of shadow and arcane within its ebon walls. Shrouded in the perpetual night, its towering spires stood as imposing sentinels guarding the secrets concealed within. Here, Phoenix Shadowwalker, the harbinger of discord, returned to the heart of his province.

As they tread upon the cold, stone streets of Fel Thalor, the high priestess extended her welcome, her reverence tinged with dread. Like a whispered chant to forbidden deities, her voice acknowledged the darkness that had taken root within this realm. Phoenix, an enigmatic figure not of their kind but reigning supreme over the Druchii, responded with a solemn nod, his chilling gaze casting an eerie crimson luminescence that seemed to draw strength from the shadows.

Guided by the high priestess, they went through dimly lit corridors until they arrived at the city's ominous heart—the library. Within its expansive chamber, the essence of arcane wisdom hung like an oppressive shroud. Countless scrolls and ancient tomes graced towering shelves containing enigmas and illicit knowledge. Phoenix, a human from the distant Flameford and mastermind of evil forces, led Qellaun and Lyra deeper into this abyss of forgotten lore.

With a single command, he urged them to begin their work, their mission set to unveil the enigmatic truths of the Eladrin, the cryptic E'vahona, and the revered Goddess of Light herself. As the siblings immersed themselves in the scrolls, their surroundings faded into the periphery of history, while Phoenix turned and resolved to explore the city.

The streets of Fel Thalor, where darkness clung tenaciously to the very stones, resonated with his muted footsteps. Here, he traversed the dominion of the unyielding will of the Druchii, a race steeped in the shadowed depths of their desires. Yet, dormant secrets would stir beneath the facade of unrelenting cruelty, awaiting resurrection in the relentless pursuit of ultimate power.

Chapter 19

Unveiling the Past: In the Halls of Knowledge

In E'vahona, the enchanting forest realm of the Eladrin, the first rays of morning light transformed the lofty treetops into a canvas adorned with radiant gold and amber hues. It was as if the heavens had dipped their brushes in sunlight, painting the world above in celestial splendor. Towering edifices, seemingly woven from the very essence of nature itself, graced the cityscape. These majestic structures, hewn from living wood, swayed in gentle unison with the rustling leaves, their leafy canopies melding seamlessly into the opulent verdure of their surroundings.

Throughout the city, magnificent waterfalls cascaded with ethereal grace, their crystalline waters gleaming like liquid gemstones beneath the early sun's tender caress. As the morning light danced upon the cascades, they seemed to shimmer with magical enchantment, their every drop a glistening jewel in the forest's crown. Elaborate gardens, meticulously cultivated and nurtured, infused bursts of vivid color and luxuriant foliage into the lush tapestry of E'vahona. Here, flowers of a thousand hues swayed in harmony with the gentle breeze, and the sweet fragrance of blossoms perfumed the air, creating an intoxicating sensory symphony.

It would come as no surprise to witness animal companions like Pumpkin, the sleek black panther, or even wolves wandering amidst these gardens. The animals moved elegantly, their fur and feathers blending seamlessly with the vibrant flora. Amidst the foliage, they played and frolicked, adding a touch of wild enchantment to this carefully curated paradise.

Residences, equally breathtaking in their design, were fashioned from a harmonious fusion of crystals and nature's bounty. They stood above the forest floor, interconnected by intricate walkways and graceful staircases that spiraled skyward. These homes seemed like crystalline sanctuaries, their facades reflecting the hues of the forest canopy and their windows framing views that were nothing short of divine. From these lofty vantage points, the panorama unfolded, bestowing breathtaking vistas that stretched for miles, unveiling the pristine beauty of the cherished realm of the Eladrin.

In the heart of E'vahona, Ong was utterly entranced by the ethereal splendor enveloping him. As Keisha guided him through this majestic Eladrin forest realm, the morning sun imbued the treetops with a palette of gold and amber. Towering arboreal edifices, artfully crafted from living wood, entwined harmoniously with the natural world, their leafy crowns merging seamlessly with the surrounding foliage.

However, what indeed left Ong breathless was the visionary architecture that elevated these homes above the forest floor. Stairways resembling glistening glass meandered gracefully between the branches of colossal trees, uniting the abodes in a magnificent design choreography. Each step was a journey through an arboreal wonderland, and as Ong ascended, he couldn't help but feel like he was climbing a staircase to the heavens themselves. From these elevated perches, one could partake in vistas of unparalleled grandeur, unfolding across the horizon for endless miles, revealing the awe-inspiring panorama of E'vahona's unspoiled environments. It was a world where nature and artistry danced in perfect harmony, a realm of enchantment that defied imagination.

Yet, it was not solely the breathtaking aesthetics that held Ong captive. As he meandered through the city, his senses were trapped by the presence of companions, akin to Keisha's cherished Panther, Pumpkin, and an array of other creatures, wandering freely through the lush gardens and cobblestone streets. The symbiosis between the Eladrin and the natural realm was an exquisite spectacle. Panthers, wolves, and myriad other creatures moved with a grace that seemed an intrinsic part of the city's daily existence. Each creature was a living testament to the harmonious coexistence of civilization and wildness, a living embodiment of the realm's delicate balance.

Ong's profound admiration for this wondrous place surfaced as he turned to Keisha, his voice tinged with reverence. "I can discern why this realm remains concealed," he reflected, his eyes gleaming with adoration. "It would be a grievous travesty to witness the despoilment of this sanctuary, where beauty and serenity intertwine." His words were like a solemn vow, a pledge to protect and preserve the sanctity of this magical realm.

Touched by his sentiments, Keisha bestowed a warm smile and leaned in, her lips meeting his in a kiss that conveyed affection and profound understanding. It was a kiss that spoke of their reverence for E'vahona and their bond amidst its enchanting beauty. However, their reverie was gently interrupted by the arrival of Lord Karrenen, who approached them with due respect. His presence reminded them that matters required their attention even in this paradise, and the intricate tapestry of E'vahona held many secrets yet to be unveiled.

Offering apologies for the intrusion, Lord Karrenen elucidated the purpose of his visit and extended an invitation to Ong. The time had come for the warrior to partake in his inaugural meeting with the council, an event they sought to conduct in seclusion. It was an honor that Ong had not anticipated but was eager to embrace, for he understood the significance of this moment within the heart of E'vahona.

As Ong exchanged a meaningful glance with Keisha, her silent support served as an unspoken assurance. He consented to Lord Karrenen's entreaty with newfound determination and anticipation for the chapter that awaited him within the hallowed council chambers. Ong followed the Eladrin leader with resolute steps, ready to embark on a fresh odyssey in his journey within E'vahona.

As Ong and Lord Karrenen traversed the path leading to the council chambers, the Eladrin denizens of E'vahona acknowledged them with respectful nods. Each nod was a silent affirmation of the council's decision, and Ong felt a growing sense of acceptance among these mystical beings. Lord Karrenen, in particular, engaged in brief conversations with his fellow

Eladrin, frequently uttering a phrase in their melodious tongue: "Lotesse i' anar 'shine' ilyamenie no' lle."

Intrigued by the unfamiliar words, Ong couldn't resist inquiring about their significance. Lord Karrenen's eyes shimmered with warmth as he imparted the translation, "May the sun shine always upon you." A simple and profound sentiment resonated with Ong, underscoring his sense of camaraderie and unity with the Eladrin. It was a blessing that transcended language, a wish for eternal light and warmth.

Grateful for this insight into their culture, Ong conveyed his appreciation with a nod to Lord Karrenen. Their pilgrimage continued until they reached the grand entrance to the council chamber, where Lord Karrenen gestured for Ong to enter, signifying the commencement of the warrior's meaningful encounter with the Eladrin council.

The massive doors to the council chamber swung open with deliberate majesty, unveiling the sacred realm within. As Ong and Lord Karrenen crossed the threshold, they were met by three additional Eladrin, their ethereal grace evident in every fluid gesture. These Eladrin were the custodians of the council's inner sanctum, and their presence lent an air of solemnity to the proceedings. Lord Karrenen, with a regal flourish, ushered Ong into the chamber, a gesture that marked the initiation of the human warrior into the inner sanctum of the Eladrin council. It was a moment of great significance, where the realms of two worlds converged, and Ong stood on the precipice of a destiny entwined with the fate of E'vahona.

Taking his designated place at the table, Lord Karrenen cleared his throat, a sound that seemed to resonate with authority and sagacity, commanding the attention of all present. The room fell into a reverent hush as his voice, akin to a haunting melody interwoven with the very fabric of the room, began the introduction.

"Esteemed members of the council," Lord Karrenen began, his words carrying the weight of centuries of wisdom, "it is with the utmost honor that I present to you Ong Swifthammer, a brave warrior from the human realm. He has undertaken a perilous journey to E'vahona to pursue an alliance with our kind." The gravity of Lord Karrenen's introduction emphasized the significance of this moment, where the fates of two worlds hung in the balance.

With the introduction concluded, Ong stood before the council, his posture resolute, awaiting their judgment and the opportunity to articulate his purpose and intentions. The council chamber, bathed in the soft glow of ethereal light, seemed to hold its breath in anticipation.

Lord Karrenen, an embodiment of otherworldly wisdom and power, introduced the council members seated around the table, each distinguished by their unique attributes and virtues. "Allow me to present to you," Lord Karrenen commenced, his words reverberating with commanding authority, "Lady Elowen, a paragon of diplomatic finesse, whose skills in negotiation know no equal, and Lord Galadon, a dauntless guardian of our people, celebrated for his unyielding valor." Each council member exuded an aura of extraordinary grace and purpose, their presence a testament to the nobility of the Eladrin.

As Ong acknowledged each council member with a respectful nod, Lord Galadon took up the mantle of speech. His voice, a resounding manifestation of unassailable strength, permeated the chamber like the harmonious notes of a sacred hymn. "It is evident, as you stand within E'vahona's embrace, that you have successfully fulfilled the initial requisites outlined by our council." His words were both an acknowledgment of Ong's journey and a recognition of his determination.

In unison with Lord Galadon's sentiment, Lord Karrenen inclined his head, his luminous gaze unwavering as it remained trained upon Ong, an expression of solemnity etched into his ageless countenance. Turning his attention to the human warrior, Lord Karrenen requested that Ong reaffirm the oath he had previously sworn. The ancient traditions of E'vahona demanded this solemn commitment, a covenant forged in the presence of the Eladrin council, serving as a testament to Ong's unwavering dedication to allying with their illustrious kind.

Within the august presence of the Eladrin council, amidst the tranquil grandeur of E'vahona, Ong Swifthammer's voice, charged with unyielding resolve, echoed through the chamber as he reaffirmed his solemn vow. The room seemed to absorb his words, carrying them like a sacred chant that resonated with the very heart of the realm.

"In the face of such dire circumstances," Ong commenced, his voice imbued with the gravity of his commitment, "where Keisha's life teeters on the precipice, and the price demanded is the revelation of E'vahona's sanctuary, I would shoulder the weight of that decision with profound sorrow. Yet, I would remain steadfast in safeguarding our concealed realm. I would firmly rebuff the request, fully aware of the consequences. Nevertheless, I would tirelessly explore every conceivable alternative to secure Keisha's freedom, diligently searching for paths that preserve her life and the secrecy of E'vahona. In my heart, I would nurture the fervent hope for a resolution that spares both, understanding the gravity of the oath I strive to uphold and the sacrifices it might entail."

A contemplative hush enveloped the chamber, the solemnity of Ong's words reverberating within the sacred space. The council members of the Eladrin regarded him with a blend of approval and scrutiny, their unyielding gazes probing the authenticity of his pledge. It was a moment that transcended mere words, a moment of profound commitment that echoed through the ages.

In this chamber, pregnant with anticipation, Ong Swifthammer stood before the venerable assembly of the Eladrin council. Lord Galadon's words, rich with a sense of finality, resounded like the harmonious strains of a celestial symphony.

"I have faith in your words," Lord Galadon commenced, his voice a comforting serenade, "In the depths of your eyes, I perceive the unwavering commitment behind your vow. Therefore, we welcome you, Ong, into E'vahona's embrace." His words were an affirmation of trust, a recognition of Ong's unwavering dedication to the sanctity of E'vahona.

A synchronized nod of concurrence rippled through the council members, acknowledging Ong's sincerity and his pledge's resoluteness. Lord Karrenen leaned forward, his countenance expectant, as if awaiting the next chapter in the unfolding saga of Ong Swifthammer's journey within E'vahona.

"Now, Ong, speak freely," Lord Karrenen implored, his gaze penetrating for insights. The council's focus shifted onto Ong, eager for the revelations that would shape the destiny of their alliance. The room seemed to hold its breath, the weight of Ong's words about to ripple through the sacred chamber.

In the heart of E'vahona, enveloped by the mystical splendor of the Eladrin's forest realm, Ong Swifthammer embarked on the retelling of Vacari's tragic tale. His voice, laden with the weight of his words, held the undivided attention of the gathered council, their eyes fixed intently upon him.

"In the grand city of Goldmoor," Ong commenced, his voice resounding like the echoes of age-old prophecies, "ruled by King Alex and Queen Jeanne, a shadow of darkness has descended. Phoenix Shadowwalker, a formidable warlock, has laid siege to their citadel, ensnaring the sovereigns within the abyssal depths of a shrouded dungeon." His words were like the somber notes of a lament, painting a vivid picture of despair and tyranny.

His words painted a vivid portrait of the dire situation, the essence of power that Phoenix brandished akin to a double-edged sword. "Phoenix, driven by an insatiable thirst for dominion, seeks to conquer Goldmoor and cast it into the throes of chaos." A dangerous threat loomed over their realm, threatening to plunge it into darkness.

Ong continued each word, weaving an intricate thread into the tapestry of their shared history. "He has forged an unholy alliance with the Druchii, a malevolent pact that not only endangers Goldmoor but looms as a grave menace to the entirety of Vacari." The gravity of this alliance hung heavy in the air, a dark cloud that threatened to eclipse their world.

With the council's unwavering collective gaze upon him, Ong plunged deeper into the heart of the matter. "Phoenix's unquenchable thirst for knowledge has driven him to seek information about the enigmatic Eladrin and the hidden realm of E'vahona. He believes that these secrets hold the key to absolute power." His words resonated with urgency, a call to action that could not be ignored.

His voice resonated with the weight of concern as he surveyed the council, imploring them to grasp the gravity of the situation. "We must thwart his efforts to unite our peoples and safeguard our concealed sanctuary, E'vahona." It was a plea, a declaration of their shared destiny, and a vow to protect their realms at any cost.

Within that sacred chamber of the Eladrin, the fate of their realms teetered on the precipice, and Ong Swifthammer's words became a rallying cry, an emotional proclamation of their intertwined destiny. The council members exchanged solemn glances, fully aware of the magnitude of the threat that loomed over Vacari and their pivotal role in shaping its future.

Amidst the intricate deliberations, Ong's voice remained resolute, outlining the daunting landscape of their challenges. "Your determination is admirable, Lord Galadon," Ong replied earnestly. "However, we tread upon dangerous ground. The whereabouts of Queen Jeanne remain a mystery, and King Alex, bound by his love for her, refuses to act until she is found. Furthermore, Phoenix Shadowwalker's power has surged, rendering him a formidable adversary. Crystal Vale is actively searching the realm for Queen Jeanne, but we must proceed cautiously until we possess that vital information."

Lord Karrenen leaned forward, his silvery eyes locked onto Ong. "Tell us, Ong, what can you reveal about Phoenix? Do you know the origins of his power?"

Ong cast a wary glance at Lord Karrenen, his visage etched with deep concern. "Phoenix Shadowwalker hails from Flameford, a city starkly distinct from your enchanting E'vahona," he commenced. "He is human, wielding dark sorcery and nurturing ambitions that imperil our world. While his origins lie in Flameford, his alliances have ensnared the Druchii, making him a formidable presence within Vacari. His motives shroud themselves in darkness, but his thirst for power knows no bounds."

Lady Elowen's eyes widened with concern as Ong confirmed Phoenix's origin. "Did you say Flameford?" she inquired, her voice trembling.

Ong nodded solemnly, sensing the weight of the revelation. "Yes, Lady Elowen, Phoenix Shadowwalker is indeed from Flameford."

Her face paled, and she turned to the council members with a heavy sigh. "Do you remember the warlock that commanded the Druchii years ago, the one who came from Flameford?" she asked. "He sought the same information we guard about E'vahona, which cost Keisha's parents their lives. Was it not rumored that he had a son, a child whose dark ambitions were interrupted by Serena's heroic sacrifice? Could this Phoenix be that same child?"

Lord Karrenen's expression darkened with realization. "If that is so," he said, his voice low and measured, "this Phoenix is a formidable opponent.

We must ensure he never learns of Keisha's existence or the information she carries. His thirst for power may lead him to seek her out, and that is a threat we cannot afford to underestimate."

Ong's concern deepened as he disclosed the truth. "I must inform you that Phoenix does know about her. The Druchii pursued us relentlessly, driven by their insatiable hunger for her capture. But I swear by my honor and love for her that I will never allow them to lay a hand on Keisha."

Lord Karrenen nodded, acknowledging Ong's unwavering commitment to protect Keisha. "Very well, Ong. You should return to her side. We shall commence our investigations and gather information about this Phoenix. Rest assured. We will do everything in our power to ensure the safety of E'vahona."

Ong gave a grateful nod and took his leave. His heart filled with determination and concern for the safety of his beloved Keisha, knowing that the fate of E'vahona and Vacari hung in the balance.

In the dimly lit library of Fel Thalor, where the air was heavy with the scent of ancient tomes and the weight of forgotten knowledge, Qellaun and Lyra, the Druchii siblings, stood as stark contrasts to the shadowy surroundings. Their obsidian skin and silver hair set them apart as they meticulously scoured scrolls and dusty manuscripts. Their quest for elusive information about the enigmatic Eladrin, the secrets of E'vahona, the shrouded Goddess of Light, and the mysterious figures Eldric and Serena drove them to comb through cryptic texts like seekers of hidden truths in a world veiled in darkness.

Beyond the towering spires of Fel Thalor, the evil presence of Phoenix Shadowwalker prowled like a sinister specter confined to a cage. His echoing footsteps reverberated ominously through the gloomy streets, and the city's dark architecture seemed to mirror the contours of his sinister ambitions. With each stride, he absorbed the hostility in the air, his restless energy materializing as eerie, flickering shadows that danced around him, like loyal familiars attuned to his nefarious desires.

Within the cavernous confines of the library, Phoenix's presence loomed like a titanic force, a shadowy colossus cast by his evil intentions. His eyes, resembling twin orbs of malevolence, scanned the sprawling collection of scrolls and tomes with a ravenous hunger for knowledge rivaling avarice's greed.

Approaching the diligent Druchii, Lyra, and Qellaun, he inquired about their findings, his query laced with dark curiosity. Qellaun began to speak, his voice laced with trepidation, but Lyra seized the moment, her words resonating through the chamber like the whisper of an ancient enigma finally unveiled.

As Lyra unveiled the name of the elusive Goddess of Light, Kadona, the library seemed to hold its breath solemnly. Cloaked in myth and legend, her presence emerged as the guardian deity, a sentinel of the Eladrin, and the bestower of E'vahona, the hidden jewel of their realm. She was the embodiment of secrets buried deep within the tapestry of their world, a celestial muse whose name resonated with a profound sense of awe and wonder. At that moment, the essence of E'vahona and its mysteries hung in the balance as the Druchii siblings and Phoenix Shadowwalker delved deeper into the enigma of the Eladrin and their hidden realm.

Phoenix absorbed this revelation with a calculating nod, his mind a churning cauldron of dark designs. The newfound knowledge had ignited a fervent ember within him, becoming the nucleus of his insatiable hunger for power and dominion. Leaving the Druchii siblings to their esoteric research, he retreated into the bleak labyrinth of Fel Thalor's streets, where the weight of Kadona's name hung like a looming storm cloud, foreboding and pregnant with sinister intent.

In the dimly lit recesses of the library, Qellaun and Lyra found themselves trapped by the seductive allure of their curiosity, a potent defense against the encroaching abyss that threatened to engulf their world. As the echoes of Phoenix's footsteps dissolved into the enigmatic shadows of Fel Thalor, the siblings exchanged triumphant glances, their eyes sparking with the satisfaction of evading the wrath of their evil master.

Qellaun, once marked by trepidation, now wore an expression of quiet fulfillment, a testament to his sister's impeccable timing and profound connection. They shared the burden of their inquiry in hushed tones, wrestling with the enigmatic enigma of cryptic scrolls and concealed knowledge.

Like spectral denizens of twilight, the unspoken question lingered between them, a palpable reminder of their precarious existence. They were, after all, offspring of darkness, irrevocably bound in servitude to the infamous Phoenix. Yet, the revelation of the Goddess of Light's involvement with their Eladrin adversaries unsettled them.

As rare as it was mirthful, Lyra's laughter shattered the silence, a fragile beam of light piercing the oppressive shadows. Her words, tinged with bitter irony, acknowledged the twisted paradox of their predicament, where a deity of radiant glow had offered aid to their sworn foes. The hostility that infused her statement lingered like a malevolent steam, a stark reminder of the labyrinthine intricacies of fate that ensnared their every step.

Determined to unearth more secrets concealed within the labyrinthine tomes and scrolls that surrounded them, the Druchii siblings redirected their unwavering focus to the relentless pursuit of knowledge, their unbreakable bond a beacon of unity in a world teetering on the precipice of chaos.

In the heart of Fel Thalor's sprawling library, the enigmatic whispers of parchment and the dusty scent of aged tomes formed an ethereal cocoon around Qellaun and Lyra. Illuminated solely by the soft, eerie glow of sconces, the siblings remained ensconced in the eternal quest for enlightenment, delving into the realms of possibility and intrigue.

As they meticulously sifted through the myriad scrolls and manuscripts, a lingering question hung in the air, a query that seemed to resonate with the gravity of uncertainty: why had Keisha, an Eladrin, embarked on a journey alongside the formidable Swifthammer and entwined her fate with that of humans? The enigma of her presence in Goldmoor, her alliance with the human warrior, and her intricate ties to the Eladrin gnawed at their insatiable curiosity.

Lyra's response, delivered with a wry smile that betrayed the undercurrent of her intentions, hinted at a covert strategy. Keisha's secrets could become a weapon for the Druchii, a tactical advantage they could exploit in the obscure theater of shadowy conflict. The notion of capturing Keisha, leveraging her affections, and manipulating her vulnerabilities planted a treacherous seed that might bear the most bitter fruits in the dark realm of espionage.

Their conversation plunged even further into the dangerous abyss of their mission, where the flow of information resembled a treacherous river, its submerged currents concealed from view. Lyra's question, laden with curiosity and wariness, acknowledged the inherent dangers they navigated. In the intricate dance between the Eladrin and the Druchii, every step they took on the path of discovery harbored the potential for unforeseen repercussions.

Returning to their solemn task, they left the question like a tantalizing riddle. This puzzle would continue to mold their actions and decisions in the relentless pursuit of knowledge and power.

Lyra's tireless exploration bore fruit in the dimly lit chambers of Fel Thalor's library, where the wisdom of ages lay shrouded within the recesses of ancient tomes. A fragment of parchment, weathered by time and imprinted with the fingerprints of countless scholars, had unveiled a shard of the cryptic puzzle that was E'vahona. Her excitement radiated through the shadows as she awaited Phoenix's approach, her discovery poised to tip the power scales.

As Phoenix advanced toward her, an aura of quiet menace enveloped him like a cloak of darkness. He personified unrelenting ambition, and the information Lyra held was a potential key to unlocking the darkest of his desires. Her voice quivered with anticipation as she presented her findings to the warlock, aware that the seeds of intrigue and dominion lay within this parchment.

Phoenix, the consummate master of manipulation, inquired about the elusive whereabouts of E'vahona, his yearning to conquer it etched upon his countenance. With a sigh of reluctant admission, Lyra confessed the absence of that vital detail. Yet, her words held profound significance that piqued Phoenix's interest, a thread of knowledge that could unravel the secrets of the hidden realm.

The revelation was simultaneously enthralling and vexing: E'vahona, the hallowed Eladrin realm, transcended mere concealment; it was a place of profound divine connection. The Goddess of Light cast her benevolent gaze upon it, imbuing it with an arcane resonance that defied mortal understanding. Within the realm's enigmatic confines lay sanctuaries where the boundaries between gods and magic intermingled, weaving a tapestry of power that beckoned with untold potential.

The air in Fel Thalor's library hung heavy with the scent of ancient tomes and the weight of unattainable knowledge. Qellaun and Lyra, the Druchii siblings, labored diligently amidst the cryptic scrolls and manuscripts, their quest to uncover the secrets of E'vahona and the Eladrin shrouded in darkness.

As they delved into their research, the question of Keisha's involvement with humans and her ties to the Eladrin gnawed at their curiosity. Lyra's wry smile hinted at a potentially treacherous strategy to use Keisha's secrets as a weapon against their enemies.

The Druchii siblings were well aware of the dangers inherent in their mission, where every step they took in the intricate dance between the Eladrin and the Druchii had the potential for unforeseen repercussions. Still, they pressed on, leaving the question of Keisha's role as an enigma to ponder.

Lyra's tireless exploration yielded a fragment of knowledge about E'vahona, and Phoenix's ominous presence added urgency to their quest. The warlock's unrelenting ambition and desire for power were palpable as he sought the key to E'vahona. Lyra's revelation about the realm's connection to the Goddess of Light ignited Phoenix's determination to uncover its secrets.

With Phoenix's command, the siblings continued their research, knowing that the location of E'vahona would not be found within the fragile pages of dusty tomes. The library safeguarded secrets too profound to be disclosed by mere ink, and the path to E'vahona's heart was fraught with peril and sacrifice.

As they grappled with their frustration and resentment towards the Eladrin, the siblings pressed forward, driven by their unquenchable thirst for knowledge and the understanding that the key to E'vahona's secrets lay concealed in the shadows, waiting to be unearthed.

Chapter 20

The Eladrin Joins the Alliance

The grand assembly in the heart of the Emeraldwoods exuded a sense of solemnity and hope as dignitaries and representatives from various Eladrin realms gathered beneath the lush canopy of ancient trees. Lord Karrenen and Lady Elowen, the Eladrin's foremost ambassadors, commanded a regal presence, embodying the gravity of the occasion.

King Manard of Crystal Vale led his delegation, known for his wisdom and impartiality. His chosen council member, an emissary of the elven nobility, symbolized sagacity and balance.

The absence of Alaric and Gareth, the representatives from besieged Goldmoor, was a cause for concern, casting a shadow over the assembly. The safety of their city and its leaders hung as an unspoken question in the minds of those gathered.

Amidst this assembly, Ong and Keisha stood together, their love as unbreakable as the ancient roots of the towering trees surrounding them. Pumpkin, their feline companion, moved among them with the grace of a guardian spirit, watching the proceedings.

The grand stone table amid the lush Emeraldwoods was adorned with crystal chalices, wines infused with elven enchantment, and exquisitely crafted pastries. This lavish spread symbolized goodwill and unity in the face of uncertainty as representatives from various Eladrin realms and the hidden realm gathered for negotiations.

Alaric and Gareth, the emissaries of Goldmoor, arrived with a sense of urgency, their apologies sincere and their commitment unwavering. They expressed their regrets for their tardiness and their determination to contribute to the negotiations.

At the head of the table stood King Manard, a figure of wisdom and diplomacy, radiating warmth and authority. He initiated the proceedings with gratitude for the gathered representatives and emphasized their common purpose – confronting the looming threat of Phoenix Shadowwalker.

"As allies bound by a common purpose," King Manard continued, "we must address the shadow of Phoenix Shadowwalker and his evil designs on Vacari. Our unity is our strength, and together, we shall forge a path towards a brighter future for our realm. But before we delve into the details of our alliance, let us first share the latest developments and information from our respective cities and realms. Knowledge is the foundation upon which our decisions shall be built."

King Manard's sweeping gesture encompassed the eclectic assembly, uniting Eladrin, Goldmoor, and Crystal Vale delegates beneath a verdant canopy of ancient trees. Shafts of dappled sunlight filtered through the emerald leaves, casting a mesmerizing dance of light and shadow upon the gathered dignitaries. The lush, vibrant foliage of the Emeraldwoods served as a breathtaking backdrop to their solemn gathering.

"Our lands witness events that necessitate collaboration, empathy, and unity," King Manard proclaimed, his voice carrying like a gentle breeze through the forest. His words resonated with the harmony of nature itself, the very essence of the forest responding to his call. "The looming specter of Phoenix Shadowwalker casts its menacing shadow, and it is our collective duty to shield our people and the cherished values we hold."

As King Manard spoke, the ancient trees seemed to sway in agreement, their leaves rustling softly in the breeze. The assembly, bathed in the ethereal play of light and shadow, listened with rapt attention. Each pair of eyes met the king's gaze with a solemn acknowledgment of the gravity of their alliance.

"Today, our discussions transcend the mere signing of documents," King Manard continued, his words a tapestry woven with threads of hope and determination. "They are a solemn pact—a bond founded on trust, camaraderie, and a shared destiny that will endure the forthcoming trials.

Together, we shall craft a future where the radiant unity of our purpose dispels the oppressive darkness of tyranny."

As he concluded his eloquent overture, King Manard's eyes shimmered with expectation, like the glistening dewdrops that adorned the leaves above. The forest seemed to hold its breath, awaiting the responses and contributions that would shape the destiny of Vacari amidst the ancient, towering trees.

Gareth, a stalwart representative of Goldmoor, strode forward with unwavering purpose, his every step echoing with the weight of his kingdom's plight. His bearing exuded regal authority, and his oratory possessed a rare blend of conviction and eloquence that held the assembly in thrall.

"Ladies and gentlemen, esteemed envoys of Crystal Vale, and the revered Eladrin," Gareth began, his voice like a resounding hymn of unity in dire times, "I extend my profound gratitude for this crucial confluence." His words carried the resonance of ancient chants that invoked solidarity in the face of adversity.

"Within the borders of Goldmoor," he continued, his voice unwavering, "we have endured the relentless siege, an evil storm conjured by the sinister warlock known as Phoenix Shadowwalker. This unrelenting siege has trapped us in a dire predicament, leaving our grasp on the well-being of our beloved monarchs, King Alex, and Queen Jeanne, at the mercy of Phoenix's caprice."

Gareth's voice transformed into a clarion call to action, its urgency mirroring the kingdom that teetered on the brink. "Let us fully grasp the weight of our circumstances; time slips away like leaves in the autumn wind, and the lives of our allies, friends, and sovereigns dangle precariously in the balance. We must not entertain hesitance or uncertainty."

His unwavering gaze mirrored the resolute resolve coursing through his words. "At this very moment, we find ourselves at the crossroads of destiny. With unwavering determination, we must forge a bedrock of trust and cooperation. It is upon this bedrock that we shall unearth the elusive truth, shatter the siege that enshrouds Goldmoor, and dismantle the nefarious designs of Phoenix Shadowwalker."

Gareth's words reverberated through the assembly, each syllable an urgent summons for unity and unwavering action in the face of the formidable tribulations they shared.

Lady Elowen, the embodiment of diplomacy and sagacity within the Eladrin delegation, glided forward with an aura of venerable wisdom that transcended the boundaries of time itself. Her presence seemed to evoke the whispers of centuries past, and as she approached the assembly, her voice resonated like a haunting melody of history's echo.

"Ladies and gentlemen, revered emissaries hailing from the cities of Crystal Vale and Goldmoor," Lady Elowen began, her voice a melodic river winding through the annals of time, "we, the Eladrin, stand in profound reverence for the inclusion in these pivotal negotiations." Her words carried the weight of countless ages, rich with the wisdom that had weathered the centuries. "Throughout the eons, we have chosen the mantle of seclusion, nestled within the hidden realm of E'vahona, zealously safeguarding our mysteries and the sanctity of our way of life. Yet, the tides of destiny have ushered forth an era where our solitude can no longer persist."

A momentary pause followed, her words etching themselves into the minds of those who listened, like ancient runes waiting to be deciphered. "In this hallowed gathering, where alliances are forged in the crucible of necessity and shared interests, we proffer our willing cooperation," she continued, her gaze unwavering as she emphasized E'vahona's secrecy. "Yet, let the immutable truth be acknowledged—E'vahona, our sanctum, must remain cloaked, even from the eyes gathered here."

Lady Elowen's ethereal gaze traversed the assembly, her eyes meeting each delegate's with an unspoken resonance reverberating through the depths of the soul. "With unwavering resolve, we pledge our allegiance to this alliance. Tirelessly, we shall labor to unshackle Goldmoor from its dire straits and thwart the nefarious designs of Phoenix Shadowwalker. United in purpose, we shall surmount the tribulations that assail us, safeguarding the well-being and prosperity of our cherished realms."

Her words found resonance in the hearts of those present, creating a symphony of understanding and reverence, a testament to the delicate harmony between cooperation and the preservation of the most closely guarded secrets.

King Manard's presence, a beacon of authority and regal grace, filled the chamber as he stepped into the forefront of the assembly. Deep and commanding, his voice resonated like the sonorous chime of a sacred bell, captivating the undivided attention of all those present.

"In gratitude, Lady Elowen, for your wisdom and grace," King Manard intoned, a subtle bow signifying his understanding of the Eladrin's concerns. "We stand acutely aware of the gravity carried by the shroud of E'vahona's secrecy and the exquisite balance it necessitates. Be assured, we not only grasp the imperative of shielding your realm's existence from prying eyes but hold it as holy as the most sacred relics."

Turning his gaze toward Ong and Keisha, who stood as the living embodiment of unity and harmony, King Manard's expression transformed into profound admiration. "Indeed, we gather in this influential assembly through the unwavering courage and tireless endeavors of our cherished friends, Ong and Keisha. Their indomitable spirit in the face of adversity has kindled a fire of unity within our realm—a fire that burns brighter than any we could have envisioned."

The monarch's gaze returned to Lady Elowen, his eyes conveying deep empathy and understanding. "The alliance we aspire to forge rests upon trust, empathy, and unwavering support. In this sacred gathering, we endeavor to safeguard the essence of Vacari and extend the hand of friendship and solidarity to our new and longstanding allies. We revere the secrecy of E'vahona and the Eladrin's cherished way of life."

Taking a moment of reflective silence, King Manard allowed his words to resonate in the hearts and minds of those in attendance, letting the weight of their shared purpose sink in. "Together, we shall confront adversity with the courage that defines our collective spirit. We shall secure the future of Vacari, and through the strength of our unity, we shall illuminate a path toward a brighter dawn for all."

His words hung in the air like the echo of a resounding promise, a testament to the gravity of the moment and the shared destiny that now bound them all.

Alaric, a representative of Goldmoor, emerged from the sea of silent contemplation like a beacon of curiosity and genuine concern. His demeanor was one of humble inquiry, a seeker of clarity amidst the veils of uncertainty.

In measured tones, he began to voice his thoughts, his words akin to a thread of genuine curiosity, "The sentiments conveyed in this hallowed assembly are deeply appreciated, yet my heart harbors a question, one that I suspect reverberates within the hearts of many gathered here today. It is not merely the immediate liberation of Goldmoor and the rescue of our revered monarchs that stir my concern, but the enduring strength of this newfound alliance."

His query, like a lantern in the darkness, illuminated the chamber with its earnestness. Alaric asked, "How do we forge bonds that transcend the confines of crisis? What actions can we take to cement this alliance, to ensure that it stands unwavering against the tests of time? I believe that understanding our collective dreams and aspirations for the future is as pivotal as addressing the challenges that confront us in the present."

With those words, a contemplative hush swept over the room as the assembly grappled with the gravity of Alaric's inquiry. Like a distant horizon, the future of their alliance beckoned with uncertainty, and Alaric's voice had raised the compass of their shared aspirations.

Lord Karrenen, known for his sagacity and measured eloquence, stepped into the unfolding dialogue. His words were like the wisdom of ages, spoken with a resonance that compelled attention.

"Lord Alaric has posed a question that resonates deeply within our shared contemplation," he acknowledged, his gaze briefly connecting with Alaric's, a silent affirmation of their shared intent. "While our immediate actions are essential to overcome our current challenges, we must also turn our gaze to the horizon of our aspirations."

His gaze encompassed the representatives from each realm, acknowledging their distinct contributions. "In this alliance, trust, friendship, and unwavering support are the bedrock upon which we stand. Yet, to fortify our unity beyond the immediate, we must recognize and embrace each city or realm's unique strengths and attributes to our collective cause."

With those words, Lord Karrenen summoned the assembly to explore the richness of their shared destiny, unveiling a path that would lead them through the present darkness and into a brighter, enduring future.

Amid the forest, Lord Karrenen's commanding presence seemed to echo like a spell, the power of his words a tapestry woven from the threads of destiny itself. As he paused, a hushed reverence fell upon those in attendance, the weight of his words settling like a majestic cloak upon their shoulders.

"From the hidden sanctum of E'vahona," he began, his voice a melodic chant, "we offer not mere magic but a sanctum of unparalleled, arcane potency. E'vahona, a realm enshrouded in the ethereal glow of the Eladrin, beckons us with the promise of secrets and enchantments that can bolster the sinews of our combined strength."

His gaze, like a shimmering beacon, then turned to Goldmoor, the jewel of the alliance. "Goldmoor, under the wise leadership of King Alex and Queen Jeanne, stands as a bastion of unyielding resilience and unwavering determination. Your city's indomitable spirit, a flame that burns brighter in the face of adversity, is a radiant source of inspiration for us all."

But the lord's gaze did not linger; his words were like the wind, touching upon each representative present. Turning to the envoys from Crystal Vale, his voice became a soothing, harmonious melody. "In King Manard's realm, Crystal Vale, unity and coexistence with nature are not mere words but a living testament. Your city, a harmonious symphony with the land, possesses a connection so profound that it beckons the very spirits of the forest. Like ancient treasures, your resources shall prove invaluable in our quest."

As Lord Karrenen concluded his oration, his words became a resounding declaration, echoing through the forest and etching itself into the hearts of those assembled. "Together, we stand as a formidable force, forged from the crucible of two distinct cities and a realm cloaked in mystery. Our unity, a binding spell that transcends time, shall guide us through the treacherous waters of today's trials and illuminate the path to a future where our strength knows no bounds."

In the heart of the ancient Emeraldwoods Forest, King Manard, a figure of majestic poise, cast his discerning gaze upon the assembly, his eyes finding Alaric, the harbinger of the unspoken challenge that now hung in the air like a blade unsheathed. With a measured grace, he adjusted the regal drapery of his attire, a mantle of authority befitting his station, and cleared his throat. These resonant tones followed, bearing the weight of both monarchy and responsibility.

"As Alaric so astutely raises," King Manard began, his voice a sonorous decree, "the veritable crucible of this alliance lies not in the temporary brilliance of words or the fleeting oaths we utter but in the crucible of time itself. It is simple to extol promises when the moment's enthusiasm burns hot; however, it is an altogether sterner trial to uphold them when adversity casts its ominous shadow upon our path."

He then permitted a pregnant silence to envelop the assembly, allowing his words to linger like the first snowfall of winter, settling upon the hearts and minds of those who listened. "What we seek here," he intoned, "is not a temporary coalition but an enduring union, one wrought in the fires of trust, kindred purpose, and the irrefutable alchemy of mutual respect. This alliance must transcend the immediate storm in Goldmoor, becoming a radiant lighthouse of hope and an unbreakable bond that shall endure even in the darkest hours."

King Manard continued With gravitas akin to an old sage, "I contend that true alliance cannot be encapsulated solely within written parchment or the labyrinthine corridors of diplomacy. It is born from the connections we painstakingly forge, the friendships we tend as cherished gardens, and the steadfast support we proffer one another."

He shifted his regal gaze from Alaric to Lady Elowen and then to Gareth, a silent testament to his envisioned unity. "In the fullness of time, it will be our deeds, not our words, that resonate like the tolling of a bell, defining the indomitable strength of this alliance. The bonds of trust we now sow shall serve as the mighty roots from which our collective strength will draw sustenance. May we not only find solace in each other's shelter when the storm rages but also revel in shared jubilation and prosperity when the sun graces our realm."

With an affirming nod, King Manard concluded, his voice a decree cast in unyielding stone, "Thus, while I cannot presume to predict the vagaries of the future, I can solemnly pledge that Crystal Vale stands poised to honor every commitment to bolster our allies in their darkest hour, and to toil with unwavering devotion toward the triumph of this alliance. Let our actions be the crucible in which the mettle of our unity is forged, and in so doing, may we secure a luminous tomorrow for all our realms."

His words hung in the air like profound magic, and in that sacred moment, the very fabric of Vacari seemed to respond. It was as if the Emeraldwoods themselves whispered their approval, their leaves rustling with ancient wisdom. The flames of unity ignited in the hearts of those assembled, and in that shared resolve, the alliance of Vacari was not merely sealed; it was transmuted into a bond of unbreakable strength.

The alliance of Vacari was no longer a promise; it was a living, breathing force, an entity born of shared purpose and fortified by their collective determination. Together, they would face whatever trials the future held with unshakable unity. In Emeraldwoods, Vacari stood as one at this moment, a testament to the enduring power of trust, friendship, and the indomitable spirit of alliance.

Chapter 21

Veiled Alliances: A Hushed Gathering

Amidst the enchanting backdrop of the twilight-draped Emeraldwoods, Ong's gaze, like a flickering ember, found Keisha, who responded with a luminous smile, a beacon of warmth amid the gathering shadows. She nodded in silent accord, a silent prelude to the momentous revelation that hung heavy in the air. Ong, his heart stubborn, extended his hand, drawing her closer until their souls seemed to merge in a dance of cosmic significance.

In the heart of this ancient forest, where the canopy of emerald leaves filtered the fading light into a tapestry of dappled shadows and ethereal hues, the scene unfolded like a trance. The gentle rustling of leaves and the distant song of forest creatures lent a magical serenade to the profound moment about to be unveiled.

"We had harbored intentions of withholding this revelation, awaiting the liberation of Goldmoor from its shackles," Ong began, his voice resonating with a quiet, dignified strength. The words emanated from him like a melody woven into the very fabric of the forest's enchantment. "Yet, in the tapestry of destiny, we find threads interwoven with moments such as this. I believe today is the right juncture to unveil the proclamation that lies within our hearts."

His words, like a river of starlight, flowed forth, each syllable etching a vow in the minds of those who bore witness. As he spoke, the shadows seemed to dance to the cadence of his voice, weaving an intricate pattern of anticipation and wonder. "Our plans had always revolved around the moment Goldmoor would stand liberated, but as I stand before you, the shadows of uncertainty cast aside, I am compelled to decree that an engagement celebration is a shared jubilation we can all embrace."

The profound gravity of his following words settled upon the assembly like a resplendent celestial body descending from the heavens. It was as if the very trees held their breath in reverence. "Our engagement," he declared, "is a sacred bridge that spans the chasm between elves and humans. It is a pledge that love shall transcend the confines of our hearts and the boundaries of our realms."

With the undivided attention of all those present, Ong continued his voice with an unwavering cadence, a rhythm of unity. The forest seemed to listen intently, and the rustling leaves stilled by his words. "Today, I stand not only as a warrior from Crystal Vale but as a vessel of hope and understanding. Keisha and I believe with unwavering conviction that love, like the most potent elixirs, knows no bounds. It is our solemn duty to forge connections, to mend the fractures that may have marred our shared history, and to build bridges that shall unite Goldmoor, E'vahona, and Crystal Vale in a symphony of harmony."

In the ancient Emeraldwoods, the words spoken by Ong and Keisha seemed to resonate not only in the hearts of those present but also within the soul of Vacari itself, a testament to the power of love and unity to transcend all boundaries.

A profound hush enveloped the assembly as if the forest leaned in to listen. The ancient Oak Heart Tree, with its gnarled and wise branches, stood sentinel over this sacred gathering, casting a dappled pattern of twilight across the scene. Shafts of fading sunlight pierced the canopy of leaves, creating a mesmerizing interplay of light and shadow.

In this sacred moment beneath the ancient Oak Heart Tree, Ong and Keisha's commitment became more than just a union of hearts; it became an anthem of trust, a melody of unity that echoed through the hearts of allies and reverberated in the depths of Vacari's soul. The air seemed charged with the occasion's significance as if the forest itself had become a witness to history.

Ong's proclamation hung in the air like a shimmering mist, a revelation that demanded contemplation from all who had gathered. The idea of an engagement celebration, a harmonious union between a valiant human and a graceful elf, resonated profoundly in this confluence of three realms. It was a concept as ancient as the trees themselves, a symbol of unity that transcended the boundaries of race and realm.

Beside Ong, Keisha radiated an air of serenity, her demeanor a testament to her unwavering resolve. Her presence mirrored her agreement, a silent pledge to see this commitment through to its fruition. The potential for their union to serve as a living emblem of unity transcending the intricate webs of politics and diplomacy was a powerful concept. It was a tangible bond, wrought not in ink on parchment but in intertwining two hearts.

Lady Elowen, the Eladrin diplomat of E'vahona, acknowledged the potential inherent in Ong and Keisha's audacious proposal with a regal nod. Like pools of ancient wisdom, her eyes held a deep understanding that extended beyond the surface. King Manard, the steadfast emissary from Crystal Vale, and Gareth, the Goldmoor delegate of unwavering loyalty, exchanged thoughtful glances. In their contemplation, they weighed the implications of this unprecedented development.

The alliance evolved, transcending the ephemeral realm of words and agreements. It was now anchored in the personal commitment of two individuals, their love and dedication tangible as the ancient oaks that surrounded them. At this moment, the air seemed to breathe with the hope that this union would inspire others, igniting a chain reaction of interconnectedness and solidarity among their realms.

The Oak Heart Tree, the silent witness to their words and vows, seemed to stir as if acknowledging the profound significance of this moment. With its ancient wisdom, the forest stood as a living testament to the power of unity and the enduring bonds forged beneath its leafy canopy.

Gareth, once the voice of skepticism, offered a slight but genuine smile, a silent acknowledgment of the profound significance of this gesture. Once clouded with doubt, his eyes held a glimmer of hope, recognizing the transformative power of connection and devotion in nurturing bonds that would endure through the ages. Alaric, who had doubts about the alliance's endurance, felt the thawing of his reservations. In the glow of Ong and

Keisha's love, he recognized the transformative power of connection and devotion in nurturing bonds that would endure through the ages.

In the peaceful forest, where the weight of destiny hung heavy in the air, Lord Karrenen, the venerable Eladrin magic master, had maintained a contemplative silence as though drawing upon the boundless reservoirs of centuries-old wisdom that flowed within him. His voice emerged as a sonorous symphony of ancient truths when he finally chose to break that silence.

"We often discover," Lord Karrenen intoned, his voice like the soft murmur of a timeless river, "that the most potent elixir of unity and understanding flows from the wellspring of love. If, in the sacred bond of this union, we find the alchemy to bless and fortify this alliance, then it shall indeed stand unwavering against the relentless currents of time."

With these words, the assembly, united not by decree but by shared conviction, reached a tacit agreement. The impending celebration of Ong and Keisha's engagement would transcend mere merriment and signify their profound commitment, symbolizing the unity they aspired to cultivate among their realms. It was as if the threads of love and friendship had become the foundation upon which this alliance would be exquisitely woven.

King Manard, the regal representative of Crystal Vale, nodded in royal approval, his eyes alight with the kindling flame of enthusiasm. "A splendid and visionary plan, Ong," he commended, his voice resounding with the warm assurance of unity. "We shall eagerly await this joyous occasion and utilize the time to fortify the bonds that bind us even further. The sacred enclave of the Emeraldwoods Forest shall serve as the ethereal backdrop for the engagement ceremony, while the grand ballroom of Crystal Vale shall play host to the following feast. Together, we shall celebrate this engagement, a testament to the strength of our alliance. And as the chapters of time unfurl, we eagerly anticipate the day when Goldmoor stands free, and we may convene once more to witness the blossoming of your love into a union of unbreakable dedication."

The forest, a silent witness to their decisions, seemed to respond with a gentle rustle of leaves, as if offering its blessings to this momentous occasion. The air was charged with anticipation and the promise of a brighter future for Vacari, where unity, love, and unwavering friendship would guide them through the trials and tribulations.

Two days had elapsed since Ong and Keisha's announcement, and in that time, preparations for the engagement ceremony had been in full swing. The heart of Emeraldwoods Forest, where nature's wonders merged seamlessly with the enchantments of elven magic, had been transformed into a realm of ethereal beauty in honor of the upcoming celebration.

The night sky, a celestial vault painted with the luminescent strokes of countless stars, shimmered like a tapestry of dreams. The air was thick with the weighty wisps of fog that spewed forth from between the trees, an interlacing canopy that led to heaven. These astral sentinels cast their benevolent light upon the forest floor, bestowing a silvery luminescence upon the gathered assembly. Like elusive will-o'-the-wisps, mystical lanterns adorned the verdant branches and drifted here and there on currents of wind where they alighted and illuminated the proceedings.

As the assembly gathered beneath the towering trees, it was clear that these two days had been filled with meticulous planning and dedicated effort. Once an ordinary part of the landscape, the archway at the forest's threshold now stood as a magnificent portal adorned with ivy and resplendent blossoms, inviting all to step into enchantment.

Elven musicians had practiced tirelessly, their melodies now weaving a symphony that seemed to transcend the mortal realm. The mystical lanterns, carefully placed among the branches, cast a soft and otherworldly glow, creating an ambiance of wonder and reverence.

The scene was a breathtaking fusion of the natural and the mystical, where the boundaries between reality and fantasy blurred, and the forest seemed willing to participate in celebrating love and unity.

Keisha, a living embodiment of eldritch beauty, stood beneath the archway, an ethereal presence that seemed to transcend the mortal realm. Her gown, a masterpiece forged by the skilled hands of elven artisans, shimmered with a captivating palette of colors. Rich shades of green flowed through the fabric, adorned with a tapestry of intricate embroidery in hues of blue and gold. These delicate threads told silent stories of ancient sagas, woven into the very fabric of her attire.

Upon her crimson tresses rested a circlet of regal bearing. It was a masterpiece of pure silver, skillfully twisted into graceful vines that encased a bed of gemstones. These stones captured the essence of starlight itself, their iridescent glow a testament to their otherworldly origin. They nestled amidst the delicate filigree of the celestial crown, as if they had been plucked from the midnight gardens of an enchanted realm and placed upon her head with the utmost care.

Adorning her slender neck was a silver circlet necklace, a radiant symbol of Ong's affection. It formed a perfect circle, representing eternity, and upon it, heart-shaped gemstones of deepest purple were nestled with deliberate elegance. These hearts, aglow with the fiery passion of their love, were framed by intricate crystals that seemed to dance like scattered stardust. As Keisha moved, the sleeves of her gown cascaded like silken waterfalls, creating a mesmerizing flow that rendered her a living legend—a vision that could only belong to the most enchanting of elven tales.

Ong, a paragon of masculine elegance, stood tall and commanding in his finely tailored black suit. The fabric clung to his imposing frame, accentuating his chiseled contours. Along the lapels, golden buttons gleamed brightly, adding a regal touch to his attire. Intricate green embroidery traced its way along the seams, an artistic flourish that mirrored the richness of the Emeraldwoods. Draped over his shoulders, a royal blue cape cascaded down his back, a gift from Lord Karrenen himself, signifying the unity between their realms.

At his right hip, a gleaming sword glistened in its scabbard. Keisha bestowed this weapon on him, symbolizing their shared journey and unwavering commitment. Every element of Ong's attire spoke of his stature, self-assuredness, and inner strength, a fitting match for his enchanting betrothed.

As this momentous union unfolded, the envoys from the Eladrin and Crystal Vale realms bore witness, including the esteemed trio of Lord Karrenen, Lady Elowen, and King Manard. Their attire was a living embodiment of their realms' grace and grandeur, each garment reflecting the essence of the alliance they aimed to forge—a harmonious blend of diversity and unity.

Lord Karrenen and King Manard, the custodians of tradition and unity, delicately unfurled gossamer strands of golden ribbons with profound reverence. These ephemeral threads, like strands of destiny, were destined to bind the hands of Ong and Keisha, symbolizing the unity of realms and the profound love that had ignited between the two souls.

Ong's voice, infused with profound emotion, reverberated through the forest's ancient trees, his solemn vow to Keisha echoing like a sacred chant. His words transcended mere speech, promising to cherish and protect her through all the lifetimes yet to unfold. His pledge was woven with threads of unyielding devotion and enduring affection, a testament to the love that had blossomed in their hearts.

In response, Keisha's voice, radiant with the luminescence of love, flowed like a musical stream, delivering her vow with unwavering grace. Her words wove a tapestry of trust and unswerving dedication to Ong, a promise that their shared future would be illuminated by the radiant glow of their love and guided by the dreams they held in common.

With their vows exchanged and their hands gently bound by the golden ribbons, the world seemed to hold its breath, as if nature paused to witness this pivotal moment. Then, with shared grace, Lord Karrenen and King Manard delicately unfurled the ribbons, a symbolic act that marked the beginning of Ong and Keisha's journey together—a journey bathed in the radiant light of love, bound by the unbreakable ties of unity, and supported by the unwavering strength of their realms.

In the heart of the elven forest, where the ancient trees whispered secrets in the language of time, the venerable elven elders and leaders approached the radiant couple. With solemn grace, they invoked the profound wisdom and enchantment of the ancient forest, where the very roots of existence intertwined with the ethereal aura of Crystal Vale, their legendary city. Their words, spoken with a reverence that transcended mere speech, carried the weight of countless centuries. Each chant was a thread, binding Ong and Keisha's destiny to the luminous tapestry of their world, an eternal bond forged in the crucible of history.

As the glorious ceremony reached its zenith, Ong, the gallant hero, and Keisha, his ethereal betrothed, mounted their noble steed, Thunder, a loyal companion on their shared journey. Together, they embarked on a timeless voyage toward the realm of Crystal Vale, where the celestial vault above bore witness to their love—a love destined to be written among the stars.

A magnificent feast awaited in Crystal Vale, a veritable banquet of unity where representatives from all three realms converged. Here, beneath the open sky and the ancient trees' boughs, they celebrated the sacred bond of Ong and Keisha and the unbreakable ties that bound Goldmoor, Crystal Vale, and the Eladrin together. This engagement ceremony was more than a mere celebration of love; it was a symbol—a glorious emblem of unity between realms. It stood as a steadfast testament to their unwavering commitment, their shared quest to free Goldmoor from the shadowed clutches of Phoenix Shadowwalker, and their firm belief that love, trust, and unity would shine as beacons in the darkest times.

The grand ballroom of the Crystal Vale Palace had undergone a breathtaking metamorphosis, evolving into a realm of enchantment that defied the boundaries of imagination. A ceiling adorned with crystals of myriad hues hung like a celestial tapestry, capturing the essence of distant galaxies in their prismatic depths. These gems bestowed upon the room an otherworldly luminescence, casting enchanting reflections across the space as though inviting guests to dance upon the shimmering surface of dreams.

Elaborate flower arrangements, their petals like fragments of rainbows, adorned every corner of the ballroom. Their fragrances, a symphony of nature's sweetest offerings, mingled harmoniously with the enchanting aromas of the myriad candles that dotted the room. Lord Karrenen, master of magic, had woven his ethereal touch into the very fabric of the atmosphere. The result was an ambiance that whispered of romance and jubilation, an enchantment that seemed to emanate from the very heart of Vacari itself.

In one corner, a troupe of elven and human musicians, a harmonious embodiment of unity, played a symphony that seemed to transcend the bounds of reality. Handcrafted from the finest wood and adorned with glistening strings, their instruments conjured melodies that intertwined like the destinies of realms, symbolizing an unbreakable unity.

The tables, draped in elegant white linens, played host to a cavalcade of bouquets, each an exquisite testament to the splendor of nature. Crystal centerpieces, their facets catching the soft, enchanting light, glistened like fragments of starlight captured in earthly form. Guests, an amalgamation of elves and humans, mingled in harmonious conversation, their faces aglow with the radiant warmth of the enchanted candles that bathed the room in a soft, otherworldly light.

At the heart of this enchanting tableau stood a magnificent stage, a symbol of unity itself. Here, a grand feast awaited, a wealthy tapestry of delicacies that spanned the realms—from the ethereal delights of the elven table to the hearty fare of humanity. The tantalizing aromas, an olfactory symphony, wafted through the air, beckoning all with the irresistible promise of a sumptuous repast.

Their engagement ceremony unfurled as a tapestry woven with poetic declarations of love, casting a spell of enchantment that set the tone for a night brimming with joy and the radiant promise of a shared future.

Ong and Keisha, standing side by side, their hands entwined in a knot of unbreakable love, were poised to embark on the next chapter of their shared journey. The engagement ceremony forged an unshakable bond and united the realms they represented. This night, bathed in the radiant glow of celebration and love, heralded the promise of a brighter future that they would face hand in hand, hearts aflame with the magic of their love.

As the final notes of the engagement ceremony faded into the ether and the unity candle bathed the chamber in its radiant glow, the atmosphere within the palace ballroom seemed to shimmer with an ethereal warmth—an embodiment of love and unity that transcended mere words. In the hands of the assembled guests, crystal goblets, brimming with the most exquisite wines harvested from the vineyards of Crystal Vale, stood ready, poised for the toasts that would etch this moment into the annals of memory.

King Manard lifted his wine glass skyward, bearing himself with regal grace and a kind smile that spoke volumes. Glistening with paternal pride, his eyes found their anchor in Ong and Keisha, the embodiment of love's power to bridge divides and unite hearts.

"To Ong and Keisha," he declared, his voice a resonant blend of authority and genuine warmth, "May your love be as enduring as the ancient emerald woods, a testament to the boundless strength of unity. May your union, like a fertile seed planted in the soil of our shared destiny, bring forth prosperity that shall flourish throughout the realms."

The gathered guests, their hearts alight with the shared hope for a future intertwined with love and unity, echoed his sentiment with a hearty and resounding "To Ong and Keisha!" Their voices, harmonizing like a chorus of celebration, seemed to echo through the very veins of the palace, sealing this special occasion in a symphony of joy and promise.

The palace's cavernous hall was alive with the resonance of merriment, a symphony of clinking goblets and joyous laughter that danced among the guests like ephemeral spirits. The engagement feast was in full splendor, an opulent tableau of gastronomic delights and enchanting ambiance—an ode to love and unity that reverberated through the very bones of the palace. It was a vivid emblem of the radiant future that beckoned Ong, Keisha, and the triumvirate of realms they represented: Goldmoor, Crystal Vale, and the Eladrin.

Lady Elowen, the graceful envoy of the Eladrin, lent an air of elegance to the jubilant atmosphere of the engagement feast. Her presence, imbued with wisdom and diplomacy, had played a pivotal role in weaving the realms together, and her words now bore the weight of unity and harmony.

As Lady Elowen addressed the assembly, her eyes sparkled with a knowing smile, like a hidden wellspring of understanding. "In the spirit of unity and love that we commemorate this eve," she began, her voice as lyrical as a tranquil brook, "there exists among the humans a tradition—a tradition of profound beauty, I must aver. It is the custom for the betrothed couple to partake in their first dance, which symbolizes the inception of their journey as an engaged pair."

Her words found resonance among the assembly, and the collective gaze turned to Ong and Keisha. The couple, their hands entwined, and hearts synchronized, prepared to embark upon this inaugural step together. Ong led Keisha to the very nature of the grand ballroom, nestled in the gentle luminescence bestowed upon it by the enchanting decor of crystals and magical embellishments.

As elven and human melodies intertwined like two souls in love, Ong and Keisha moved as if guided by the unseen hands of destiny. Their dance was a symphony of hearts in harmony, a celestial dance where the boundaries of realms and races faded into insignificance. In this enchanted moment, they appeared as the solitary inhabitants of a world where nothing else existed, and their love shone brighter than the most glorious stars.

Their dance was a tribute to unity, a testament to the fusion of diverse realms, races, and cultures united under the unwavering banner of love. As they twirled and embraced, their smiles became radiant beacons, illuminating the room with the brilliance of their affection, as if the universe had conspired to shrink itself, leaving only the two of them in this transcendent moment.

One by one, the guests joined the dance; humans and elves, Eladrin, and Crystal Vale's elite came together to celebrate this remarkable union. The dance floor, now a tapestry of unity and camaraderie, bore witness to an alliance sealed not only in the crucible of politics but also in the sacred bonds of love, trust, and friendship.

Under the celestial canopy of the palace ballroom, Ong and Keisha's inaugural dance became an emblem of hope—a promise for a brighter future that would transcend the borders of three realms. The engagement feast surged forth with laughter, jubilation, and a profound sense of unity destined to buoy them through the adversities yet to come.

Karrenen, ever a presence of dignified authority, ascended once more, his mere fact commanding the attention of all in the chamber. The official declaration of the Eladrin council's decision to join the alliance was met with thunderous applause and fervent words of agreement, the collective spirit of unity growing in magnitude like a rising tide.

King Manard, the sagacious sovereign of Crystal Vale, also rose from his seat, his countenance reflecting profound conviction. "From this juncture onward," he declared, his voice resonating like the tolling of a resolute bell, "humans and Eladrin are not disparate entities but singular entities. While our customs and traditions may bear distinction, we shall forever stand as one, an unbreakable union in times of need, forging a bond that no adversity can sunder."

His words echoed among the assembly, fortifying the dedication to the alliance. The guests, attuned to the gravity of this moment, nodded in unison, fully aware that this union stood as a beacon of hope in the face of the encroaching darkness that had threatened their respective realms.

Ong and Keisha exchanged a final, meaningful glance as the engagement feast continued its joyous crescendo, then discreetly withdrew from the grand ballroom. The night had unfurled as a breathtaking celebration of love and unity, and now, they sought the serenity of their private moments to savor this extraordinary juncture in their lives.

The guests dispersed to their respective chambers, their hearts imbued with the radiant optimism of the morrow. They departed, knowing that the trials ahead would be met not as separate entities but as allies bound by the unbreakable cords of friendship and love.

Chapter 22

Espionage and Reconnaissance Missions

In the shrouded embrace of night's dark cloak, two elven silhouettes, resplendent in ebony robes that seamlessly melded with the obsidian tapestry of the forest, emerged on the outskirts of Goldmoor. Their presence was a whispered secret, their steps an ethereal dance, as if the earth trembled to reveal their passage.

The first elf, Seraphina, possessed eyes as profound as the abyss, mirroring the starless expanse above. Her movements were a spectral ballet choreographed by the whispers of the nocturnal zephyrs. A silver dagger, glimmering with an otherworldly luminescence, hung at her side, a sentinel of her deadly finesse.

Beside her, Thalorin was an enigma unto himself. His emerald orbs glinted with an inner conflagration, a defiance that mirrored the forest's unyielding resistance to the encroaching darkness. A subtle aura of magic clung to him, a communion with the hidden secrets of nature as he trod upon the earth.

United by their unwavering loyalty to Karrenen and the kingdom they hailed as their own, they embarked on their undercover mission. The heart of Goldmoor beckoned, heavy with the weight of tension and uncertainty. Mere whispers in the night, they delved into the fortress's core, determined to unearth the hidden truth.

Their quest? To ascertain if King Alex languished in the dungeon's abyss, as rumor's shadow had suggested—a silent beacon of resistance against the tyranny that had ensnared their land. The stakes soared to dangerous heights, and the specter of betrayal loomed large in the moonlit air as they pressed on, guided by the silvery radiance of the moon and driven by an unswerving sense of purpose.

Deeper into the heart of Goldmoor, Seraphina, and Thalorin advanced with a cautious, almost mathematical precision. The moonlight, a delicate sieve filtering through the dense canopy above, painted intricate, shifting patterns upon their ebon cloaks, trapping them in a mesmerizing ballet of light and shadow.

The city itself appeared to pulse with an uneasy vitality; faint echoes of revelry and stifled laughter whispered from the taverns and alleyways. Yet, beneath this facade of normalcy, an insidious tension coiled like a sleeping serpent. The Druchii's influence slithered through every stone and cobbled street, their malevolence whispered by the rocks beneath their feet.

As elusive as phantoms, the elven duo deftly evaded the vigilant patrols of Druchii soldiers and the piercing scrutiny of Phoenix, who ruled his dominion with the vigilance of a hawk perched high on its watchful branch. They navigated the labyrinthine alleyways and narrow side streets, always looking for the faintest glimmer of a clue that might unravel the secrets in the dungeon's depths.

Time flowed like liquid shadows, hours slipping away like fleeting specters, yet Goldmoor's enigmas remained securely locked. Undeterred by the challenges, they conversed in hushed, clandestine tones. Thalorin's whispered communion with the earth guided them through a treacherous maze, avoiding snares and barriers laid by their oppressors.

Every step into the city's heart, the atmosphere grew increasingly pregnant with trepidation. Each corner turned, each threshold crossed, seemed to teem with the potential for discovery. Nevertheless, Seraphina and Thalorin, steadfast in their mission, pressed forward, driven by an unyielding determination to locate King Alex and deliver a beacon of hope to a city overshadowed by the relentless pall of despair.

In the deepest, most shadowed recesses of Goldmoor's intricate labyrinth of streets, the fortune of Seraphina and Thalorin took a dangerous twist. In an alley that seemed to promise sanctuary, fate unveiled two Druchii sentinels who had strayed from their designated path.

These Druchii guards, consumed by their clandestine discourse, remained oblivious to the intruders in their midst. Seraphina and Thalorin exchanged a knowing glance, and in a balletic display of swiftness and silence, they closed the gap.

Thalorin led the dance of death, his blade an extension of his very will, finding its mark with a gleaming certainty in the heart of one of the guards. The Druchii's eyes widened in stark surprise as life's luminance drained from him, leaving him to crumple upon the cobblestone without uttering so much as a whisper.

Seraphina's movements mirrored the elegance of her companion, lethal in their grace. With a subtle twist of her wrist, a concealed dagger found its mark in the second guard's throat. His eyes bulged in silent agony as he clutched at his neck, futilely attempting to staunch the crimson vitality slipping through his trembling fingers.

Their actions were a seamless, macabre ballet. With swift and eerie grace, they concealed the lifeless bodies in a nearby shadowed alcove, where they would languish, hidden from the world, until the sun's golden embrace kissed the city awake. The scene unfolded like a morbid sonata, and as they stood over the concealed corpses, Seraphina and Thalorin shared a moment of somber satisfaction, recognizing that their silent victory had propelled them one stride closer to their elusive objective.

The overheard conversation led the elven duo to a clandestine gathering of Goldmoor's inhabitants, huddled in the cloak of obscurity. A grizzled man, his visage marred by a patchy beard, wove the tapestry of the dungeon's legend, narrating its infamy and the formidable guardian statues that barred entry. His words trembled with a potent mixture of fear and reverence, for none dared challenge the stoic stone sentinels to save for Phoenix himself.

Bolstered by newfound resolve, Seraphina and Thalorin ventured toward the location indicated by the informant. There, bathed in the dim luminescence of a flickering street lantern, they beheld the two colossal guardian statues. These grim sentinels, hewn from somber stone, depicted armored warriors whose eyes radiated with an eerie, otherworldly luminescence. Each colossal figure clutched a monumental sword, poised as if to mete out judgment upon any audacious trespassers.

Thalorin, the bolder of the pair, tentatively advanced. His outstretched hand hovered mere inches from the invisible barrier that separated them from the sentinel guardians. It was as if an invisible force held him at bay.

Seraphina joined her companion, her penetrating gaze scouring the statues for concealed mechanisms or cryptic clues. In the silence of their mutual understanding, they acknowledged the colossal challenge that loomed before them, which whispered promises of triumph and peril in the heart of Goldmoor's complicated puzzle.

In the hushed communion of their voices, Thalorin spoke with a timbre that carried the weight of uncertainty as though whispering secrets to the very stones themselves. "It appears we stand before a formidable magical ward, one meticulously woven by Phoenix's hand."

Seraphina, her dark eyes pools of determination, nodded in concurrence. "Indeed, but where magic casts its veil, the thread often exists to unravel it. Let us gaze upon these sentinel statues; within their stony visages may lie the key, concealed in plain sight."

Together, their fingers gently caressing the intricate carvings and runes etched into the stone, they embarked upon an intellectual dance fueled by the urgency of their mission. Their thoughts raced, their wills unyielding as they sought the elusive solution that would unlock the cryptic heart of Goldmoor.

As Seraphina and Thalorin delved into the contemplation of the guardian statues, a buried memory, a treasure trove of wisdom imparted by Lord Karrenen himself, stirred within Thalorin's mind—the mentor who had mastered the alchemy of magic and lore.

"Hold," Thalorin breathed, his voice scarcely louder than the leaves rustling in the night's breeze. "I recall Lord Karrenen's teachings, a recollection of statues akin to these. They serve not merely as sentinels, but as riddles, puzzles awaiting the embrace of intellect."

Seraphina shifted her gaze towards her companion, her eyes aglow with a spark of anticipation, like twin stars in the velvety tapestry of the night. "What manner of puzzle?"

Thalorin, momentarily closing his eyes in reflection, summoned his mentor's wisdom. "The statues harbor an enchantment, a sequence, a melody. Each step we tread becomes a note within that symphony. To unseal our path, we must mirror the sequence precisely, and in its echo, the statues shall yield."

Seraphina's brow knits with contemplation, her thoughts like elusive fireflies in the forest's depths. "A misstep could awaken a trap or summon the Druchii's wrath?"

Thalorin's solemnness affirmed her concern. "Precisely. We must be vigilant and discerning. Let us embark upon the deciphering of this elusive melody."

They dissected the statues meticulously, capturing their poses' subtleties, nuances, and grace. Slowly, like alchemists toiling over a volatile concoction, they assembled the sequence, note by note.

In the timeless continuum of their efforts, Thalorin advanced, replicating the symphony with flawless precision. A subdued growl resonated from the statues, followed by the mystical dissolution of an unseen barricade.

Seraphina's heart echoed with a tumultuous symphony of relief and trepidation. "You have unlocked the path, Thalorin."

He nodded, his gaze an unyielding sentinel fixed upon the now-accessible entrance. "Remember, dear Seraphina, this is the opening verse in a symphony of challenges. If Phoenix has expended such artful measures to safeguard his secrets, we must anticipate that more formidable trials lie ahead. Caution must be our closest companion, for we shall encounter the unknown."

With an unwavering resolve etching their countenances, Seraphina and Thalorin embarked on their maiden steps into the labyrinthine heart of Goldmoor's enigmatic dungeon, mindful that each heartbeat drew them nearer to the core of the riddle, where answers awaited their relentless pursuit.

As they navigated the treacherous second tier of the dungeon, Seraphina and Thalorin confronted an unforeseen adversary. Seraphina, advancing with a careful, feline grace, her watchful eyes sifting through the gloomy corridor's secrets, encountered an insidious betrayal by the ancient stones beneath her. Swift as a lightning bolt, Thalorin's agile reflexes jerked her from the precipice of an unfathomed abyss, sparing her from an inky descent into darkness.

Seraphina's heart hammered against the walls of her chest like a caged bird yearning for freedom. She gathered her shaken composure, the profound gratitude for Thalorin's swift intervention shining like stars in her eyes. "Thank you," she whispered, a tremulous elegy of relief and lingering astonishment.

Thalorin nodded, his vigilant gaze remaining ever fixated upon the treacherous floor. "We must proceed with a diligence befitting scholars of ancient texts," he counseled, his mental cogwheels churning for a viable solution. "For these cunning trapdoors may conceal themselves anywhere, and their activation would not only herald our presence to potential adversaries but might also become the harbinger of our undoing."

Together, they embarked on an intricate inspection of the floor, a meticulous quest to discern the subtle discrepancies or vestiges that might betray the presence of concealed trapdoors. Each step was a calculated maneuver, taken with a surgeon's precision, and they communicated in the silken whispers of conspirators, determined to surmount this newly arisen challenge and unveil the truth veiled by King Alex's enigmatic incarceration.

Upon ascending to the enigmatic third tier of the dungeon, Seraphina and Thalorin bore witness to a beguiling tableau. Their journey through the winding passageways led them past a mesmerizing tapestry of arcane runes intricately etched into the stone floor beneath their feet. In a brief crescendo of mystic energies, a solid stone barricade unfurled itself, accompanied by an ethereal hum that cast an eerie incandescence upon the inscribed symbols.

The two elven intruders, possessed of grace and poise, came to an abrupt halt, their eyes riveted to the newly formed barrier. It was an unmistakable sign that they had breached yet another layer of enigmatic defenses safeguarding this clandestine realm.

Thalorin's brow furrowed with the weight of contemplation as he parsed their intricate predicament. "These runes, undeniably, are the catalyst," he ruminated, his voice a flowing river of thought. "Our path lies in the deciphering of their purpose or the discovery of their counter."

Her breath a whisper on the threshold of these arcane wonders, Seraphina dared to approach the runes. Her nimble fingers hovered, trembling in the aura of the inscribed mysteries, unwilling to make direct contact. Her gaze, an alchemist's crucible of scrutiny, delved into the symbols, seeking the alchemical keys to unlock their true purpose. "There must be a way to circumvent their vigilance," she declared, a glint of resolute determination sparking in her eyes. "The teachings of Lord Karrenen have fortified us for trials such as these."

With minds as keen as the sharpest of elven blades and an intimate familiarity with the arcane arts, they embarked on the intellectual deconstruction of the runes, each chant, and sigil a cipher hiding the secrets of passage.

In the sacred chamber of their contemplation, Seraphina's memory ignited with a gleaming ember of wisdom bestowed by Lord Karrenen during their ardent training—a memory of a specific rune, the Rune of Concealment. With newfound assurance, she turned to Thalorin, her voice a fervent whisper that danced with the flame of revelation. "Thalorin, I recall," she confided, her eyes alive with the fire of realization. "A means to traverse these runes without rendering them inert exists—a Rune of Concealment."

Thalorin's eyes widened, the significance of her words resonating deeply within him. "Indeed! Lord Karrenen's teachings in the secrets of concealment. Let us employ it."

Seraphina retrieved a small, intricately wrought rune from her concealed pouch—a token of their shared training and preparation. With a profound reverence for their craft, they advanced and activated the Rune of Concealment. As they approached the runic barrier, an invisible shroud enfolded them, veiling their presence in shadows and granting them passage through the runes without awakening further arcane sentinels.

In seamless communion, they continued their descent into the labyrinthine depths of the dungeon, their passage now unimpeded by the arcane sentinels that had guarded its secrets. With every footfall, they drew nearer to their coveted objective, the elusive truth concealed within the shadowed annals of Goldmoor's enigmatic past.

As they ventured deeper into the dungeon's murky embrace, their mission's gravity clung to the air, a silent specter that weighed heavily upon them. Seraphina's voice, an echo of hope and apprehension, pierced the quiet that enveloped them.

"Thalorin," she began, her words laden with the gravitas of their quest, "with each layer of protection we've encountered, the likelihood of King Alex's presence here grows more palpable. Yet, we both know that 'likely' is a currency Lord Karrenen would not accept as proof."

Thalorin nodded, his visage etched with unyielding determination. "Your wisdom is undeniable, Seraphina. We must unearth irrefutable evidence. Let us forge onward in our pursuit."

Their footfalls reverberated softly through the dimly illuminated corridor, each step propelling them toward the elusive truth, a beacon of hope they yearned to kindle within their kingdom's heart. The enigmas of Goldmoor's subterranean labyrinth unfurled before them like a tome waiting to be unsealed, its secrets poised to divulge their truths.

Thalorin's gaze, an ardent explorer's beacon, traversed the intricate, winding passageway they had entered, and a sarcastic smile, subtle as a secret, graced the contours of his lips. He turned to Seraphina, an ember of amusement glinting in his eyes.

"Remember those lessons on mazes, Seraphina? I held a particular aversion to them, always feeling as though I'd wander through them for an eternity."

Seraphina's laughter, soft as the murmur of a hidden brook, danced through the corridor, her eyes twinkling with mirth. "Ah, Thalorin, you weren't alone in that sentiment. It appears that the tangled mysteries of our past once again confront us. Let us intertwine our thoughts, as in those lessons of the old days, to navigate this enigmatic puzzle."

With an unspoken pact of concurrence, they ventured into the winding labyrinth, their footfalls a symphony of echoes as they threaded their way through the convoluted passages. It was a crucible of intellect and cooperation, a gauntlet of their mettle they were determined to surmount in their relentless quest to unveil the elusive truths buried within Goldmoor's subterranean depths.

With its erratic twists and turns, the labyrinth tested their patience, casting them adrift in recursive contemplation as they retraced their steps thrice before finally deciphering the enigma of the correct path. Their triumph was a testament to their unwavering resolve and unyielding tenacity, a phoenix-like rise from the ashes of frustration.

A luminous sense of achievement bathed them in its radiance as they emerged victorious from the labyrinth's depths. Seraphina, her brow kissed by a glistening bead of sweat, exchanged a knowing glance with Thalorin. Together, they had conquered the labyrinthine riddles, embodying their shared resolve.

Thalorin's words hung in the air like a specter, dark and foreboding as they descended on the precipice of descending to the dungeon's lowest tier. "I shudder to contemplate the perils that await us below," he murmured, his voice a tapestry woven with equal parts anticipation and trepidation. The dungeon's unknown and malevolent denizens lay in ambush, and their arduous journey had merely scratched the surface.

The grotesque chimeras, ghastly and otherworldly, stood as sentinel guardians before the door, evoking shivers that coiled down Seraphina and Thalorin's spines. These eerie creations bore witness to Phoenix's twisted maneuverings, a testament to his deranged conception of security.

Seraphina's voice, a tranquil river amidst turbulent thoughts, graced the shadows with its wisdom. "Phoenix leaves naught to chance," she whispered. "How shall we breach their vigilance and gain ingress to the sanctum where the vital knowledge resides? We must explore every avenue."

Thalorin, his countenance creased with contemplation, hatched a plan to scatter the shadows of their impending challenge. "A diversion," he proposed sotto voce. "We require a spectacle to lure these chimeras away from their post, affording us the clandestine ingress we need."

Their gazes converged, a silent covenant of mutual understanding passing between them like a whispered secret. In the breathless interlude that followed, they recognized the precipice upon which they stood—a precipice that promised either triumphant ascent or a dangerous descent into the jaws of danger.

Thalorin's brave scheme bore the aura of daring, a gambit that Seraphina perceived as a beacon of potential success. With synchronized nods of accord, they orchestrated their plan to trap the chimeras' attention.

With resolute purpose, lighting their eyes, they emerged from the shadowy sanctuary, deliberately drawing the grotesque creatures into their focus. Thalorin, like a pied piper of the dark, led one of the chimeras in a whirlwind chase to the right, while Seraphina, embodying elven skill and grace, wove a tapestry of evasion in her flight to the left.

The chimeras, reacting with visceral menace to the sudden intrusion, pursued their respective prey with a terrible determination. Through a labyrinthine ballet, Seraphina and Thalorin, sculptors of their fate, employed their intimate knowledge of the terrain to elude the looming specters.

After a meticulously measured interval, they executed a flawlessly synchronized maneuver to outmaneuver their pursuers. Thalorin, like a phantom reclaimed by the shadows, melded into the inky abyss. Meanwhile, Seraphina invoked the art of concealment magic, her form vanishing from the chimeras' predatory gaze. Their ire seething, the grotesque guardians found themselves in a futile quest, hissing in frustration at the phantom specters that had eluded their grasp.

With the pathway to the door unburdened by malevolent sentinels, Seraphina and Thalorin ventured cautiously into the entrance, their footsteps hesitant as they crossed the threshold. They had achieved a hard-won victory in their battle of wits with the chimeras, yet the crucible of challenges ahead remained shrouded in an enigma, guarded by the unyielding hand of Phoenix.

Upon breaching the sanctum, their arrival did not escape the gaze of King Alex, and his initial response unfurled as a storm of emotions, an intricate tapestry woven from threads of fear and anger. Mistaking Seraphina and Thalorin for Druchii, his voice extended like a storm within the chamber, a tempest echoing with unbridled ire.

"Vile Druchii spawn! What evil machinations bring you here?" King Alex's voice resounded like a war horn, the repercussions of his rage engulfing the chamber in a tempestuous symphony.

Undaunted by the thunderous outburst, Seraphina shook her head with resolute authority, her demeanor a bastion of unwavering purpose. "Your Majesty," she proclaimed with a voice that commanded attention, "we are not of Druchii lineage. We are Eladrin, emissaries dispatched by Lord Karrenen. Our mission is twofold: to confirm your presence and to unveil the snares set by Phoenix, ensuring your swift rescue when the hour arrives."

Incredulity glistened in King Alex's eyes as he scrutinized their features more closely, the iridescent light of truth gradually penetrating the veil of his initial fury. His countenance, once a storm of anger, morphed into a mélange of hope and astonishment.

"You are Eladrin? Authentically so?" he stammered, his voice ringing with a newfound spark of hope.

Upon crossing the threshold into the chamber where King Alex languished, Seraphina and Thalorin's perceptive eyes alighted upon a chilling tableau. The stone floor beneath them, slick with the evil glint of water, sent shivers that cascaded like a spectral waterfall down their spines. King Alex, his visage etched with the weariness of captivity and the shadows of despair, urgently sounded a somber warning. "Mind your every step. Deadly serpents serenade the floors of this chamber, and lurking in these aqueous depths, a grotesque sea monstrosity awaits—an abyssal aberration that defies nature."

Within the dimly lit confines of the chamber, King Alex's words hung like a shroud, their weight bearing down upon the fragile equilibrium of the moment. The aura of foreboding in the room pressed upon them, and the mere contemplation of confronting serpentine threats and an abhorrent sea monstrosity sent an icy current rippling through their very souls. In this treacherous enclave, the specter of misstep loomed like a harbinger of doom, a single footfall potentially heralding their downfall.

With a profound gratitude that resonated in their hearts, Seraphina and Thalorin acknowledged King Alex's dire warning. In cautious unity, they closed the distance to where their sovereign was unjustly incarcerated. As they approached, their acute, elven senses discerned the subtle presence of a shimmering, arcane barrier that trapped him.

Thalorin, the precursor of insight, scrutinized the sinister purpose of this spectral wall. He leaned in close, his voice a velvet whisper that embraced Seraphina's ears. "To dispel this barrier would doubtlessly unshackle the serpents and awaken the abhorrent fiend. Prudence must be our guiding star; our every move a careful dance."

The ominous specter of potential catastrophe weighed upon them, their actions bound by the precarious balance of life and peril.

With a respectful bow to their imprisoned sovereign, Seraphina and Thalorin pledged their departure, their gaze an unspoken promise of the role his revelations would play in the imminent liberation of Goldmoor and his emancipation from Phoenix's clutches. King Alex, a beacon of gratitude amid adversity, implored them to tread the path of caution and prioritize the safety of Queen Jeanne.

Leaving King Alex to the confines of his aqueous prison, Seraphina and Thalorin retraced their steps through the labyrinthine maze, emerging once more into the concealed arteries beneath Goldmoor's heart. Their mission had yielded invaluable intelligence and unveiled but a fraction of the enigmatic trials awaiting them on the horizon.

In their wake, King Alex exhaled a sigh of relief, his heart wrapped in the belief that the Eladrin would be the beacon of hope for Goldmoor and his beloved Queen Jeanne. A mental vow emerged within him—a vow to personally extend his gratitude to Ong Swifthammer and Keisha, the architects of his salvation.

Under the shroud of nightfall, Elna and Rarum descended upon Flameford, and the city greeted them with a macabre embrace of eerie darkness. The architecture of this enigmatic realm stood in stark defiance of the human settlements they had known. Tall and imposing buildings assumed the role of somber sentinels, their presence tinged with an unsettling aura, accentuated by the foreboding palette of black and crimson that draped the cityscape.

Their first trial materialized in the form of the city gate, a formidable threshold lined with obsidian amulets that radiated unsettling energy—a collective whisper of warning from Flameford itself. It was as though the city, aware of its venom, resisted their intrusion, a spectral hand urging them to acknowledge the peril that thrived within its boundaries. Yet, in the face of this spectral resistance, Elna, her resplendent blonde locks framing eyes as blue as a summer sky, and Rarum, his earth-toned visage a mirror of unwavering determination, pressed forward.

Every step in this shadowed realm bore the weight of careful calculation, each footfall a ballet of subtlety. They understood that their clandestine foray into Flameford was a dance with danger. In hushed yet unwavering tones, they exchanged a conversation as much a pact as a strategy.

Elna, her voice a musical whisper, initiated the discourse. "The intelligence we've gathered thus far suggests that Flameford should be a desolate expanse due to Phoenix's relentless siege on Goldmoor. However, we must not underestimate the cunning of Phoenix. Druchii, by nature, are masters of deception. They may have left insidious surprises and traps in their wake. Caution must be our constant companion as we tread this treacherous path."

Rarum, the steadfast guardian by her side, nodded with resolute agreement. While the city appeared as a desolation of the forsaken, the specter of the Druchii's malevolence remained an ever-present shadow. Through the veiled alleys and shadowed lanes, they advanced with senses heightened, their mission unfurling in the chilling embrace of a city that refused to surrender its secrets willingly.

Elna and Rarum, like elusive specters navigating the labyrinthine streets of Flameford, had forged an unspoken agreement regarding their destination. The timbre of Elna's voice resonated with unwavering purpose as she voiced their path forward. "Our quest leads us to the palace," she intoned, her words like a clarion call in the gloom. "Within its hallowed halls, the legacy of Phoenix's father, a warlock who once ruled Flameford, may conceal the keys to our mission's success."

With shared resolve etched upon their countenances, they advanced, resolute in their intent to wrest the enigmatic truths from the very heart of Flameford's brooding citadel.

Elna's discerning gaze followed the trajectory of Rarum's stare, and her keen eyes were drawn to the towering edifice that loomed as a dark sentinel amidst the city's nocturnal tapestry. Its austere contours demanded attention, its silhouette cutting a stark contrast against the obsidian canvas of the night. She pondered for a fleeting moment, then turned to Rarum, her voice a thread of unwavering conviction in the hushed symphony of the night.

"That tower," she remarked, her words a barely audible but resolute declaration. "It exudes significance. If secrets of consequence exist within Flameford, that spire is the crucible wherein they are held. Let us proceed with measured caution, ascend its precipitous heights, and unravel the mysteries that may aid our struggle."

With a synchronic nod that bore witness to their shared accord, they embarked on their clandestine pilgrimage toward the ominous tower. Through the labyrinthine streets of Flameford, they moved with the stealth of phantoms, unwavering in their pursuit of knowledge to tip the scales in the looming battle against Phoenix.

An ominous undercurrent permeated the atmosphere as Elna began her ascent of the tower's stairs. It manifested in a low growl, an auditory harbinger of the peril lurking nearby. With a reflex as swift as shadows converging, Rarum's stalwart grasp seized Elna, pulling her back into the sanctum of darkness, where secrets and danger were entwined in an eternal dance.

Amidst the dimly lit stairwell, Elna's gaze pivoted with unnatural swiftness, pinpointing the origin of the unsettling disruption. There, an aberration of the natural order manifested—a monstrous and evil entity. Its ocular orbs radiated an unholy malevolence, casting a baleful luminosity across the obsidian corridor. The contoured weaponry of its claws glistened with a nefarious gleam, the polished instruments of an impending confrontation. It was a grotesque symphony of fear, a grotesquery that could neither be ignored nor denied. Elna recognized that to advance further, they must confront this nightmarish apparition.

Rarum, a colossus of unyielding resolve, assumed his battle-ready stance in response to the spectral guardian's ominous challenge. With sinews tensed and weapon unsheathed, he heralded the commencement of a harrowing contest—an impending maelstrom of strength and spirit. Undeterred by its mortal adversary, the creature surged forth, a torrential onslaught of maleficent fury. Rarum's prowess and training converged as his sword met the creature's rending claws in an explosive clash. This battle transcended the physical realm, a theater of survival and dominance within the dimly lit stairwell.

From the sanctuary of shadows, Elna observed with a breathless reverence, her arcane knowledge poised for invocation at the crucial juncture. The battle surged like a symphony, an opus of existence and destruction, and Elna awaited the crescendo when her arcane verses would intermingle with the harmony of conflict. The destiny of their ascent into the tower's abyss depended on the outcome of this ethereal confrontation.

The battle continued, unyielding and unrelenting, the maelstrom of combat unfurling like a tapestry of fate. Elna's incantations wove a delicate web, a dance of words that unraveled the creature's defenses and ensnared its movements, a lyrical subjugation of malice to the will of ancient magic. Each blade stroke from Rarum carried the weight of destiny, a symphony of steel and sinew that inexorably eroded the creature's resilience. Blow by blow, they penned the eulogy of their formidable adversary until, with a final, immaculately executed strike, Rarum laid low the monstrous sentinel.

As the silence of triumph unfurled like a funeral shroud, Elna approached the tower's portal, her aura imbued with the echoes of the arcane. Her astute understanding of mystical arts discerned the presence of intricate locks, formidable barriers forged in the crucible of arcane mastery. Her initial attempts to unbind the portal yielded no fruit, and a furrow of frustration creased her brow.

Rarum, his breath returning like a tempestuous tide, found amusement in Elna's vexation. His mirthful rumination wove through the ether like a haunting melody. "Elna, could it be they wish to safeguard a treasure behind this impervious gate?"

Elna's response was a wry, knowing smile, for the enigma of the locked door now became irrefutable. "Indeed, Rarum. It seems we stand at the precipice of revelation. Let us weave our wills into unlocking the guarded secrets beyond this door." Together, they turned their resolve to the enigmatic barrier, their determination aflame to conquer the riddles and mysteries in the tower's heart. Rarum's earlier endeavor to rend the door asunder through sheer might had yielded naught but a resounding rebuke—an interlude in their quest that bore testament to the complexity ahead, for this was a challenge that transcended the boundaries of mere physical force.

Elna took her place before the door that guarded the tower's secrets, an enigma deciphering enigmas. Her discerning eyes traced the arcane runes and sigils that wove a mystical tapestry upon the door's surface. Their intricate design spoke volumes of the architects' commitment to safeguarding the cryptic treasures held within. Her nimble fingers danced like whispers upon the enchanted etchings, a reverent caress of secrets long veiled. "They have spared no expense in protecting what lies beyond," she observed, her voice a musical resonance against the mystic silence. "We must tread with grace to unravel these enchantments."

In the dappled twilight of their secret vigil, Elna immersed herself in the artistry of magic, delving deep into the reservoir of her knowledge and intuition. Rarum, the stalwart guardian, remained vigilant, his unwavering trust in Elna's arcane prowess akin to an unbreakable bond. Together, they forged a pact with destiny, relentlessly pursuing unraveling the mysteries veiled by the enigmatic door.

Elna's dexterous fingers painted runes upon the door's surface, each symbol a note in a symphony of enchantments. Her scholarly devotion to ancient rituals and their esoteric symbols bore fruit as the door acquiesced to her delicate ministrations. It yielded with a hesitant sigh, parting its enigmatic veil to unveil the passage that beckoned them forth.

In acknowledgment of her arcane mastery, Rarum, the vigilant guardian, nodded in solemn approval. "Your expertise shines, Elna."

Together, they ventured into the sanctum of the tower, shadows draped about them like a shroud of revelation. Within, Elna's senses found purpose, guiding her toward a collection of scrolls neatly arrayed upon a wooden dais. Each parchment was a potential key to unlocking the mysteries of Phoenix's past and his unholy dalliance with the dark arts.

One by one, Elna unrolled the scrolls, her eyes etching the words into her consciousness. The knowledge they held was a treasure trove of insight into the enigmatic warlock's dark history. The words were a river of revelations, flowing toward understanding, and as they meandered through the ancient text, the puzzle pieces of Phoenix's evil power and nefarious ambitions began to align.

Elna's azure eyes widened in the dim chamber, her fingertips caressing the text as if feeling the pulse of its revelation. The scroll whispered a chilling tale of dark rituals and thwarted designs. It told of a human infant, a vessel chosen to bear the legacy of a dread power, and the inception of a rite intended to infuse him with the eerie mantle of his warlock ancestor.

As Elna's voice wove the tale of the Eladrin archer and the child's near escape from the abyssal ritual, the chamber seemed to reverberate with the weight of destiny's intricate design. Rarum, his eyes like ancient stones weathered countless storms, listened with awe and realization. The narrative unveiled a tapestry of not only Phoenix's dark history but also the presence of an enigmatic Eladrin archer whose actions had disrupted the course of evil fate.

With a thoughtful pause, Rarum ventured a question that echoed shared curiosity. "Who was this Eladrin archer, Elna? And what became of the child, spared by fate's capricious hand?"

Elna's fingers gently traced the words on the aged parchment as she unraveled the scroll's cryptic message. Her voice carried the weight of a narrative still unfolding. "The identity of the Eladrin archer remains shrouded in mystery, a shadowy figure who left no trace behind. As for the child, he was swept away in the chaos that ensued. The scroll hints at a hidden refuge, where he was taken to be safeguarded from the relentless pursuit of the warlock and his dark conspiracy."

Rarum's contemplative gaze shifted from the scroll to Elna, his thoughts like shifting sands that concealed and revealed their enigmatic truths. "Could it be that this child, spared by fate and sheltered by the Eladrin archer, grew to become the warlock known as Phoenix? If so, the circumstances of his upbringing may hold the key to understanding his motivations and the darkness that clings to his soul."

Elna nodded in agreement, her eyes shimmering with the wisdom of discovery. "Indeed, Rarum. The past may hold the answers we seek, and this chamber may reveal more about Phoenix's origins and the enigmatic Eladrin archer who intervened in his fate. Let us continue to unravel the secrets hidden within these scrolls, for they may illuminate the path forward in our quest to confront Phoenix and safeguard our realm from his malice."

Elna and Rarum delved deeper into the scrolls, their quest for knowledge and revelation guiding them through the labyrinthine corridors of history. In the heart of Flameford's palace, amidst the whispers of forgotten truths, they sought to unearth the enigmatic past that had given rise to the shadowed present.

Rarum nodded, his rugged features etched with determination. "Indeed, Elna. The revelations we have uncovered here are but pieces of a larger puzzle. Crystal Vale awaits, and in the presence of King Manard, we shall assemble the fragments of our knowledge into a coherent narrative. The truth about Phoenix's past and dark ambitions may be the key to our realm's salvation."

Elna carefully rolled up the scroll and returned it to its rightful place among the ancient tomes and records in the hidden chamber. The weight of their discoveries hung in the air, a reminder of the path they had embarked upon, filled with peril and enigma. "Before we leave this place," she began, her voice steady, "we must ensure that we leave no trace of our presence. Flameford's secrets must remain concealed until the hour of reckoning."

Rarum, always attuned to the practicalities of their mission, nodded in agreement. Together, they meticulously ensured that the chamber was restored to its hidden state, with the tapestry concealing their entrance again. As they departed the room and descended the tower's stairs, the enigmatic darkness of Flameford embraced them once more, its secrets intact but its future uncertain.

Their journey would now lead them to Crystal Vale, where they hoped to find answers and allies in their quest to confront Phoenix. With each step, they left behind the shadowed city of Flameford, encouraged by the knowledge they had unearthed. They forged ahead toward the regal chambers of King Manard in Crystal Vale, where the next chapter of their saga awaited.

Chapter 23

Unveiling the Power of the Phoenix

In the concealed heart of E'vahona, a realm veiled from the prying eyes of mortals, Lord Karrenen stood as the harbinger of a revelation draped in the weight of destiny itself. Like a looming thundercloud, King Manard's message had cast its ominous shadow over Vacari and all the realms nestled within its cosmic embrace.

The knowledge he held resembled a dormant serpent coiled deep within the annals of secrecy, poised to strike and unleash untold chaos. Its venomous truth whispered the name of Maelgrim Shadowwaker, the enigmatic warlock whose legend resonated through the corridors of time. Maelgrim, the ancestor of Phoenix Shadowwalker, harbored an ambition as chilling as the depths of a winter's night – one that could tip the precarious balance of power within Vacari.

Amidst the shroud of whispered conspiracies, Maelgrim had beseeched the Druchii high priestess to choreograph a nefarious rite upon his flesh and blood, his son, Phoenix. The sinister contours of this dark design were wrought to ensure that the young warlock would inherit not just his father's potent legacy but an augmentation of it – a quantum leap towards becoming the most formidable sorcerer in all of Vacari.

The ritual, a brewing storm of hostility, had been set into motion, its arcane energies coiling and writhing in a macabre empowerment dance. Yet, fate's capricious hand intervened when Serena, an Eladrin archer with a heart ablaze with a vengeance, intruded upon this shadowy theater. The agony of Maelgrim's decree fueled her determination, for it had once ordained the death of her beloved, Edric.

Her arrows, guided by the unrelenting pursuit of retribution, found their mark with a precision that defied mortal skill. But in the eleventh hour, a shadowy figure among the Druchii moved with unnatural speed, snatching Maelgrim from Serena's deadly embrace. Vengeance eluded her grasp on that fateful day, slipping away like the ethereal specter of a fleeting dream.

Undaunted, Serena embarked on an unyielding quest, her unwavering resolve leading her to the elusive sanctuary of Maelgrim. In an explosive clash orchestrated by fate, she exacted retribution for her beloved by extinguishing the evil warlock's life. However, her triumph exacted a grievous toll, as her existence was claimed by the abyssal void that had devoured her.

In the aftermath of the disrupted ritual, Maelgrim seethed with an infernal rage, his very being aflame with the burning desire to witness his nefarious design come to fruition. He turned once more to the Druchii priestess, imploring her to clandestinely convey his son, Phoenix, to Fel Thalor, the labyrinthine heart of Druchii dominion. Phoenix would remain shrouded in obscurity until the fateful day ordained for the ritual's resumption—a rite destined to imbue him with the indomitable legacy of his father's arcane mastery.

Yet, the priestess's devotion extended beyond mere compliance. She nursed her clandestine ambitions, birthed in the stygian depths of the abyss itself. As Phoenix matured, she solemnly vowed to amplify his burgeoning power by interweaving her very abyssal essence into the tapestry of his soul. With this evil fusion, she aspired to forge Phoenix into a harbinger of unparalleled might, a scourge capable of eradicating the Eladrin, a persistent thorn in the side of the Druchii for centuries.

Amidst this intricate tapestry of secrets, shifting allegiances, and unspeakable ambitions, the fate of Vacari is dangled by the most fragile threads. Shrouded in darkness and complexity, the loom of destiny had been painstakingly threaded, and Lord Karrenen found himself at its epicenter. His duty was to unravel the enigmatic patterns it wove and shield the realm from the storm that loomed ominously on the horizon.

Within the sanctified chambers of his contemplation, Lord Karrenen grappled with the dire imperative that now clung to their world, a vice of uncertainty. Undeniably, it was imperious to ascertain whether the sinister ritual had unfurled its evil wings, ensnaring Phoenix within its abyssal embrace. The allure of unimaginable power summoned a specter that loomed at the very fringes of comprehension.

Phoenix's malevolent schemes had woven a shadowy tapestry, ensnaring King Alex and Queen Jeanne in a web of captivity. Goldmoor, once a radiant beacon, now languished beneath Phoenix's dominion, its spirit crushed beneath the oppressive yoke of tyranny.

The cogitations of the council member navigated the labyrinthine corridors of his thoughts as he pondered who would embark on the perilous odyssey into the very heart of darkness – Fel Thalor, the enigmatic citadel of the Druchii. In its labyrinthine recesses lay the arcane secrets of the sinister ritual and the elusive specter that was Phoenix himself.

Lord Karrenen acknowledged that Ong and Keisha, unyielding and stubborn, would eagerly undertake this treacherous mission. Yet, the prospect of dispatching Keisha into such dire peril gnawed at his heart, for Phoenix had already decreed her capture. Her worth to him surpassed that of a mere pawn; she held the key to the hidden city of E'vahona, a sanctuary concealed from the world's prying gaze for countless centuries. He also worried about the hidden magic harbored within Keisha – elemental magic intertwined with her father's magic – a potent combination that would undoubtedly place her in even graver danger.

Turning the pages of possibilities within his mind, Lord Karrenen contemplated the potential of Seraphina and Thalorin, two of his most promising proteges. Their return from Goldmoor carried the weight of invaluable intelligence. This quest had plunged them into the abyssal depths of the dungeon, unveiling the cryptic truths behind King Alex's imprisonment. The council eagerly awaited their report, their vitality sapped by the arduous journey, rendering them temporarily unfit for an immediate departure.

The council member teetered at the precipice of decision, his resolve unwavering, yet the shadow of indecision loomed large. Time, that most enigmatic and elusive of currencies, crept inexorably onward, urging him to designate champions to brave the storm of darkness that awaited within the cavernous depths of Fel Thalor.

In the contemplation chambers, Lord Karrenen bore the weight of his responsibility as if he were the world-weary Atlas himself, the burden of choice etched into the furrows of his brow. He knew, with the grim certainty of fate's decree, that there was but one course of action, a path fraught with peril and shadowed by uncertainty.

His journey led him through the dimly lit streets of E'vahona, where he crossed the threshold of Ong and Keisha's abode—a sanctuary bathed in the soft radiance of companionship. As he entered, his eyes fell upon a sight that offered a fleeting respite from the gathering storm. Pumpkin, the ebony panther, stretched lazily, a sentinel of the shadows, embodying the feral grace of the untamed.

As wise as ever, Ong sensed the gravity that clung to Lord Karrenen like a somber shroud. He beckoned the council member within with a gracious welcome, though the furrowed concern on his face betrayed his keen intuition.

"What brings you to our hearth, Lord Karrenen?" Ong inquired, his words laced with a quiet intensity.

Lord Karrenen revealed the harrowing mission that loomed like a storm on the horizon with a sigh that carried the weight of worlds. His gaze shifted to Keisha, the embodiment of resilience and determination and the guardian of Pumpkin, her steadfast companion.

"I beseech you both," he implored, "to undertake a dangerous odyssey. Your destination is none other than Fel Thalor, that citadel shrouded in darkness, and your quest carries nothing less than the gathering of enlightenment. This knowledge revolves around Phoenix, the enigmatic harbinger of our prevailing uncertainty. You must unearth whether the sinister ritual has unfurled its dread wings and whether Phoenix now bears the culmination of his evil might."

Ong's gaze shifted to Keisha, a silent communion of understanding flowing between them like a clandestine oath. Keisha's resolve remained steadfast, her determination etched in the unyielding line of her jaw.

"We shall embark upon this treacherous journey," he proclaimed, his eyes unwavering, "for the sake of Vacari and to unveil the enigma that obscures our path. Though I hold reservations about taking her into that city," he added, his gaze momentarily flickering toward Pumpkin.

Lord Karrenen nodded in solemn appreciation, his voice laden with the moment's seriousness. "I understand your apprehensions, and I commend your bravery. The council and all of Vacari stand indebted to your noble sacrifice."

With those words, he turned to depart, his footsteps resonating through the chamber like the solemn refrain of destiny's inevitable call. The council awaited his return, their fates inextricably woven into the enigmatic tapestry of Fel Thalor, where darkness and light clashed in a battle that would determine the destiny of realms untold.

Within the dim-lit confines of their home, Ong's gaze bore the weight of a thousand unspoken fears as he turned to Keisha. The flickering lamplight cast wavering shadows upon his furrowed brow. His voice, a soft plea born of love and apprehension, reverberated through the room like a whispered prayer in the stillness of the night.

"My love," he began, his words laced with a poignant blend of longing and concern, "I harbor profound unease at the thought of you venturing into the depths of Fel Thalor. Yet, I am acutely aware that your spirit is as untamed as the wind, and my heart understands the futility of trying to tether you. But I implore you, as the rope to my heart, to avoid unnecessary risks, for my world finds its center in your smile."

Keisha, a vision of unwavering courage and grace, met his gaze with a smile that danced like sunlight upon still waters. Her response, a testament to the unspoken bond that bound their souls, carried the wisdom of ages within its simplicity.

"Yes, of course," she affirmed, her voice a soothing balm to the lingering disquiet, "I am wise enough to heed your counsel. We must prepare for this treacherous mission, for time is as elusive as a phantom, and our destiny awaits."

Ong's heart swelled with love and the weight of his promise in the stillness of their exchange. As he watched her, a silent vow passed between them, spoken only in the language of eyes locked in unwavering devotion. He whispered, invoking the protection of the stars, "I will keep an even closer watch over her."

Turning away, he collected the tools of their quest, a silent guardian lurking in the shadows, his determination mirroring the unwavering love that bound their destinies.

As the impending moment of departure hung heavy in the air, E'vahona's tranquil veil seemed to hold its breath in rapt anticipation. The couple, united by purpose and burdened by the gravity of their mission, steeled themselves to venture beyond the concealed boundaries of the city and into the realm of profound uncertainty. Pumpkin, a creature of both shadow and grace, joined them, a mute sentinel of the nocturnal realm.

Keisha sought to offer Ong a glimmer of solace with a wistful smile that gleamed like a rare gem amidst the dimness. Her words floated upon the breeze, carrying the promise of a memory yet to be etched into the tapestry of their lives. "With Pumpkin by our side, we may steal moments within the embrace of Emberwood Forest. There, beneath the ancient boughs, we shall find comfort."

Though tinged with a rueful shake of his head, Ong's response bore a glimmer of humor, a fleeting ember in the encroaching darkness. "I suppose that is something, my love," he conceded, his voice a blend of acceptance and affection.

Yet, concern lingered in his eyes, the unspoken dread of the unknown casting a somber shadow over their resolve. "Do you possess any inkling of where the knowledge we seek might reside?" he inquired, his words weighed with the seriousness of their quest.

Keisha's response was measured, her voice a steadfast beacon of determination. "Most likely, our answers lie within the heart of Fel Thalor, concealed in the labyrinthine depths of its interior—the library, a repository of secrets veiled in the obscurity of ages past."

Ong's muttered rejoinder, accompanied by a wry twist of his lips, conveyed a unique blend of exasperation and reluctant resignation. "Such is our fortune," he mused, his tone tinged with subtle irony, "to be led through the heart of the city as if fate conspires to test the depths of our resolve."

Their uttered words, carried on the breath of hushed anticipation, resonated far beyond the boundaries of E'vahona. The impending journey into Fel Thalor was poised to become a testament to their love, courage, and unwavering resilience—a story yet to be inscribed in the grand tapestry of Vacari's unfolding destiny.

Upon reaching the lush fringes of Emberwood Forest, a profound transformation in the tableau of their surroundings unfurled before them. Ong's perceptive gaze, attuned to the subtleties of nature, swept across the woodland expanse, revealing a sight that stirred a symphony of wonder in his heart. The forest, cradled within the warm embrace of autumn, cast its enchantment upon him, a realm where the very essence of magic danced amidst the falling leaves.

He stood in awe of the surreal transformation that had woven the once-verdant canopy into a tapestry of fiery orange and passionate red hues. It was a forest that defied comparison, its essence set ablaze by the spectral touch of a celestial artist. The air itself seemed to shimmer with the flickering brilliance of its resplendent foliage.

"I have never beheld a forest adorned in such resplendent attire," Ong remarked in a soft murmur that resonated like the gentle rustle of fallen leaves stirred by an ethereal breeze.

Keisha, her eyes alive with the wisdom of the land, offered an explanation that skillfully wove together the threads of nature and geology. Her smile, a reflection of the forest's boundless beauty, held a touch of melancholy for the profound forces that had shaped this magnificent tableau.

"It is the hallmark of this region," she elucidated, her voice a lyrical cadence of understanding, "where the realm of volcanoes embraces the domain of forests. The earth here breathes fire, and its passionate embrace has painted the world in vivid oranges and passionate reds. It stands as a testament to the ceaseless dance of nature and the formidable forces that shape its grandeur."

Ong's smile mirrored the forest's resplendence as he absorbed the breathtaking panorama. "Indeed," he concurred, his words an affirmation of profound appreciation, "it is a symphony of colors, a living canvas that sings of the wonders of our world."

With hearts ablaze and the forest as their silent confidant, they ventured deeper into the heart of Emberwood, each step an ode to the boundless beauty of Vacari and each moment a testament to their indomitable resolve. Before them lay Fel Thalor, a citadel cloaked in shadows and guarded by secrets, a destination known only to the most intrepid souls.

Amidst the enchanting embrace of Emberwood, a singular moment of serendipity unfolded, akin to a fleeting interlude in the grand symphony of their journey. Ong, with eyes finely attuned to the hidden treasures of nature, stumbled upon a bloom of profound elegance—a crimson blossom, vibrant as a phoenix's wing, cradled amidst the verdant foliage.

Time seemed to hang in suspended animation like a patient specter as Ong paused before this living testament to nature's artistry. The flower, in its delicate glory, whispered secrets of the woodland, and Ong, in silent communion with its tranquil beauty, allowed his thoughts to drift like leaves upon a serene stream.

After a reverie that danced on the precipice of eternity, he extended his hand, a bridge between worlds, and plucked the radiant flower from its earthly sanctuary. It nestled there, cradled in his palm, a fragment of nature's poetry, and in that ethereal moment, he perceived its actual abode—resting within the glorious tapestry of Keisha's radiant hair.

With the grace of a courtly knight, he approached her, presenting the scarlet bloom as a token of his admiration and devotion. Like the notes in a love ballad, his words flowed from his lips, each syllable carrying the profound weight of his affection.

"A beautiful flower for my beautiful lady," he intoned, his voice a melody that resonated through the hallowed halls of the forest.

Keisha flushed with the flower's hue she now possessed and offered her gratitude in the soft language of a gentle kiss. Now an exquisite adornment in her crimson tresses, the bloom whispered tales of their love to the forest's ancient trees, who stood as silent witnesses to this enchanting moment.

Hand in hand, hearts intertwined like the roots of the ancient trees, they ventured deeper into Emberwood—a forest alive with secrets, where every step was a testament to the enduring magic of their love.

Within the wooded realm of Emberwood, where the ancient trees whispered secrets and the air held echoes of forgotten lore, Ong's senses detected a spectral murmur amid the rustling leaves and sighing winds, sharp as a hawk's eye. His instincts, honed by a lifetime in the heart of Vacari's untamed wilderness, kicked into action.

With a silent grace that befits a forest dweller, he tugged Keisha gently into a secluded grove, a sanctuary of dappled light and rustling shadows. There, beneath the arboreal canopy, they became one with the secrets of the woods, waiting like sentinels in the twilight for the enigma to unravel.

The origin of the elusive whispers finally revealed itself: a contingent of Druchii—a race renowned for their cunning and enigmatic demeanor. Like a solemn drumbeat, Ong's heart quickened with the realization that they were drawing ever nearer to Fel Thalor, their ultimate destination and the enigmatic nature of darkness itself.

A sigh, borne of resignation and a seasoned familiarity with the perils ahead, escaped Ong's lips. He knew the Druchii to be as elusive as they were relentless in their pursuit. As the shadowy figures passed by, akin to phantoms drifting through the forest's ethereal veil, he held his breath, his gaze trapped by the intricate dance of shadows and moonlight.

When the final echoes of their presence dissolved into the emerald depths of the woodland, Ong and Keisha, their eyes locked in unspoken accord, resumed their journey. Yet now, their steps bore a heightened awareness, and their senses were finely tuned to the secrets woven into the very fabric of Emberwood.

The ever-enigmatic forest enveloped them once more, its whispered secrets echoing like a haunting refrain that accompanied them along their path. The lingering presence of the Druchii lingered like a spectral afterimage, a constant reminder that in Emberwood, every shadow concealed a tale, and every rustling leaf held the dual promise of both adventure and peril.

As they approached the outer fringes of Fel Thalor, the citadel shrouded in shadows and enigmas, Ong's astute strategic mind sought refuge in the comforting embrace of night. He recognized that the veil of darkness would serve as their most stalwart ally, concealing their every movement within the obsidian enigma of the evening.

With a wisdom that mirrored the age-old knowledge of the forest, Keisha, their guide through the labyrinthine mysteries of Emberwood and beyond, unveiled a concealed sanctuary—a grove hidden in the murky heart of the woods. It was a place where moonlight cascaded through the leaves like liquid silver, and ancient trees stood as solemn sentinels, guarding the secrets of their refuge.

Within this hidden bower, a tapestry of twilight and whispered secrets, Ong contemplated their situation, a thoughtful furrow etching his brow. His gaze shifted to the horizon, where the sun's descent heralded the imminent arrival of their cloaked ally—night itself.

"Perhaps," he mused, his voice a low timbre infused with strategic insight, "we shall fare best beneath the veiled protection of nightfall. The shadows shall be our confidants, and through Fel Thalor, we shall navigate, unseen, if the fates favor our endeavor."

Keisha, an unwavering beacon of determination, nodded in agreement, her trust in Ong's sagacity as stubborn as the roots of the ancient trees. With the sun's descent, they settled into the grove, awaiting the moment when darkness would emerge as their most trusted ally and the enigmatic heart of Fel Thalor would lie within their grasp. She gently smiled at Ong and remarked, "Now, you see why Emberwood is often advised against. Though it holds breathtaking beauty, it is equally treacherous, especially with the presence of the Druchii."

Ong nodded in understanding, his gaze fixed on the approaching night. "Yes," he admitted, "I now comprehend the wisdom of such advice."

Night unveiled its majestic tapestry within the serene grove, draping the world in its inky shroud. The moon, a vigilant sentinel in the star-studded heavens, gazed upon them with benevolent eyes. The world seemed to hold its breath, an expectant hush settling over the land as the intricate dance of shadows and secrets extended its beguiling invitation.

As Twilight's celestial tapestry unfurled, the world transformed into a realm of mystery and concealment. Ong and Keisha, akin to elusive phantoms, embarked upon their journey toward the very heart of Fel Thalor, the citadel of enigmas. Enveloped in the obsidian embrace of the night, they seamlessly merged with the darkness, becoming an integral part of the obscurity that veiled their purpose.

Ong, armed with the seasoned wisdom of a veteran scout, led them along the periphery of Fel Thalor's enigmatic expanse. They moved as silhouettes within the tapestry of shadows, every step a testament to their mastery of the intricate terrain woven from secrets and obscurity. More than once, they seamlessly melded into the cloak of concealment as vigilant patrols glided past, resembling specters in the night.

Keisha's keen eyes discerned the presence of a Druchii patrolling along the outer wall, and she swiftly alerted Ong to the situation. He sighed, resigned but willing to act. "Stay here. I'll handle it," he whispered.

She shook her head in response. "Yes, I know you could, but my method is quicker." With graceful ease, she retrieved her longbow, expertly nocked an arrow, drew it back, and released it fluidly. The arrow found its mark with uncanny precision, and the Druchii sentinel fell silently upon the wall. She turned to Ong, a triumphant sparkle in her eyes.

Ong couldn't help but smile. "Alright, I'll concede that one to you."

Keisha's archery skills had proven to be an invaluable asset, and they continued their journey into the heart of Fel Thalor, confident in their ability to navigate the shadows and secrets surrounding them.

Their odyssey, fraught with peril and uncertainty, had finally brought them to their coveted destination—the library, a sanctuary of concealed knowledge and veiled verities. However, what lay within its dimly illuminated chambers left them breathless, their hearts burdened by a foreboding that eluded immediate comprehension.

Scrolls, ancient and weathered by the relentless passage of time, lay scattered upon the library's stone floor like fallen leaves in the aftermath of an arcane storm. These scrolls, relics of forgotten wisdom, bore the weight of centuries within their parchment, their inked secrets murmuring tales of both power and peril.

Ong and Keisha exchanged silent glances, their eyes mirroring the disarray that enveloped them. In this chamber of age-old sagacity and abandoned memories, the tapestry of fate seemed to dangle by a precarious thread, yearning for their touch to weave a new chapter into the chronicles of Vacari's history.

Ong's nimble fingers descended as a bridge between the annals of time and the knowledge repository within the dimly illuminated library chamber. He plucked a scroll from the scattered mosaic of forgotten wisdom. The parchment, a relic of ages past, felt frail and heavy with enigmatic secrets as though it bore the weight of countless centuries upon its aged surface.

He passed the scroll to Keisha, a wordless exchange that spoke volumes in the peaceful stillness of the library. Her eyes, twin pools of curiosity and apprehension, roamed over the arcane script that danced upon the parchment's canvas. As her gaze traversed the inscribed words, an unspoken comprehension coursed between them, akin to a secret exchanged in the sacred sanctum of the night's silence.

"This," she whispered, her voice a gentle ripple in the profound stillness, "holds within it knowledge of the Eladrin and fragments of E'vahona's hidden lore. It seems that someone was driven to unearth secrets long veiled in the obscurity of history."

Ong added his discerning insight by offering a solemn nod to acknowledge the undeniable truth. "It's clear that more than mere scholarly curiosity guided the hand that sought this knowledge. A darker purpose seems to have been the driving force."

Shifting her gaze from the scroll to meet Ong's eyes, Keisha couldn't help but voice the suspicion that hung like an impending storm. "Any wagers on who might be behind this insatiable thirst for information?"

Ong's affirmative nod mirrored her unspoken thoughts. "It's a wager I'd gladly take. My bet, my lady, rests upon Phoenix's doorstep—or, at the very least, someone entangled with his ominous legacy."

As the weight of their discovery settled, Ong and Keisha were entangled in a web of intrigue and uncertainty.

With the fire of determination flickering in her eyes, Keisha embraced the challenge. "Then let us unravel these scrolls and pierce the shroud of secrets that Phoenix fervently guards. We shall seek the truth about the ritual and unveil the shadows concealing his intentions."

In the library's solemn silence, forgotten lore and knowledge became their allies, each parchment an enigma waiting to be unraveled, each word a key to the mysteries entwining Phoenix Shadowwalker and the enigmatic ritual.

In the labyrinthine expanse of ancient scrolls and dusty tomes, the quest for answers had become an arduous odyssey, a journey through the annals of lost wisdom that appeared as elusive as the wisps of moonlit mist. Ong and Keisha, two relentless seekers of truth, delved deeper into the dusty repository, their determination unwavering, even as the scrolls conspired to guard their secrets. They stood at the edge of disillusionment, teetering on the brink of despair, but their resolve remained unbroken.

And then, as if carried on the ethereal breath of fate itself, Ong's vigilant eye caught sight of a half-destroyed scroll—a relic of knowledge that had weathered the relentless march of time and deliberate acts of sabotage. He retrieved it with a reverence reserved for the most precious of treasures, his fingers tracing the frayed edges as though they held the remnants of a map leading to salvation.

Though marred and fragmented, the scroll bore traces of something profound—a tapestry of ink and symbols that hinted at an incantation or a spell of great import. Ong passed it to Keisha, who studied the surviving words with eyes that sparkled like stars in the nocturnal heavens.

Her voice, gentle and harmonious within the silence, broke the tension that had gripped them. "These words, Ong, bear the mark of an incantation, a spell woven with intent and purpose."

Ong, ever the meticulous observer, noted a broken glass sphere nearby—a shattered vessel of mysteries that mirrored the scroll's fragmented state. His sigh, a lament for the secrets just beyond their grasp, lingered in the air like a mournful dirge.

"It seems," he contemplated, "that someone went to great lengths to erase the trail we sought to follow. They shattered not only glass but the path to understanding as well."

The mystery deepened, the shadows within the library echoing the enigma surrounding Phoenix and his nefarious ambitions.

In the library's dim illumination, Ong and Keisha stood at the crossroads of revelation and obstruction, their quest for answers akin to a riddle waiting to be unraveled. The fragments of knowledge, tantalizing and incomplete, bore witness to the dark forces that guarded their secrets. Yet, beneath the ruins of shattered glass and fragmented scrolls, the truth lay in wait—a phoenix of knowledge, poised to rise from the ashes of obscurity.

Within the sanctified chambers of the library, Ong and Keisha, concealed like phantoms in the twilight, deliberated their next course of action. Their voices, a quiet and veiled symphony, carried the weight of their contemplations as they grappled with the enigma that lay before them, like explorers in the uncharted territory of the arcane.

Then, as if orchestrated by the hand of destiny itself, the portal to their sanctuary—the library's door—creaked open, unleashing a torrent of possibilities and perils upon their concealed figures. Like elusive forest creatures retreating to the cover of shadowed woods, they sought refuge in the cloaked embrace of the room's dim recesses, where silence became their sacred shield.

With the vigilance of watchful sentinels in the abyssal night, their eyes locked onto the intruder—a Druchii priestess, her presence an enigma of fascination and foreboding. With a grace born of secrets and shadows, she approached the fragmented scroll and the shattered glass sphere, her fingers delicately tracing the remnants of enigmas, her lips curling into a sly smile, a precursor of unveiled mysteries.

Within the tranquil confines of the library, she whispered to the very fabric of existence, her voice a confidential communion shared with none but the unseen witnesses. "Lyra," she breathed, a name that hung in the air like a wisp of ethereal melody carried by the whims of the wind, "bestowed this sphere upon Phoenix Shadowwalker, along with the incantation to awaken his latent power."

With methodical movements, the priestess gathered the fractured shards of the glass sphere, each fragment reflecting a destiny torn asunder. She tucked them away, a covert pledge to safeguard the secrets they harbored. Her words, an offering to the abyss, resonated like an oath sworn to ethereal forces. "The Druchii," she contemplated, "have fulfilled their promise to Maelgrim. His progeny, a phoenix of untapped power, now soars higher than his sire's loftiest dreams."

As Ong and Keisha observed the sorceress in the library, she began to speak, her voice a soft cadence that seemed to resonate with ancient secrets. "Lyra," she murmured, a name that hung in the air like a wisp of ethereal melody carried by the whims of the wind, "bestowed this sphere upon Phoenix Shadowwalker, along with the incantation to awaken his latent power."

The mention of Lyra's involvement in Phoenix's quest for power sent shivers down Ong and Keisha's spines. It was now clear that Lyra had played a significant role in Phoenix's pursuit of arcane mastery. Yet, the true nature of her connection to him and her allegiance remained in mystery, leaving them to wonder whether she was an ally or an adversary in their relentless pursuit of the truth surrounding the sinister ritual and Phoenix's intentions.

Ong and Keisha emerged in the dimly lit chamber with the sorceress gone and the library's secrets still concealed. Their clasped hands, entwined like the threads of fate, spoke of their unwavering commitment to one another and the shared quest that bound their destinies.

Ong's voice, a soothing whisper in the stillness, promised renewed purpose. "Let us depart this enshrouded sanctuary before the first light of daybreak, my love. Though veiled in shadows, our path beckons us beyond these confining walls."

In the tranquil moments of their secluded refuge, they stood together, silhouettes against the backdrop of night, their hearts aligned in their determination to uncover the enigma that had led them to Fel Thalor. The journey ahead promised more profound revelations and significant challenges, but they faced it with resolute unity, their love a guiding light in the darkest times.

In the tranquil haven of E'vahona, Ong and Keisha found a respite from the relentless pursuit of knowledge and the enigmas that had woven their destinies into the tapestry of Vacari. Here, amidst the whispered secrets of the hidden city, time flowed differently, offering them a precious moment of rest.

As they settled into their dwelling, the soft radiance of E'vahona's mystical aura enveloped them, casting a soothing spell upon their weary souls. The shadows whispered tales of ancient wisdom, and the gentle breeze carried the scent of untold mysteries. It was a place where dreams and reality danced in harmonious union.

Ong and Keisha, hand in hand, embraced the sanctuary of their haven. Ong's voice, a comforting presence in the stillness, filled the space between them. "Rest, my love," he murmured, his words a gentle lullaby, "for tomorrow is a new chapter in our quest, and we shall face it with renewed vigor."

Keisha, her eyes reflecting her gratitude, nodded with a serene smile. In the heart of E'vahona, they surrendered to the embrace of slumber, knowing that their dreams promised further revelations and that their love would remain an unwavering anchor in the uncharted seas of uncertainty.

Chapter 24

Council of Shadows

The Council Chambers of E'vahona, an ethereal jewel nestled within the enigmatic realm of the Eladrin elves, stood as a masterpiece of elven artistry, its architecture a testament to the millennia of craftsmanship that had birthed it. The grand entrance beckoned them with arched doorways intricately adorned in sinuous vine-like carvings as the council members assembled, guiding them into a spacious chamber bathed in an otherworldly luminescence. Moonlight filtered through magnificent stained-glass windows, casting kaleidoscopic hues upon the polished marble floors, creating a mosaic of colors that seemed plucked from the very dreams of the night sky.

Within this sanctified sanctuary, history whispered its tales through the hallowed stones. The gleaming marble floors reflected the soft, ethereal glow of crystal chandeliers suspended like constellations of celestial stars. Towering alabaster columns, regal and slender, rose like timeless sentinels, bearing the weight of the elven realm's legacy upon their meticulously sculpted shoulders.

Seated in a harmonious circle, the council members assumed their positions elegantly, befitting their ancient lineage. At the head of the table, Lord Karrenen, a paragon of wisdom and responsibility, claimed his throne. His ageless visage, etched with the knowledge of centuries, served as a living testament to his enduring leadership. Beside him, Lady Elowen embodied grace, her gaze as sharp as a warrior's blade, and her silvery tresses cascading like liquid moonlight.

To Lord Karrenen's left, Lord Galadon exuded a quiet authority that held firm amidst the swirling currents of politics and power. Completing the quartet, Lady Lythia, renowned for her razor-sharp intellect and unwavering determination, graced the chamber with her presence. Her silvery gown shimmered like the starlight that danced through the stained glass, a living embodiment of the celestial wonders that adorned their sacred haven.

Lord Karrenen's voice, like a resonant bell tolling through the hallowed chamber, broke the silence of the opulent cocoon. "Esteemed members," he began, his timbre carrying the weight of centuries of leadership, "we are convened today to receive two sets of reports, each laden with gravity. As Ong and Keisha return from their perilous journey, Seraphina and Thalorin have delved into the abyss of danger."

Witnessing countless deliberations that had shaped Vacari's destiny, the council chamber held its collective breath, the air thrumming with anticipation. The revelations poised on the precipice promised to cast shadows far beyond the hallowed halls of Goldmoor, shaping the fate of their realm.

Lord Galadon leaned forward, his eyes alight with insatiable curiosity, and directed his inquiry towards Lord Karrenen with measured eloquence. "Before we delve into the intricate threads of these reports, might we begin with a broader overview of the grand tapestry that Seraphina and Thalorin have woven?"

His words possessed a resonance that commanded the rapt attention of all present. Lord Karrenen responded, "Indeed, Lord Galadon. Seraphina and Thalorin embarked on a dual-pronged quest. Firstly, they journeyed to Goldmoor, the principal city within Vacari, to ascertain the whereabouts of King Alex with unwavering certainty. Secondly, they undertook the formidable task of scrutinizing the ramparts of security enshrouding our captive sovereign, gathering a wealth of intelligence crucial to our future strategies."

The words hung in the air, laden with the gravity of their mission. The council members understood implicitly that confirming King Alex's location and assessing the enemy's vigilance was pivotal in the intricate realm of politics and the art of war within Vacari.

Within the serene chamber, where thoughts flowed like a river of wisdom, Lady Elowen, the embodiment of grace and sagacity, interjected with a finesse that mirrored the gentlest breeze caress. "Might it be prudent, esteemed colleagues, to commence with the chronicles of Seraphina and Thalorin? Their odyssey, intricately interwoven with King Alex's fate and the enigmas concealed within Goldmoor's formidable walls, is the linchpin of our endeavor to liberate Goldmoor from the clutches of Phoenix's darkness."

Lord Karrenen, the venerable patriarch presiding over the council, dipped his head in agreement, silently endorsing Lady Elowen's insightful suggestion. With a solemn nod, he summoned Seraphina and Thalorin, their moment of revelation poised just beyond the grand doors of the chamber, where destiny and secrecy converged.

As the colossal doors parted, revealing a portal to anticipation and intrigue, the council members turned their unified gaze, their collective breath held in taut silence. Seraphina and Thalorin entered, their presence akin to a regal procession, bearing the weight of their sacred mission like a celestial crown.

Seraphina, a vision of ethereal beauty and unwavering resolve, moved with the fluidity of a forest stream. Her obsidian hair, a cascade of midnight silk, framed her countenance, which bore the weight of responsibility with regal grace. Beside her walked Thalorin, a figure bathed in silver luminescence, his silken locks shimmering with an otherworldly glow. The undying ember of resolute determination gleamed in their eyes, mirrored by the council members eagerly awaiting their revelations.

With Eladrin's innate grace and a purposeful presence, Seraphina and Thalorin embarked on their report, their voices resonating through the hallowed Council Chambers of E'vahona like a harmonious symphony.

"Esteemed council members," Seraphina began, her silver tresses flowing like a cascade of moonlight, "from our journey to Goldmoor, we bring tidings of utmost significance. King Alex, the rightful sovereign of Goldmoor, indeed languishes within the somber confines of their dungeon. We had the privilege of engaging in discourse with him, and while his demeanor retained the luster of royalty, it was not bereft of the burdens he carries."

Thalorin's raven hair mirroring the ambient glow of the chamber continued the narrative, "We surmise that his disquiet stems from the enigma surrounding Queen Jeanne's whereabouts. Our interactions with the king have revealed that her destiny remains a riddle to him. We believe this mystery exacerbates the turmoil that besets him."

Their words wove a tapestry of imagery and emotion, akin to a masterful painting depicting their clandestine meeting with the imprisoned king and the shadows looming over Goldmoor's once-resplendent halls. The Council of E'vahona, trapped in the unfolding revelation, found themselves entangled in a narrative where the fates of kingdoms and monarchs hung in the balance.

Thalorin, his countenance graced by a respectful nod, continued their chronicle, his words like offerings of gratitude and admiration bestowed upon their venerable mentor. "Before we plunge into the labyrinthine corridors of Goldmoor's dungeon, we wish to tender our deepest gratitude to our revered teacher, Lord Karrenen. His unwavering instruction and mastery of arcane arts have served as the compass guiding our success in traversing the labyrinth of challenges that beset our path."

Lord Karrenen, a living tome of wisdom and experience, received their sentiments with a gentle smile, his eyes alight with the spark of a mentor's pride. In that moment, he beheld his pupils, now transformed into capable and resourceful individuals, poised to confront the intricate tapestry of their world's complexities.

Seraphina's voice, reminiscent of a serenade sung by the ancient forests themselves, commenced the vivid tableau of their odyssey. "As we delved into the abyss of Goldmoor's dungeon, our first encounter loomed at the threshold—a pair of colossal Guardian Statues. Carved with meticulous artistry, these stone sentinels stood as formidable custodians, barring passage to the complicated puzzle that lay beyond."

Thalorin's words flowed like a river, meandering with a grace that belied the treacherous path they trod. "With the utmost wariness, we advanced, for we were aware of the ancient enchantments that stirred when intruders dared to approach. As we drew near, their eyes blazed to life, their scrutiny an intensity that seemed to pierce the very essence of our souls."

Together, their voices wove a tale of suspense and peril, inviting the council members to visualize the daunting presence of these Guardian Statues, who guarded the cryptic secrets of Goldmoor's hidden depths.

Seraphina continued her narrative, her words a symphony of tension. "Upon bypassing the watchful gaze of the Guardian Statues, we ascended to the dungeon's second level. A more sinister challenge awaited here—a labyrinth of cunningly concealed trap doors lurking beneath the timeworn, creaking floorboards."

Thalorin's voice seamlessly intertwined with Seraphina's, their narrative a duet of enchantment. "The trap doors, fashioned from somber wood and carrying the faint whisper of bygone eras, seemed deceptively innocent as if woven seamlessly into the very fabric of the architecture itself. Yet, beneath their veneer of tranquility lay treacherous abysses, ever ready to trap those who ventured heedlessly."

The council members, now captivated by the tale, found themselves transported to the scene, their minds enshrouded in the looming presence of these trap doors, poised like silent sentinels, awaiting to plunge Seraphina and Thalorin into the abyss of uncertainty.

"As we delved deeper into the labyrinthine heart of the dungeon," Seraphina continued, her words an incantation that conjured the vivid image, "we ascended to the third floor, where a different peril lay in ambush. Mysterious runes, pulsating with arcane vitality, adorned the walls like constellations in a celestial tapestry. These intricate symbols posed a riddle, their true purpose veiled in the cloak of enigma."

Thalorin, imbued with the wisdom of their mentor's teachings, added, "Recognizing the latent danger, we summoned the knowledge imparted to us by Lord Karrenen. With deft hands, we inscribed a Rune of Concealment, a key of our crafting, to unlock the mysteries of this beguiling enchantment."

Their words painted a vivid tableau—a chamber illuminated by mesmerizing, luminous runes, where the air bore the scent of ancient magic. Through the narrative, the council members could almost taste the ghostly energies intricately woven into the fabric of the dungeon's defenses.

"As we ascended to the fourth floor," Seraphina admitted, a subtle note of chagrin in her melodious voice, "we were confronted with a labyrinth of a different type, a maze not constructed from stone and mortar, but woven from the intricate threads of enchantments and illusions. This challenge tested our intellect and mastery of ancient elven magic, a test of wits and wisdom."

Thalorin's voice carried the resonance of retrospection as he mused, "Perhaps, in hindsight, a more attentive approach to our lessons on navigating enchanted mazes would have been prudent. Nevertheless, in moments of uncertainty, our training served as a compass guiding us through the labyrinth of illusions. We unraveled the veils of deception, revealing the true path amidst the convoluted riddle, much to our profound relief."

Their vivid descriptions conjured an image of the council members standing at the heart of a magical labyrinth, where the walls danced and shifted like capricious specters, weaving a disorienting puzzle. It was a testament to their indomitable determination and the power of their shared knowledge that they had triumphed over this enigmatic crucible.

"As we ascended to the final floor," Seraphina continued, her countenance now etched with solemnity, "we harbored the belief that our trials neared their conclusion. Yet, the whims of fate held one last examination in reserve for us. Standing sentinel at the threshold of the exit were two formidable Chimeras, creatures of myth forged in the crucible of fire and fury. These chimeras bore the forms of lion heads and serpentine coils, their bodies a nightmarish blend of regal ferocity and serpentine cunning. Their wings, unfurled like those of majestic eagles, added an unsettling grandeur to their monstrous visage. These grotesque amalgamations of creatures from both heaven and hell seemed to defy the very laws of nature, standing as horrifying guardians of the warlock's sinister domain."

As the tale unfolded, the council members remained entangled in the web of Seraphina and Thalorin's harrowing journey. The vivid descriptions of the mythical Chimeras, the treacherous chamber with lurking serpents, and the complex magical barrier left them hanging on every word, their imaginations transported to the depths of Goldmoor's dungeon.

Thalorin's gaze hardened, his recollection tinged with the memory of that encounter. "These guardians were no mirage or mere trap; they were living embodiments of legend, tasked with protecting the secrets concealed behind that door. In the face of this ultimate trial, we were compelled to act with swiftness and unwavering resolve to prove our mettle and surmount this formidable barrier."

Their narrative painted a tableau of the mythical Chimeras, their eyes blazing with a flicker of arcane intelligence, their forms both majestic and terrifying. The council members found themselves inexorably drawn into the suspenseful narrative woven by Seraphina and Thalorin, where the threads of destiny hung in a precarious balance.

"Upon stepping into the chamber," Seraphina continued her hushed serenade, "an unexpected tableau greeted our senses. The chamber lay veiled in ankle-deep waters, a seemingly tranquil expanse that concealed a lethal secret. With each cautious step, a sinister hiss serenaded our ears, and a chorus of serpentine whispers reverberated through the room, weaving a symphony of dread."

Thalorin's voice resonated with the gravity of their encounter. "Beneath the deceptively calm surface of that chamber, a treacherous nest of venomous serpents lay in wait, their fangs poised with deadly intent. Each step we took had to be measured and deliberate, for a single misstep would have sounded the lament of our venture."

Seraphina acknowledged his words with a solemn nod, her eyes reflecting the unforgettable memory. "And there, nestled in the dangerous embrace of that chamber, we beheld King Alex. As we approached, he lay shackled to the very floor, his eyes a turbulent vortex of relief and dread. Yet, what truly arrested our senses was the presence of a monstrous sea behemoth, a Leviathan forged from the annals of myth and legend. Its colossal form cast a shadow over our captive sovereign, an ominous sentinel."

Their narrative painted a tableau of peril—a room teeming with lurking serpents, the looming presence of the Leviathan, and King Alex, a prisoner of these dangerous guardians. The council members leaned in, trapped by the compelling drama that unfolded.

"Indeed," Thalorin continued, his tone a somber sonnet, his gaze unwavering in the face of adversity. "The final crucible we confronted was the most formidable—a magical barrier that cocooned King Alex. This enchantment was an intricate tapestry demanding an intimate comprehension of the arcane arts. While our magical prowess is substantial, we were acutely aware that attempting to dismantle the barrier would court grave peril."

Seraphina interjected, her voice tinged with urgency, "The very instant we contemplated the removal of the barrier, we realized the potential cataclysm it could unleash. The sea behemoth and its ominous retinue, the eerie denizens of the deep, would have sensed the weakening of the enchantment and descended upon King Alex with ruthless celerity, ready to exact their dire retribution."

Their words painted a harrowing canvas—a delicate equilibrium between freeing King Alex and the looming menace of the sea behemoth and its malevolent acolytes. The council members exchanged knowing glances, their minds grappling with the precipice upon which Seraphina and Thalorin had stood.

Seraphina pressed on, her voice unwavering, "Yet fear not, esteemed council members, for we exercised prudence. We refrained from tampering with the barrier, understanding that its removal would precipitate immediate peril for King Alex. Our paramount concern was his safety."

Thalorin nodded in concurrence. "We prioritized the well-being of King Alex above all else, resisting the temptation to dismantle the magical enclosure. Instead, we gathered crucial intelligence about his predicament, a strategic choice guided by our unwavering commitment to ensuring his welfare."

Their explanation offered a glimmer of hope amid the darkness of their trials, reassuring the council that Seraphina and Thalorin had navigated the labyrinth of danger with sagacity and courage, with King Alex's safety as their unwavering lodestar.

The council members, their voices a symphony of wisdom and determination, collectively acknowledged the gravity of the situation and the need for cautious, meticulous planning. Their exemplary performance validated Lord Karrenen's choice of Seraphina and Thalorin for the mission, and it was clear that the liberation of King Alex would require a carefully orchestrated effort.

Seraphina and Thalorin, their heads held high with a sense of accomplishment, took their leave from the council chambers, their mission fulfilled for the time being. They knew their respite would be brief, for the shadows of impending tasks loomed on the horizon.

Lord Galadon, ever the sage, continued to steer the discourse toward a path of strategic insight. "It is evident that the road ahead is fraught with challenges. Phoenix's cunning and the formidable security surrounding King Alex demand our utmost attention. We must assemble a team of mages and strategists, those well-versed in the arcane arts and the art of war, to unravel the enigmas of the dungeon and secure our sovereign's release."

Lord Karrenen, the guardian of knowledge, nodded in agreement. "Indeed, Lord Galadon. The mission to liberate Goldmoor requires a fusion of arcane expertise and tactical brilliance. We must gather our most skilled mages and strategists to form a formidable alliance that can decipher the intricacies of the dungeon's defenses and execute a daring rescue."

Lady Lythia, the embodiment of intellect, added her insight to the deliberation. "Let us remember the importance of gathering intelligence as well. Before embarking on such a dangerous mission, we must learn as much as we can about the dungeon's layout, its guardians, and any hidden secrets. Knowledge will be our greatest weapon in this endeavor."

Lady Elowen, the pinnacle of grace and sagacity, concurred. "Wisdom and preparation shall be our guiding stars on this journey. Let us convene the most adept mages, strategists, and scholars in our realm, pooling our collective expertise to craft a comprehensive plan for King Alex's rescue."

The council members, united in purpose, exchanged determined glances, fully aware of the challenges ahead. The liberation of King Alex was a matter of utmost importance, requiring the utmost diligence, skill, and resolve. As they continued their deliberations, the fate of Vacari hung in the balance, and the shadows of Phoenix's influence loomed ever more prominent on the horizon.

Lord Karrenen's gaze shifted as if wielding a scepter of authority back to Lord Galadon. "As for Ong and Keisha," he continued, his voice now bearing the weight of ancient wisdom, "they ventured into the very heart of darkness in search of Phoenix, that nefarious warlock whose malevolent presence has repeatedly cast a looming shadow over Vacari's security. Their journey took them through treacherous domains, yet their courage and indomitable spirit shine as beacons, illuminating the path forward."

As the council's attention turned towards the imminent report from Ong and Keisha, Lord Karrenen's gaze, like a regal scepter, shifted to Lord Galadon, the embodiment of sagacity. The ancient elven leader's posture conveyed both authority and a profound understanding of the gravity of the situation. When he spoke of Ong and Keisha's mission, his voice bore the echoes of ages past, a reminder of the enduring battle against the evil forces that threatened Vacari.

The grand doors of the chamber swung open with an almost reverent hush, allowing Ong and Keisha to make their entrance. Their arrival was a study in contrasts—Ong's cerulean eyes, alight with determination, met Lord Karrenen's gaze with reverence. At the same time, Keisha, draped in a verdant cloak that rustled like leaves in the wind, exuded an otherworldly grace. The assembly bore witness to their presence, acknowledging the significance of their mission with bated breath.

The stage was set, and the council was poised to hear the tale of Ong and Keisha's journey into the heart of darkness, where the evil shadow of Phoenix loomed, threatening the security of Vacari.

In the hallowed chamber of the council, Lord Karrenen, a living repository of wisdom, acknowledged Ong and Keisha's presence with a subtle inclination of his regal head. His gesture carried the weight of centuries of leadership, an unspoken recognition of the significance of their mission. With a commanding gesture, he beckoned them to begin, his voice a harmonious blend of authority and sagacity that resonated through the chamber.

Ong, bearing the gravitas of their mission, cleared his throat before embarking on the narrative. His words flowed like a steadfast river, unwavering in their resolve. "Our sacred duty led us deep into the heart of darkness, into the malevolent citadel known as Fel Thalor."

Keisha, her eyes an enchanting shade of emerald, took up the mantle of the story with an eldritch allure that sent shivers down the spines of the council members. "Our objective was to unearth the truth about Phoenix's inheritance—to ascertain whether he now wields the full measure of his progenitor's shadowed legacy, the sinister powers of Maelgrim Shadowwalker."

Her words, delivered with the poise of an Eladrin, carried a weight of solemnity that hung in the air like a mysterious mist. The mere mention of Maelgrim Shadowwalker's name sent ripples of unease through the assembled council.

Lord Karrenen's visage, etched with a subtle furrow of brows, reflected a mix of curiosity and apprehension. The invocation of such potent malevolence marked a pivotal moment that demanded their undivided attention. His commanding gesture urged Ong and Keisha to unveil the intricate layers of their revelation.

Ong's narrative unfolded like a dark tapestry, each word resonating with the gravity of their dangerous mission. "Deep within the dark heart of Fel Thalor, we moved with stealth through labyrinthine alleys, cloaked in enigma. Our mission bore the weight of discerning whether Phoenix, the heir to the ominous mantle of Maelgrim Shadowwalker, had harnessed the evil tendrils of his progenitor's sorcery. Regrettably, during our sojourn, the elusive presence of Phoenix remained beyond our grasp."

As Ong's words hung in the air, a collective shiver coursed through the council members, their faces reflecting the deep-seated dread that clung to the legacy of the Shadowwalker lineage. The absence of a direct encounter with Phoenix left them in an unsettling state of uncertainty, where shadows concealed more than they unveiled.

Keisha, her countenance bathed in an almost mystical allure, interjected with a tone that resonated like an eldritch incantation. "Nonetheless, we ventured along the ashen trails of his presence, following traces of haunting remnants of shadow magic that bore witness to his unholy communion with these formidable powers. Yet, his motives persist as a riddle veiled in obscurity."

The council members, their expressions resembling an intricate tapestry woven from threads of apprehension and unwavering resolve, absorbed this newfound revelation. It was increasingly apparent that the realm's shadows concealed secrets yet to be unveiled, and the true extent of Phoenix's dominion over these murky depths remained an enigma that cast a long shadow over their deliberations.

Intriguingly, Keisha's eyes took on an ethereal luminescence as she continued her account. "In the stygian depths of Fel Thalor's heart, amid the winding corridors that seemed to mock the very concept of reason, and within the forbidden libraries whose tomes whispered forbidden knowledge, we stumbled upon yet another disquieting revelation. It appeared that an unseen hand had ventured into the archives of history, plumbing the depths of the tomes to unearth secrets concerning the Eladrin and our clandestine sanctuary, E'vahona."

Like the breath of the very tapestry of time, a silken hush enveloped the council chamber. A whispered symphony of unease coursed through the assemblage, its tendrils of concern entwining their thoughts like creeping vines. The sanctuary of E'vahona, a realm veiled in the most profound secrecy, had been revealed to prying eyes. The significance of this revelation hung like a storm cloud over their hearts, casting a shadow of trepidation.

Ong's oratory, imbued with a resonance that spoke of unwavering resolve, bestowed gravitas upon their discovery. "Undoubtedly," he affirmed with steadfast conviction, "the trail we followed points, with disconcerting clarity, toward a nexus that binds those in pursuit of this esoteric lore to Phoenix."

Among the council members, their exchanges of knowing glances were silent dialogues echoing with shared apprehension. The intricate threads of intrigue and peril were converging into an enigmatic tapestry, and its weaver concealed within the very shadows they sought to unveil.

Lord Karrenen, the patriarch of wisdom, bent his regal head, a visage painted with hues of gratitude and worry. "Your report, Ong and Keisha, is a revelation cascading like a waterfall in the fate river. You both hold pivotal roles in this intricate weaving of destiny, and your performance thus far is commendable."

His gaze, filled with a paternal warmth transcending mere words, bore into their souls. "In these trying hours, the gift of rest is as precious as the rarest gem. I counsel that you embrace this respite, rejuvenating your spirits and fortifying your resolve. The storm may grow fiercer, and we need your unwavering strength."

With a parting nod, Ong and Keisha gracefully exited the council chamber, their footsteps echoing the solemn cadence of their duty, the burden of their mission casting a shadow upon their shoulders.

As the grand tapestry of the council's deliberations drew to a close, Lord Karrenen, the sentinel of sagacity, proffered his prudent counsel. "It suits us to regather on the morrow to deliberate the specter of Phoenix and this emerging threat that haunts our realm's doorstep. With measured thought and gathering all knowledge, we shall chart the course of our response."

The somber yet resolute countenances of Lady Elowen and Lord Galadon echoed their consent, their brows etched with the gravity of their duty. Lady Lythia, the luminary of intellect, contributed, "Verily, we must not underestimate the looming specter that shrouds our realm in shadows. The safeguarding of our land rests upon the fortifications of our attention."

With a shared recognition that their realm's destiny hung in the balance, the council members dispersed into the twilight of their tasks. Each bore their mantle of responsibility with the knowledge that their choices would forge the very fabric of their realm's future.

Chapter 25

The Rising Threat

In the heart of E'vahona, cradled amid the ethereal splendor of the Eladrin city, the first rays of dawn stretched their golden fingers across the horizon, stirring Ong and Keisha from their slumber. The avian choristers' melodies, their celestial sonnet songs, wove a harmonious tapestry that roused the lovers from their dreams. Their chambers, adorned in the finest Eladrin craftsmanship, seemed to breathe with life, their walls draped in silks that shimmered like liquid stardust, telling intricate tales of ancient valor and enchantment.

As they prepared for the day, the chamber's opulence danced with the allure of Eladrin's artistry. Keisha, her fiery mane cascading like molten copper, was resplendent in an elegant gown that shifted through hues of pale greens and ocean blues with every graceful step, each movement a living canvas of colors. Beside her, Ong, his warrior's physique clad in armor of intricate design, glimmered like a sentinel of strength, a sentinel against the room's soft and ethereal hues.

Hand in hand, they descended grand staircases, their footsteps soft as the whisper of secrets upon polished marble floors. Their journey led them to the very heart of E'vahona—the enchanting garden. In this realm, the air bore the delicate fragrance of blossoming lilies and exotic blooms, which seemed to embody an eternal spring.

This garden was more than a mere reflection of nature; it was a testament to the Eladrin's profound connection with the living world. Graceful willow trees swayed perfectly with the caressing breeze, their leaves tenderly grazing crystalline ponds adorned with floating lilies. Sunlight-kissed petals unfurled in opulent arrays, a symphony of color set against the tapestry of emerald foliage. Butterflies, their wings a shimmering mosaic of iridescence, danced from petal to petal, crafting living brushstrokes of beauty.

Amidst the splendor of this natural haven, hidden alcoves along labyrinthine pathways beckoned Ong and Keisha. Elaborately carved benches, fashioned from alabaster and silver, bore plush cushions and delicate filigree, inviting moments of reprieve. Each nook unveiled a unique vista of the natural wonders—an idyllic pond where koi darted beneath lily pads, miniature waterfalls cascading over glistening stones, or arbors adorned with vines that created canopies where dappled sunlight played.

Ong and Keisha selected an alcove bedecked with glorious wisteria blooms in their quiet retreat. As they settled upon the alabaster bench, Keisha's fiery tresses framed her ethereal features, and Ong's robust, earthbound physique spoke of his human lineage. In the tender embrace of E'vahona's tranquility, they reveled in the timeless beauty of their love. This love transcended worlds, bringing them to this enchanted sanctuary where solace and joy found a home.

Enveloped by the harmonious symphony of nature and the gentle kiss of sunlight filtering through the leaves, Ong and Keisha realized that E'vahona was not just a city; it was a sanctuary where their love flourished—an oasis of serenity and a testament to their indomitable bond. In the heart of the hidden realm, they cherished the present, their souls interwoven with E'vahona's enchantment.

As they marveled at the tranquil beauty of their surroundings, a vibrant tableau unfolded before them. Pumpkin, their steadfast panther companion, reveled in the pure joy of her element. Her sleek, obsidian fur shimmered in the morning light as she playfully pounced and chased kaleidoscopic butterflies. Each bound and leap displayed her lithe grace, and her exuberant laughter harmonized with the trills and warbles of her airborne playmates.

Watching their loyal friend's carefree antics, Ong and Keisha exchanged knowing smiles. Pumpkin embodied the spirit of freedom and exhilaration, a constant reminder of E'vahona's limitless wonders.

Their idyllic reverie came to an abrupt halt with the arrival of Lord Karrenen, the venerable sage of E'vahona. He approached with regal grace, his silver mane reflecting the golden sunlight, and his eyes, akin to twin pools of ancient knowledge, gleamed with profound wisdom. The atmosphere was steeped in deep respect and reverence as he entered the garden, adding an aura of solemnity to the tranquil setting.

With a graceful incline, Lord Karrenen acknowledged the sacredness of their moment and extended his heartfelt apologies for the interruption. Like a melodic river of wisdom, his voice flowed through the air like a soothing breeze rustling the leaves. "I beg your pardon for this intrusion," he began, his words carrying the weight of ages. "But I come bearing a matter of utmost importance. The council convenes later today, and the growing power of Phoenix shall be at the forefront of our deliberations."

Ong and Keisha exchanged resolute glances, the tranquil contentment of their sanctuary giving way to an unwavering determination. Keisha's unshaken and determined voice rang out like a clarion call, a declaration of their shared understanding that they must confront the looming specter of Phoenix head-on. "We shall be in attendance," she affirmed, their mutual commitment to facing the encroaching threat clear in her words.

Lord Karrenen took his leave with a bow of deference, allowing them to return to their garden sanctuary. As he departed, Ong and Keisha knew that the tranquil respite of E'vahona was but a fleeting reprieve. The ascendant power of Phoenix would cast its ominous shadow even over the hidden realm, and they were prepared to meet the challenges ahead with unwavering love, unbreakable loyalty, and indomitable resolve.

Within the evil depths of Goldmoor's sinister throne room, Phoenix held court, his dark dominion shrouded in dread. The chamber's walls, adorned with macabre tapestries that chronicled cruel conquests and ominous rituals, seemed to throb with malice, casting serpentine shadows that slithered and writhed upon the frigid stone floor. Phoenix's throne, a nightmarish creation carved from obsidian and etched with cryptic symbols, stood as a brooding horror, its malevolence palpable within the chamber.

Against this backdrop, a Druchii soldier clad in ebony armor that gleamed with an unsettling aura hastened into the throne room. His echoing footsteps reverberated through the dim, oppressive atmosphere, thick with a sense of impending doom. Phoenix, the master of this wicked realm, perched atop his twisted throne, his crimson eyes aflame with a vicious fire that felt like it could sear one's soul.

The soldier approached, his voice trembling with trepidation as he delivered his report, "Lord Phoenix, we have uncovered the lifeless forms of two Druchii concealed within a shadowy alcove of our city."

Phoenix's lips curled into an evil smile, revealing teeth as sharp as serrated blades. His command was swift and unrelenting, a decree that sent shivers of terror coursing through the heart of Goldmoor. "Initiate a comprehensive scouring of our realm," he hissed, his voice dripping with menace. "Every dwelling, every residence, must undergo meticulous inspection for the presence of interlopers. Those discovered must be swiftly and unmercifully brought to the palace."

As his dark proclamation reverberated through the throne room, the air grew colder, the hostile grip of Goldmoor tightening like an oppressive vise. In that chilling moment, it became painfully clear that no secrets would remain concealed, and no intruders would elude the all-seeing gaze of Phoenix. Goldmoor, a city veiled in shadows, would yield nothing to the curious, and its master would stop at nothing to maintain his dominion over the abyss.

Through the dimly lit labyrinthine thoroughfares of Goldmoor, Druchii soldiers moved with unwavering resolve, their footfalls a grim cadence echoing through the murky alleyways. Their eyes gleamed with an unsettling intensity as they approached each residence, their steps imbued with the weight of their ominous task. The air seemed heavy, saturated with the palpable intrusion that hung like a poisonous fog in the depths of night.

As they crossed the thresholds of Goldmoor's dwellings, they did so without mercy, leaving no corner unexamined. Their gloved hands tore through rooms, upending furniture and desecrating tapestries in their relentless pursuit of any sign of intruders who might have infiltrated the city's shadows under the cloak of darkness. Drawers were wrenched open, wardrobes stripped bare, and every conceivable hiding place within each dwelling was ruthlessly scrutinized.

The Druchii soldiers executed their task with unwavering determination, their vigilant eyes scouring every nook and cranny for the faintest trace of foreign presence. The flickering torchlight cast eerie and grotesque shadows upon the walls, weaving a disquieting tapestry that draped the atmosphere with an unsettling aura. Their diligence knew no bounds in their relentless quest to fulfill their lord's chilling command.

As time passed, the search became an unending ordeal, house after house, street after street. Yet, despite their tenacity, the soldiers' stoic expressions gradually betrayed the creeping tendrils of frustration. The elusive intruders remained frustratingly concealed from their grasp as if they were phantoms woven into the city's dark tapestry.

Finally, one of the soldiers returned to Phoenix, his demeanor a silent testament to the fruitless nature of their endeavors. He reported that no intruders had been unearthed within the sinister embrace of Goldmoor's boundaries, leaving the kingdom seemingly untouched by foreign presence.

Phoenix's countenance darkened as he absorbed the disturbing news, a pervasive disquiet settling like an ominous cloud upon his shoulders. The shadowed city had yielded no answers, and the enigma of the deceased Druchii persisted, casting a sinister veil of uncertainty over his evil rule.

Phoenix's thoughts swirled in a maelstrom of disquiet, a storm that raged within the confines of his mind as he ascended from his imposing throne. The revelation of the two lifeless Druchii soldiers had cast a persistent pall of doubt, an enigmatic specter refusing to yield to the light of understanding. What if these shadowed intruders harbored a covert purpose, an insidious mission to liberate King Alex from his chains? The notion clawed at him like a relentless wraith haunting the innermost sanctums of his consciousness.

With unwavering determination, Phoenix traversed the labyrinthine corridors of his malevolent castle, his presence akin to a blade that cut through the air, parting the way for his relentless advance. His obsidian robes, adorned with runic sigils that pulsed with ominous energies, billowed around him like an ethereal shroud as if the very fabric of the void itself clung to his form.

He arrived at the forbidding entrance to the dungeon, where darkness reigned supreme and despair was the only constant. The ponderous iron door groaned, revealing the chilling and damp chamber within. King Alex, a once-proud figure now marked by the ravages of captivity and torment, sat upon the unyielding stone floor, his visage etched with the weight of his enduring imprisonment.

"Why do you persist in your intrusion?" King Alex's voice, a weary echo of its former strength, carried a bitter undertone from years of isolation. "Can you not depart and grant me the solitude I so desperately crave?"

Phoenix's eyes narrowed, a disconcerting glimmer of malevolence swirling within their depths. He did not heed the king's question, driven by an insatiable curiosity that gnawed at him like a relentless predator. "Have there been any who have ventured into your presence?" he demanded, his voice a subtle undercurrent of menace.

King Alex hesitated, a fleeting contemplation dancing across his worn countenance. Then, with a profound sigh and an air of reluctant acquiescence, he responded, "No, Phoenix. No one has visited me."

Like dark tendrils of a looming storm, the warlock's suspicions refused to abate. His fingers, imbued with the latent power of malevolence, tingled with a sinister anticipation that lurked just beneath the surface of his skin. The temptation to delve deeper into the recesses of King Alex's thoughts, to unveil the hidden truths through his sinister powers, threatened to overwhelm him.

Without warning, Phoenix unleashed a storm of psychic torment upon the imprisoned king, a relentless deluge of anguish that sought to shatter the fortress of his will. Yet, King Alex clung firmly to his denial, his fortitude unwavering, like a lone sentinel against the dark tide.

With a guttural growl of frustration, Phoenix retreated, his evil power receding like the ebbing tide of a tumultuous storm. The king's defiance had not wavered, and Phoenix, like a defeated tempest, could extract no more from the impenetrable depths of his captive's mind.

In the turbulent wake of his confrontation, Phoenix seethed with an inner tempest as he stormed away from the oppressive dungeon, leaving King Alex to dwell in solitude once more. The once-resolute king, battered and bruised in both body and spirit, exhaled a breath he hadn't realized he'd been holding. Phoenix's relentless onslaught of torment had thrust him into yet another harrowing ordeal, but it had not succeeded in shattering his indomitable spirit. While encroaching darkness, a glimmer of hope persisted like a solitary ember on the blackest night.

King Alex sighed in relief, for Phoenix's malevolent powers had failed to unveil the clandestine truth—he remained unaware that a pair of Eladrin had ventured into his presence. Moreover, his keen senses had not detected the subtle disablement of the traps that guarded the path to the dungeon, an artful ploy executed by the Eladrin with the hope that Phoenix would remain oblivious. Their intent was clear: to avoid the necessity of turning off these treacherous mechanisms once Queen Jeanne was safely in their care, and together, they embarked on the journey to reclaim the city.

Yet, as Phoenix retreated, burdened by his unresolved suspicions, his footsteps resounded through the labyrinthine halls of his malevolent stronghold. Each echoing footfall resonated like a lament, an ominous omen heralding the relentless pursuit of his enigmatic purpose. His destination beckoned from the heart of his shadowed domain, a realm of knowledge and secrets concealed deep within the castle's core—the library.

In the dimly lit expanse of the library, Qellaun and Lyra, an enigmatic pair marked by otherworldly qualities, stood as sentinels amidst the labyrinth of ancient tomes. The flickering candles that lined the rows of books cast their ethereal glow, revealing spectral silhouettes that danced like wraiths upon the tapestry of knowledge. As Phoenix, the master of darkness, entered this chamber of enigmas, Qellaun turned to face him, his countenance as tranquil and composed as a star-studded night sky.

Within the confines of this sanctum, where the boundaries between the human and the arcane blurred, the urgency in Phoenix's voice reverberated like a clarion call, a plea for solace amid the storm of his relentless inquiries.

"Have you discovered anything?" he implored, his words a prayer to the cosmos, a yearning for respite from the ceaseless torment of uncertainty.

Qellaun, bearing the weight of regret like a cloak of shadows, responded with a solemnity befitting this sanctum of ancient wisdom. "I regret to inform you, Phoenix," he began, his words laden with the somber truth, "that our exhaustive search has yielded no further revelations regarding E'vahona or the veiled secrets it guards. The archives remain as enigmatic and impenetrable as the celestial void."

Phoenix's frustration, a tempestuous maelstrom churning within him, manifested in the clenching of his fists—each digit a vice grip upon his insatiable ambition. "E'vahona," he muttered bitterly, an utterance of both desire and vexation. It hung in the air like an unresolved melody, a haunting refrain that echoed through the cavernous depths of his psyche. "How can an entire realm persist in eluding my grasp?"

Lyra, her voice a gentle melody that resonated with ancient wisdom, wove her words into the tapestry of the conversation. "The knowledge of E'vahona," she began, her words like notes from a celestial harp, "has forever been veiled in mystery, an enigma woven into the very fabric of our existence. It is whispered to exist beyond the realms known to our kind, a sanctuary untouched by the relentless march of time or the prying gaze of outsiders."

Phoenix, a storm of resolve and unbridled ambition swirling within him, fixed his gaze upon the elusive horizon of knowledge. His eyes, twin orbs of relentless determination, blazed like twin supernovae, their radiance illuminating the depths of his insatiable hunger for the forbidden wisdom that had remained tantalizingly just beyond his reach. "Complacency," he hissed, the word a venomous serpent that could not find purchase in his heart. "E'vahona holds the key to my ascent, and rest is a luxury I cannot afford."

As he cast a fleeting glance toward Lyra, his crimson eyes bore into her very essence. "Continue your search," he commanded, a solemn decree that brooked no refusal. "But do more than that. Delve into the enigma of the Eladrin, this Keisha. Uncover her secrets, for they may yet serve my purpose."

Qellaun, bearing the weight of truth like an anchor in a stormy sea, interjected cautiously. "My Lord," he began, his words a shield against unchecked ambition, "even if we were to uncover secrets about Keisha, Swifthammer and her people guard her like the most sacred relic. They would sooner move mountains than allow you to approach."

Phoenix's response was a scorching glare, a wordless testament to the depths of his intent. As he turned away from the ancient library, the echoes of untapped power and the enigma of E'vahona's secrets whispered in the recesses of his mind. The pursuit was unending, a relentless quest that led him to the precipice of shadow and light, where the truths hidden within the veil of obscurity would mold his very destiny.

Lyra's gaze shifted, her eyes grazing the countless tomes that lined the library's shelves, their ancient pages housing secrets that had defied revelation. Her sigh was a lament for the weight of their task, a burden that pressed upon her like the stone foundations of their dark citadel. "But E'vahona," she murmured, the name a whisper that carried the weight of generations of fruitless searches. "It has lingered beyond the grasp of our kin for untold eras. How can he harbor the belief that we will succeed where countless others have faltered?"

Qellaun's response bore the quiet resignation of one who has glimpsed the vastness of their leader's ambitions and the shadows that envelop them. "Lyra," he intoned, his voice an elegy to the futile pursuit of the unknowable, "Phoenix's heart is a furnace that burns with unquenchable fire. He champions the improbable, for he has wrested triumph from the jaws of impossibility. The reasons behind his pursuit of E'vahona may remain cloaked in an enigma, but we must carefully navigate the treacherous currents of our quest. For in the uncharted depths, we may unearth the keys to unlock a power beyond mortal imagination."

The library bore witness to their solemn conversation, its atmosphere heavy with the weight of their leader's insatiable demands. The quest for E'vahona's secrets persisted, a journey fraught with danger and uncertainty, where the shadows concealed not only the mysteries of the realm but also the price that would be exacted to unveil them.

Lyra's gaze swept across the sprawling labyrinth of shelves that lined the library's grand chamber. Each tome, ancient and weathered, held within its pages the accumulated wisdom and elusive secrets of a thousand ages. She sighed a melancholy exhalation that echoed through the cavernous chamber like the tolling of a solemn bell. It was a sigh born of their burdens, the weight of their unending quest pressing upon them like the immovable foundations of their dark citadel.

"But E'vahona," she whispered, the name escaping her lips as a fragile breath carrying the weight of generations of Druchii's fruitless pursuits. Her mournful lament voice hung in the air like a mournful dirge. "It has remained an elusive specter, just beyond our reach, for countless eras. How can he believe that we will succeed where countless others have faltered?"

Qellaun's response was a solemn acknowledgment, his words imbued with the resignation of one who had ventured deep into the abyss of Phoenix's ambitions and glimpsed the relentless shadows that shrouded them. His voice, a steady elegy to the ceaseless pursuit of the unknowable, resonated through the ancient library, a sanctuary of enigmas.

"Lyra," he intoned, his words a melancholy ode to the pursuit of the impossible, "Phoenix's heart is an inferno that consumes the boundaries of possibility. He champions the improbable, for he has wrested victory from the jaws of the unimaginable. The reasons behind his relentless quest for E'vahona may remain concealed in an impenetrable enigma, but we must carefully navigate the treacherous currents of our journey. For in the uncharted depths of our pursuit, we may yet unearth the keys to unlock a power beyond mortal imagination."

The library, a silent witness to their conversation, bore the weight of their leader's insatiable thirst for knowledge. Its atmosphere, thick with untold secrets, hung like a heavy shroud. The quest for E'vahona's hidden truths persisted, a perilous odyssey fraught with danger and uncertainty, where the shadows concealed not only the mysteries of the realm but also the toll that would be exacted to unveil them.

Chapter 26

Whispers in the Wind

In the heart of Crystal Vale, cradled within the verdant embrace of majestic oaks and towering maples, the palace stood as a glorious testament to the harmonious union of human artistry and nature's awe-inspiring grandeur. The very essence of the land seemed to conspire in favor of the palace's existence, as if the ancient trees had willingly bent their branches in homage. Colorful banners, adorned with the proud emblem of the kingdom, fluttered in a choreographed dance with the gentle breeze, their vibrant hues weaving a tapestry of whispered legends.

Approaching this architectural marvel, two gallant soldiers of Crystal Vale embarked on a journey through an enchanted threshold. The stone archways, meticulously adorned with motifs that appeared to narrate the very history of the land beneath their feet, extended an irresistible invitation. Each stride upon the polished marble staircase was a deliberate step toward the monumental double doors of the palace, their wooden panels intricately etched with sagas of human heroes and historic triumphs.

Upon crossing that threshold, the soldiers found themselves cradled within the sanctuary of the palace's hallowed halls. Here, the regal authority of the monarchy waltzed in perfect harmony with the soulful warmth of human craftsmanship. Elaborate tapestries, painstakingly woven by the skilled hands of artisans, depicted tales of courage and unity. Their vibrant colors radiated life within the solemn confines of the chamber, as if the walls had absorbed the essence of courage and heroism, now releasing it back as an unspoken promise of hope.

And at the heart of this rich tapestry of existence, King Manard held court from the throne of Crystal Vale. He was not merely a sovereign but the living embodiment of his city's essence. His presence transcended the boundaries of mere authority, exuding wisdom and compassion like a haunting melody that tugged at the heartstrings of all who beheld him. His keen eyes, reminiscent of ancient sages peering into the depths of the human soul, mirrored a profound understanding of his subjects' needs. It was as if the very land whispered its secrets into his willing ear, forging an unbreakable bond between king and city.

Kneeling with an earnestness that rivaled the fervor of mystics at an ancient altar, the soldiers presented themselves before the throne. Their voices carried the weight of undeniable destiny, resounding like the clarion call of fate itself. With unwavering determination etched upon their faces, they wove a tale of their recent voyage to the forsaken island—an accursed lagoon, besieged by the untamed and the formidable. Sea serpents, hydras, and dragons, titans of the deep, had cast their ominous shadows over this desolate land, rendering it off-limits to all who dared to approach.

Amidst this maelstrom of chaos and primal fury, a solitary tower stood as an enigmatic sentinel amidst the stormy sea. Its silhouette against the turbulent horizon whispered secrets even the waves dared not divulge. The culmination of their report hung in the air, an unspoken question, like a hidden riddle seeking an answer in the depths of the king's eyes. King Manard, his regal bearing untouched by the tremors of uncertainty, nodded solemnly, his voice resonant like the measured footfalls of a solitary traveler through a moonlit forest. "Thank you for unveiling this puzzle," he said. "We shall delve deeper into this mystery. Perhaps we are one step closer to reuniting Queen Jeanne with King Alex."

In that pivotal moment, Crystal Vale held its breath. Its historic tapestries rendered mute witnesses to the birth of a new chapter in their kingdom's annals. The path ahead was fraught with the shadows of uncertainty. Still, King Manard, a beacon of unwavering resolve, was poised to illuminate those shadows and restore their beloved land's harmonious cadence.

As King Manard strode through the grand halls of the Crystal Vale palace, his thoughts raced like a storm, stirred by the sinister actions of

Phoenix and the ever-present specter of Queen Jeanne's safety. Frustration swelled within him like a surging tide, for the lack of immediate communication with Lord Karrenen left him grasping for swifter means to convey his concerns. None of the territories offered a method of contact that did not stretch across days or weeks, and their difficult situation demanded a more expeditious conduit for exchanging vital information.

The relentless hunger for reliable information gnawed at King Manard's consciousness like an insatiable, otherworldly beast. The fate of Goldmoor and the enigma of King Alex's whereabouts remained inextricably bound to the liberation of Queen Jeanne. A faint glimmer of hope had emerged as his soldiers unearthed a slender thread of possibility, but the impassable chasm separating them from the Eladrin elves threatened to eclipse it. The fingers of King Manard, laden with the weight of a kingdom's destiny, drummed impatiently upon the ornate marble balustrade, the rhythmic cadence a reflection of his inner turmoil. Frustration furrowed his brows like thunderclouds heavy with the impending storm, and every passing moment without news from Lord Karrenen deepened the abyss of his unease.

Like a longing poet searching the heavens for inspiration, his gaze turned toward a towering window that framed the azure sky. Amidst the vast expanse of cerulean, a spectacle of pure wonder unfolded. A magnificent bird, transcendent in its ethereal splendor, soared with the grace of celestial ballet amongst the cotton-candy clouds. Its feathers shimmered, a cascade of colorful hues defying the laws of nature, and its wings pulsed with an arcane vitality that marked it as an entity apart from the mundane avian realm.

An elderly advisor, an oracle of knowledge and lore, sensed the king's enraptured gaze and approached him with measured steps, like a sage summoned to reveal ancient truths. "Your Majesty," he began, his voice a symphony of reverence, "that is an Etherwing, a being of legend within our realm. It possesses a wondrous gift, the power to bear messages across the sprawling tapestry of Vacari's domains, guided by the mystical currents of magic."

King Manard's curiosity kindled, like a dormant ember awoken by a breath of enchantment, and he prayed to the advisor to illuminate the secrets of these ethereal beings. The advisor, his wisdom a river flowing through the annals of time, shared the lore of the Etherwings. These majestic creatures had long served as messengers and guardians of Vacari's intricate web of mystical connections, weaving through the ether like celestial weavers of destiny. They could penetrate even the most remote and clandestine corners of the realm, guided by an innate communion with the magical ley lines that crisscrossed Vacari's heart.

As the lore sang, their feathers bore the ancient enchantments of ages past, a gift that allowed them to harness the pulsating currents of magic, making them swifter than the wind and more agile than the fastest arrow. They were not mere messengers but custodians of Vacari's most jealously guarded secrets. They were a living testament to the enduring bond between the realm and the mystical forces that coursed through its veins. In the eyes of the people, they stood as symbols, emissaries of a realm's unwavering connection to the enigmatic parties that flowed through the very fabric of its existence.

The advisor's words unveiled the enigmatic nature of the Etherwings, beings discerning as the most selective fine art connoisseurs. To bridge the chasm between mortal and ethereal, one needed a profound comprehension of the arcane and an innate communion with the very soul of Crystal Vale. Only the elite, often mages or those whose souls bore the indelible mark of affinity for the mystical energies coursing through the realm, found themselves on the cusp of these majestic beings' recognition. Building an accord with an Etherwing was akin to a delicate dance, demanding the steps of patience, the notes of respect, and the unwavering commitment to guarding Vacari's most coveted enigmas. With the wisdom of ages etched upon his countenance, King Manard grasped the weight of this undertaking and the necessity of selecting the perfect candidate for this pivotal role.

In the days that followed, Crystal Vale embarked upon a clandestine odyssey, an intricate web of exploration woven through the tapestry of the city to unveil those whose souls bore the elusive gifts required to commune with the Etherwings. An august council assembled, comprising sages, mages, seers, and scholars, each a luminary in their own right, to sift through the voluminous reservoir of hopeful aspirants. These extraordinary individuals would need a mastery of magic and a profound and unassailable connection to the land's essence and the ethereal energies that wove through it like threads in an ancient loom.

The quest spanned every nook and cranny of Crystal Vale as whispers and rumors of potential candidates trickled in from the city's farthest reaches. From the humble village healers, gifted with the uncanny ability to mend wounds with but a gentle touch, to reclusive hermits dwelling deep within the forest, said to commune with the spirits that lingered in the ancient woods, no stone remained unturned. Those anointed few who would bear the solemn responsibility of approaching the legendary Etherwings and weaving the threads of trust with these enigmatic entities emerged from this painstaking process. The gravity of their calling was an invisible mantle, for upon their shoulders rested not only the fate of Queen Jeanne but the very equilibrium of the territories they held dear.

The air thrummed with anticipation and hope as Crystal Vale's brilliant minds sifted through the multitudes. The voyage to unlock the Etherwings' well-guarded secrets had embarked upon its inaugural steps, and the entire domain held its collective breath, awaiting the emergence of those destined souls poised to embark on this monumental odyssey of connection and revelation.

In the heart of Crystal Vale, where the sun's shining rays filtered through the time-scarred boughs of ancient oaks, weaving an intricate tapestry of dappled light and shadow upon the verdant, emerald carpet that graced the forest floor, King Manard presided, a colossus of anticipation. At his side, a trinity of mages—Zeveus, Orius, and Idos—stood, their robes agleam with the vivid hues of amethyst, sapphire, and emerald, a vibrant testament to the arcane mastery coursing through their very beings.

The Etherwings, celestial beings of legendary grace and enchantment, perched upon the outstretched branches of a colossal oak, their plumage aglow with the shifting colors of twilight's embrace. A gentle breeze caressed the leaves, and the atmosphere hummed with an otherworldly current as if the very earth held its breath, awaiting the profound union that was to unfold.

King Manard, a paragon of regal poise amidst this spectral confluence, turned his gaze upon Idos, the first among the mages. With the gravity of eons and the resonance of ancient chants, Idos advanced, his voice a sonorous echo laced with the words of eldritch power. His fingers traced arcane sigils through the air, weaving a tapestry of spells that transcended human understanding. A melodic, ethereal, and transcendent chant cascaded from his lips, resonating through the forest like a symphony of nature.

As the crescendo of the incantation reached its zenith, the luminous orbs that were the Etherwings' eyes locked onto Idos, their iridescent plumage stirring with spectral grace. The forest seemed to bow reverently, each leaf and twig poised in rapturous obeisance.

Yet, in an instant, a collective gasp rippled through the onlookers. The Etherwings, with an elegance akin to celestial bodies descending from the sky, took wings, their mighty pinions cleaving the air with otherworldly grace. They ascended into the heavens, leaving a trail of mystic light that painted the sky in hues of ethereal luminescence. It was as though the cosmos had beckoned, and the celestial emissaries heeded the siren call without hesitation.

Idos, bearing the weight of disappointment and the bittersweet taste of resignation, watched their ascent, his outstretched hand slowly descending to his side. The forest, a sanctuary of ageless wisdom, returned to its natural rhythm. Still, the memory of that brief enchantment lingered, a poignant testament to the profound quest for unity and salvation ahead.

King Manard, bearing upon his countenance the gravity of a monarch entrusted with a decision that could sway the very course of destiny, turned toward his counsel and the two remaining mages, Zeveus and Orius. The relentless pursuit of the one who could forge a communion with the Etherwings, a celestial bridge between realms, pressed onward. In this persistent quest, the luminous promise of a brighter future dangled precariously, its radiance balanced upon the edge of a fragile precipice.

Orius, enrobed in the splendor of sapphire that rippled like the fathomless depths of an inner ocean, extended his arms heavenward as if beckoning the very stars to partake in his arcane symphony. His voice, a mellifluous incantation, rippled through the forest, each note akin to a serenade offered unto the heavens. His nimble fingers wove intricate patterns, an ancestral tapestry of a magical lineage traced back eons—his chant, an ethereal loom, interlaced with the very fabric of the enchanted glade.

The Etherwings, their plumage a shimmering tableau reminiscent of the twilight sky, regarded Orius with a gaze that held the secrets of epochs past. For a fleeting heartbeat, the forest, attuned to the celestial harmonies, seemed to hold its breath in collective anticipation. It was as if the spirits of the land itself had joined this ethereal chorus, their presence palpable amidst the verdant embrace.

Yet, the instant that Orius's hand extended to bridge the distance and establish that profound connection, the Etherwings, with a fluid grace that mirrored the elusive dance of moonlit wraiths, deftly eluded his touch. Their movements, a symphony of fluidity and evasion, left naught but a tantalizing wisp of their presence in their wake.

A collective gasp, as if the air itself exhaled disappointment, resonated through the assembly, their hopes momentarily dashed against the jagged cliffs of uncertainty. Orius, his sapphire gaze soon shadowed by the cloak of thwarted aspirations, withdrew his hand. The Etherwings, seated upon their arboreal throne, appeared to turn their gaze skyward as if beseeching answers from the boundless cosmos, leaving the city's fate suspended in the delicate balance of possibility.

Though the weight of a second failure pressed upon his heart like a mountain's unyielding bulk, King Manard's resolve remained steadfast, a beacon of unwavering light amidst the encroaching shadows. He understood that the odyssey to unite their fractured realms was a tapestry woven with threads of adversity, and the path ahead lay shrouded in a veil of enigmatic uncertainty. With a resolute nod that echoed like a solemn oath, he turned to his advisors and the last remaining mage, Zeveus, and the quest to find the one who could commune with the Etherwings pressed on, each moment a luminous ember of hope glowing brighter in the gathering dusk.

As the sun, a molten sphere of glory, dipped below the horizon, bestowing its final, golden benediction upon the day, the forest of Crystal Vale stood sentinel, holding its breath in palpable anticipation. Zeveus, the last of the chosen mages, strode into the waning light. Cloaked in robes that mirrored the ever-shifting hues of twilight, he radiated an aura of tranquility, a serene lake cradling the tender whispers of evening's breeze.

The Etherwings, their ethereal forms aglow with the soft, silvery luminescence of the moon, regarded Zeveus with eyes that mirrored the unfathomable depths of the night sky. Each feather upon their majestic wings bore a glimmer of starlight as though they were woven from the cosmic fabric that stitched together the heavens. Their presence exuded an aura of ancient wisdom as if they were sentinels guarding secrets that spanned epochs.

With a grace that transcended the limitations of mere mortals, Zeveus raised his hands, his fingers tracing intricate patterns in the air, a celestial dance mirroring the constellations above. His voice, a melody that resonated with the very heartbeat of the earth, wove through the forest, a harmonious duet with the murmurs of the ancient trees. The enchantment he summoned transcended the tangible world, reaching out to caress the very essence of the Etherwings.

In that fleeting, eternal moment, the forest held its collective breath again, suspended in a delicate breath between worlds. And then, as if the stars had aligned in celestial agreement, it happened—the Etherwings, their trust forged in the crucible of magic and destiny, allowed Zeveus to approach. One among them, a glorious creature whose feathers glistened like moonlit pearls, descended in a choreography of grace, alighting upon Zeveus's shoulders.

The assembled witnesses, their breaths hushed in awe and wonder, bore witness to a communion forged in the realms of possibility and the ethereal. Zeveus, his fingers a master's brush on the canvas of magic, touched the Etherwing's iridescent feathers, sending ripples of arcane energy cascading through their newfound connection.

In that transformative instant, Crystal Vale and its enigmatic citizens discovered a beacon of hope, a bridge to the undiscovered realms, and a guardian of secrets that had eluded them for eons. As the Etherwing, with a celestial twinkle in its eye, conveyed its trust to Zeveus, the destinies of their realms converged, setting the stage for an extraordinary journey into the uncharted territories of magic and wonder.

King Manard's voice, a resonant command that rivaled the authority of the whispering winds in their might, poured forth with words heavy as the burdens of responsibility and trust. "Zeveus, Guardian of the Etherwings," he intoned, each syllable etched with the gravity of leadership and the profound weight of purpose. "Your singular bond with these enigmatic beings has unveiled a path to our shared destiny. By the power vested in me, a sacred trust from the hearts of the people of Crystal Vale, I now anoint you as the Warden of Mystical Connections."

The title reverberated through the chamber, echoing like the refrain of destiny—a mantle of profound responsibility that Zeveus embraced with the humility and grace befitting a true mage. In solemn reverence, the mages and courtiers bowed their heads, paying homage to the birth of a new era.

King Manard extended a delicate scroll, its parchment infused with the essence of their realm's hopes and fears. He held it aloft, the words adorning it aglow with latent enchantment, shimmering like stardust suspended in the celestial void. "Zeveus," he instructed, his voice a lyrical cadence woven with ancient wisdom, "deliver this message to our trusted Etherwings. Let them be the carriers of our collective hopes, the messengers who bear our most cherished dreams upon their celestial wings."

With a profound sense of purpose and a heart brimming with unspoken gratitude, Zeveus accepted the scroll with a respectful bow. His eyes, mirrors of deep connection, mirrored the immense gratitude that words alone could not encompass. In that poignant moment, he ascended to the role of the conduit between realms, a bridge spanning the chasm of uncertainty and reuniting their fates in the boundless tapestry of destiny.

In the heart of E'vahona, where the luminous trees stood sentinel, their ethereal glow casting a celestial luminescence upon the land, Lord Karrenen stood in contemplation by a tranquil pond. The calm waters mirrored the ever-shifting tapestry of his emotions, and each ripple reflected his inner turmoil. His scholarly robes, spun from the finest silks native to the realm, flowed like spectral tendrils in the gentle breeze, imbuing him with an otherworldly air.

As he beheld the serene splendor of his hidden realm, Karrenen's acute elven senses caught a faint glimmer—a mere mote of light that danced within the verdant canopy of the ancient arboreal giants. His keen eyes, attuned to the subtle harmonies of nature, followed the path of this unexpected luminescence, tracing it back to its elusive source.

There, amidst the verdant boughs of a majestic Etherwing tree, a regal emissary of the Eladrin realm held court. The creature, a paragon of otherworldly beauty, possessed feathers that shimmered with an iridescence so profound that each hue melded seamlessly into the next, like colors in a painter's dream. The bird's gaze bore into Karrenen with an intelligence that transcended the ordinary as if it held the very secrets of the cosmos in its gleaming eyes.

Karrenen approached the Etherwing with a hushed reverence, his heart a symphony of curiosity and trepidation. He extended a slender hand, fingers like tendrils of starlight, and the avian sentinel, recognizing him as both a renowned mage and the guardian of E'vahona, permitted the approach. From the bird's delicate beak, Karrenen received a message—a miniature scroll bound with a ribbon of silver.

With an elegantly deft motion, he unfurled the scroll, his keen, elven eyes deciphering the words King Manard of Crystal Vale had meticulously penned. Like an icy breath from the abyss, the message was clear and chilling—a report detailing the existence of a solitary tower amidst a realm besieged by the chaos of sea serpents, hydras, and dragons. An island shrouded in mysterious danger and unfathomable secrecy, where Queen Jeanne, the cherished wife of King Alex, might be held captive, her fate entwined with the evil forces that lurked therein.

Karrenen's heart plummeted like a fallen star, descending into the abyss of despair as he fully comprehended the profound gravity of the situation. The potential fate of Queen Jeanne, a luminous linchpin in the intricate machinations of Vacari's stability, hung like a Damoclean sword over their world, casting a looming shadow that threatened to engulf their existence. It was a moment when the churning tides of destiny swirled with ominous portent.

With measured resolve, he recognized that the hour had come to convene the council, to gather the minds and wisdom of Vacari, and to deliberate not only on this newfound peril that had breached their sanctum but also on the burgeoning tempest of Phoenix's ascendance—a storm they had anticipated, yet whose full fury remained an enigma.

As he delicately refolded the message, the parchment bearing the weight of worlds, and secured it within the silken folds of his robes, Lord Karrenen couldn't help but be awed by the grand tapestry of fate, intricate and sprawling, that unfolded before him. The destinies of kingdoms, cities, and realms swayed on the precipice of uncertainty, their delicate balance teetering like a tightrope walker on a steep edge. He, a venerable mage and guardian of E'vahona, understood that he was a weaver of threads, entrusted with shaping their shared destiny, his actions a reflection of the cosmic loom upon which their world hung.

Chapter 27

The Mystique of the Noble Dragons

The Council Chambers of E'vahona, a sanctuary of Eladrin craftsmanship beyond compare, unfurled before Lord Karrenen like the pages of a time-worn, enchanted tome. Its architecture stood as a triumphant symphony of ethereal beauty, a celestial ballet of purpose and artistry intertwined. Celestial tapestries spun with the finest threads of magic adorned the walls, their intricate patterns weaving the tale of E'vahona's storied history in hues so vivid they appeared to waltz with a life all their own. Each stroke of color upon these woven canvases narrated a chapter in the realm's illustrious past, akin to the stars that form an epic constellation.

Above, crystal chandeliers, reminiscent of celestial bodies, hung suspended in the vaulted sky of the chamber. Their radiant luminance enveloped the space in a gentle, otherworldly glow, bestowing an enchantment that defied mortal comprehension. It was as if the very stars, moved by some cosmic benevolence, had descended from the night sky to grace this hallowed ground with their presence, infusing it with a mystic energy that transcended the grasp of mere mortals.

As Lord Karrenen strode into the chamber, his entrance cast an additional layer of gravity upon the already electrified atmosphere. The expectant gazes of his council comrades converged upon him like constellations in an ocean of cosmic wisdom. Lord Galadon, the venerable sage, occupied the very heart of their assembly, his eyes aglow with the ancient sagacity honed across countless eons. He stood as the living vault of

E'vahona's history, a sage whose knowledge spanned epochs, and his mere presence served as a monument to the indomitable legacy of their people.

Lady Elowen, an embodiment of grace itself, stood in his company, her tresses of golden hair cascading like liquid sunlight. Her regal bearing and ethereal beauty symbolized E'vahona's eternal allure. Beside her, Lady Lythia, a paragon of strength and commanding presence, seemed to encapsulate the very essence of their realm's unyielding fortitude. Together, they forged a triumvirate of wisdom, elegance, and power, poised to navigate E'vahona through the trials ahead.

As Ong and Keisha crossed the threshold into these sanctified council chambers, a palpable aura of reverence permeated the air as if the walls murmured age-old secrets to those who dared to venture within. Like sentinels of enlightenment, the council members acknowledged their presence with solemn nods, their eyes alight with the radiant spark of a shared purpose transcending time. In this chamber of destiny, the legacy of E'vahona came to life, an immersive tapestry of wisdom, power, and ancient secrets woven into the very fabric of their existence.

The council chambers themselves were a hallowed bastion of sagacity, where the tapestries of time interwove with threads of destiny. Elaborate murals graced the walls, each a magnum opus of artistry and narrative. These intricately wrought depictions spun the epic yarn of E'vahona's history, where courage and enchantment engaged in an eternal waltz.

In the very core of this celestial sanctum, the council members held their court, their presence akin to that of divine beings descended from the stellar expanse. Every nod and gesture bore profound significance, as though the universe conspired in their favor. Ong and Keisha, like interlopers in a realm of legends, were shrouded in the council's solemn acknowledgment, poised to assume their roles in the unfolding odyssey of E'vahona.

Seated at the splendid table, Lord Karrenen's entrance into the council chamber mirrored the arrival of a celestial maestro prepared to conduct a symphony of fate. As he assumed his position, a profound hush descended upon the assembled council members, their eyes mirroring the myriad emotions swirling within the chamber—anticipation, apprehension, and an unwavering determination to confront the impending storm.

The venerable mage, Lord Karrenen, emerged as the epitome of wisdom and resolve, his presence akin to the guardian of an ancient grove, anchored in time yet ever-watchful. His voice, reminiscent of the melodic song of a silver-throated nightingale, resonated through the chamber—a clarion call to unity and purpose. He wove a tapestry of awareness with every word, crafting the portrait of Phoenix, a looming storm poised to shroud the realm in shadow.

"In this sacred conclave of the present day," Lord Karrenen commenced, his words an eldritch incantation that bound their hearts and minds, "we stand united to confront the specter of Phoenix, a harbinger of darkness whose malevolence casts its ominous shroud over our beloved realm."

The council members, Lady Elowen, Lady Lythia, and Lord Galadon, stood as the vigilant sentinels of Vacari's destiny, their gazes unwavering as they absorbed the profound gravity of the moment. The sands of time flowed inexorably through the hourglass, and the council comprehended that their realm's fate hung delicately in the balance, awaiting their united determination to tip the scales toward a brighter tomorrow.

Within the hallowed confines of the council chambers, the atmosphere throbbed with palpable anticipation, reminiscent of the charged silence before a storm unleashed its elemental fury. As they assembled around the splendid table, the council members exchanged knowing glances, their eyes heavy with unspoken anxieties.

Lord Karrenen, the venerable sage, inaugurated the discourse with a voice akin to the gentle whispers of ancient trees, conveying both the solemnity of their predicament and the promise of boundless wisdom. He delved deep into the abyss of Phoenix's ascendant power; each uttered a masterful stroke on the canvas of their comprehension, unveiling the intricate tapestry of darkness woven by the warlock.

"The threat of Phoenix," Karrenen solemnly proclaimed, "is a storm that swells in strength with each passing day, an unyielding maelstrom poised to engulf our realm in shadow. Like the relentless surge of the tide, his dominion rises unabated, and we must find a means to stem this ever-mounting deluge."

The council members, Lady Elowen, Lady Lythia, and Lord Galadon, leaned forward with undivided attention, their countenances echoing the trepidation gripping their souls. The destiny of Vacari rested squarely upon their shoulders, and the urgency of their task bore down upon them, an unyielding weight that would define the course of their realm's history.

As they delved into the mysteries of the half-incantation uncovered by Keisha, the chamber seemed to throb with an enigmatic energy akin to an uncharted realm waiting to be unveiled. They exchanged conjectures and insights, untangling the arcane threads of the magic. Lord Galadon's eyes, reminiscent of ancient scrolls, bore the weight of countless millennia of knowledge as he unveiled their discoveries.

"This fragmentary incantation," he expounded, "offers but a glimpse into the abyss, a key to unshackling powers that lie beyond our mortal comprehension. It is as though Phoenix endeavors to tether his essence to the heart of darkness, drawing upon its malevolence to fuel his unquenchable ambition."

Around the table, the council members contemplated the profound implications of their revelation, their collective musings akin to constellations in the night sky, forming intricate patterns of enlightenment. They apprehended the arduous path ahead in this crucible of intellect and wisdom. Nevertheless, their resolve remained unwavering in the face of the looming threat.

As the council members deliberated within the hallowed chamber, the air seemed to shimmer with an arcane tension, an invisible tapestry of destiny weaving their fates together. Lord Karrenen's voice, a commanding elven sonnet, resonated throughout the room, unveiling the nefarious designs of Phoenix and his unquenchable thirst for power.

With each revelation, the council's thoughts danced like flames in an eternal night, casting fleeting shadows of apprehension upon their countenances. The awareness that Phoenix, akin to his malevolent precursor Maelgrim, harbored designs upon the enigmatic E'vahona weighed upon their hearts like a curse from ages past. In their unity and sagacity, they recognized that although the hidden realm's whereabouts remained a riddle, the warlock's sinister intent loomed on the horizon like an impending storm, casting a shadow of uncertainty over their future.

Ong and Keisha's discovery of scattered tomes within the Druchii library, chronicling Phoenix's relentless pursuit of E'vahona, cast a grim shadow upon the path ahead. The council members exchanged somber glances, their countenances etched with the stark realization that the warlock's motivations transcended their comprehension. Even without direct knowledge, the mere fact that he sought spoke volumes about the unfathomable depths of his ambition.

Their concerns, akin to crystalline fragments reflecting a fractured reality, were intricate and intertwined. As they embarked on their quest to solve the Phoenix enigma, they recognized that unveiling the warlock's true intent was their foremost imperative. The road ahead remained uncertain, yet the council stood unwavering, their unity forged in the crucible of a shared mission and steadfast determination.

Amidst the council's contemplative discourse, Lady Lythia's voice, as musical as a nightingale's serenade, pierced the weighty atmosphere, bearing the gravity of their most pressing apprehension. Her words wove through the chamber like a tapestry of hope and trepidation, resonating like a call to action.

With a graceful inclination of her head, Lady Lythia posed the question that hung in the air like an unbroken thread of destiny: "Do we wield the strength and numbers requisite to liberate Goldmoor, reunite its captive monarchs, and confront the looming specter of Phoenix and his Druchii confederates?"

Lord Karrenen, his gaze laden with the weight of objective truth, sighed like the wind that courses through the ancient forest, bearing the secrets of innumerable ages. The significance of his words, akin to stones cast into tranquil waters, rippled through the collective consciousness of the council, heralding the gravity of the path they were destined to tread.

"It is a somber reality," Karrenen acknowledged his elven voice, a melancholic symphony infused with unwavering resolve. "Our formidable forces may not suffice to accomplish these objectives simultaneously. To liberate Goldmoor, to safeguard its sovereigns, and to thwart Phoenix's insidious aspirations, we must exercise prudence and strategy in our choices."

The council's epiphany hung heavily in the chamber, akin to the rising sun revealing the expanse of their world. Their quest, fraught with peril and uncertainty, demanded unwavering bravery and a meticulous, considered approach. Their decisions would mold their realm's destiny in the impending days, a weight upon their hearts commensurate with the gravity of their responsibility.

During the council's profound deliberation, Ong's voice, resonating with the authority of a battle-hardened warrior, cleaved through the somber atmosphere. His inquiry, a beacon of hope amidst the gathering storm, hung like a guiding star.

With a subtle nod of acknowledgment, Lord Karrenen recognized the wisdom in Ong's suggestion. Like a constellation of minds, the council momentarily halted their discourse, their thoughts converging like stars forming a new constellation in the night sky.

In the ensuing silence, the council members contemplated the delicate equilibrium between seeking external aid and safeguarding their realm's autonomy. They weighed the potential alliances and pondered the far-reaching consequences of each choice, aware that their decisions would reverberate through the annals of time, shaping the destiny of their realm.

As the collective gaze of the council shifted toward the horizon, their minds ventured into the unknown like intrepid scouts on the verge of an extraordinary odyssey. Fueled by unwavering determination and guided by the stars of unity, their quest would lead them to distant allies and uncertain allegiances, weaving a tapestry of bonds and loyalties in their shared pursuit of hope and salvation.

Amidst the council's ongoing discourse, Lord Galadon's voice, as resonant as the age-old trees of E'vahona, ascended with a question that reverberated through the chamber. His words, akin to leaves stirred by a gentle breeze, rustled through the minds of the gathered council members, kindling a spark of intrigue.

"What of the Noble Dragons?" Lord Galadon inquired, his voice laden with the wisdom of eras past. His gaze, as keen as the talons of the dragons he invoked, sought answers in his peers' eyes.

Lord Karrenen, the venerable sage, regarded Lord Galadon with a pensive nod. His measured and contemplative response resonated through the chamber like a profound, mystical incantation. "It is conceivable," he admitted, his words serving as a bridge between hope and uncertainty, "that we may be able to persuade the Noble Dragons to lend their formidable might to our cause."

Keisha, her fiery spirit akin to a phoenix in ascendancy, demanded clarity, her voice slicing through the shroud of ambiguity. "What do you mean by 'conceivable,' Lord Karrenen?" Her eyes, brilliant and stubborn as a starlit night, held him in unwavering scrutiny.

Lord Karrenen's reply, imbued with his profound understanding of the enigmatic nature of dragons, washed over the council like a gentle revelation. "The Noble Dragons," he commenced, his voice echoing with the ancient cadence of long-forgotten legends, "have long receded from the tumult of our realm, seeking solace in their secluded domains. Persuading them to intervene in our struggles is a delicate endeavor that demands diplomacy and unwavering patience."

Keisha nodded, her gaze shifting from Lord Karrenen to the council. "But they remain a part of Vacari?"

Lord Karrenen affirmed his response like a tranquil river of wisdom. "Indeed, they are integral to Vacari, and their ties to our realm endure. Yet, centuries ago, they withdrew to their secluded realm, even though Vacari remains their home."

The council members bore the weight of Lord Karrenen's words, their countenances a tapestry of expressions. Their pursuit of dragon allies was an odyssey into the enigmatic, a quest where alliances would be forged through the crucible of diplomacy, and their realm's destiny hung in precarious equilibrium, poised to sway with the whims of fate.

Ong's inquiry, stubborn as a warrior forging a path through the densest of forests, pierced the chamber's solemnity. His words, akin to a beacon in the twilight, beckoned Lord Karrenen to illuminate their path ahead.

"What measures must we undertake to beseech the aid of the Noble Dragons?" Ong's voice, steadfast and unwavering, lingered in the air like a drawn sword awaiting its decisive strike.

Lord Karrenen, his eyes gleaming with the age-old wisdom of epochs past, met Ong's gaze with a measured nod. Like the opening of a long-forgotten tome, his response unveiled the secrets of an uncharted journey. "To approach the Noble Dragons," he began, his voice a river of knowledge winding through unknown lands, "one must journey beyond the confines of the Emeraldwoods into the realms that cradle the very portals of magic. There, you must seek the legendary gateway to The Hidden Isles."

The council members, their attention captured with the tenacity of a forest's undergrowth, leaned forward in eager anticipation. Like a mirage on the distant horizon, The Hidden Isles had perpetually remained an elusive realm cloaked in the mists of ancient legends.

Lord Karrenen's voice persisted, a guiding beacon illuminating the cavernous depths of uncertainty. Yet, caution permeated his words, akin to flickering shadows dancing in the warmth of a fire's glow. "However," he cautioned, "locating the portal marks just the commencement. It is a conscious entity, a sentinel guarding its enigmatic secrets, and not all who chance upon it are granted passage. The journey to secure the alliance of the Noble Dragons is fraught with dangers and problems, a crucible of will and intellect that will stretch our determination to its utmost limits."

The council, like an impending storm, absorbed Lord Karrenen's words. Their quest for the dragons' aid was a dangerous odyssey that would propel them beyond the familiar boundaries of their realm, where the very forces of magic and destiny would arbitrate their fate.

Keisha's inquiry, a glimmer of curiosity that shimmered within the chamber's sacred ambiance, remained poised like a glistening dewdrop upon a leaf. Lady Elowen, her golden tresses symbolic of grace and discernment, contemplated the question with a measured gaze, her thoughts unfolding like the petals of a delicate bloom.

"Who," ventured Keisha, her voice tinged with subtle anticipation, "would stand as the most likely to gain passage through the portal?"

Lady Elowen, the epitome of wisdom and elegance, leaned forward, her words a meandering stream of contemplation coursing through their midst. "The Noble Dragons," she began, her voice as musical as a woodland brook, "are beings deeply attuned to the natural world. They revere nature in all its forms, and their guardian of the portal shares in this reverence."

Shining with the revelation of profound truth, Keisha's eyes met Lady Elowen's gaze. The connection between herself and the realm of nature ran as deep as the ancient oaks of Emeraldwoods.

"You mean," Keisha articulated, her voice resounding with astonishment and affirmation, "someone like me would have the greatest chance of securing passage?"

Lady Elowen's response, gentle as the breeze that rustled leaves in a tranquil meadow, bore the weight of potential. "Indeed," she affirmed, her words a whispered assurance of hope, "your affinity with nature may well be the key to unlocking the path to The Hidden Isles."

Keisha's declaration, resonant as the musical notes of a distant songbird, lingered in the air, a decision solidified by unwavering determination. Ong, his protective instincts akin to the towering oaks of Emeraldwoods, shifted his gaze toward her, his eyes aflame with devotion. He vowed in a voice as stubborn as the age-old roots anchoring their realm, "You shall not journey alone. I pledged to safeguard you, my beloved, and I shall accompany you."

The council members, their countenances a mosaic of approval and admiration, observed as the bond between Keisha and Ong, a connection woven with threads of love and unswerving loyalty, was reaffirmed in the face of formidable trials. Karrenen, the venerable mage, nodded with a wisdom that had weathered countless storms, acknowledging the indomitable strength of their determination.

"Prepare yourselves for the impending journey," he advised, a guiding light in the gathering shadows. "And might I propose that you bring Pumpkin?" A shared laughter, as heartwarming as a sunbeam piercing the forest's canopy, filled the chamber. "As if we could ever consider leaving her behind," Keisha responded, reflecting on the bond between her and her cherished feline companion.

Beneath the emerald canopy of E'vahona, Keisha stood, her bow cradled in her hands, her fingertips caressing the gleaming wood as she inspected its polished surface. Brimming with arrows crafted from the realm's finest materials, her quiver hung at her side, a testament to her prowess as an archer. Each arrow bore vibrant fletchings, a cascade of colors that promised nothing less than precision and unerring accuracy.

Ong, her resolute guardian, had honed his blades to a razor's edge, ensuring that his weapons would serve him faithfully in the trials ahead.

His armor, etched with runes of protection, bore the scars of battles past, a testament to his unwavering dedication.

Pumpkin, their feline companion, nuzzled Keisha's leg, her emerald eyes radiating curiosity and affection. The bond between them was unbreakable, a silent accord that transcended words.

As they prepared to depart from the familiar embrace of E'vahona, Keisha's fingers tightened around her bow, symbolizing her unwavering resolve and commitment to their quest. The ancient and sagacious forest murmured its blessings, and with Ong by her side and Pumpkin as their steadfast guide, they ventured onto the path leading to the elusive Hidden Isles, where dragons lurked in the shadows and destiny beckoned.

Chapter 28

Forging Alliances with Dragons

The Emeraldwood forest sprawled before them like an ancient sentinel, its towering arboreal sentinels reaching skyward in silent reverence. Dappled sunlight filtered through the verdant canopy, casting a mesmerizing tableau of shifting shadows and ethereal beams upon the forest floor. It was a realm of awe and enchantment, where the air seemed to hum with the hallowed secrets of the land.

As they ventured deeper into the forest's heart, the symphony of nature enveloped them—a harmonious chorus of avian melodies, the rustling cadence of leaves in whispered conversation, and the distant murmur of a hidden stream's song. The emerald leaves overhead wove a resplendent tapestry, their lush hues twirling in graceful cadence with the wind's gentle caress.

Ong, ever vigilant, scanned their surroundings keenly and turned to Keisha, his voice a low, reassuring rumble interwoven with the forest's symphony. "Have you ever glimpsed a dragon?" he inquired, his curiosity matched only by the reverence that the mere mention of such magnificent beings invoked.

Keisha's gaze wandered into the depths of the woods, her memories summoned by Ong's question. "Once," she began, her voice imbued with reverence, "I beheld a wondrous silver dragon, so colossal it appeared to touch the heavens. Yet, that was years past, and it vanished into the heart of these woods, concealed from mortal sight."

Ong cast a contemplative glance at Keisha, and a question that had been gnawing at him since the outset of their journey escaped his lips. "Aren't you apprehensive about encountering these dragons we're about to seek? After all, they possess extraordinary abilities and powers, not to mention their colossal size, dwarfing us by four or fivefold."

Keisha's smile radiated with quiet confidence as she responded, her words flowing like a soothing melody. "No, I harbor no fear of these Noble Dragons. You're correct; they possess unique abilities and powers, but these are beings of nobility, aligned with the light. Dragons, like us, exhibit a spectrum of alignments. There are Noble Dragons, Neutral Dragons, and even those of malevolence. You'll come to understand that the Noble Dragons can be our allies. If we succeed, they have the potential to turn the tide of battle and reshape the fate of Vacari. Many believe that dragons have departed our realm, but if we can persuade them to return, it may become the turning point in our quest to liberate Goldmoor."

Ong nodded in understanding, his thoughts a silent echo of the enigmas concealed within these woods. They continued their journey, each step bringing them nearer to the concealed portal where the guardian of the Hidden Isles awaited. The forest, an ancient sentinel, whispered its ageless secrets, and the promise of dragons lingered in the air, an alluring enigma that urged them forward.

Beneath the emerald canopy of the Emeraldwood forest, Ong and Keisha traversed in communion with the venerable trees, their footsteps a gentle rhythm upon the mossy ground. The forest seemed to eavesdrop on their conversation, its ancient wisdom humming in the rustling leaves and the distant song of a concealed stream.

Ong's gaze shifted towards Keisha, mirroring both curiosity and empathy. "I recall inquiring before about your unique connection to nature," he began, his voice a gentle current of understanding, "but I'm curious if this connection has ever presented challenges for you or if people have placed higher expectations upon you."

Keisha responded with a subtle nod, her thoughts a murmur amidst the woodland's quietude. "There have been moments when I've felt things," she admitted, her voice bearing the weight of her extraordinary gift, "but nothing impossible, at least not yet. And yes, people tend to expect more from me, perhaps because they know this connection."

A crease of concern furrowed Ong's brow, his empathy extending to the complexities of Keisha's abilities. "Does it ever trouble you," he gently inquired, "when these expectations weigh upon you?"

Within the dappled embrace of the forest's light, Keisha's gaze met Ong's, her eyes reflecting emotions. "At times, yes," she confessed, her voice tinged with vulnerability, "but then I realized that perhaps this is my purpose. After all, they cared for me when I was a child."

Ong drew her close, his embrace a testament to his unwavering support. "I won't hinder your path in the forests, but I won't allow you to venture alone any longer," he vowed. "I made a promise and intend to honor it, for you mean the world to me." He sealed his promise with a kiss, and they resumed their journey together.

In the heart of the ancient forest, Ong and Keisha moved in harmony with nature's whispers. Towering trees leaned closer, their branches forming a natural canopy overhead. Sunlight filtered through the leaves, casting a dappled mosaic of light and shadow upon the forest floor. As they continued through the woods, their connection deepened, a bond that transcended the forest's embrace and the expectations on their shoulders.

Continuing their journey, Ong's curiosity flowed like a gentle stream through the forest, his words weaving through the rustling leaves and whispering foliage. "Why do you suppose these dragons retreated to this hidden location instead of remaining in Vacari?" he pondered, his gaze mirroring the mystery of their vanished allies.

Keisha contemplated the question, her connection with nature as a fount of introspection. "Perhaps," she began, her words a tapestry of reflection, "there were lessons we needed to learn, challenges we had to face on our own, without relying on them for intervention."

Ong nodded in agreement, his understanding etched upon his furrowed brow. "It makes sense," he acknowledged, "but now, more than ever, we require their assistance."

Keisha's response was firm, her gaze unwavering as she spoke of the looming threat that had set them on this path. "Indeed," she affirmed, her voice laden with the gravity of their mission, "especially with Phoenix and the dire peril he represents."

In the heart of the ancient forest, their shared purpose and determination took root, a bond of unwavering resolve that would guide them through the trials ahead. The secrets of the Hidden Isles awaited, as did the uncertain alliance with the noble dragons, all in the name of safeguarding their realm from the encroaching darkness.

In the heart of the ancient forest, their footsteps created a gentle rhythm upon the earth as Ong and Keisha ventured deeper into the green embrace of the Emeraldwood. The rustling leaves whispered secrets from ages past, and the sunlight filtered through the dense canopy, casting a golden tapestry upon their path.

Suddenly, a low growl pierced the air, a warning from their loyal companion, Pumpkin. The faithful hound's hackles stood on end as she fixed her gaze upon a concealed presence lurking behind a tree. With instincts honed by years of vigilance, Ong placed a cautious hand on Keisha's shoulder.

"Slowly," he advised, his voice scarcely louder than a leaf's rustle, "let us ascertain what it is. Phoenix's Druchii still scours these woods for you."

Keisha nodded in comprehension, her senses alert to the palpable tension in the air. Ong took her hand, their fingers intertwining in a reassuring clasp, and they advanced toward the tree from which Pumpkin's growls emanated.

Ong unveiled the enigmatic item nestled in the underbrush with a gentle foliage push. Keisha's face blossomed into a knowing smile, and in hushed tones, she whispered, "This is the hidden portal."

In that quiet moment, the portal lay before them like a forgotten relic, its purpose veiled in mystery. The forest seemed to hold its breath as if the trees anticipated their decision. It was a doorway to the unknown, a threshold leading to the Hidden Isles where the noble dragons resided. Their quest teetered on the brink of revelation, and the fate of Vacari hung suspended in the balance.

The guardian, a figure of silver-haired elegance, emerged gracefully from the portal's side. Clad entirely in shimmering silver, his presence exuded otherworldly beauty as he approached Keisha and Ong. Curiosity sparkled in his silver eyes, akin to moonlight on still waters.

With measured grace, he asked, "May I inquire about your purpose here?" His voice, a musical whisper, carried the weight of ages, inviting trust and caution in equal measure.

Ong exchanged a glance with Keisha, and she stepped forward, her determination unwavering. "We seek the guardian of this portal," she explained, her words infused with respectful resolve. "We aim to request an audience with the Noble Dragons in the Hidden Isles. A sinister force threatens Vacari, and we implore their assistance."

The guardian's silver gaze shifted between them and then, with a touch of intrigue, toward Pumpkin, the loyal panther companion. "Is she your companion?" he inquired, his words as serene as a tranquil forest. Keisha nodded, her affection for the panther evident in her eyes. "She has been my steadfast companion since she was but a cub, and now she shares her loyalty with Ong and me."

The guardian's decision was swift, his authority unchallenged. "I shall grant you entry into the Hidden Isles," he declared, his voice a soothing melody. "Seek out Kimras, the golden dragon, and request an audience. May your quest find favor with the Noble Dragons, and may the winds of fortune guide your steps."

As the guardian uttered these words, the portal before them came alive with a shimmering vitality as if it held the essence of newfound possibilities. Keisha and Ong stepped boldly into the mystical realm of the Hidden Isles, where their destinies would be intricately woven into the tapestry of fate, entwined with the enigmatic dragons.

Emerging from the portal, Ong, Keisha, and Pumpkin stood on the Hidden Isles' threshold. Before them unfurled a breathtaking panorama of unparalleled beauty and enchantment, a realm where nature's grandeur stood on full display, leaving them momentarily breathless.

The Hidden Isles unveiled its unparalleled beauty with a flourish of natural wonders that stunned visitors. The waterfalls stood as the true marvel of this extraordinary realm, each a breathtaking masterpiece of nature's artistry. These cascades descended gracefully from towering cliffs with an ethereal elegance, a testament to the profound beauty hidden within the Hidden Isles.

Some of these waterfalls descended like delicate veils, their silken streams trailing behind them in the gentle breeze reminiscent of ethereal ribbons adorning the landscape. Others roared with a thunderous might, their tumultuous waters creating iridescent mists that caught the sun's rays, painting the air with vibrant rainbows like ephemeral bridges to other realms.

Amongst the lush and vibrant landscape, meandering rivers and serene pools had formed at the base of these majestic waterfalls. Crystal-clear lakes sparkled like precious gems, their pristine waters holding an otherworldly clarity that reflected the essence of purity and tranquility. Below the surface, graceful silverfish darted about with a serenity that added to the enchanting spectacle, their presence a reminder of the delicate balance of life within this magical realm.

In all its splendor, the Hidden Isles played host to a symphony of nature, where life and magic harmonized in a melody that resonated within the hearts of all who ventured into this sacred land. Above them, benevolent dragons soared through the cerulean skies with a grace that defied gravity, their colossal wings casting fleeting shadows that danced upon the fertile earth below, a living testament to the boundless wonders of this realm.

In such breathtaking beauty, Ong, Keisha, and Pumpkin stood at the threshold of a realm where wonder and enchantment intertwined with every facet of existence, a world where the boundaries of imagination seemed limitless, and the promise of an audience with the Noble Dragons held the key to their realm's salvation.

In the verdant embrace of the Hidden Isles, a magnificent copper dragon named Caelum, resplendent in his own right, spotted the newcomers as they entered this enchanted realm. With a regal sweep of his majestic tail, he beckoned them forward, his gaze curious yet welcoming, like a wise elder inviting seekers into his sanctum.

"Can I assist you, travelers of the mortal realm?" Caelum inquired, his voice as musical as the soft rustle of leaves in the breeze, a voice that seemed to carry the ancient wisdom of centuries. Ong and Keisha exchanged meaningful glances before embarking on their purpose—a noble quest to meet Kimras, the Golden Dragon, and implore his aid in their dire need.

Caelum, the benevolent guardian of this celestial sanctuary, nodded in understanding, the gleam of acknowledgment mirrored in his emerald eyes, which held the ageless secrets of the Hidden Isles. "Very well," he replied, a regal assurance in his words. "Follow me, and I shall lead you to Kimras."

With measured reverence, the trio followed Caelum as he guided them up a towering spire, a structure that seemed to aspire to touch the very heavens themselves. As they ascended, their eyes were met with a breathtaking spectacle—a colossal Golden Dragon, shining in all its glory, its scales gleaming like molten gold beneath the ambient light as if forged by the gods themselves. Once a palace of mortal design, the dragons had transformed the tower into a beacon of majesty and grandeur that glistened in the sun, a testament to the magic and wonder that thrived within the Hidden Isles.

Caelum, the ever-gracious guardian of the Hidden Isles, conducted himself with the poise and dignity befitting his esteemed role. He turned to Kimras, addressing the Golden Dragon with profound respect, his words a tribute to the grandeur of their surroundings. "Kimras, honored guests have graced our realm with their presence," he announced, his voice resonating through the chamber like a melodic symphony. Kimras, a living embodiment of magnificence, swiveled his colossal head with regal grace, acknowledging their arrival with a nod that bespoke wisdom and benevolence.

"Approach, seekers of our counsel," Kimras declared, his deep, sonorous rumble resonating in the Hidden Isles' marrow. Ong, Keisha, and Pumpkin advanced with reverence and anticipation, traversing the distance to stand in the presence of a creature whose power and sagacity dwarfed all mortal comprehension.

Kimras, the Golden Dragon, surveyed the trio with the timeless wisdom of ages past. His luminous scales, like liquid gold set ablaze, cascaded in a glorious spectacle that mirrored the brilliance of their surroundings. His eyes, twin pools of boundless knowledge, held a tranquil and ageless intelligence that gazed into the very depths of their souls.

" Why, Eladrin, do you seek our audience?" Kimras inquired, his voice a profound and resonant melody that filled the chamber like an orchestral opus. Keisha, momentarily taken aback by the dragon's familiarity with her heritage, exchanged glances with Ong, their expressions blending astonishment and intrigue.

Kimras, the epitome of grace and potency, released a musical laughter that reverberated through the chamber like the harmonious notes of a celestial choir. "Eladrin," he continued with a knowing smile, "why should you be surprised? I sensed your essence when you approached."

Keisha's heart quickened, and she stepped forward, her gaze unwavering and resolute. "We seek an alliance with you," she replied to Kimras, her voice carrying the gravitas of their mission, "because of the shadow cast by Phoenix Shadowwalker and the darkness that threatens to engulf Vacari."

As Keisha's words lingered in the chamber, an expectant hush seemed to drape over the Hidden Isles as if the very soul of the realm held its breath in anticipation. Kimras, the majestic Golden Dragon, regarded Keisha with a gaze that transcended mere size, his decision poised on the brink of destiny, ready to mold the fate of Dragonkind and the realm of Vacari itself.

Turning his regal head, Kimras, the embodiment of wisdom and magnificence, directed his gaze toward the council members gathered around him – a pantheon of dragons, each representing a unique facet of their ancient race. As he introduced them, these dragons exuded an aura that bespoke their individuality, their very presence a testament to the profound power and knowledge they embodied.

"To render an enlightened judgment," Kimras commenced, his voice a solemn cadence befitting the gravity of their deliberation, "allow me to acquaint you with the esteemed Dragon Council." With a graceful nod, he beckoned their attention to the first among them, Silvara, the gentle and nurturing silver dragon. She radiated an aura of serenity that could quell even the fiercest storms of the heart. Her scales gleamed with a soft, silvery luminescence that appeared to hold the very essence of moonlight within it.

Kimras then directed their regard to Dirona, the bronze dragon whose wisdom was renowned throughout their realm. Her eyes, ancient and unfathomable, contained the wisdom of countless eons, and her presence exuded an aura of profound contemplation and insight as though she were a living library of knowledge.

Next in line was Hespherus, the imposing brass dragon known for his indomitable power and charismatic charm. His stature was impressive, and his regal bearing matched the intensity of his fiery breath. In his presence, one could sense the awe-inspiring might that was the hallmark of his kind.

Finally, Kimras's gaze landed upon Caelum, the mischievous and clever copper dragon who had guided Keisha, Ong, and Pumpkin to this auspicious audience. Caelum's demeanor sparkled with a playful and quick-witted nature, and his eyes twinkled with a knowing mirth. His presence served as a reminder that dragons, despite their awe-inspiring grandeur, could possess vibrant and spirited personalities, defying the stereotype of solemn aloofness.

Amidst the venerable assembly of dragons, Keisha and Ong stood as mortal representatives, their presence resonating with the accumulated wisdom and might of the Dragon Council. The chamber itself seemed to pulsate with the profound forces of fate, and the destiny of Vacari, perhaps even the broader world, now rested within the grasp of this council, their choices woven into the intricate tapestry of existence.

Silvara, the silver dragon whose essence exuded gentleness and nurturing care, acknowledged the encroaching darkness with eyes that shimmered like moonlit pools of understanding and empathy. Her wisdom, a balm to troubled souls, hung like a comforting melody, harmonizing with the shared concern for their beleaguered realm.

Kimras, the Golden Dragon and esteemed council leader, concurred with Silvara's astute observations. His voice, a sonorous resonance akin to distant thunder, rolled through the chamber. "Before we proceed," he intoned, "I would request the names of our esteemed guests."

Stepping forward with unwavering determination, Ong Swifthammer, the brave soul whose roots reached Crystal Vale but had since found his home in E'vahona, introduced himself. "I am Ong Swifthammer," he declared with palpable pride. "Originally hailing from Crystal Vale, I now reside in E'vahona. At my side is Keisha, an Eladrin archer and the love of my life," he gestured to her with a warmth that transcended mere words.

"Lastly," he added, pointing to their ever-loyal companion, "this is Pumpkin, our faithful panther."

Kimras, bearing the weight of their names with a regal nod, acknowledged their presence. As their identities reverberated within the chamber, the council of dragons contemplated the significance of these mortal visitors and the gravity of their plea. The destiny of Vacari dangled on the precipice, poised to be sculpted by the forthcoming decisions in this sacred enclave.

In the hallowed chamber of dragons, Dirona, the bronze dragon of wisdom and majesty, injected a question that carried the gravitas of a potential alliance. Her words flowed like a cascading river of ancient knowledge, her gaze akin to molten metal, drilling into Kimras as she probed the nature of their proposed collaboration.

"Before we pledge our aid," she commenced, her voice a comforting symphony of bronzed wisdom, "may we inquire of their intentions? Do they seek us to wage their battles or envision a partnership where we fight as one? Should unity be their aim, I would consent, on the condition that archers and wielders of magic ride our backs when we take to battle."

In response, Keisha, an embodiment of their determination, didn't hesitate to address Dirona's inquiry. She turned to Kimras with unyielding resolve, her unwavering gaze a beacon of conviction amid the council of dragons.

"We harbor no desire for you to fight in our stead," she affirmed resolutely. "Rather, we aspire to join your ranks, to sit upon your mighty backs in battle as allies." Her words, a testament to their commitment to unity, forged a covenant between Eladrin and dragons, binding them in the shared destiny to confront the looming darkness threatening their cherished realm.

Kimras, the grand and glorious Golden Dragon, acknowledged their plea with a graceful nod, his massive form shimmering like a beacon of hope against the backdrop of the Hidden Isles. His eyes, like pools of molten gold, radiated wisdom and assurance.

"Come, Keisha," Kimras beckoned, extending one immense wing as an invitation. "Let us take a ride, and I shall gauge your prowess. If your skills match the promise I see in you, we shall offer our assistance." With that, Keisha climbed onto Kimras' back, her determination radiating like a beacon of light.

Ong, who watched with concern and pride, received Kimras' reassuring words with gratitude. As Keisha soared through the sky on Kimras' mighty wings, they executed daring maneuvers and spins, their flight a graceful ballet of unity and shared destiny. Keisha's longbow, a silken extension of her will, sang with each arrow loosed, striking true as Kimras guided their flight. Together, they became a force of nature, a fusion of Eladrin skill and dragon might, as they showcased their aerial prowess amidst the vast expanse of the Hidden Isles.

Upon their return, as Kimras gently lowered Keisha to the ground, Ong couldn't contain his admiration. He whispered to her like a tender breeze in the Hidden Isles, "You were magnificent, my love." A smile, radiant as the morning sun, graced his lips as he continued, "There is no way I could do what you just did."

Kimras, now a steadfast ally, turned his attention to the pair, his voice carrying the weight of an enduring commitment. "We pledge our aid to your cause. Send word when you require our presence, and we shall answer the call. An alliance has been forged, one that shall endure for all eternity." The bond between Eladrin and the dragons had been sealed, and together, they stood ready to confront the encroaching darkness that threatened their realm.

With hearts full of gratitude, Ong and Keisha bade farewell to Kimras and the noble dragons of Hidden Isles, their words of thanks resonating with the profound importance of the alliance they had forged. As they embarked on their journey back to their homeland, their spirits were buoyed by the knowledge that a powerful force now stood by their side, ready to face the encroaching darkness.

Upon their return to E'vahona, they sought out Karrenen, the venerable mage who had guided them on this path. Upon hearing the news, his smile spoke volumes of the hope that had been kindled within him. He nodded approvingly and then, with a tone that conveyed both reassurance and urgency, informed them that the council had another matter to discuss.

With the weight of newfound responsibility resting upon their shoulders, Ong and Keisha retreated to their home, knowing that the road ahead was fraught with challenges. Rest was a precious commodity, one they would need to replenish their strength for the trials yet to come. The bond between Eladrin, dragons, and the fate of Vacari had been irrevocably woven, and their destiny awaited them like a shimmering tapestry of possibilities, rich and untold.

Chapter 29

Phoenix's Obsession with E'vahona

The heart of Goldmoor, where the radiant palace stood as a marvel of human artistry and craftsmanship, was a living testament to the divine union of creativity and the splendor of their realm. Within the opulent chambers adorned with tapestries woven from artists' dreams, an intricate dialogue unfurled between Lyra and her brother, Qellaun. In this epicenter of the grand city, their voices were not mere words but resonant echoes imbued with the weight of a difficult revelation.

Lyra, her countenance etched with deep furrows of concern, turned to Qellaun, her eyes akin to twin crimson stars ablaze with an intensity that could rival the sun. She posed a question that hung like an ancient, heavy shroud, each word pregnant with the weighty secrets of a tyrant's relentless aspirations.

"Have you been privy to the latest developments concerning Phoenix's unwavering pursuit of E'vahona?" Her words were not just spoken; they were an incantation, a conjuring of dread and fascination woven into a single breath.

Qellaun, his silken tresses cascading like liquid moonlight over his shoulders, leaned in with a measured curiosity, his voice a sonorous river flowing with an undercurrent of trepidation. "Nay, dear sister, what infernal designs has he hatched now? What new web of intrigue does he unfurl?"

Lyra's gaze remained trapped by the distant horizon, where the Purplefire Woods loomed like an enigmatic sanctuary cloaked in mystery and magic. "He has dispatched a squadron of Druchii, their shadowed figures poised to scour every leaf and twig of the Purplefire Woods, hunting for the elusive entrance to E'vahona," she revealed, her words carrying the sad weight of a mission fraught with dire consequences.

Qellaun sighed, a deep and weary exhalation echoing the burdensome gravity of their predicament. "Indeed, Lyra. His hunger for E'vahona's secrets appears unquenchable, even as we inch closer to unraveling its enigmas."

Lyra's lips curled into a sardonic smile, her voice dripping with venomous sarcasm as potent as any dragon's breath. "Determination, you say? I would sooner dub it an insatiable obsession."

In the glorious halls of Goldmoor, where shadows whispered ancient truths and the relentless pursuit of an enigmatic leader shaped the destiny of a realm, the siblings contemplated the treacherous road that lay ahead—a path fraught with peril, secrets, and the unyielding flames of Phoenix's all-consuming fixation.

In the heart of the forbidding Purplefire Woods, Caedon Parquette, a battle-hardened Druchii warrior of unparalleled experience, was trapped within the intricate tapestry of ancient trees. A heavy sigh, laden with the weight of their ceaseless quest, escaped his lips like a spectral wisp. It was as though the very woods conspired to exhale secrets, their leaves rustling with the echoes of untold sagas and the seductive promise of veiled truths.

Phoenix's unrelenting pursuit of the elusive Eldarin city, "E'vahona," loomed over them like a spectral shroud of enigma. Caedon's penetrating gaze roamed the impenetrable undergrowth veiled by skepticism and the enduring doubt that had plagued their kind for eons.

Turning to his fellow warrior, the forest's twilight shadows pirouetting on their implacable countenances, Caedon vocalized the question that gnawed at his soul. "Can he truly harbor faith in the existence of this fabled realm? We have been whispering these rumors for years, yet the Druchii have never laid bare its enigmatic secrets."

The response from his comrade resounded with a conviction that hinted at Phoenix's unyielding resolve, a force as invincible as the encircling trees. "Indeed, he clings to his belief. The siren call of the unfathomable power rumored to reside within E'vahona has trapped his soul."

Caedon's sigh was a solemn pact with destiny, echoing through the timeless woods. With each deliberate step into the heart of the forest's enigma, he plunged deeper into the labyrinthine mysteries of E'vahona, propelled by his leader's unwavering will, unwavering even in the face of seemingly insurmountable odds.

Amidst the glorious throne room, Phoenix, the relentless and insatiably power-hungry leader of the Druchii, occupied his imposing seat like a looming specter cast upon the backdrop of luxury. His ebony eyes, aflame with an unquenchable thirst for dominion, pierced the chamber's dimness, awaiting the latest message in his ceaseless quest for E'vahona.

As Qellaun and Lyra, siblings bound by unwavering loyalty to their dark master, entered, Phoenix's contemplative demeanor gave way to steely anticipation. He inquired, his voice a chilling echo of authority, "What news do you bring?"

Qellaun, the bearer of the weighty burden of their fruitless search, replied with somber gravity, "I regret to inform you, My Lord, there is none."

Phoenix's impatience flared, his yearning for the elusive realm gnawing at the core of his being. "I demand possession of that realm!" His proclamation cut through the air like a blade, a chilling decree of relentless desire.

Lyra, her composure tempered by the wisdom of reason, attempted to quell the hunger within him. "We are aware of your desire, My Lord. However, as I have previously conveyed, even the Druchii of antiquity failed to unearth E'vahona."

Phoenix's ire ignited, and he fixed his smoldering gaze upon her, his patience waning and desperation setting the stage for an ultimatum. "Seize Keisha, now! She shall divulge the location, or she shall meet her demise!"

Qellaun, aware of the dangerous history entwining Keisha and her lineage, dared to voice a cautionary note to their leader. "My Lord, your father, Maelgrim, attempted that with her father and met his end at the hands of her mother. An Eldarin, sworn to defend E'vahona at all costs, is not to be trifled with."

Phoenix's incredulous glare met their words, his voice tinged with frustration. "Why would they choose to die in defense of a realm? Such a notion defies all reason."

Qellaun, his words laced with an understanding born of ancient wisdom, replied, "It is a belief that transcends reason, My Lord. The Eladrin comprehend the dire perils that would accompany E'vahona falling into the wrong hands, and thus, they have pledged to safeguard it from such calamity."

Phoenix's exasperation boiled over, and in a sudden eruption of anger, he hurled an object from the nearby pillars across the room. This violent act manifested the fierce storm within the recesses of his heart, a turbulent testament to his unquenchable thirst for control and the unattainable secrets of E'vahona.

Enveloped by the all-consuming obsession for E'vahona, Phoenix stormed out of the dark and foreboding palace, his footfalls reverberating ominously through the cold, echoing stone corridors. He embarked on a relentless march towards Zylron, his colossal red dragon, with an unyielding resolve to extract the coveted knowledge from an unexpected wellspring: Queen Jeanne, the wife of King Alex.

With a single command, Zylron ascended to the heavens, soaring above the vast expanse of Serpent's Lagoon. The dragon's descent was a breathtaking spectacle as Phoenix materialized into the tower room, his arrival shattering the delicate, ethereal surroundings that enveloped Queen Jeanne. Startled and disrupted by the intrusion, she recoiled in shock, a momentary disturbance in the calm facade of her spectral realm.

Phoenix, his cruel laughter resonating through the chamber like a malevolent symphony, took perverse pleasure in witnessing the spectral torment that clung to Queen Jeanne. "I possess the power to quell these haunting specters," he declared with a chilling calm, "but only if you surrender the secrets of E'vahona."

Desperation etched deep lines upon her face as Queen Jeanne vehemently shook her head, her voice trembling sincerely. "Phoenix, I have told you repeatedly—I am bereft of knowledge concerning that enigmatic realm."

Phoenix's glare intensified, his patience eroding with each passing heartbeat. "Very well," he spat, his words dripping with venom, "if you persist in your obstinacy, I shall magnify your torment." With that ominous pronouncement, he mounted Zylron and issued the command to return to Goldmoor, leaving behind Queen Jeanne's anguished screams and heart-wrenching pleas for respite. The relentless apparitions continued their cruel assault, a manifestation of Phoenix's unquenchable lust for power and the elusive secrets harbored by E'vahona.

Upon his return to the grim and foreboding city of Goldmoor, Phoenix's insatiable hunger for the enigma of E'vahona intensified. He issued a chilling edict to his Druchii forces entrenched within the town: interrogate the citizens anew and, this time, show no mercy. Answers were demanded, and they were to be procured without delay.

The Druchii, renowned for their ruthless efficiency, executed his orders with zealous enthusiasm. Once-thriving streets were transformed into a cacophonous symphony of anguish, echoing with desperate pleas for clemency. Homes were pillaged, and citizens were dragged from their sanctuaries to face relentless grilling. Fear and panic constricted the hearts of the innocent, trapped in the ruthless machinations of their evil ruler, a city cast into shadows by the insatiable thirst for dominion and the impenetrable mysteries of E'vahona.

Even King Alex, known for his benevolence, could not ignore the agonized wails emanating from the dungeons' abyssal depths. These desperate cries reached out like spectral tendrils, tugging at the very strings of his heart. A somber melody played upon his conscience, which compelled him to act. He knew in the marrow of his bones that he must find a way to halt Phoenix, shield his beloved subjects from further torment, and defy the sinister machinations that loomed over their realm like storm-laden clouds.

The return of Caedon Parquett and his companions to Goldmoor carried with it the crushing weight of failure. As they trudged wearily through the city's shadow-draped avenues, the lines etched upon their countenances bore witness to the twin burdens of exhaustion and frustration. The mission entrusted to them, the quest to unearth the elusive portal to E'vahona concealed within the heart of the Purplefire Woods, had morphed into an impossible trial.

Caedon entered the palace, a palpable despair weighing heavily upon his heart. His footfalls reverberated through the cold, stone corridors, echoing like the tolling of a funeral bell. In the oppressive presence of Phoenix, he braced himself for the inevitable clash that loomed on the horizon. The air in the throne room grew pregnant with stifling anticipation as Phoenix's incisive gaze bore down upon him like a blade honed to a ruthless edge.

Caedon's voice, tinged with the bitter aftertaste of remorse, relayed the harsh truth, a truth that would surely stoke the fires of Phoenix's unrelenting wrath. He recounted the torturous odyssey of their futile searches, the relentless forays into the heart of the impenetrable forest that had yielded naught but despair. His confession hung like a lament, an admission that ushered a tempest of unbridled fury. In the crucible of Phoenix's anger, Caedon was reduced to a crumbling edifice, and his essence was wrapped with an agony that transcended the physical realm.

Finally, after what seemed like an eternity, the torment abated. Caedon, battered and broken, was summarily dismissed from the throne room. He staggered away from the presence of his tyrannical overlord, his body trembling like a leaf caught in the storm, thankful to have emerged with his life intact yet haunted by the indelible scars of his failure.

Phoenix's insatiable thirst for knowledge propelled him into the labyrinthine depths of the dungeon, his heart ablaze with a genuine desire to wrest the coveted information from King Alex's reluctant grasp. The rhythmic percussion of his footsteps reverberated through the suffocating darkness, a grim overture to the impending clash of wills.

Within the unforgiving confines of his cell, King Alex braced himself for the storm that approached. He sensed the palpable aura of anger and desperation radiating from Phoenix, a vortex that threatened to engulf everything in its inexorable path. As the dungeon door swung open with an ominous, grating creak, King Alex met the dreaded gaze of his captor with unyielding fortitude, his regal bearing undiminished by the shadows surrounding him.

Without a single utterance, Phoenix unleashed his wrath upon King Alex, his cruelty a relentless tide that crashed upon the prisoner's resilience like unyielding waves against a solitary rock. The torment was a tangible specter, an evil presence that King Alex endured in silence, steadfast in his determination not to yield to the unrelenting storm. Amidst the savage onslaught, Phoenix's insistent demand for the coveted knowledge loomed like a chilling, ever-present specter.

Compelled by his all-consuming obsession, Phoenix persisted in his relentless quest, oblivious that King Alex was devoid of the enigma's location. "I tire of this game!" he roared, his voice thunderous in the chamber's dank depths. "The location of E'vahona, I demand it now!" He cast a fleeting, venomous glance back at King Alex. "You have but a week to divulge this information, or Queen Jeanne shall pay the price with her life. And if you persist in your silence, your life shall also be forfeit." With a committed turn, he departed the dungeon, his footsteps a haunting echo of his ominous decree.

Battered and bruised, King Alex could only offer a sorrowful prayer for the safety of his beloved queen as Phoenix retreated from the dungeon, leaving him trapped in solitude and shrouded in an aura of relentless uncertainty.

Enthroned upon his dark, foreboding seat at the very heart of the palace, Phoenix cast a long and brooding shadow that seemed to engulf the entire chamber. The obsidian walls of the grand hall, like sponges for his evil thoughts, absorbed his sinister musings, imparting an eerie and unsettling ambiance to the surroundings. His eyes, twin flames of a vengeful spirit, flickered with an intensity that could incinerate the soul of those who dared to meet his gaze.

Amid the dark tapestry of his reverie, Phoenix's voice, a sinister murmur laden with foreboding, pierced the oppressive silence. "E'vahona shall be mine by any means necessary. Its power shall be the crucible of my ascension." His words hung in the air like a sinister invocation, resonating ominously within the chamber as though they were the chants of his relentless obsession.

Phoenix's thoughts meandered to his father, Maelgrim, a cryptic figure from the annals of the past whose aspirations had ultimately eluded him.

However, Phoenix had yet to succeed in mirroring his predecessor's failures. "I shall triumph where my father faltered," he declared with a persistent voice that dripped with unwavering determination. "Even if it means rending the very fabric of our realm asunder and shattering the fragile peace of the Eladrin, I shall unearth the enigmatic secrets of E'vahona. It shall bow to my will or be consigned to oblivion."

With his resolve steeled and his ambition kindled into a blazing inferno, Phoenix remained seated upon his ebony throne, a tyrant whose unwavering determination was poised to propel him towards his sinister objectives, heedless of the toll it might exact upon the world around him.

Chapter 30

Songs of the Deep: Secrets of the Merfolk

In the concealed realm of E'vahona, the clandestine city of the Eladrin, the council chambers stood as a sanctum of veiled secrets cloaked in an ethereal aura. The chamber, hewn from the heartwood of an ancient arboreal giant, radiated with an iridescent luminescence as though the essence of twilight had chosen this place as its eternal dwelling. The Eladrin's artistry in architecture wove an intricate tapestry of enchantment, casting ever-shifting patterns of moonlight and star shine upon the chamber's every facet.

At the epicenter of this mystical sanctum, an oval table sculpted from obsidian wood, adorned with Eladrin runes etched in the ancient script of bygone eras, stood as a symbol of unity among the diverse races that called this realm home. Gathered around its dark, enigmatic surface, the council members were a living canvas of opulent hues that seemed to dance and transform with each breath drawn. Lord Karrenen, bearing the weight of a regal bearing that transcended the limits of time, held his position at the head of the table, his gaze an unspoken testament to the boundless wisdom that had steered the Eladrin through countless millennia. By his side sat Lady Elowen, a living embodiment of grace and elegance, her emerald eyes veiled in an aura of enchanting mysticism.

Across the table, Lord Galdon, a colossus of a man whose laughter reverberated like distant thunder in the heavens, reclined with an authoritative approachability. Beside him, Lady Lythia, an enigmatic scholar, exuded a profound serenity that mirrored the tranquil stillness of a secluded forest clearing, a scholar's haven amidst the grandeur of E'vahona.

Within the august assembly, two figures stood in stark contrast to the otherworldly beauty of the Eladrin. Keisha, her tresses ablaze with the fiery hues of a raging inferno, exuded an aura of unwavering determination that transcended her mortal form. Beside her, Ong, a colossal human warrior, a testament to unyielding strength and resolute courage, his very presence a testament to humanity's indomitable courage. Seraphina and Thalorin, both Eladrin mages of exceptional prowess, had been summoned to partake in this momentous gathering.

In this concealed enclave, a sacred realm where enchantment and enigma wove an intricate tapestry, the fate of the entire realm dangled precipitously in the balance. The council convened with a gravity that echoed through the very core of E'vahona, a weighty resonance that seemed to emanate from the very roots of the ancient city.

Amidst the dazzling luminescence that bathed the E'vahona council chambers, Lord Karrenen, his voice a resonant symphony akin to the ancient elder trees swaying in a mystical breeze, ascended to the assembled council. Like fathomless pools of boundless wisdom, his eyes held the council members in thrall as he wove a tapestry of words imbued with arcane significance, each syllable pregnant with the import of the realms' destinies.

"In the realms where the tapestry of fate is meticulously woven, we have uncovered a swifter path of connection, a gossamer thread that binds us more tightly than ever. Behold, the Etherwings," he proclaimed, unveiling a pair of winged amulets that sparkled with an ethereal shimmer. A collective nod and a murmur of approval cascaded through the council like leaves stirred by a gentle breeze.

However, Lord Karrenen's countenance bore an added weight, a veil of concern that overshadowed the initial euphoria. Like twin constellations, his eyes delved deeper into the chamber's profound depths as he continued, "Yet, as the threads of destiny unfurl, so too do they unravel the enigmatic tapestries of distant lands. A message borne upon Crystal Vale's winds ushers hope and trepidation."

A peaceful stillness settled upon the council, a profound silence gripping the chamber with solemnity. Lord Karrenen's words painted a vivid canvas of perilous shores and shrouded isles. "In a land beset by the evil wrath of the Hydra, the seething fury of sea serpents, and the scorching breath of dragons, there stands a lagoon veiled in eternal darkness. At its core, an ominous tower, a sentinel of malice."

He paused, allowing the gravity of his revelation to descend upon his audience like a funereal shroud. "King Manard of Crystal Vale suspects that the radiant Queen Jeanne, trapped by the cruel design of the Phoenix, languishes within the shadowed confines of that accursed tower. Yet, even his valiant warriors could not draw near, for the perils that guard the isle are as ancient as the annals of time."

The visages of the council members transformed into a kaleidoscope of emotions, ranging from sad reflection to unyielding determination, mirroring the tumultuous skies beyond the chamber's enchanted windows. In that pivotal moment, it became abundantly clear that the destinies of kings and queens, realms and rulers, were intricately interwoven, akin to the very fabric of the cosmos, and the council stood poised to thread the needle of fate itself.

As Lord Karrenen's words lingered in the chamber, their resonance akin to the faintest echo of an incantation whispered across the ages, Lord Galadon emerged from the cloak of contemplation. His voice, a resonant symphony of authority, unfurled like the notes of a sacred melody played upon an elder tree harp. His eyes, resembling polished orbs of onyx, ensnared the council's undivided attention as he spoke with the sensible wisdom of countless lifetimes.

"Esteemed council members," he intoned, his words like the haunting refrain of a timeless ballad, "we find ourselves standing at the juncture of destiny, where the threads of time and the caprices of fate intertwine. But before we dare to weave the tapestry that shall unshackle Goldmoor from the clutches of the Phoenix, we must embark upon an urgent quest—the rescue of Queen Jeanne."

His proclamation, a clarion call to the noble virtues of honor and chivalry, echoed through the chamber like the solemn tolling of a revered bell. The council members nodded in somber unison, their collective resolve coalescing into a binding pact as enduring as the ancient oaths that bound them.

Lady Elowen's presence, an embodiment of the Eladrin's grace and wisdom, lent her voice to the unfolding symphony of deliberation. Her words, as delicate as the moonflower's petals yet pregnant with prophetic insight, drifted through the chamber like a fragrant breeze.

"But let us not be ensnared by the flames of our zeal," she cautioned, her emerald eyes shimmering with a prescient illumination. "Just as the Phoenix cunningly laid traps within the dungeons that ensnare King Alex, so shall the tower that incarcerates Queen Jeanne be a labyrinth of treacherous design. We must tread with the vigilance of a forest creature stalking elusive prey, for the shadows conceal manifest and hidden perils."

Her words lingered in the air like the fading luminescence of a dying star, a reminder that courage must be tempered by prudence and that the path to salvation was fraught with treacherous hazards. The council, their shoulders burdened by the weight of responsibility, gazed out upon the foreboding horizon, aware that their fates were inexorably entwined in the shadows and secrets of their world.

As the council's deliberations unfolded like the unfurling of ancient scrolls, Ong, the towering human warrior whose voice resonated like the mighty rush of a river's current, interjected with an audacious notion as striking as a sudden thunderclap rending the silence of a moonlit night. "What of our newfound alliance with the dragons?" he posed, his words as potent as the smoldering embers borne upon a dragon's fiery exhalation.

His suggestion lingered in the chamber's atmosphere like the span of a dragon's wing, a daring proposition that ignited a spark of intrigue among those assembled. However, before this nascent idea could take root and blossom, Lord Karrenen, the venerable guardian of the council's arcane lore, raised his hand, and his words flowed like a river of age-old wisdom.

"A notion as brilliant as a solitary star in the vast midnight sky," he conceded, his eyes gleaming with an acknowledgment of the warrior's insight. "But to unveil our alliance with the dragons at this juncture would be akin to baring one's chest to an unseen adversary. The element of surprise, my dear Ong, stands as a weapon as formidable as any forged steel."

Ong, the brave warrior whose heart mirrored the nobility of a dragon's spirit, nodded in silent agreement. He comprehended that timing was as crucial as the celestial constellations in the intricate choreography of their strategic dance. Thus, with a shared understanding, the council consigned the notion of invoking the dragon alliance to the depths of prudent consideration, recognizing that in the intricate tapestry of their schemes, secrets were the threads that intertwined and held fast the fabric of their destiny.

Amidst the council's muted deliberations, Keisha, her voice a resonant sonata of unyielding determination, strode forward like a stormy ocean wave crashing upon a distant shore. Her hair, an incendiary cascade rivaling the fiery hues of a burning sunset, framed her countenance like a wreath of smoldering embers as she spoke, each word carrying the weight of unspoken alliances.

"What of the fathomless depths of the sea, where the merfolk reign?" she inquired, her words as fluid and relentless as the ceaseless ebb and flow of the tide. "Adrianna, the daughter of King Oceanous, is my cherished friend. Beneath the watery abyss, secrets and potential allies await; in her, we may discover a key to unraveling the mysteries of that forsaken isle."

The council listened, their collective gaze converging upon Keisha like a forest bending beneath the caress of whispering winds. Her proposition, a shimmering beacon of hope amidst the looming storm of uncertainty, hung within the chamber's atmosphere like a glistening pearl suspended beneath the surface of an unfathomable abyss.

Lord Karrenen, his wisdom akin to the profound depths of oceanic trenches, regarded Keisha with a knowing gaze as though he perceived the intricate currents of destiny swirling around her. "The merfolk, beings of both enigmatic allure and majestic power, may indeed possess the elusive key to unlock the secrets of that accursed isle," he contemplated, his voice a reverent incantation.

The council's contemplative silence within the chamber mirrored the tranquil calm that often precedes the tumultuous arrival of a storm at sea. Keisha's proposal, a luminous beacon of hope piercing the gathering shroud of despair, had stirred the waters of possibility. The council was keenly aware that their salvation might yet find its course in the uncharted depths of the unknown.

As the council's discourse continued, a storm of ideas akin to a disruption in the heart of a burgeoning storm, Keisha, standing as a bastion of determination amidst the gathering shadows, raised her voice to address the council once more. Her words were like haunting notes of a mermaid's song, rising to claim the full attention of those assembled.

"While the merfolk's enchantments may bestow upon us the means to traverse the serpents' aqueous domain, the dragons pose as tempestuous a challenge as the fiercest tempest," she reasoned, her voice an intricate dance of waves and currents, a melody of the sea itself. "The tower's snares, akin to the intricacies of fate, demand a deft hand and an intimate familiarity with the elusive world of shadows. We require the expertise of those who tread the path of subtlety."

In response, Lord Karrenen, his smile akin to a crescent moon piercing through the shroud of a storm, shifted his gaze toward two of his most promising disciples, Seraphina and Thalorin. Like the first rays of dawn after a tumultuous night, their presence infused the chamber with renewed hope.

"Seraphina and Thalorin," Lord Karrenen proclaimed, his words a benediction from the tapestry of destiny, "possess the skills we so desperately need. Their talents, as boundless as the night sky, and their comprehension of the arcane arts, as profound as the ocean's abyss, render them our most cherished assets."

Ong, the warrior whose discernment was as sharp as the edge of a finely honed blade, lent his sagacious counsel. "Before we embark upon the uncharted seas," he suggested, as unyielding as a ship's resilient hull, "should we not first ensure that the merfolk can navigate the treacherous waters leading to that forsaken isle? The foundation of our plan must rest upon the bedrock of certainty."

Constantly vigilant and wise, the council concurred with Ong's prudent advice. With her fiery mane and profound connection to the merfolk, Keisha emerged as the chosen emissary. Her journey, a quest into the enigmatic unknown, would carry her across the mystical domains of the Shimmering Coast, where the waves murmured secrets and the stars waltzed upon the cerulean canvas of the boundless sea.

Ong, the unwavering human warrior, resounded with a declaration, his voice a resounding bell amidst the council's deliberations. His words were as resolute as a sentinel standing guard at the gates of a kingdom.

"Keisha shall not undertake her voyage to the Shimmering Coast in solitude," he proclaimed, his words a fortress of unwavering determination. "I shall stand beside her, a guardian of her fiery spirit and a blade unsheathed against the enigmatic unknown."

Ong continued with a sweep of his gaze that encompassed the council, "I have another matter to address. While I acknowledge that Keisha is often the most suitable choice for missions, the practice of sending her alone ceases here and now. Such actions put her in needless peril. I shall accompany her on future missions unless an alternative candidate is better suited. But I insist that she never embarks on a mission alone again."

Like a forest swaying to the wind's call, the council acknowledged Ong's commitment with solemn nods. Keisha, the embodiment of unwavering determination, bore a smile of gratitude, illuminating the chamber like a comet streaking across the night sky.

Their union, a pact forged in the crucible of loyalty, love, and friendship, painted a portrait of courage and camaraderie destined to withstand the trials of time and tide. Within that consecrated chamber, the council bore witness to the genesis of a dangerous odyssey and the reinforcement of bonds prepared to endure through the ages.

As Ong and Keisha readied themselves for their impending journey, the atmosphere in the chamber was electric with anticipation. The council members watched them with eyes brimming with hope and expectation. Beyond the ornate doors lay a world teeming with mysteries and perils concealed within the shadows, ready to test the mettle of these two brave souls.

Chapter 31

Whispers of the Tides: A Merfolk's Pact

Beneath the expansive cerulean sky, Ong, Keisha, and Pumpkin found themselves standing on the verge of the Shimmering Coast. Here, the boundaries between the terrestrial and the aquatic realms coalesced in breathtaking harmony. The shoreline before them promised a grand adventure, an ancient map that had yet to be charted, where the forest's whispered secrets entwined with the ocean's gentle murmurs.

The sea stretched like an endless tapestry, its waves performing an enchanting ballet of light and shadow. Overhead, seagulls, the winged custodians of the coastline, executed their graceful pirouettes in the boundless cerulean expanse. Their cries harmonized like a celestial symphony, a chorus celebrating the freedom of exploration.

Leading the way, Keisha's fiery mane cascaded down her back, reminiscent of Twilight's passionate embrace. She moved gracefully toward the water's edge, her steps causing the sands beneath her feet to shimmer like fragmented stardust. Ong, the stalwart warrior, followed in her wake, a sense of reverence washing over him as if he were crossing the threshold into a legendary kingdom.

Surveying the boundless sea ahead, Ong couldn't help but express his awe. "I have never encountered a merfolk before," he confessed, his words carried away by the gentle sea breeze, a testament to the uncharted territory ahead.

Keisha, a repository of knowledge about the ocean's enigmatic depths, graced him with a knowing smile. Their shared voyage of discovery was only beginning. "The merfolk of the Shimmering Coast hold knowledge and power that can shape the destinies of entire realms."

With the ocean's tender embrace framing their tableau and the shimmering sands as their stage, Ong, Keisha, and Pumpkin stood at the threshold of a new chapter in their epic saga. Here, between the realms of land and sea, the unknown beckoned like a distant lighthouse, its radiant beacon guiding them toward secrets yet unveiled.

Beside the tranquil shoreline, where the lush forest met the expansive sea, Keisha stood as a living ember against the serene blues of the Shimmering Coast. Her fiery mane billowed in the ocean's caress, a vivid contrast to the azure horizon. As her gaze ventured beyond the gentle waves, she spotted a graceful silhouette gliding through the crystalline waters—a form so harmonious with the sea that it seemed a natural extension of the waves.

With a graceful sweep of her hand, Keisha beckoned to the denizen of the depths, a mermaid whose beauty rivaled the ethereal radiance of moonlight filtering through the dense forest canopy. Golden hair flowed like liquid sunlight, sea-green eyes held the secrets of boundless depths, and a mermaid tail adorned in regal purples enveloped her form. She embodied the very enchantment and allure of the sea, a siren born of the coastal realm.

As the mermaid, Adrianna, drew nearer to the shore, her movements transformed into a ballet of ethereal grace, the water around her parting like a tender lover's embrace. Her voice, as melodious as the gentle lapping of waves upon the shore, welcomed Keisha with a chorus that echoed the haunting melodies of a hundred sea shanties.

"Keisha, friend of the land," Adrianna sang, her words enchanting as the ocean's serenade, "what brings you to our shores on this auspicious day?"

With a radiant smile, Keisha replied, her joy as bright as the noonday sun. "Adrianna, seeing you again is both a pleasure and an honor."

Emerging beside Adrianna was another figure, an imposing merman named Aqilus. His mermaid tail adorned in a symphony of azure hues cascaded like liquid sapphire beneath the moon's luminescent glow. His sea-green eyes held a resolve as unyielding as the ocean's depths, and his physique bespoke his role as a sentinel of the merfolk's realm.

With a graceful gesture, Adrianna introduced her mate to Keisha. "This is Aqilus, guardian of our realm's secrets and keeper of our ancient wisdom."

Ever the diplomat, Keisha stepped forward to facilitate introductions. "Aqilus, this is Ong, my intended and a valiant warrior of the land."

Their meeting, a convergence of disparate worlds, stood as a testament to the enduring bonds forged amidst the enigmatic currents of the Shimmering Coast. Here, amid the pristine beauty of the natural world, the realms of land and sea, humans, and merfolk, merged into a living embodiment of unity and cooperation—a testament to the boundless possibilities arising in response to destiny's call.

Within the hushed secrets of the Shimmering Coast, Keisha leaned closer to her mermaid friend, Adrianna. As gentle as a lullaby, the sea breeze ruffled Keisha's fiery tresses, carrying her words like the sacred notes of an ancient chant.

"Adrianna," Keisha began, her voice a whispered melody, "I beseech you for a favor."

Adrianna, her sea-green eyes reflecting the boundless depths of the ocean, nodded with an expression of steadfast friendship. "Anything, my dear friend," she replied, her words a soothing lullaby. "What do you wish of me?"

Her gaze bore the intensity of a tempest gathering on the horizon. Keisha spoke of an island veiled in enigma and peril, painting a vivid portrait of its dangers—the serpents that prowled its depths, the Hydra's venomous wrath, and the looming tower that cast an ominous shadow. "We have reason to believe," Keisha continued, her voice unwavering, "that the Queen of Goldmoor may be imprisoned there."

Aqilus, the sentinel of the merfolk realm, listened intently, his sea-green eyes deep pools of ancient wisdom. "The island you describe," he interjected, his voice resonating like the abyss itself, "sounds akin to Serpent Lagoon. I possess knowledge of a concealed passage that will allow me to approach the location unnoticed."

Ong, the brave warrior, voiced his inquiry with a resolute tone. "But how can we confirm the Queen's presence within that place?"

Adrianna, her gaze drifting toward the distant horizon, pondered the possibilities. "It would depend upon the tower's design," she mused, her words as elusive as the ocean's secrets. "If a window is facing the water, we may have a chance to catch a fleeting glimpse of her."

Aqilus, resolute and steadfast in his commitment, proclaimed, "I shall embark on this investigation and ascertain the secrets concealed within the tower. However, for the safety of all, I must insist that you remain here until my return."

As the sun dipped toward the horizon, casting shimmering reflections upon the waves, the trio and their newfound merfolk ally readied themselves for a venture into the unknown. In the twilight's tender embrace, their fates intertwined like the currents of the deep sea, and they stood on the precipice of an extraordinary quest, poised to unravel the mysteries of the Serpent Lagoon and, perhaps, rescue a queen from the clutches of darkness.

With a graceful nod of agreement, Aqilus slipped beneath the sea's surface, his powerful tail propelling him toward the concealed cave. The ocean swallowed him whole, and Keisha, Ong, and Pumpkin were left on the shore, their fates hanging in the balance like delicate bubbles in the vast expanse of the unknown.

Beneath the boundless canopy of the cerulean sky, where the ocean's whispers danced upon the shoreline, Ong's eyes sparkled with curiosity. His gaze meandered between Keisha, the fiery-haired enchantress by his side, and Adrianna, the mermaid whose beauty rivaled the limitless depths of the sea. A tranquil hush had descended upon them as they awaited Aqilus's return, and it felt like an opportune moment to quench his thirst for knowledge.

"I have a question," Ong began, his voice as profound as a hidden wellspring of wonder. "Given that we find ourselves in this interlude, waiting for Aqilus to resurface, it seems a fitting time to inquire."

Keisha beckoned him forward with a gracious nod, her eyes gleaming with the allure of shared revelations. "Pray, what is your question, dear?"

Ong, with an unwavering gaze, traversed the sea's expanse between Keisha and Adrianna and back again, his curiosity rising. "How did your paths cross, and how did you forge such a steadfast friendship?" he inquired, his voice tinged with intrigue.

Adrianna, the mermaid who held the wisdom of the sea and a laugh that echoed like the timeless rhythm of waves, turned her gaze toward Keisha, her sea-green eyes dancing with playful mischief. "Shall I regale the tale, or would you prefer, dear Keisha?"

With a smile as radiant as the sun's first embrace of the morning waves, Keisha graciously deferred to Adrianna. "Please, Adrianna, the floor is yours."

With a knowing laugh that resonated through the air like the lyrical refrain of a sea shanty, Adrianna directed her attention toward Ong, ready to recount their tale. "This is a narrative as whimsical as a shell adrift upon the tide," she began, her words flowing as gently as the sea's caress upon the shore. "In the days when Keisha was yet a youth, and I, still an inhabitant of the ocean's depths, fate conspired to bring our paths together."

She continued, her eyes alight with the memory of that pivotal day. "Keisha had wandered away from her home, her steps guided by the lure of the Shimmering Coast. Enchanted by the siren call of the sea, she ventured into its waters for a swim. Yet, as fierce as the ocean can be, it bore her further from shore than her young strength could handle."

A tender smile graced Keisha's lips as she recollected that moment. "And that's when my dear friend Adrianna became my savior. She witnessed my struggle, heard my cries for aid, and guided me safely back to the shoreline with the elegance of a sea nymph."

Adrianna's laughter rang out like the chiming of distant seashells, adding the final flourish to their shared narrative. "Thus, we became fast friends, our bond forged by that day's secret. It's a story known only to us until now."

Brimming with gratitude, Ong turned first to Keisha and then to Adrianna. "Adrianna, I am profoundly thankful for your heroic act that day," he conveyed, his words as sincere as the most solemn knight's oath. In that poignant moment, amidst the serenading whispers of the sea and the threads of friendship, a new strand was woven into the tapestry of their shared destiny.

In the depths of Serpent's Lagoon, where the air vibrated with tension and menace, Aqilus emerged from the concealed cave. The world unfurled before him, a living tapestry of ancient fears made flesh—the writhing serpentine heads of the Hydra, the leathery wings of dragons casting ominous shadows, and the curved forms of sea serpents, all converging in a chaotic ballet of malevolence.

With the fluid grace of a sea deity, Aqilus moved through the dangerous waters, his sapphire tail slicing through the turbulent currents with effortless finesse. His eyes, keen as a raptor's piercing gaze, scoured the surroundings for any glimmer of hope amidst the encroaching darkness.

And then, as if summoned by fate, he looked up towards a towering window in the ominous tower. Within the suffocating gloom stood a lady in captivity, her form as ethereal as moonlight. A regal crown graced her brow, symbolizing her enduring grace, while cascades of brown hair framed her visage. Yet, like a haunting melody, her cries of terror pierced the very soul, baring the torment that held her captive.

Heavy with the weight of his revelation, Aqilus bore witness to the imprisoned Queen of Goldmoor, trapped within the heart of this forsaken realm. With an unshakable sense of purpose, he turned and retreated into the concealed cave, vanishing into the depths with the secrets of Serpent's Lagoon clutched tightly within his heart.

Returning to the Shimmering Coast, he carried the burden of his discoveries and the promise of hope. In the presence of Keisha, Ong, and Adrianna, he would unveil the grim truth of the Queen's captivity. Together, they would carve a path toward a kingdom's salvation and rekindle a realm's shattered dreams.

Amidst the tranquil beauty of the Shimmering Coast, Aqilus, the harbinger of destiny's revelation, stood in solemn audience with Keisha and Ong. Like ancient tomes containing the secrets of the abyss, his sea-green eyes held a profound wisdom that mirrored the ocean's depths. The sun, a molten orb of gold, hung low in the sky, casting long shadows upon the shoreline as if nature paused in anticipation of the forthcoming revelation of fate.

With a measured cadence that echoed the ebb and flow of the tides, Aqilus recounted his harrowing discoveries—the menacing presence of the

Hydra, the vigilant patrol of the dragons, and the sinister sea serpents that guarded the lagoon like monstrous gatekeepers. But above all, his words bore witness to the Lady of the Tower. Her anguished screams were a mournful lament that pierced the hearts of all who dared to listen.

Ong, the relentless warrior whose spirit burned as fiercely as the sun's dying embers, expressed his gratitude to Aqilus, his voice an unwavering beacon of resolve amidst the gathering storm of uncertainty. "Indeed, it seems likely that the Queen is imprisoned there," he conceded, his gaze never wavering from the distant horizon. "Yet, the looming question remains: how do we tread upon that treacherous isle?"

In the silent communion of shared purpose, Aqilus and Adrianna, the merfolk guides of this audacious expedition, exchanged a meaningful glance—a glance that spoke of hope entwined with peril. "We have devised a plan," Aqilus began, his words like the gentle surge of a tide on the shore. "The two mages among your party shall ride upon our dolphins and wait just off the coast of Serpent's Lagoon. Adrianna shall wield her command over the serpents, urging them to withdraw."

With a sea-green fire in her eyes that mirrored the determination of a tempest-tossed sea, Adrianna added her voice to the unfolding strategy. "Aqilus shall do his utmost to restrain the Hydras while I shall conjure a storm to bewilder our draconic adversaries. But even in the chaos, we cannot be assured of escaping their ever-watchful gaze."

A somber hush descended upon the assembly as the weight of their impending perils settled like an ominous shroud. Aqilus pressed on, the gravity of their mission etched deeply into his being. "As for the tower itself," he continued, "the mages shall hold the key. They must dismantle the traps and free the imprisoned Queen. Time, my friends, is our enemy, and we must act with swiftness born of desperation."

Ong, the embodiment of unwavering resolve, nodded with solemn purpose, his gaze unwaveringly fixed upon the shimmering horizon. "We shall convey our plan to Lord Karrenen," he declared, his voice resonating like the promise of a storm's fury. "We shall return with the mages in tow, ready to orchestrate the liberation of the Queen."

And so, beneath the watchful gaze of the Shimmering Coast, where the sea whispered ancient secrets and the sun dipped below the horizon, a grand design was set into motion—a daring rescue mission wherein land and sea would unite. Courage would serve as the guiding star through the stormy night.

Chapter 32

Planning for the Queen's Rescue

The council convened with a gravity rarely matched in the heart of Crystal Vale, a city that reached for the heavens with its towering spires and labyrinthine streets teeming with human ambition. King Manard, a sovereign known for his wisdom and fortitude, presided over this gathering with regal solemnity. Crystal Vale, a symbol of humanity's resilience, had flung open its gates to welcome the Eladrin council and Ong and Keisha, who bore the weighty news of an audacious rescue mission.

Within the council chamber, where tapestries depicted sagas of bravery and conquest, an air of somber anticipation hung like a veil. Lord Karrenen, bearing the burdens of leadership etched upon his visage, emerged as the voice of the Eladrin council. Lady Elowen, the embodiment of grace and sagacity, radiated tranquility amid the impending storm.

Lord Galadon, ever the strategist, contemplated the unfolding drama while Lady Lythia, her eyes like ancient wellsprings of knowledge, observed with the discerning gaze of a seer.

Ong, the unwavering human warrior, stood tall, his presence a testament to human courage. By his side, Keisha, her fiery tresses a beacon of determination, embodied strength and grace.

The Eladrin mages, Seraphina and Thalorin, who would wield the magic needed for the impending rescue, exuded an aura of arcane might. Their robes, woven from threads of moonlight, whispered secrets of spells yet to be cast.

As the council assembled, the chamber seemed to hold its breath, aware that within its hallowed confines, the destiny of Queen Jeanne hung in the balance, trapped within the clutches of unfathomable darkness. It was a gathering of disparate races and divergent fates, united by a singular, complex purpose—a purpose that would test their mettle and forge bonds that transcended realms. In this poignant moment, Crystal Vale stood as a bastion of hope, its decisions echoing through the annals of history.

Amid the luxury of the Crystal Vale council chamber, where chandeliers bathed the room in a radiant glow matching the city's ambitions, Ong rose to deliver news that had traversed land and sea boundaries. Like the tolling of a sanctified bell, his words reverberated through the chamber.

"Aqilus," Ong began, his voice as unyielding as the granite cliffs that guarded their shores, "a merman hailing from the depths of Coraluna has confirmed our gravest fears. Queen Jeanne is incarcerated on an island, an accursed realm known as Serpent Lagoon."

As his words fell upon the council like a shroud of foreboding, Ong's eyes met those of the assembly, each member bearing the mantle of responsibility in their countenance.

With a solemn nod, Keisha added her voice to the melancholy chorus. "Aqilus dared to approach the island for a preliminary survey. His findings have affirmed the presence of evil forces—deadly sea serpents, formidable hydras, and vigilant dragons. Moreover, he bore witness to the Queen's anguished cry."

In the aftermath of Keisha's revelation, Lord Karrenen, his gaze akin to a vigilant sentinel surveying the vast horizon, gave voice to his foreboding thoughts. "If Aqilus could hear the Queen's anguished cries during his initial reconnaissance," he mused, "it stands to reason that malevolent specters, or other sinister entities, may dwell within the accursed confines of that tower."

In that pivotal moment, the council chamber bore witness to the gravity of destiny, as the combined might of land and sea committed to a noble quest that would lead them through the shadowed heart of darkness, testing their courage and unwavering resolve. Amidst the glorious city of Crystal Vale, the die had been cast, and the fate of Queen Jeanne hung over them like a lingering specter, waiting for the heroes to heed its haunting call.

Within the sanctified chamber of Crystal Vale, where the tapestries silently chronicled tales of courage and triumph, Lady Lythia's presence, as ethereal as a moonbeam's glow, broke the contemplative silence. Her voice, akin to the hushed secrets of distant stars, bore the wisdom of ages past.

"Before we embark upon the treacherous journey to rescue Queen Jeanne," Lady Lythia began, her words flowing like a measured stream of time itself, "we must secure a sanctuary—a bastion of safety where she can find respite until the day Goldmoor is liberated."

King Manard, his noble heart kindled with compassion, stepped forward like a guardian of realms. "You may bring her here to the shelter of Crystal Vale," he offered, his voice as unwavering as the fortress walls that encircled his city. "We shall protect her with the steadfast strength of our citadel until the dawn breaks on the day of her triumphant return to her husband and the throne of Goldmoor."

A solemn nod from Lady Lythia sealed the pact, an unspoken agreement forged in the crucible of shared determination.

Ong posed a question that hovered in the chamber like an unspoken covenant. "Yet, how can we guarantee that Phoenix, the evil warlock, will not return to Serpent's Lagoon only to discover Queen Jeanne's absence? Secrecy is our shield, for we dare not expose King Alex to his vengeful fury."

Lady Elowen's eyes, as profound as ancient woodlands, redirected her gaze to Keisha. "Keisha," she inquired, her voice tinged with anticipation, "do you believe that the merfolk can conjure storms capable of dissuading Phoenix from venturing to Serpent's Lagoon? These disturbances could cloak our actions, veiling the truth from his watchful eye."

Keisha took a moment to contemplate the gravity of the proposition. "I shall consult with Adrianna," she confirmed, her voice resonating with the allure of the submerged realm. "Or perhaps I shall suggest that she implores her father, King Oceanous, to awaken the storms and start weather turbulences that even Phoenix would hesitate to challenge."

Within the sanctified chamber where destinies intertwined, the components of a grand plan were laid bare—an alliance forged with land, sea, and the very elements themselves. Their quest was nothing short of rescuing a Queen and outsmarting the shadowy forces poised to shroud an entire kingdom in darkness.

Lord Galadon, the strategist whose eyes gleamed with tactical insight, shifted his attention to Ong. Like the piercing beacon of a lighthouse on the distant shore, his inquiry sought to illuminate the path ahead.

"Now that we've set the foundation," Lord Galadon began, his words a measured march, "could you explain the details of Aqilus and the merfolk's intentions? What role awaits us, and what do they request of us?"

Ong, the resolute guardian, nodded in solemn recognition, his determination unyielding as the citadel's mighty walls. "The merfolk shall embark upon a treacherous odyssey," he began, his words carrying the gravitas of their impending destiny. "They shall traverse a concealed waterway, a submerged route spanning from the depths of Coraluna to the accursed heart of Serpent Lagoon."

Ong's voice remained unwavering as he unveiled the merfolk's intricate strategy. "Adrianna and her mermaid sisters will harness their mermagic, a formidable force born from the very depths of the sea, to command the serpents that coil protectively around the island. Like sirens of legend, their voices will become an enchanting chorus that beckons the serpents to withdraw, creating an opening in the dangerous heart of this forsaken domain."

As Ong pressed on, his words painted vivid images of bravery and determination. "Aqilus, with a dauntless spirit and unwavering determination, will embark on a dangerous endeavor to subdue the fury of the hydras—those multifaceted monstrosities that defy easy control. With the unwavering support of his fellow mermen, they shall strive to restrain these formidable adversaries for a limited time."

He paused, the gravity of Aqilus' caution resonating through the room like a solemn echo. "But hydras are capricious creatures, their moods as unpredictable as the shifting tides. The merfolk have wisely readied a contingency—a tactical retreat that will lure the hydras deeper into the boundless ocean should their control falter."

The council chamber stood in collective silence, the intricate threads of their plan weaving a tapestry of daring and sacrifice. Ong's narrative continued each word a brushstroke on a canvas of courage and unwavering commitment as the heroes prepared to face the treacherous path ahead.

Keisha, her fiery presence illuminated by the chandeliers' opulent glow, stepped into the narrative with a resonant melody of unwavering resolve. "With the serpents' graceful withdrawal from the island," her words carried the weight of destiny, "Adrianna and her mermaid sisters shall conjure a tempest—a tempest designed to confound the vigilant dragons that patrol the skies above Serpent Lagoon."

Her eyes blazed with the fierce determination of her conviction as she continued. "Yet, let it be known that vigilance must be our constant companion, for the dragons possess a keen vision capable of piercing even the veil of a storm electrified by lightning. Thus, we shall lean upon the talents of our two Eladrin mages, Seraphina and Thalorin, masters of the arcane and adepts in the art of concealed passage."

Keisha's words lingered in the air, a testament to the delicate interplay between natural forces and the artful cunning of the arcane. Their plan, born from the unity of land, sea, and magic, had been forged in the crucible of necessity. In the heart of Crystal Vale, destiny unfolded its intricate design—a path fraught with peril and promise, where courage and unity would guide their way.

The councilors and their allies stood like figures etched upon the canvas of fate, their gazes fixed on Seraphina, a manifestation of arcane elegance. Like the magic of an ancient spell, her voice wove threads of magic into the air they breathed.

"As we navigate the treacherous waters of Serpent's Lagoon," Seraphina began, her words a whispered pledge of mysteries yet to be unveiled, "Thalorin and I shall approach astride two dolphins, our ethereal steeds guiding us through the liquid realms. Our destination—a forbidding tower where the hostility of Phoenix lurks in ambush."

Thalorin, the master of arcane arts, continued the narrative with the precision of a well-practiced incantation. "Within the shadowed chambers of the tower, we shall unearth the nature of Phoenix's enchantments, the spells that safeguard the Queen's captivity. With her mystical mastery, Seraphina shall unravel these traps and wards that stand sentinel along our path."

As the councilors listened, their attention unwavering, Lord Karrenen, the font of wisdom and foresight, took on the mantle of guidance. "We shall equip them with the instruments necessary to breach any magical barriers obstructing their advance," he affirmed, cementing their faith in the mages' capabilities.

He added, his tone resolute, "Their mission is one of swift and unwavering purpose—to extract Queen Jeanne without delay. We must avoid entanglements with the spectral and the arcane, for time is our most precious and dwindling resource."

The chamber resounded with their shared determination, the plan crystallizing like a beacon amidst encroaching shadows. United in purpose, they prepared to confront the challenges of Serpent's Lagoon, where the salvation of the Queen gleamed like a fragile gem amid the shrouded depths.

As Ong once more stepped into the spotlight of their council's collective resolve, he wove a vivid tapestry of their daring rescue plan—a symphony of intricate movements, where each note resonated with peril and promise.

"If fate smiles upon us and our efforts bear fruit," Ong proclaimed, his voice an unwavering call to action, "Seraphina and Thalorin shall accompany Queen Jeanne from the tower's accursed grasp, riding upon the backs of the graceful dolphins that have pledged their alliance in this perilous enterprise."

His narrative continued firmly as the steeds that awaited them. "Upon reaching the embrace of the Emeraldwoods, the stalwart warriors of Crystal Vale shall stand prepared, their steeds as swift as coursing rivers, to convey the Queen to safety within the impenetrable walls of Crystal Vale."

Ong's gaze shifted toward the merfolk, those enigmatic dwellers of the deep. "The merfolk shall maintain their vigil, awaiting the moment when Seraphina and Thalorin have spirited the Queen away from the cursed island. Then, in harmony with King Oceanous himself, they shall conjure hurricanes and unleash the sea's fury, a veil to shroud our actions until the hour is ripe for the liberation of Goldmoor."

Lord Galadon, the master strategist, bestowed his blessings, his words laden with the weight of hope and unwavering faith in their grand design.

"May the stars above guide your path through the intricate shadows, and may the winds of fortune carry your spirits aloft."

With that, the councilors dispersed, each departing to prepare for the impending rescue of Queen Jeanne. This brutal crusade would test not only their mettle but also the bonds of their unity and the fabric of their intertwined destinies. In the heart of Crystal Vale, beneath the watchful gaze of the celestial heavens, they embarked upon a quest to shape the future of Vacari and measure the resilience of heroes.

Chapter 33

The Daring Rescue of Queen Jeanne

Amidst the hallowed confines of Emeraldwoods Forest, where the towering arboreal giants stood as stoic guardians, Seraphina and Thalorin materialized from the obscurity, bathed in the dappled radiance that streamed through the foliage like fragments of celestial glass. In this mystic woodland, where the air resonated with the whispers of time-worn spirits, they stood at the precipice of fate.

Before them materialized, two mermaids, their tails shimmering with the ethereal luminescence of moonlight caressing the ocean's surface. These mermaids, ethereal as the misty veil of dreams, exuded an aura of solemn purpose. Their presence echoed the serene depths of the ocean itself.

As Seraphina and Thalorin descended into the crystalline waters, a profound transformation overcame them. Their terrestrial limbs, once attuned to solid ground, now embraced the sinuous elegance of the underwater realm. With effortless grace, they mounted the sleek forms of two dolphins, their loyal companions, in this aqueous odyssey.

The mermaids and their cetacean comrades moved in perfect unison, a fluid ballet that bridged the divide between sea and sky, between realms intermingled and destinies intertwined. Seraphina and Thalorin, perched atop their aquatic steeds, embarked on a journey away from the accursed Serpent's Lagoon—a voyage toward redemption and the epicenter of their audacious scheme.

They remained poised in the boundless expanse of sea and sky, suspended between two worlds. Seraphina and Thalorin, ever-watchful like the darkest of nights, and the mermaids, epitomizing aquatic elegance, held their positions, measuring the moments until their allies would converge with them on this treacherous expedition.

Beneath the cerulean depths of Coraluna, where the refracted sunlight painted the ocean floor with shades of sapphire and gold, Aqilus and Adrianna guided their fellow merfolk like stewards of the aqueous domains. Each mermaid and merman moved with the grace of balletic oceanic performers, their tails swaying in perfect harmony, orchestrating a symphony of aqueous artistry.

Their odyssey guided them inexorably towards the ominous maw of a cavern, a yawning portal to the mysterious core of Serpent's Lagoon. Aqilus, relentless as the unyielding cliffs that guarded the sea, assumed the role of a vigilant guardian at the cave's entrance. His eyes, akin to sea glass, gleamed with a blend of determination and circumspection, reflecting the peril that lay ahead. His voice, a sonorous beacon amid the subterranean susurrus, compelled his companions to step gingerly onto this treacherous path.

"Exercise utmost vigilance," Aqilus admonished, his words reverberating like ancient incantations within the aqueous chamber, "for we embark on a journey through the difficult abyss of this cavern."

The merfolk, their eyes aglint with the ethereal allure of the abyss, heeded his caution as they advanced, a procession of aquatic enchantment. Their destination beckoned—a forsaken isle where serpentine creatures lay dormant in an ominous hush, a domain fraught with peril and enigma.

Adrianna assumed the vanguard role with unwavering purpose as the sun's golden embrace danced upon the water's undulating bosom. Her tail, adorned in regal purples reminiscent of amethyst's majesty, glided through the aqueous medium with the fluid grace of an underwater queen. As she forged the path towards the enigmatic island, her comrades trailed in her wake, a tableau of unity and resolute purpose.

In the heart of this aqueous realm, where the cavern's concealing shadows yielded to the enigmatic depths of Serpent's Lagoon, the merfolk embarked on a mission that would strain their resolve and unveil the arcane enigmas shrouded beneath the waves. The journey had commenced, and destiny steered their course towards the island's mysterious shores, where secrets long buried would soon be unfurled.

Within the aqueous tapestry of Serpent's Lagoon, where the moonlight pirouetted upon the water's surface like the glistening threads of a cosmic loom, Adrianna spared a momentary glance towards Aqilus. Her eyes, the color of unfathomable sea-green depths, betrayed a complex tapestry of emotions, a fusion of unwavering resolve and a hint of veiled apprehension.

"May fortune favor us," she murmured, her words a tender, silken embrace of the underwater currents, " thus, our journey commences."

With resolve etched upon her aquatic visage, Adrianna, a regal sovereign among her mermaid sisters, charted her course toward the looming presence of the serpents. These sinuous behemoths, their serpentine forms coiling like spectral guardians in the abyssal depths, awaited her arrival. In this aqueous procession of otherworldly allure, the mermaids, an ensemble of ethereal beauty, mirrored her movements with unwavering grace.

As they drew closer to the serpents, their tails moved in a hypnotic cadence, a siren's call resonating with the deep-sea creatures' essence. Each swish and undulation of their tails seemed to beckon, to summon. With mermagic coursing through them like the rhythmic tides of the sea, they wove their beguiling enchantments, their voices reverberating through the watery expanse like sacred hymns within an underwater cathedral. In this mesmerizing aquatic ballet, the mermaids enacted a harmony of artistry and mysticism, forging an unspoken bond with the serpentine denizens of the abyss. This silent agreement transcended the confines of mere words.

Amidst the very core of Serpent's Lagoon, where arcane sorcery intertwined with the enigmatic depths, the mermaids' mermagic reigned supreme. The serpents, erstwhile sovereigns of this cryptic domain, succumbed to the resonant chorus of voices that enticed them away—an awe-inspiring testament to the might of unity and the indelible legacy of the merfolk beneath the aqueous veil.

In this mystical heart of the lagoon, where the boundaries of enchantment and obscurity blurred, the mermaids' magical arts held dominion. The serpents, once unchallenged rulers of this realm, now consented to the harmonious symphony of voices that lured them from their ancient throne—a living testament to the unyielding potency of solidarity and the timeless heritage of the merfolk beneath the undulating waves.

Beneath the vaulted expanse of Serpent's Lagoon, where Merfolk wielded the elements with the mastery of arcane virtuosos, Aqilus spearheaded an audacious charge toward the colossal behemoths known as Hydras. These creatures, monstrous and twisted, embodied a primal force, their forms a living nightmare etched in the depths of the abyss. The Hydra, a terror with somewhere between six and one hundred heads, each supported by a long neck, coiled around each other or fanned out, ready to attack challengers from every conceivable angle.

Aqilus, his unwavering gaze unflinching beneath the undulating strands of kelp that framed his visage, harnessed the age-old mermagic that coursed through his being—a magic as ancient as the very ocean itself. Initially, their enchantments enshrouded the Hydras, weaving a tapestry of aqueous dreams, an imaginary ballet that sought to subdue these titanic adversaries.

Yet, the Hydras, embodiments of unyielding vigor and primordial chaos, defied such attempts at control. With a fury akin to nature's wrath unleashed, they shattered the ethereal bonds with a ferocity that transcended mortal comprehension.

With a sigh of resignation, Aqilus, the stalwart guardian of the abyss, rallied his brethren, his voice a resounding call amidst the tumultuous aquatic tempest. "So be it, fellow mermen," he proclaimed, his words a testament to unwavering determination, "draw the Hydras into the abyss's inky depths, where the void devours all."

The merfolk, radiant in their aquatic grace, encircled the Hydras, luring them with a beguiling proximity, their tails aglow with the muted luminescence of the abyss. As the Hydras gave chase, akin to tempestuous maelstroms seeking elusive quarry, the mermen guided them deeper into the ocean's unfathomable embrace.

In the shadowy abyss of Serpent's Lagoon's depths, the mermen enacted a dangerous dance, a choreography of courage and self-sacrifice. They enticed the Hydras further, their forms vanishing into the eternal obscurity of the ocean's enfolding darkness. Amidst the chaotic turmoil, they fulfilled their sacred duty, propelled by the unbreakable bonds of brotherhood and the understanding that their actions paved the path to salvation.

Amidst the aqueous realm of Serpent Lagoon, where the sea and sky entwined in an ever-shifting embrace, Adrianna and her mermaid sisters summoned their mermagic once more. This time, their enchantments wove a symphony of tempestuous might—a meteorological ballet that conjured the wrath of the elements.

Once serene and crystalline, the azure skies overhead darkened in response to their ethereal commands—thunderous clouds assembled like titans of old, their looming presence a warning of impending tumult. Lightning, akin to divine spears hurled by celestial warriors, streaked across the heavens in blinding splendor.

Torrential, relentless, and unforgiving rain descended from the heavens in cascading sheets. It was as if the tears of the gods themselves fell upon the island, a deluge that pounded the earth in a relentless cadence—a symphony of nature's unbridled fury echoing through the stormy heart of the lagoon.

As Adrianna's gaze locked onto the two Eladrin mages, a subtle nod of affirmation traversed the space between them—an unspoken covenant of shared purpose. With a choreography of grace and precision, the mages dismounted their sleek aquatic companions, their feet alighting upon the rain-slicked sands of the island's shores.

Amid the storm they had summoned, Seraphina and Thalorin embarked upon the concluding chapter of their voyage. The island, a realm cloaked in enigma and peril, beckoned them forward. Amidst the tumultuous symphony of thunder and rain, they moved with an almost spectral quality, ethereal figures traversing a world bathed in the elemental turmoil they had conjured.

Seraphina, carrying over the howling winds and torrential downpour, remarked to Thalorin, "Behold the might of the merfolk, masters of sea and sky, who have bent the disruption to our will. The elements conspire with us, my dear friend, as we tread the precipice of destiny."

Their mission unfurled within the tempestuous symphony of nature's unrestrained might—a fragile ballet of shadows and secrets, where the tumultuous storms above concealed their covert odyssey into the very heart of Serpent Lagoon's enigmatic depths.

Within the obsidian recesses of the tower, Seraphina and Thalorin navigated a treacherous labyrinth interwoven with malevolent flora. This otherworldly garden, a testament to the unforgiving nature of Phoenix's enchantments, served as a symbolic bulwark—a sinuous tapestry of thorns and venom woven with sinister intent to trap and hinder all who dared to intrude.

As they delved deeper into the tower's core, the toxic flora confronted them, each malicious presence an embodiment of the evil forces that imprisoned Queen Jeanne. Every vine, petal, leaf, and stem seemed imbued with the essence of darkness, forming a disorienting kaleidoscope of eerie and unnatural hues.

Seraphina and Thalorin, their senses acutely attuned to the hostile environment, acknowledged the looming peril posed by the poison that hung in the air. Each breath they drew felt like an offering to an evil deity, thick with the haunting specter of death.

In this harrowing tableau, Thalorin's intellect raced, a wellspring of wisdom and unwavering resolve. He recalled a vial of elixir bestowed upon them by Lord Karrenen—an alchemical concoction steeped in ancient understanding and arcane mastery. With indefatigable diligence, he applied the elixir to the maleficent flora, its essence a soothing counterforce against the encroaching venom.

Like the dark tide yielding before the radiant dawn, the malevolent flora withered and receded, their nefarious intent thwarted by the alchemical antidote. Once a fortress of despair, the tower bore the indelible scars of their confrontation—its pernicious guardians vanquished, defeated by the potent magic of knowledge and the unwavering power of purpose.

In the heart of this enigmatic tower, Seraphina and Thalorin forged ahead on their quest, their spirits ablaze with renewed determination, their path now unburdened by the deadly clutches of poison. They ventured onward, stalwart sentinels of hope amidst the shrouded recesses, driven by an unrelenting resolve to free Queen Jeanne from her spectral prison.

Seraphina and Thalorin confronted yet another labyrinthine challenge within the tower's enigmatic depths. This intricate and bewildering maze appeared as if conjured by Phoenix's penchant for enigmatic and vexing traps.

As they stood before the labyrinth's confounding entrance, their gazes locked in a silent communion of resolute purpose, Thalorin couldn't suppress a muttered curse that escaped his lips. "Cursed be Phoenix," he grumbled, his words a testament to the exasperation that these mazes invoked. The warlock reveled in weaving these bewildering puzzles, each a tribute to his cunning and malice.

With measured determination, they embarked on their odyssey through the labyrinth—a journey fraught with serpentine twists and disorienting turns akin to the convoluted path of fate itself. They navigated corners, retraced their steps, and confronted dead-ends that seemed to mock their progress.

Yet, a sense of mastery gradually emerged with each obstacle surmounted and every erroneous turn rectified. Seraphina's laughter resonated through the labyrinth's winding corridors like the tinkling chime of a long-forgotten melody. "We are improving," she remarked, a glimmer of optimism in the face of adversity.

In this ever-shifting enigma, where time appeared as elusive as a fleeting phantom, they pressed forward, guided by the twin beacons of unwavering determination and steadfast camaraderie. Each intricate twist and bewildering turn brought them closer to their ultimate objective, a testament to their indomitable spirit and the unyielding pursuit of Queen Jeanne's liberation.

Amidst the labyrinth's enigmatic embrace, Seraphina and Thalorin stood as living proof of the resilience of the Eladrin spirit—a living testament to the belief that even the most confounding of mazes could be unraveled with unwavering resolve and the luminous torch of camaraderie to illuminate the way.

In the aqueous expanse of Serpent Lagoon, an unrelenting pursuit unfolded as the mermen continued to lure the wrath of the Hydras upon themselves. Like tempestuous thunderheads of fury, the colossal beasts pursued with a primal intensity that defied the very laws of nature.

Aqilus, a merman of unyielding resolve, maintained a telepathic communion with Adrianna, their thoughts a silent symphony that spanned the realm between the terrestrial and aquatic domains. Like a message carried upon the inexorable tides themselves, his inquiry resonated through the watery depths, a search for tidings of the Eladrin's progress.

Amidst the tumultuous pursuit, Adrianna's response, a mere whisper in the boundless ocean of shared thoughts, reached him. "They still reside within the tower," she conveyed, her words carrying an urgency that mirrored the relentless cadence of the Hydras' pursuit.

In response, Aqilus executed a graceful pivot, his majestic form guiding the Hydras deeper into the ocean's abyss. Like a luminescent beacon amidst the obsidian expanse, his hope rested upon the swiftness of the Eladrin—the anticipation that they would soon liberate Queen Jeanne from her spectral confinement and, in doing so, quell the explosive rage of the pursuing Hydras.

In this symphony of pursuit and evasion, courage and desperation, Aqilus and the mermen transformed into a living tempest within the shadowed depths of Serpent Lagoon. Their selfless sacrifice, akin to an offering to the capricious tides of fate, was the overture to a grand opera of salvation—a queen's liberation and the resounding triumph of hope amidst the abyss.

Aqilus, their unwavering leader, imparted a solemn directive to his fellow mermen as they navigated the problematic ballet with the Hydras. "Stay clear of their heads and tails," he admonished, his words a clarion call for caution. "We are not here to engage these titans in battle; our purpose is to divert and distract, to buy time with our lives."

In response to his wise counsel, the mermen adjusted their positions, mindful to remain outside the treacherous reach of the Hydras' fearsome appendages. Like masterful choreographers, they orchestrated a mesmerizing dance of evasion and allure—a rhapsody of sacrifice in the face of invincible adversaries.

As the relentless pursuit and selfless sacrifice unfolded beneath the murky depths, it became a testament to the indomitable spirit of those who dared challenge the abyss. Their actions resonated as a haunting melody, a requiem for those who risked all to uphold the mantle of hope amidst the fierce tides of Serpent Lagoon.

In the heart of the tower's enigmatic depths, where enshrouded secrets lurked and shadows wove their cryptic dances, Seraphina and Thalorin confronted another formidable challenge. Guardians of an origin veiled in mystery, beings of ethereal design and mysterious purpose, stood as sentinels of the arcane, staunchly barring their passage.

Before the threshold of the tower's inner sanctum, Thalorin's lips curled into a sardonic smirk—an ironic recognition of the trials ahead. "Here we go again," he mused, his voice a mere whisper amidst the labyrinthine mysteries of the unknown.

At this moment, teetering between trepidation and unwavering determination, they confronted their latest trial, akin to knights at the entrance of a fabled dragon's lair. The guardians, their forms a mosaic of shimmering energies and age-old enchantments, bore witness to the unyielding resolve of the Eladrin.

With measured strides and the weight of destiny draped upon their shoulders, Seraphina and Thalorin steeled themselves to confront these enigmatic sentinels. Like the keyholders to a hidden realm, the guardians held the secrets that awaited their mastery. In this clash of wills and the arcane, they aimed to unlock the door leading to Queen Jeanne's salvation, thereby reclaiming hope from the heart of darkness.

Within the sanctum of the tower, Seraphina and Thalorin faced these enigmatic guardians, their determination unwavering, their recollections of Goldmoor's trials serving as guiding stars in this moment of peril.

With meticulous precision, they tread the same path they had once traversed in the distant halls of Goldmoor. Like scholars deciphering the cryptic script of an ancient tome, they scrutinized the guardians with the discerning eyes of seekers, unraveling the intricacies of their sculpted forms.

Every detail, every subtle nuance etched into the guardians' stone visages, became a fragment of a grand, unsolved puzzle. This puzzle was the key to unlocking the path before them. They traced the lines of those sculpted limbs, their movements mirroring a symphony of cautious analysis.

Time, in its relentless flow, stretched into an eternal tapestry as they methodically pieced together the intricate sequence, step by step. Each movement bore a testament to their mastery, a tribute to the unity of their purpose and their shared intellect.

Then, as if kissed by the hand of arcane magic, Thalorin advanced, his movements mirroring the carefully deciphered sequence with flawless precision. In response, the statues, like ancient sentinels acknowledging the arrival of the worthy, rumbled with a sonorous resonance, granting passage to those who had unlocked the secrets of their enigmatic guardianship.

As the last echoes of the resonant rumble faded, an invisible barrier dissolved, revealing the path forward—a portal into the core of the tower's enigma. In this triumphant moment, where adversity yielded to their intellectual prowess and unwavering determination, Seraphina and Thalorin assumed their roles as champions of intellect and perseverance, poised to confront whatever challenges the tower yet concealed in its shadowy depths.

At the zenith of their arduous odyssey, Seraphina and Thalorin stood before the majestic door guarding the sanctum within the tower—a door cloaked in enigma and sealed by the very hand of magic itself.

Their discerning eyes and nimble fingers sought the implements entrusted to them by Lord Karrenen, the justice of arcane wisdom. Like relics from a bygone era, these tools held the key to unraveling the intricate lock that obstructed their path.

With the utmost delicacy, they embarked upon this final trial, mindful of the dire consequences that an errant move might incur. Like a guardian of long-forgotten enigmas, the door appeared poised to thwart any intrusion with its evil magic.

In the peaceful ambiance of the tower's inner sanctum, they labored in concert, their fingers deftly manipulating the tools with a precision that mirrored the delicate choreography of celestial bodies. With each calculated motion, they inched closer to unlocking the door's hidden mechanism, keenly aware of the specter of failure hovering over them.

Their shared determination shone as a beacon amidst the encroaching darkness. The door, as silent as a whisper in the night, submitted to their mastery, its magic conquered, and its secrets unveiled.

In this pivotal instant, Seraphina and Thalorin stood as beacons of hope, poised to reveal the truths concealed beyond the threshold. These truths bore the promise of Queen Jeanne's deliverance and the liberation of Goldmoor from the clutches of malevolence.

With the arcane seal of the door undone, Seraphina and Thalorin stood upon the brink of the unknown, their hearts resolute and their purpose unshaken. As the door groaned open, a cacophony of anguished wails rent the air, akin to the mournful lament of countless lost souls.

Their gazes met in silent acknowledgment, and with unwavering determination, they braced themselves against the haunting cries that reverberated through the tower's shadowed chambers. Spectral and ethereal, the denizens of this nightmarish realm swirled around them like restless phantoms, their forms elusive, their torment palpable.

With measured steps, Thalorin approached the figure amidst the spectral throng—a figure whose ethereal visage bore the unmistakable aura of a queen, her presence a testament to her regal grace and harrowing captivity.

In a voice that resounded with authority and compassion, Thalorin addressed Queen Jeanne. "We are Eladrin," he proclaimed, his words a beacon of truth amidst the noise of deceit surrounding her. "We have come to liberate you from this tower, to return you to your cherished city. Please, come with us."

In the queen's eyes, once pools of despair, a newfound hope flickered like a lone star in the encroaching night. In this delicate balance between decision and destiny, amidst the twilight of shadows and specters, Seraphina and Thalorin, the Eladrin mages who had navigated the labyrinthine depths of the tower's secrets, now stood as sentinels of salvation, ready to guide Queen Jeanne from the abyss of captivity into the radiant embrace of freedom.

As Queen Jeanne descended the spiral stairs of her ancient prison, the guidance of Seraphina and Thalorin led her to the threshold of liberation. Once encased within the unyielding stone walls, her gaze extended to the distant island, a place of torment and isolation.

In this moment of newfound liberty, the queen's heart fluttered like a caged bird yearning for the boundless skies, seeking escape from the desolation that had defined her world.

A gentle smile adorned Seraphina's lips as she addressed Queen Jeanne, her words a soothing balm to the captive soul. "Fear not, Your Majesty," she reassured, her voice an unwavering melody of assurance. "We have dolphins waiting to carry us away. Place your trust in them, and Thalorin shall stand as your stalwart guardian. But time is our adversary; we must hasten our escape."

In this pivotal juncture, as Queen Jeanne prepared to embark on a journey from darkness into the radiance of hope, Seraphina, Thalorin, and the loyal dolphins became harbingers of redemption and deliverance. With their combined strength and resolve, they would navigate the dangerous waters and lead the queen back to the welcoming embrace of her cherished city—a city that longed to reclaim its lost queen.

With Queen Jeanne under the watchful care of Thalorin, Seraphina, guided by the whims of destiny, set forth on the voyage to escort the queen beyond the ominous shores of Serpent's Lagoon. A silent nod exchanged with Adrianna, a testament to the unbreakable bond forged in the crucible of adversity, set in motion a chain of events that would culminate in salvation.

As they traversed the outskirts of Emeraldwoods, the ancient forest stood as a sentinel, its venerable trees whispering secrets of epochs past. Like a ribbon of hope unfurling, the path to safety stretched before them, leading the way to the sanctuary of Crystal Vale—a city where Queen Jeanne's heart could finally find solace.

As Seraphina and Thalorin approached the outskirts of the majestic Emeraldwoods, the forest's ancient sentinels whispered secrets of time immemorial. Here, beneath the verdant canopy, a pivotal moment of destiny awaited. Thalorin's solid and sure hands gently assisted Queen Jeanne as she disembarked from the noble dolphin, a creature that had become their ally in a realm where alliances were forged by courage.

Like knights of old, the warriors of Crystal Vale stood in solemn honor of their rescued monarch. With deference befitting royalty, they bowed in unison, paying homage to the queen whose return would herald a new dawn for Goldmoor. "This way, Your Majesty," they spoke with unwavering resolve, their words a pledge of safeguarding her until the kingdom could be reunited.

Amidst this tableau of loyalty and courage, Queen Jeanne walked forward, her regal bearing a testament to the indomitable spirit that had sustained her in captivity. The path to Crystal Vale lay ahead, a sanctuary where she would find refuge and from whence her journey would eventually lead her back to the embrace of her beloved king and people.

For Seraphina and Thalorin, their task was fulfilled, and the weight of their mission was lifted from their shoulders. With the queen now safe in the hands of her protectors, they turned their steps homeward to E'vahona, the hidden realm of the Eladrin. There, they would convey the news of Queen Jeanne's rescue to the council, setting the next chapter of their epic tale in motion.

Adrianna, the mermaid with an ocean's depth of wisdom, silently acknowledged Seraphina's departure. Her telepathic connection with Aqilus, the guardian of the deep, became the conduit through which tidings of their success were relayed. The steadfast and resolute mermen continued their daring mission, their every stroke of fin propelling them further from the grasp of the relentless Hydra.

As the mermaids and mermen reunited at Serpent's Cove, a sacred meeting ground for their kind, anticipation hung in the air like the cresting waves of the sea. King Oceanous, the ruler of the aquatic realm, awaited their return, his presence a beacon of unity and purpose.

In the intricate tapestry of this grand quest, threads of fate intertwined, weaving together the destinies of merfolk and Eladrin, of land and sea. The queen's salvation marked a turning point in their tale—a testament to the enduring power of courage, friendship, and unwavering determination.

In the presence of King Oceanous, the sovereign of the abyssal depths, the very fabric of the world seemed to bend to his will. With his trident, a relic of immeasurable power, he harnessed the elemental forces at his command, unleashing a symphony of chaos upon the world above.

The skies, once serene, were rent asunder by jagged lightning, like fiery tendrils reaching down to touch the earth. Each bolt was a reminder of the merfolk's determination, a promise etched in electric brilliance that no prison, no malice, could withstand the united might of sea and sky.

The waters surrounding the island became a tempestuous maelstrom, churning with the fury of the deep. Like titanic serpents, waves rose and fell with unrelenting force, crashing upon the shore with thunderous resonance. The sea seemed to rebel against the evil grip that had held it captive.

As the island trembled beneath the onslaught of King Oceanous's wrath, the skies darkened, shrouding the land in an obsidian cloak. The day turned to night, and the world seemed to hold its breath, awaiting the verdict of destiny.

This storm, this cataclysmic display of nature's fury, would persist until the warriors of Goldmoor had defeated their oppressors and reclaimed their city. It was a testament to the merfolk's unwavering resolve, a promise etched in storm and lightning that the battle for Goldmoor would be fought and won.

Chapter 34

Tides of Destiny: Preparing for the Final Battle

Amidst the enigmatic embrace of the Hidden Isles, veiled in an otherworldly mist, this ethereal realm emerged as a bastion of breathtaking beauty—a jewel adrift in the uncharted vastness of the untamed sea. Hidden alcoves, bathed in the mystical aura that enshrouded the isles, concealed secrets that predated the very fabric of existence.

Upon this mystical stage, a council of diverse beings convened beneath the sanctuary of ancient trees whose gnarled branches whispered ageless secrets to the ever-curious wind. Each tree stood as a sentinel of knowledge, their leaves rustling with the collective wisdom of ages untold. It was beneath this verdant canopy that the council of realms came together, their presence a testament to the unity of worlds, the convergence of destinies, and the mysteries yet to be unveiled.

Gathered together, this council of beings from different realms and races came to confluence, their fates tightly interwoven in the looming shadow of an impending darkness. The air around them crackled with the electric charge of myriad possibilities as they embarked on the formidable task of untangling the intricate threads of fate, which were perilously close to snaring the Kingdom of Goldmoor.

Lord Karrenen and Lord Galadon, emissaries of the Eladrin Council, epitomized the regal elegance that their kind was renowned for. Like mirrors reflecting the ages, their eyes bore the weight of countless decisions made in the name of their realm's welfare, carrying within them the echoes of bygone eras.

King Manard, the sovereign of Crystal Vale, a bastion of humanity ensconced amidst the enchanting wilderness, brought with him the wisdom of generations past. His presence radiated authority and benevolence—a guiding light amidst the encroaching darkness.

Ong, the unyielding warrior, and his betrothed, Keisha, the flame-haired Eladin, represented the bridging of worlds within Vacari—a testament to the enduring bonds that transcended boundaries and united the realm's denizens.

Seraphina and Thalorin, Eladrin mages of profound wisdom and unparalleled magic, exuded an aura of deep reverence. Their mere presence was a living testament to the eternal interplay of light and shadow within the heart of the Eladrin realm, where balance was both a pursuit and a way of life.

And then there were the dragons—Kimras the Gold Dragon, Silvara the Silver Dragon, Dirona the Bronze Dragon, Hespherus the Brass Dragon, and Caelum the Copper Dragon. They stood as majestic sentinels of boundless power and timeless wisdom. Their resplendent scales shimmered like treasures coveted by kingdoms, and within the depths of their ancient eyes, one could glimpse the unfathomable knowledge of ages long past.

Amidst the council's deliberations, their voices became the skilled hands of a master weaver, deftly intertwining threads of strategy and finesse. Every spoken word was akin to a painter's delicate brushstroke on the canvas of destiny, layering meaning upon meaning, crafting a tapestry of intricate design and purpose.

In the heart of the deliberation chamber, the first step toward Goldmoor's salvation crystallized—the liberation of King Alex. Time, that ever-watchful sentinel, held its breath, poised to witness the intricate dance about to commence. Each step taken within the labyrinthine dungeons would herald liberation's triumphant crescendo or the mournful dirge of ruin.

An air of urgency prevailed within the chamber, like a tempest brewing on the distant horizon. The council, their envoys Seraphina and Thalorin, felt the weight of their deliberations like an impending storm. In this chamber of destiny, the threads of time tightened, and the very fate of Goldmoor teetered upon their fingertips.

Seraphina and Thalorin, those resplendent Eladrin mages, stood as shimmering sentinels of arcane mastery amid the council's assembly. Their eyes, deep and enigmatic pools of mystical knowledge, radiated an unwavering determination. Like architects of salvation, these two bore the weighty responsibility of unlocking the prison that held King Alex captive.

Seraphina's words hung in the chamber like a prelude to a grand symphony. "Before we can free King Alex," she began, her voice carrying the resonance of purpose, "we must navigate treacherous waters and face formidable foes. Serpents and sea monsters guard his prison, a testament to the darkness that shrouds him."

A nod of acknowledgment rippled through the council. Lord Karrenen, representing the Eladrin Council, spoke with gravitas, "Seraphina speaks the truth. These challenges are formidable, but they are the crucible through which our salvation must pass."

Seraphina, her gaze unwavering, added, "King Alex shall be the catalyst upon which this battle hinges. His fate and the fate of Goldmoor are intertwined."

In this chamber of destiny, words and resolve collided, forging the path forward to confront the darkness that held the king captive.

During their deliberations, the council turned its attention to the intricate assignment of their forces. With each division defined, a tapestry of clarity began to weave itself within the gathering, illuminating the roles and responsibilities of each member.

Ong, a towering figure among the ground forces, stood as a symbol of leadership. His gaze, a beacon burning with unwavering determination, pierced through the air like a clarion call to action.

With a commanding presence, Ong elucidated his strategy. "The warriors of Crystal Vale," he declared, his voice akin to the resounding beat of a war drum, "shall merge their strength with the formidable Eladrin. We shall forge a united front, and you shall find Pumpkin in our ranks." A wry smile graced his lips as he continued, "Pumpkin shall be under my watchful eye." At this, Keisha's eyes sparkling with delight turned to Ong and quipped, "At least she'll keep you out of trouble."

Their words carried the weight of their impending battle, each sentence etching a promise of unwavering dedication to their cause. As they gazed towards the horizon of impending conflict, they understood that every decision forged within this sanctum of strategy would reverberate through the annals of history. They knew their resolve, like tempered steel, would be tested on the battlefield, where destiny awaited their unwavering courage.

In the sanctum of strategy, within the hallowed walls of their council chamber, these heroes stood as a formidable ensemble, their presence radiating a sense of purpose that glittered like morning dew upon a field of valor.

Caelum, the copper dragon, issued his proclamation, his voice like the resonant echoes of a mighty bell reverberating through the council chamber. He spoke of the copper dragons' intention not to carry riders on their backs. Their decision was a testament to their pursuit of freedom, a freedom that would allow them to confront the Druchii with unbridled might. Like molten pools of wisdom, Caelum's eyes held the knowledge that some of the Druchii were skilled magic users, and keeping them from converging on dragons with riders was a strategic imperative.

The copper dragons, embodiments of untamed strength, awaited their moment of glory. Their fiery breaths smoldered, contained only by the anticipation of battle. The very air crackled with the electric charge of their impending action. Their mission, to separate the Druchii from Phoenix, hung like a tapestry of fate in their collective consciousness.

Within this grand tableau of strategy and courage, the dragons prepared to unfurl their majestic wings, their presence akin to looming mountains on the horizon. The wind seemed to whisper secrets of destiny, carrying with it the weight of the approaching battle. The heroes, their resolve forged as firmly as the most demanding steel, gleamed with unwavering determination as they readied themselves for the imminent orchestration of war.

In the sanctum of strategy, the two dragon sisters, Silvara and Dirona, held a whispered conversation, their voices a symphony of wisdom and determination amidst the impending storm of battle.

Silvara, her scales glistening like moonlight on a tranquil lake, bore the weight of Lord Karrenen upon her back. Her role was clear: safeguarding the mage, a repository of arcane knowledge and the best choice to confront Phoenix's formidable magic. As they exchanged glances, her eyes held the unspoken promise that she would protect him until the crucial moment when his powers would be needed in the final confrontation.

Dirona, resplendent in her bronze majesty, assumed the mantle of leadership for her brethren. She would lead the silver and bronze dragons into battle, their magnificent forms a testament to their ancient lineage. On their backs, mages with robes reflecting the colors of their draconic partners were poised, ready to disrupt the ground-based mages that eluded the copper dragons' grasp. Like a clarion call, her voice carried the mandate that the mages must be shielded at all costs.

The sisters marveled at the mystical affinity that bound them to their human allies, the seamless fusion of magic and might that would soon transpire. The air was charged with anticipation as they prepared for the battle ahead, where destiny and courage would intertwine in the dance of war.

Amidst the grandeur of the council chamber, the golden and brass-scaled dragons stood like noble titans, their presence a testament to the alliance between the draconic and human worlds. Their regal bearing and unwavering patience marked them as the aerial vanguards, guardians of the sky who would soon forge an unbreakable bond with the archers.

In this solemn moment of communion, the archers, bows in hand, paid homage to the sacred connection they were about to form with these majestic creatures. A blazing spirit among them, Keisha garnered nods of trust and respect from her fellow archers.

The archers knew that their role was pivotal; they were the custodians of the skies, responsible for ensuring the protection of the ground forces and mages. Kimras, the golden dragon, had chosen Keisha as his partner, a decision that bore the weight of destiny. She approached to address her comrades, her voice carrying the wisdom of their impending task.

"Use your fiery arrows with caution," she advised her words like sparks of wisdom at night. "Keep the Druchii busy; make them dance to avoid your deadly rain of fire. And once Karrenen is on the ground, gather overhead to form a protective shield for him during our final assault against Phoenix."

The archers listened intently, their resolve steeled by her guidance. The air quivered with anticipation, for this alliance between archer and dragon was a pact of fire and sky, a bond that would soon be tested in the crucible of battle.

Amidst the gathering of warriors, Ong, their steadfast leader, rose to address them. His presence was like a mountain amid the community, and his words held the weight of destiny. He spoke of their mission and vital role in the upcoming battle to liberate Goldmoor.

With the wisdom of a seasoned commander, Ong outlined their strategy. They would lurk in the shadow of Goldmoor's imposing gates, hidden from sight, like a coiled serpent ready to strike. Their patience, like a well-sharpened blade, would serve them well as they awaited the emergence of King Alex from the labyrinthine dungeon.

Ong's words were a solemn reminder of their duty—to safeguard King Alex at all costs. He stressed the importance of this task, for the fate of Goldmoor rested on their shoulders.

Then, with a glint of determination, Ong shared the pivotal moment of their plan. Once within the city, the majestic and fierce dragons would descend from the skies. They would arrive like a thunderclap amid a storm, catching the Druchii and Phoenix by surprise.

The warriors nodded in understanding, and their hearts steeled for the battles ahead. The air seemed charged with anticipation, for they knew that their actions would shape the destiny of Goldmoor and the realms beyond.

In the heart of their strategic conclave, the heroes stood at the precipice of destiny, their eyes alight with the fire of purpose. Before them, the maps unfurled like ancient scrolls, each line and symbol a harbinger of battles yet to be waged. The air was heavy with anticipation, like the calm before a storm.

With a commanding presence, Ong, the stalwart leader, stepped forward. His words, like a clarion call, echoed through the chamber. He stressed the pivotal moment they had all been preparing for—the audacious push toward Phoenix, the ultimate confrontation that would determine the fate of Goldmoor.

Amid the gathering, Karrenen, the mage of arcane mastery, shared his insights. He knew that once he descended from Silvara's back, the magic battle against Phoenix would commence. The weight of this responsibility rested heavily upon him, and he turned to the mages for their aid, recognizing the necessity of their combined power.

Keisha, the fiery spirit among them, addressed the archers with fierce determination in her eyes. She emphasized their role in this critical stage, urging them to head toward Karrenen and Phoenix. Her words resonated like a battle hymn as she instructed the archers to unleash their fiery arrows around Phoenix, hoping to create a chaotic distraction.

The heroes nodded in unison, their resolve solidifying like the forging of a legendary blade. At this moment, they were the architects of fate, their actions poised to shape the destiny of Goldmoor, and all the realms entwined in its intricate tapestry.

In this chamber of destiny, each hero embodied a unique facet of the world's hope, a prism refracting the radiant light of courage and determination. Their presence was a testament to the indomitable spirit that stood unwavering against the encroaching darkness, a fire that refused to be extinguished, and a unity that fortified their ranks against the impending storm.

The air thickened with a palpable sense of purpose as they gathered, like the charge before a thunderous storm. The heroes understood that this battle transcended mere victory; it was a crucible in which hope itself would be tested and forged anew. Every gesture, every chant, and every arrow nocked bore the weight of the world's future.

Lord Galadon, the embodiment of wisdom, spoke with a gravity that resonated through the chamber. His words were not just a rallying cry but a profound acknowledgment of the interconnected destinies of Goldmoor and Vacari, realms teetering on the brink of oblivion. His voice echoed like a clarion call, a harmonious reminder that their fates were inseparable from the outcome of this imminent struggle.

As his words hung in the air, the council members, their expressions with a blend of unwavering determination and solemn resolve, understood the immense burden they carried. The impending battle was not a mere clash of arms; it was a confrontation with the encroaching darkness, a darkness threatening to engulf Vacari in despair.

Lord Galadon stepped forward, his voice rising, "Let's drive i' du tuulo' Vacari!" (Let's drive the darkness from Vacari) His declaration echoed like a rallying cry, a vow to banish the darkness and restore the light to Vacari, for the fate of realms and the essence of hope hinged on their unwavering resolve.

With fervent nods, they departed, each hero embracing their role in the coming conflict. Their hearts beat in synchrony with the urgency of the hour, for they knew that the time for action had arrived. The fate of Goldmoor, Vacari, and the essence of hope rested upon their unwavering commitment to halt the relentless advance of Phoenix's malevolence.

Chapter 35

The Calm Before the Storm

In the dimly lit dungeon of Goldmoor, Phoenix's ominous presence once again descended like a shroud of malevolence. His sinister aura clung to the stone walls, transforming the chamber into a malefic theater of cruelty. Shackled between two rugged posts, King Alex raised his gaze as his tormentor entered, his eyes wearied but harboring an unyielding determination.

Phoenix advanced with the stealth of a predator, his footsteps reverberating ominously in the confined space. His obsidian robes swirled around him like a cloak of shadows, and the flickering torchlight painted grotesque patterns upon his twisted countenance.

"I grow weary of your obstinacy, King Alex," Phoenix hissed, his voice oozing venom. "As the hour approaches, my patience wears thin. Surrender the answers I seek, and your suffering shall find its conclusion."

Despite the chains that bound him, King Alex maintained a dignity that even Phoenix's malice couldn't extinguish. "You may break my body," he retorted, his voice trembling yet persistent, "but my spirit shall forever remain unbroken. I've repeated it countless times—I possess nothing of value to offer you."

Phoenix's fury erupted in a blaze of dark magic. Cursed energy surged from his fingertips, trapping the king's psyche and subjecting him to unbearable torment. King Alex's anguished cries reverberated through the dungeon, a haunting chorus of defiance against the relentless cruelty of his captor.

As the suffering continued, Phoenix abruptly released his grip, leaving King Alex gasping for air, his body quivering with exhaustion. The dungeon seemed to exhale, its ancient stones silently witnessing the unspeakable horrors.

With a chilling promise, Phoenix drew nearer, his eyes gleaming with malice. "Your unyielding resolve betrays you, King Alex. Time dwindles for your wife, your people, and yourself. Remember, a mere three days remain for you to provide the answers I seek, lest your beloved pays the ultimate toll. The answers you possess are your sole salvation. Choose your path wisely."

As Phoenix departed, his ominous ultimatum hanging in the air like an evil specter, the imprisoned king grappled with the physical chains that bound him and the profound weight of his choices. These choices would ultimately chart the destiny of Goldmoor, a kingdom teetering on the precipice of despair.

Within the dimly lit dungeon, King Alex breathed a sigh of relief as the evil sorcerer's presence receded. His weary eyes, bearing the scars of his torment, shifted from the receding figure of Phoenix to the unforgiving stone walls that confined him.

"I can only pray that the Eladrin are diligently working to secure my wife's freedom," he murmured, a whispered lament in the cold darkness. "Her time dwindles, all because of Phoenix's obstinate belief that we possess the elusive information about E'vahona."

He sighed again, the weight of his responsibilities pressing upon him like the very stones of his prison. "Truth be told, I am grateful that I do not possess that information," he confessed, his voice a fragile echo in the lonely chamber. "For if I did, I might be tempted to surrender it to save my beloved wife and, in doing so, compromise the very essence of our realm."

Within the ancient city of Goldmoor, where shadows and secrets converged, a Druchii patrol materialized as if borne from darkness. Caedon, a loyal agent of their dark cause, embarked on a mission to locate Qellaun, the trusted advisor to the evil Phoenix. His report held the key to the unfolding narrative in this realm of intrigue and uncertainty.

In a clandestine rendezvous, Caedon found Qellaun waiting just beyond the imposing doors of the palace, a sentinel of the city's covert affairs. His nod was a gesture of silent recognition, signaling that the time for a report had arrived.

"Report," Qellaun demanded with a tone that bespoke authority and expectation.

Caedon, his voice measured and gravely delivered the findings of his patrol. "Sir, we have traversed the path around Serpent Lagoon up to Emeraldwoods Forest, yet there is no trace of Swifthammer or Keisha. However," he continued, his words carrying a note of intrigue, "we have witnessed an occurrence unlike any in memory."

Qellaun's interest piqued, and he inquired, "What occurrence?"

Caedon replied with a sense of awe tinged with trepidation, "It appears that the weather in the region has taken a turn of unparalleled severity. As we move away from Purplefire Woods, this storm of unprecedented fury rages on, a phenomenon hitherto unseen in all my years of service."

Qellaun nodded in acknowledgment, gratitude for the information apparent in his expression. "Thank you," he replied before allowing Caedon to depart.

Left alone with his thoughts, Qellaun embarked on his path of action, leading him to the dark heart of Goldmoor's power—Phoenix, the ruler whose very presence casts a shadow of dread over the land.

Phoenix, an embodiment of darkness and chaos, moved with relentless purpose through the foreboding corridors of his citadel. His ebony cloak trailed behind him, akin to the sinister shroud of his rule, and his eyes blazed with an unyielding determination that brooked no opposition.

As he approached the threshold of his grand chamber, Qellaun, his ever-loyal servant, intercepted him. In the suffocating stillness of the castle, Qellaun's voice resonated, a soft but unwavering murmur of counsel.

"My Lord," he began, choosing his words with the precision of one who bore grave tidings, "it may be prudent to delay your journey to Serpent Lagoon."

Phoenix's response was a visceral display of impatience and fury. He turned to confront Qellaun, and his visage contorted with anger, the impact of his boot on the stone floor reverberating like a dire omen.

"Why?" Phoenix's voice, barely above a menacing whisper, demanded an answer.

With unwavering resolve, Qellaun met his master's gaze, speaking with the gravity of a seer. "A tempest of unparalleled fury," he intoned, "sweeps relentlessly from the area around Serpent Lagoon up to Emeraldwoods Forest. This cataclysmic storm, not witnessed in centuries, lays waste to all in its path."

Phoenix, ever the master of fierce forces, stood in contemplation. His thoughts swirled like ominous clouds, and his decision, when it came, was swift and resolute.

"Very well," he conceded, his voice carrying the electric charge of a gathering storm, "inform me the moment the maelstrom abates." With those words, he turned and strode toward the palace, leaving Qellaun to wrestle with the capricious tempest that mirrored the turbulent depths of his soul.

In the tranquil sanctum of the library, Qellaun and his sister Lyra engaged in a conversation, their words a delicate dance amid the dimly lit and towering shelves of knowledge. The weight of secrets and intrigue hung heavily in the air, a palpable presence amid their exchange.

Lyra's eyes, reminiscent of moonlight's soft caress on tranquil waters, expressed genuine curiosity. She sought to unravel the enigmatic motives that propelled their evil master, Phoenix, into action. Her voice, a fragile melody in the castle's ominous silence, conveyed a tender inquiry.

"I comprehend," she ventured, her words laced with both apprehension and a thirst for understanding, "that his relentless pursuit revolves around gaining control of E'vahona, the very heart of our world. Yet, I question his singular fixation on the Eladrin, especially Keisha. Is it solely due to her possession of knowledge concerning E'vahona's whereabouts?"

Qellaun, the ever-loyal confidant, met his sister's gaze with a somber resolve. Heavy with the burden of dark knowledge, his eyes echoed the chilling truth he was about to impart.

"It transcends mere knowledge of E'vahona," he intoned, his voice a grave undertone in the cavernous library, "although that is undeniably a substantial part of his ambition. It is also because she has chosen to align herself with the formidable Warrior Swifthammer, daring to intervene in Phoenix's sinister machinations."

Lyra's understanding deepened as the pieces of the infamous puzzle fell into place. Her once-questioning gaze now held the clarity of revelation.

"I perceive," she murmured, her voice resounding with newfound comprehension. "It is not merely the knowledge but her unwavering allegiance to Swifthammer and, by extension, the Eladrin, that fans the flames of Phoenix's wrath." She turned toward her brother, her eyes conveying the weight of her realization. "But surely he comprehends the folly of such an endeavor. Swifthammer and her people would never capitulate to Phoenix's desires."

Qellaun chuckled softly, his laughter bearing the weariness of one who knew the depths of their master's arrogance. "We speak of Phoenix, dear sister," he replied, his voice tinged with resignation and resolve. "In his delusion, he believes himself to be all-powerful, convinced that none would dare defy his will. He plans to capture Keisha and lay claim to E'vahona with unwavering confidence, blind to the reality that awaits him."

Lyra glanced at her brother, her expression a mixture of understanding and lamentation. "Indeed," she conceded, her voice tinged with a sense of foreboding, "he may be powerful, but he underestimates the indomitable spirit of those who oppose him. Swifthammer and her people will never yield to his demands. Alas, it seems Phoenix will never accept the limits of his ambition."

In the intimate confines of that chamber, brother and sister bore witness to the chilling intricacies of their master's evil designs, their conversation revealing yet another layer of Phoenix's dark and treacherous plan.

In the opulent Throne room of Goldmoor, Phoenix brooded like a shadow cast by a stormy sky. Once a symbol of regal grandeur, the chamber now stood as a foreboding hall filled with golden tapestries that hung like sunlit banners of a bygone era. An air of trepidation and despair had usurped its former glory.

Phoenix's countenance bore the weight of his boundless wrath, his eyes burning with an intensity rivaling a tempest's fires. His fury was an unquenchable flame, and the air seemed to tremble in response.

Driven by an insatiable hunger for power and a relentless thirst for vengeance, the tyrant seethed with frustration over the formidable obstacles blocking his path to unveil the enigma of E'vahona. His grand designs were thwarted, his lofty ambitions held in check, and he had arrived at an evil decision.

He raised his dark scepter in that solemn Throne room, casting a sinister silhouette upon the gilded walls. His voice, a harbinger of impending doom, sliced through the oppressive atmosphere like a chilling gale.

"Enough is enough," he declared, each word laden with evil intent. "I shall issue a request to these trembling citizens. Two days. Two days to surrender the knowledge I seek, to unveil the enigmatic secrets of E'vahona. Should they fail me, the inhabitants of Goldmoor shall bear the weight of their defiance."

The walls seemed to shudder at his proclamation, and a dread descended upon the once-proud Throne room. In that pivotal moment, the fate of Goldmoor dangled precariously, trapped in the unrelenting clutches of Phoenix's malevolence.

Amidst the glorious emerald embrace of Crystal Vale, the warriors congregated, their armor glistening like polished gemstones beneath the dappled canopy of ancient trees. They stood as an unyielding forest, their spirits akin to the immovable oaks surrounding them.

In this serene glade, King Manard, a regal figure whose eyes bore the weight of wisdom and concern, moved through the ranks of his warriors. His steps were measured, carrying the confidence of a leader who understood the gravity of the impending storm.

He assessed his forces, each warrior a testament to unwavering resolve, a guardian of hope. Their armor, adorned with the proud sigil of Crystal Vale, gleamed like the morning dew on leaves, reflecting the glory of a kingdom united.

As vigilant as a sentinel lynx, the king's gaze rested upon each warrior, offering silent blessings and heartfelt wishes for their safety in the battles ahead. His voice, though soft-spoken, carried the profound hopes and aspirations of his realm.

"Valiant sons and daughters of Crystal Vale," he began, his words a rallying cry. "May your hearts remain resolute, your courage unwavering, and your swords as steady as the North Star. As we stand upon the precipice of this battle, we know that our spirits are as unyielding as the roots of these ancient trees. Go forth, and may fortune smile upon you in the trials ahead."

With those words, King Manard's faith in his warriors was palpable, and an aura of unwavering determination descended upon the meadow, enveloping them like a protective cloak. In the heart of Crystal Vale, beneath the towering canopies and amidst the verdant foliage, the warriors prepared to confront the encroaching darkness, bound together by duty, honor, and the sobering awareness that not all who embarked on this challenging journey would return.

In the serene realm of Hidden Isles, where the ebb and flow of time paid homage to its ethereal denizens, the dragons congregated, a breathtaking display of iridescent scales, majestic wings, and primal power. They were the celestial titans of the skies, the elemental overlords, and the vigilant guardians of their cherished domain. The air shimmered with reverence as they assembled beneath the vast, boundless expanse of the cerulean heavens.

Among them stood Kimras, the venerable Gold Dragon, a paragon of wisdom and authority among his kin. His resplendent scales glistened with a molten brilliance, and his age-old eyes bore the weight of countless epochs filled with knowledge and experience. He recognized the moment's gravity, and his voice resonated like distant thunder as he addressed the gathering of mighty dragons.

"Children of the celestial tapestry," he began, his words a harmonious symphony, "the time has come for us to defend the sanctity of our realm, to safeguard the lands entrusted to us for uncountable generations. We are responsible for the skies above and the lives that thrive beneath our majestic wings."

His gaze swept over those dragons bearing riders, understanding the profound significance of their bonds, each a testament to trust and shared destiny.

"To those who bear riders," Kimras proclaimed, carrying the weight of a sacred covenant, "I entrust you with the guardianship of your companions. Protect them as you would safeguard the very heavens we call our domain."

With the solemnity of his declaration, Kimras summoned the very essence of the celestial realm, unleashing a mighty roar that reverberated through the valley like a clarion call. His words held an unwavering determination, a proclamation of indomitable resolve.

"We shall not yield to the encroaching abyss," he affirmed, his voice an anthem to the unyielding spirit of dragons. "With wings ablaze and hearts aflame, we shall ascend into the crucible of battle. Together, we will extinguish this malevolent shadow that seeks to defile our world. Let our flames be the guiding beacon illuminating the path toward a new dawn."

At that poignant moment, beneath the boundless cerulean sky of Hidden Isles, a chorus of roaring and growling responses arose. The dragons, their spirits ignited with a resolute purpose, pledged their unwavering loyalty to the cause. Together, they would ascend like a storm, a natural force that would shatter the encroaching darkness and herald the arrival of a brighter era.

Within the sacred confines of E'vahona's mystical halls, where ancient arboreal sentinels whispered esoteric secrets and the very air thrummed with enigmatic energy, Lord Karrenen, a paragon of Eladrin nobility, orchestrated a gathering of mages. They formed a congregation of luminescent souls draped in robes that shimmered like the ethereal essence of starlight.

As Lord Karrenen's dulcet voice resonated through the otherworldly realm, it bore the twin mantles of authority and affection. His words became a harmonious cadence, carrying with them the weight of centuries of tradition and the promise of an uncharted future.

"In the annals of time," he commenced, his voice akin to a gentle breeze, "our lineage has not been beckoned to wield the fiery crucible of battle. We are the custodians of age-old wisdom, the sentinels of cryptic arcana, and the beacons of radiance in the darkest epochs."

His eyes, reminiscent of pools of liquid moonlight, penetrated the core of each mage's being, endowing them with a paternal benediction. "Yet today, the umbral tempests have encroached upon our sacred lands, and we are summoned to confront them. While our swords may bear the patina of bygone eras, our magic remains potent, and our determination stands unbroken."

With a graceful flourish of his hand, Lord Karrenen directed their attention to the boundless splendor of E'vahona that surrounded them. The mystical forest bore witness to their shared purpose, with ancient trees and glistening streams echoing the very rhythm of their realm's heart.

"Recall, dear mages," he declared, his words brimming with the essence of their noble lineage, "that we are the Eladrin. Our power surges from the very core of E'vahona, and our bond with this realm is indomitable. Stand resolute, for you embody the fortitude of our people."

At that moment, the mages acutely felt the weight of their heritage and the profound duty entrusted to them. The gentle luminescence that enveloped them seemed to intensify, a radiant affirmation of their purpose. They were not merely mages but living embodiments of E'vahona's enduring spirit.

As Lord Karrenen's gaze traversed from one mage to another, his words reverberated like a hymn of hope amidst gathering shadows. "Though the echoes of our battles have remained dormant for centuries, remember this: the radiance that guides us has never faltered. We shall illuminate the path to triumph, for we are the sentinels of light, and our magic shall pierce through the encroaching darkness."

With hearts united and spirits enkindled, the mages of E'vahona stood in readiness, their connection to their realm and lord unwavering. In the very nature of E'vahona, they became a luminous beacon of hope, poised to ignite the flames of a new dawn.

Lord Galadon, a venerable presence whose wisdom surpassed his years, addressed the assembled Eldarin warriors and archers in a separate chamber. Their forms, clad in armor adorned with the symbol of E'vahona, glistened like the starlight itself.

"My brethren," Lord Galadon's voice resonated like the clarion call of a distant horn, his words a soothing balm to their hearts. "Though centuries have passed since our kind last took up arms, we are not estranged from the embrace of the Goddess of Light. Her blessings flow through our veins, and her grace shields us from the encroaching shadows."

He raised his gaze to the heavens as if seeking divine guidance amidst the tapestry of stars that adorned E'vahona's night sky. "We may have been dormant, but we are not diminished. Our strength, our purpose, they remain as steadfast as the foundations of our realm. We stand ready to protect E'vahona and Vacari."

The warriors and archers nodded in solemn agreement, their eyes shimmering with the radiance of unwavering faith. Lord Galadon's words were a beacon of hope, a reminder that their heritage was a source of strength, not mere antiquity.

"As the darkness encroaches, remember that we are the sentinels of E'vahona," Lord Galadon continued, his voice unwavering. "With the Goddess's grace, we shall banish the shadows and usher in a new era of light. Our bows shall sing, our swords shall gleam, and our resolve shall remain unshaken."

With that solemn oath, the Eldarin warriors and archers, blessed by the Goddess of Light, stood united in purpose. In the heart of E'vahona, they became a formidable bulwark against the encroaching darkness, their spirits ablaze with the promise of a brighter dawn.

In the tranquil sanctuary of their love, Ong and Keisha sought refuge in each other's arms. The room seemed to bask in the ethereal glow of their affection, an enchanted chamber where unspoken vows and boundless devotion hung heavy in the air.

Ong, his sturdy frame radiating protectiveness, enfolded Keisha in a tender embrace that promised to shield her from the tumultuous world outside. Their lips met in a kiss that bore the weight of an eternal covenant, a pledge etched in the language of the soul. It was a kiss that tasted fiery passion, an ache of longing, and an unwavering resolve to defy the looming shadows.

"Promise me, you will come back to me," Ong implored, his gaze locking onto Keisha's with an intensity that mirrored the ferocity of their love. His gentle murmur voice carried the gravity of their shared dreams.

Amidst the cascade of Keisha's vibrant crimson hair, a veritable waterfall of fiery strands, she returned his gaze with an affectionate smile that possessed the power to heal the deepest wounds. "I can only promise to try," she whispered, her words bearing the fragile hope of a love confronted by the uncertain path that stretched before them.

Their embrace tightened as if seeking to merge their very souls into one, a testament to the profound love that bound them. In that poignant moment, amidst the warmth and tenderness, an unspoken fear lingered—a fear that the impending battle might snatch Ong away, leaving Keisha to grapple with a heartache that knew no equal.

Keisha's thoughts momentarily shifted to another cherished soul within their home—the furry and bounding presence of Pumpkin, their faithful companion. Her gaze, reflecting their profound bond, drifted towards their loyal friend, her heart heavy with their unspoken understanding.

"Promise me something," she implored, her voice carrying the gentle tremor of vulnerability. "If fate should steer me towards an uncertain path, promise that you will care for Pumpkin."

Ong nodded solemnly, his resolve unwavering, yet he couldn't resist drawing Keisha even closer, as if his embrace's sheer intensity could shield him against the looming dangers of battle. "But you will return," he insisted, the declaration an emotional testament to his boundless love. "My heart belongs to you."

In response, Keisha's words were a tender murmur, but they contained the entirety of an emotional cosmos within them. "And mine to you," she whispered, a pledge of love that transcended the boundaries of time and space.

Their hearts, bound together by an unbreakable bond, led them to seek a precious moment of normalcy amid the looming storm of battle. Together, they ventured into the garden, where vibrant blooms stood as a shining testament to the enduring beauty of life, even in the face of impending uncertainty. Amidst the blossoms, Keisha lowered herself to Pumpkin's level, her voice a gentle, earnest promise.

"Watch over Ong," she whispered to their faithful companion, embracing a tender reassurance. "And remember, take care of yourself as well, dear Pumpkin. We cherish you, too."

Pumpkin, the embodiment of joyful abandon, frolicked amidst the flora, his presence a testament to the unbroken bond between human, elf, and their furry companion. In these fleeting hours before the battle's ominous commencement, love, promises, and steadfast loyalty saturated the air, a poignant tribute to the indomitable spirit of those who dared to confront the encroaching darkness.

Chapter 36

The Final Confrontation: Battle for Goldmoor

Outside the imposing gates of Goldmoor, the Eladrin Warriors and Crystal Vale Warriors stood in a tense, determined formation. Their armor gleamed under the moon's pale light, catching the silvery glow and transforming them into spectral figures of valor. Swords and spears glistened with an almost otherworldly sheen, a testament to the craftsmanship of these resolute defenders. At the forefront of this assembly stood Ong, a formidable human warrior with black hair that seemed to absorb the moonlight, making him appear both ethereal and resolute. Beside him, a loyal and fierce companion, Pumpkin, a sleek black panther, awaited with a vigilant stance, her obsidian coat mirroring the night itself.

The atmosphere was heavy with anticipation, a palpable tension that seemed to resonate in the air they breathed. The warriors' expressions were a mix of determination and worry, and their brows furrowed with the weight of the impending rescue mission. Like keen sentinels, their eyes were fixed on the towering walls of Goldmoor, where their trusted ally was imprisoned.

Yet, time felt like an eternity as they awaited the moment when their comrade would be freed. Every second that passed seemed to stretch into an eternity, each heartbeat echoing in the night, and their hearts ached with the burden of uncertainty. They knew that the fate of Vacari rested on this moment, and the weight of their responsibility pressed heavily upon them.

Ong, the leader of this courageous group, clenched his gauntleted fists, the steel plates creaking softly with his silent resolve. His black hair rustled in the night breeze, his eyes never leaving the gates, as if, by sheer determination, he could will them to open. He was determined to see their mission through, to rescue their ally and restore peace to Goldmoor and all of Vacari. Pumpkin, his loyal companion, a magnificent black panther with sinuous muscles, mirrored his resolve, her feline form exuding a quiet yet fierce determination. Her keen senses were alert for any movement within the castle walls.

As the minutes ticked by, the warriors' emotions swirled - a potent mix of hope and fear, courage and doubt. They had come this far, fought bravely, and now stood on the precipice of a pivotal moment in Vacari's history. With hearts steadfast and swords at the ready, they waited for the moment when the gates of Goldmoor would swing open, and their ally would emerge, free once more, like a beacon of hope amidst the shadows.

In the northernmost reaches of the sky, hidden from view and masked by the ancient arts of the Eladrin, the mages and their dragon allies maintained their silent vigil. The vast expanse of the northern skies stretched before them like an open canvas awaiting the brushstroke of destiny.

Lord Karrenen, shrouded in a magical cloak of invisibility, sat regally atop Silvara, the silver dragon. Silvara's silver scales gleamed with a soft, ethereal radiance in the moonlight, their otherworldly luminescence mirroring the serene power she embodied. Lord Karrenen held his staff with unwavering resolve, the intricate runes etched into its surface glowing faintly as a testament to its arcane might. He knew their moment to descend into the battle would come when it was most crucial, a precise dance with fate guided by their ancient bond.

Beside Lord Karrenen, Dirona, the mighty bronze dragon, stood as sentinel and protector. Her massive wings, a rich bronze hue reminiscent of aged copper, were poised for swift flight, their edges sharp as finely crafted weapons. Like molten bronze, her vigilant eyes scanned the northern horizon with keen perception, tracing the subtle shifts in the night's tapestry. Dirona understood her role well – to lead the charge of the silver and bronze dragons, their presence a secret weapon waiting to be unveiled.

The anticipation of what lay ahead hung heavy as they waited in the northern skies. The bond between Eladrin mages and their dragon allies deepened their unity, a testament to ages of trust and cooperation. They remained hidden, a concealed force ready to descend upon the battlefield with the grace and fury of ancient guardians when the time was right. They held their position in the northernmost part of the skies, guardians of hope and power, awaiting their moment to shine like a constellation of hope in the darkest of nights.

In the southernmost expanse of the skies, a different scene unfolded, hidden from the prying eyes below. Keisha, the fiery red-headed Eladrin warrior known for her distinctive purple attire, sat atop Kimras, a magnificent Gold Dragon, her presence veiled by the mystic arts. The southern skies were a realm of potential and power, a stark contrast to the calm before the storm.

Resplendent in her gleaming purple armor and vibrant crimson hair, Keisha sat atop Kimras with a commanding presence. Kimras, the embodiment of golden majesty, radiated an aura of regal authority that matched the grandeur of the southern skies. Keisha held her bow confidently, its intricate designs and ethereal glow testament to its otherworldly craftsmanship. She knew she was the leader of the archers who would ride the Bronze and Gold dragons into battle against the Druchii.

Beside her, the Bronze and Gold dragons waited in disciplined formation, their massive wings shimmering like precious metals bathed in sunlight. These dragons were formidable warriors and trusted allies, ready to heed Keisha's command when the time came.

As they hovered in the southernmost part of the sky, anticipation coursed through the group like an electric current. The bond between Keisha and her dragon allies ran deep, a testament to their unity and shared purpose. They remained hidden from view, a concealed force waiting for the signal to swoop down and protect Vacari from the impending danger. They held their position, guardians of hope and courage in the southern skies, prepared to unleash their might when the call to action finally sounded, their presence a glimmer of hope in the dark tapestry of the night.

In the expansive skies, a unique strategy unfolded as Caelum, the noble copper dragon, divided his kin into two distinct groups - the East and West. Riders unburdened these dragons, their mission clear: to lend their formidable skills and powers to aid their allies and protect those who rode into battle, especially Lord Karrenen and Keisha. The skies were abuzz with the potential of their might, a silent but potent force awaiting its moment to shine.

With a keen and vigilant eye, Caelum, resplendent in his magnificent copper scales that gleamed like the richest of autumn leaves, oversaw this tactical division. His serpentine form was a testament to his ancient lineage, every curve and scale bearing the weight of centuries of wisdom. He knew that his copper dragons could make a significant difference in the upcoming conflict, their abilities a precious resource for their comrades on the battlefield.

In the East, a group of copper dragons awaited their command. Their scales shimmered with a warm, burnished metallic hue as they hovered in disciplined formation, ready to unleash their unique powers and skills upon the battlefield.

In the West, another contingent of copper dragons mirrored their Eastern counterparts. Their serpentine forms held a quiet determination, and their eyes sparkled with a readiness to defend their allies and ensure victory.

Caelum's plan was clear - these unmounted dragons would support the Eladrin mages and warriors on the ground. They would safeguard Lord Karrenen and Keisha, ensuring they could carry out their critical roles without fear for their safety.

As they held their positions in the sky, the bond between Caelum and his divided copper dragons was unbreakable. Their unity and shared purpose were the embodiment of unwavering commitment. For now, they remained hidden, a concealed force ready to descend upon the battlefield with all the might of the copper dragons when the call to action finally came, their presence a beacon of hope in the turbulent sky.

Stealthily, under the cover of the night sky, two promising Eladrin mages, Seraphina and Thalorin, moved with quiet determination toward the looming dungeon of Goldmoor. Their responsibility was to free King Alex, and their hearts beat with anticipation and resolve.

With her dark, mysterious eyes that seemed to hold the secrets of a thousand spells and a silver dagger glinting like a sliver of the moon in her hand, Seraphina led the way. Her black hair flowed like a shadowy waterfall as she moved gracefully through the darkness, her senses honed for any sign of danger. She was a master of the arcane arts and had been entrusted with this critical task.

Beside her, Thalorin, with emerald eyes that sparkled with the wisdom of ages and silver hair that shimmered like moonlight on a tranquil lake, moved with a quiet elegance that matched Seraphina's grace. He was her trusted companion and fellow mage, their skills complementing each other perfectly. Thalorin's deep knowledge of magic and keen insight were invaluable assets for their mission.

As they advanced towards the dungeon, their footsteps made no sound, and their presence was cloaked in an enchantment of stealth. Their objective was clear - to reach King Alex and secure his freedom, a pivotal moment in the battle for Goldmoor.

For now, the dungeon loomed ahead, a forbidding fortress of stone and shadow. Seraphina and Thalorin knew that within its depths, their skills and determination would be put to the test. But they were prepared, their resolve unwavering, as they ventured further into the heart of the enemy's stronghold, their every step a silent commitment to their mission.

Seraphina and Thalorin entered the dungeon, their footsteps echoing softly in the predawn silence. As the world outside bathed in delicate hues of lavender and rose, the dungeon's stone corridors seemed to absorb the essence of darkness. It was where secrets were whispered through the cool, damp air.

Eerie familiarity hung in the atmosphere like a phantom's embrace as they retraced their steps. Once animated and menacing, silent guardian statues now stood frozen, their stone forms reminiscent of forgotten titans, bearing silent witness to the passage of time.

The trap doors, once treacherous maws ready to snare the unwary, were now docile, their intricate mechanisms rendered harmless by the skilled hands of the Eladrin duo. The magic runes that had once pulsed with ominous power now lay dormant, their ethereal fire extinguished.

Confidently, they navigated the labyrinthine passages, each twist and turn a page in their shared adventure. The once-daunting maze now felt like an old, familiar tale, a story etched in the walls and floors.

The fierce and menacing chimeras had returned to their previous lair, their grotesque forms illuminated by the eerie glow of the dungeon's torches. Seraphina and Thalorin, undeterred by the looming peril, bore a resolute purpose that ignited their eyes like twin beacons of determination.

Emerging from the shadowy sanctuary of the corridor, they became the puppeteers of their fate, deliberately drawing the grotesque creatures into their dangerous dance. Thalorin, a pied piper of the dark, led one of the chimeras in a whirlwind chase to the right, his steps a haunting melody in the dimly lit labyrinth. Simultaneously, Seraphina, a manifestation of elven skill and grace, wove a tapestry of evasion as she gracefully evaded the second chimera's relentless pursuit, her movements a ballet of survival.

The chimeras, reacting with visceral menace to the sudden intrusion, pursued their respective prey with a terrible determination, their serpentine forms undulating like shadows cast by a malevolent moon. Through a labyrinthine ballet of misdirection and stealth, Seraphina and Thalorin, the sculptors of their fate, employed their intimate knowledge of the terrain to confound the looming specters.

After a meticulously measured interval, the duo executed a synchronized maneuver that defied the chimeras' relentless pursuit. Thalorin, like a phantom reclaimed by the very shadows themselves, melded seamlessly into the inky abyss, leaving no trace of his presence. Meanwhile, Seraphina invoked the ancient art of concealment magic, her form vanishing from the chimeras' predatory gaze like a whisper carried away by the wind.

The grotesque guardians, their ire seething and their hisses echoing in frustration, found themselves in a futile quest, their pursuit of phantom specters leading only to the abyss of bewilderment. Finally, Seraphina and Thalorin, their breaths barely audible, reunited at the dungeon's heart, their elusive dance complete. With renewed determination, they pressed on, their goal clear: to free King Alex from the clutches of darkness and usher in a new dawn for Vacari.

Deeper they ventured, their passage marked by the echoes of their determined footsteps. The heart of the dungeon lay ahead, cloaked in a spectral gloom. The chamber seemed to hold its breath, the water's surface rippling with an ominous tension as if it, too, remembered the past.

Seraphina and Thalorin entered the chamber, their presence a solemn symphony in the darkness. The memory of the deadly serpents lurking beneath the water's depths cast a shadow upon their hearts. Yet, this time, they were armed with a potent elixir, a magical elixir brewed from the alchemy of their determination.

With meticulous care, they poured the elixir into the water. Like a spectral dance, an otherworldly light unfurled as it merged with the inky depths, casting an eerie, ghostly glow upon the aquatic realm. The once-menacing serpents writhed and convulsed in moments, surrendering to the elixir's relentless embrace. As they met their final fate, the water transformed from an abyssal black to a pale, lifeless gray, like the fading memories of an ancient curse.

Turning their attention to the captive King Alex, Seraphina and Thalorin spoke reassuringly, their voices like soothing lullabies in the chamber's tranquil atmosphere. "King Alex, fear not, for Queen Jeanne is safe."

Relief washed over King Alex's countenance as he acknowledged their words, and his gratitude radiated from his eyes like the first rays of dawn breaking through a stormy night. Yet, as their collective gaze shifted toward the chamber's depths, a new threat materialized—an eldritch sea monster, a titanic embodiment of malevolence, slumbering beneath the inky surface, poised to unleash chaos upon the world.

In the dimly lit chamber, King Alex's inquiry hung in the air, a poignant testament to the growing urgency of their predicament. His eyes, a reflection of his captivity, danced between the flickers of hope and the shadows of apprehension.

Thalorin, the consummate strategist, pondered the impending danger with furrowed brows, his gaze locked onto the turbulent waters where the eldritch sea monster stirred. "We must find a way to defeat this monstrosity, King Alex. It shall not be permitted to menace us any longer."

Her essence pulsating with magical vigor, Seraphina turned to Thalorin with a resolute sparkle in her eyes, like a star born from the void. "Our combined strengths may be our salvation. I shall dispel the arcane barrier that ensnares King Alex. While I do so, Thalorin, you must confront the eldritch sea monster, drawing its malevolent gaze away from our sovereign."

Thalorin nodded, his demeanor reflecting the weight of the impending challenge etched upon his features. "A perilous task, indeed, but we shall protect King Alex at all costs."

As the plan coalesced, the chamber seemed to crackle with an electric energy, a cosmic battle between courage and impending peril. Seraphina and Thalorin prepared to face the eldritch sea monster, an otherworldly force of malevolence that awaited its fateful reckoning.

In the heart of that chamber, a celestial ballet unfolded, a dance of light and darkness. Seraphina approached the ethereal barrier with the grace of a sorceress, her fingertips seemingly woven from threads of arcane energy. She meticulously unraveled the barrier, freeing King Alex from his spectral cage.

Meanwhile, Thalorin, akin to a graceful acrobat performing upon the precipice of peril, led the eldritch sea monster on a treacherous and intricate chase. The monstrosity, a nightmarish amalgamation of writhing tentacles and evil intent, pursued him with a relentless fury that echoed through the haunted corridors. Each step he took was a daring gambit, every heartbeat a harmonious ballet with impending peril.

Seraphina seized the fleeting moment as the ethereal barrier dissipated into shimmering fragments. With the swiftness of a striking serpent, she yanked King Alex from the clutches of his spectral prison. Thalorin, his brow glistening with the sweat of exertion, continued to lure the eldritch sea monster closer, its monstrous form ensnared within the fading lattice of magic.

With the sea monster now imprisoned in its ephemeral cage, the trio stood as triumphant warriors, their eyes aflame with determination. Their collective gaze converged upon King Alex, a beacon of hope in the heart of this shadowed realm. "Come, Your Majesty," Seraphina implored, her voice a soothing melody amidst the discord, "The hour has arrived for you to reclaim your throne, and united, we shall stand resolute against the encroaching darkness."

With King Alex now free and encouraged, they began their journey out of the dungeon's depths. Guided by Seraphina's unwavering presence, they delivered King Alex to Ong, the stalwart human warrior, waiting beyond the labyrinthine passages. Ong's black hair seemed to absorb the surrounding gloom, his determination an unyielding fortress against the encircling shadows.

Once King Alex was safely in Ong's care, Seraphina and Thalorin embarked on their path, venturing deeper into the dungeons to reach the forests beyond. There, awaiting them like guardians of ancient legend, were a bronze and a silver dragon, their majestic forms poised for flight. With the grace of skilled riders, Seraphina and Thalorin mounted the dragons, their journey taking them toward the northern skies, where other mages and allies awaited their arrival.

The dragons' wings sliced through the air like silver and bronze crescents, carrying the duo away from the dungeons and into the vast expanse of the northern heavens. They joined the celestial symphony of allies hidden among the clouds, their united purpose a beacon of hope in a world of uncertainty.

As Ong handed King Alex a finely crafted sword, the blade gleamed with the promise of justice and liberation. Ong's voice was a steady, unwavering command as he addressed the newly freed king, "Your Majesty, they are waiting for your order. It's time to issue the charge."

King Alex nodded solemnly, accepting the sword with a firm grip. His eyes, filled with determination and a hint of sorrow for his people's suffering, bore into the city's heart. "For Goldmoor," he declared, his voice echoing with unwavering purpose.

With that rallying cry, Ong, King Alex, Pumpkin the black panther, and their warriors surged forward, their footsteps resounding like a thunderous war drum. The city's streets became a battleground, where the clash of steel against steel filled the air.

The Druchii, entrenched in Goldmoor's heart, faced a fierce onslaught as Ong and his warriors stormed through the city like an avenging tempest.

Swords clashed in a cacophony of metal, and the warriors fought with a determination that struck fear into the hearts of their foes.

Pumpkin, the black panther, moved with a predatory grace, leaping upon Druchii assailants with a ferocity that sent them reeling. His ebony fur seemed to absorb the shadows, a fitting embodiment of the darkness's impending defeat.

The battle raged on, the air vibrating with the clash of wills. The warriors of Goldmoor, fueled by King Alex's leadership and Ong's unwavering resolve, pressed onward toward the city's heart. They fought not only for themselves but for their realm's future, for the hope that had been rekindled.

A decisive battle unfolded in the city's heart, where the shadows had once held sway. Goldmoor's defenders, united in purpose, fought with bravery, determined to cast out the Druchii invaders and restore their home to the realm of light. The fate of Vacari hung in the balance, and the city's heart pulsed with the rhythm of a committed people determined to reclaim their rightful place in the tapestry of destiny.

Ong fought with courage as relentlessly as the unyielding mountains, born from an unwavering determination to defend his homeland and love that burned brighter than the fieriest of stars. His blade, a gleaming extension of his resolve, cleaved through the enemy's ranks like a divine avenger, a beacon of hope that guided his comrades through the storm of battle.

The clash of weapons, a symphony of tempered steel, the shouts of warriors like thunderclaps, and the anguished screams of the wounded intertwined into a haunting melody. This lament would forever reverberate in the annals of their memories.

Pumpkin, the agile and fierce feline, moved through the battlefield with the grace of a spectral dancer, her ebony fur a stark contrast to the inferno of battle that raged around her. She struck with the swiftness of a striking serpent, her claws tearing into the souls of enemy soldiers who dared to encroach upon Ong's path. Her presence was a source of inspiration, an emblem of loyalty and courage that kindled the hearts of those who fought alongside her, a living testament that even in the darkest moments, the light of unwavering companionship could pierce the shadows.

With every sweeping arc of their weapons and each unrelenting step forward, Ong and his warriors inched closer to reclaiming Goldmoor from the cruel clutches of darkness. The fate of their realm, an ethereal thread woven into the tapestry of destiny, hung in precarious balance. Yet, their determination was an unbreakable bond, a declaration to the cosmos that they would emerge victorious against all odds, for their love for Goldmoor and Vacari was a fire that could not be extinguished. Their courage was a beacon that could not be dimmed.

As Seraphina and Thalorin arrived on the backs of the majestic dragons, the skies above the northern part of Goldmoor became a theater of impending destiny. Lord Karrenen, the masterful mage, nodded with silent command and whispered a word of power to Silvara, the silver dragon. Silvara, in turn, communicated through an unspoken bond with Dirona, the noble bronze dragon, their thoughts interweaving like strands of destiny itself.

With a synchronized motion, Dirona and Silvara took to the skies, their colossal wingspans casting shadows upon the battlefield below. The mages riding upon their backs were poised like archons of ancient lore, their staffs aglow with arcane energy.

The arrival of the mages marked an epochal turning point in the battle, their presence transforming the battlefield into an ethereal realm of magic and mysticism. Perched upon the colossal backs of mighty silver and bronze dragons, they became an otherworldly force, weaving their incantations into the very tapestry of the conflict.

The silver dragon, Silvara, released a shimmering light cascading down like a radiant waterfall. The brilliance of her breath illuminated the darkened skies, blinding the Druchii below and disorienting their ranks. Their eldritch spells faltered, their aim disrupted by the dragon's celestial radiance.

Beside her, Dirona, the bronze dragon, exhaled a searing torrent of molten fire that descended upon the Druchii like the wrath of a vengeful deity. The flames devoured the enemy lines, leaving a trail of charred earth and chaos in their wake. Druchii warriors shrieked in agony as the fiery onslaught incinerated their ranks.

The silver dragons, their scales glistening like shards of moonlight upon freshly fallen snow, unleashed their icy breath in a deadly cone of crystalline doom. The frigid mist from their majestic jaws enveloped enemy soldiers in a bone-chilling grip, encasing them in ephemeral ice prisons. Each frosty exhalation was a testament to the dragons' power, turning the once-hallowed battlefield into a frozen wasteland of despair, where the promise of victory crumbled like fragile icicles in the face of their might.

In stark contrast, the bronze dragons, lords of the electric storm, wielded the fury of lightning with divine authority. Arcs of electricity, born from their thunderous roars, struck down Druchii warriors with devastating force. The sky seemed to bow in homage to their command as bolts of energy arced and danced like vengeful spirits, seeking out those who dared to oppose them. With each electrifying discharge, they rewrote the destiny of the battle, lighting up the night with a chaotic symphony of divine wrath.

The mages riding on the dragons' backs added formidable magic to the fray. Arcane lightning bolts crackled and danced across the battlefield, striking down Druchii spellcasters and rending the dark magic that shrouded Goldmoor.

As the mages channeled their spells through the dragons, the air around them crackled with electrifying energy, and the earth trembled beneath their collective might. Their magic, an intricate symphony of destruction and chaos, manifested their unwavering resolve to free Goldmoor from the insidious darkness that had taken root. It was as if they had become conduits of elemental forces, drawing upon the essence of the cosmos to tip the scales of fate in favor of their beleaguered kingdom.

Lord Karrenen, though positioned toward the back, contributed his mastery of magic to the battle. His spells, a fusion of fire and ice, wove together into a storm of elemental fury. Firestorms engulfed enemy formations, while freezing winds encased Druchii warriors in ice, rendering them immobile.

Together, the dragons and mages were a force of nature, an unstoppable storm of magic and might. They swept through the enemy lines like a celestial reckoning, their presence an embodiment of the realm's determination to cast out the darkness creeping upon Goldmoor.

As the battle raged below, Lord Karrenen remained vigilant, ready to support and guide his students and allies. The combined might of dragons and mages became a beacon of hope, a testament to the resilience of Goldmoor, and a harbinger of the inevitable victory to come.

In this pivotal moment, the silver and bronze dragons' arcane fury unleashed upon the battlefield transcended their roles as mere mages and dragons. They became the harbingers of hope, the defenders of light, and the architects of the kingdom's salvation. The battle raged on, but with their magic and unwavering allies, they fought as one, determined to shatter the suffocating grip of darkness once and for all.

In the northern skies, Keisha, her fiery red hair streaming behind her like a banner of defiance, and her loyal companion Kimras, the resplendent Gold Dragon, witnessed the arrival of the silver and bronze dragons with a knowing nod. They exchanged a wordless communication, their bond of trust unbreakable, and with a determined gesture, they signaled to their fellow archers.

With a majestic flourish, the Gold and Brass Dragons, their scales gleaming like molten gold in the sun's embrace, descended from the heavens. Their mighty wings sliced through the air like blades, and as they joined the battle, the very sky seemed to salute their arrival.

The arrival of Keisha and her cadre of archers marked an opulent chapter in the battle, their presence akin to a lethal ballet amidst the chaos of combat. Perched atop the mighty Gold and Brass dragons, they rode into the very heart of the conflagration, their quivers brimming with arrows that would etch the destiny of Goldmoor in the annals of time.

The tide of conflict shifted as the dragons and their riders joined the battle. The forces of Goldmoor, united in purpose and fueled by their unyielding determination, pressed forward with renewed vigor. The ground shook beneath the clash of armies, and the heavens seemed to weep for the fallen.

With their boundless strength and elemental prowess, the Gold and Brass Dragons descended upon the battlefield like avatars of justice. Their fiery breath engulfed the Druchii in searing infernos while their metallic scales deflected the enemy's desperate attacks.

Gold dragons, their scales agleam like molten ingots of the divine, became the storm of purifying flames that surged through the Druchii ranks. Their fiery breath, a torrent of infernal majesty, swept over enemy soldiers like an incendiary deluge. The air itself seemed to shimmer with the intensity of their fire, and the anguished cries of the Druchii became a mournful chorus as their very flesh was consumed by the scorching conflagration, casting grotesque, dancing shadows upon the macabre tapestry of the battleground.

Brass dragons, masters of subtler arcane arts, exhaled clouds of hypnotic mist that embraced Druchii troops in a surreal, dreamlike stupor. The enemy stumbled and faltered. Their movements were slowed by the enchanting vapors that filled the air, their wills trapped by the dragon's sorcery. And when terror threatened to clutch the hearts of the Druchii, the Brass dragons conjured billowing clouds of dread, their presence sowing the seeds of abject terror among the enemy ranks, like phantoms of impending doom.

As Keisha's archers unleashed their arrows, each shaft became a harbinger of oblivion, finding its mark with an uncanny and unfaltering precision. The skies above Goldmoor transformed into a canvas of crimson and gold as fiery arrows descended like vengeful meteors upon the Druchii horde, thinning their numbers and igniting the chaos of war with an alchemical dance of death and glory.

The archers, skilled and unwavering, lined the backs of these celestial creatures. They unleashed a relentless hail of arrows upon the Druchii below, each shot a testament to their unerring marksmanship. Arrows found their marks with deadly precision, sowing chaos among the enemy ranks.

The mages, perched upon the backs of the dragons, added their formidable magic to the fray. Arcane fire and lightning burst forth from their outstretched hands, striking down the Druchii with unrelenting fury. The archer's arrows and the mage's spells created a storm of destruction that swept through the enemy lines like divine retribution.

In the northern skies, a symphony of warfare unfolded. Dragons and archers, mages and warriors, all fought in harmony, their combined might a beacon of hope amidst the chaos. The battle was far from over, but with each passing moment, the forces of Goldmoor grew stronger, their resolve unbreakable and their determination unwavering.

In the eastern and western skies, Caelum, the majestic Copper Dragon, beheld the glorious display of power below as the silver, bronze, gold, and brass dragons, along with their riders, converged upon the battlefield like avatars of celestial wrath. With determination and a touch of pride, Caelum, resolute not to be left out, issued a silent command to his fellow copper dragons.

The battle unfolded with an unremitting fury, and the copper dragons descended upon the battlefield like titanic emblems of invincible might. Their flight through the turbulent skies was a dance of celestial grandeur. Their colossal forms starkly contrast to the explosive power they held within their very essence.

Without the encumbrance of riders, the copper dragons were free to unleash their full elemental might upon the unfolding chaos. As Caelum led the charge, they descended from the heavens like a thunderous storm, their wings sweeping through the air with a primal grace.

Caelum himself, eyes ablaze with enthusiasm, dove towards the enemy ranks with an undaunted spirit. His breath weapon, a torrent of electrified copper shards, burst like a storm, striking down Druchii warriors with unparalleled force. The copper dragons, his brethren, followed suit, their collective power cascading upon the battlefield like a cascade of cosmic lightning.

Their unleashed might rent the fabric of the battlefield, and the Druchii were left in awe of the elemental onslaught. The earth quaked beneath their electric fury, and the air crackled with the sound of their vengeance.

At that moment, Caelum and his copper dragons were a force of nature itself, a cataclysmic reckoning that the Druchii could neither anticipate nor withstand. The battle took on a surreal quality as the copper dragons, free of riders and unburdened by restraint, embodied elemental chaos, their power a testament to the unyielding spirit of Goldmoor's defenders.

Copper dragons, their scales adorned in an array of verdant and earthy hues, commanded the untamed forces of nature itself. With a single exhalation, they unleashed a cone of corrosive acid that carved a path of devastation through the Eladrin lines. Armor and flesh alike dissolved in the malevolent caress of their breath, leaving behind a desolate landscape where the earth seemed to weep at their passage.

Yet, the copper dragons possessed a second, insidious weapon—a toxic cloud of lethargy that enshrouded their adversaries. The air became thick with weariness, weighing down the Eladrin warriors with the burdensome mantle of exhaustion. The copper dragons, masters of lethargy, sowed the seeds of hesitation and uncertainty among their foes, like spectral weavers of fate, tangling the threads of bravery with the web of despair.

As they soared and unleashed their fury, the heavens seemed to bow in deference to their elemental majesty. The eastern and western skies became a theater of divine retribution, where dragons and lightning waged war against the forces of darkness, and the fate of Goldmoor hung in the balance, poised on the precipice of eternal glory.

In the eastern and western skies, the copper dragons, unburdened by riders, became a force of nature. Caelum and his brethren descended upon the battlefield with elemental fury. Their breath weapons carved swaths of devastation through the enemy lines, and the earth trembled beneath their thunderous roars.

Amidst the relentless storm of battle, the sky above Goldmoor appeared to reflect the unrest unfolding below. A brooding maelstrom of ominous storm clouds coalesced, their shadowy tendrils reaching across the expanse. Like the wrathful fury of celestial gods, lightning streaked through the heavens, casting an eerie, flickering illumination over the tumultuous tableau.

Thunder, the percussive heartbeat of war, reverberated through the air, punctuating the din of clashing steel and fervent battle cries. It echoed as if the gods had turned their divine gaze upon the battlefield, witnessing the mortal clash of forces and destinies. The skies above Goldmoor became an ethereal amphitheater, where the elements conspired to etch the tale of bravery and defiance into the annals of time, a story of a realm's unyielding spirit in the face of encroaching darkness.

Amidst the tumultuous battlefield, a grand tapestry of unity and determination unfolded. The ground forces, led by Ong, surged forward with unrelenting courage. Pumpkin, the ebony panther, was a shadowy wraith amidst the chaos, her lithe form moving with a grace and speed that defied the very essence of the night.

With his raven-black hair, Ong was a beacon of determination and love for his realm. His blade cleaved through the enemy's ranks like a scythe through ripe wheat, a harbinger of hope for his comrades. Each swing of his sword was a testament to his unwavering resolve, and his comrades followed his lead with unyielding loyalty.

The archers, perched upon the backs of Gold and Brass dragons, were a deadly rain of arrows obscuring the sun. Their volleys found their marks with unerring precision, thinning the Druchii ranks with each fatal shot. The dragons, resplendent in their metallic and golden scales, descended upon the battlefield like avatars of justice.

Riding upon the backs of silver and bronze dragons, mages wove their spells into the very fabric of the conflict. The silver dragon, Silvara, unleashed a shimmering cascade of radiant light that blinded and disoriented the Druchii. In contrast, Dirona, the bronze dragon, summoned molten fire that devoured the enemy with relentless enthusiasm.

Keisha, her fiery red hair a beacon of defiance, led her archers atop the Gold and Brass dragons. Their arrows became a relentless storm that darkened the skies, each shaft finding its target with uncanny precision. The heavens saluted their arrival as fiery arrows rained down upon the Druchii, sowing chaos and despair.

Amidst this symphony of warfare, Pumpkin, the ebony panther, danced with lightning speed through the chaos. Her ebony fur seemed to absorb the very shadows, and her claws found their marks with deadly precision, protecting Ong and his comrades from any who dared approach.

The battlefield was a living testament to unity and bravery, where the forces of Goldmoor fought as one against the encroaching darkness. It was a tumultuous mosaic of destruction and heroism, where love for their kingdom and unwavering determination drove them forward. Together, they stood as a bulwark against the forces of evil, a beacon of hope amidst the chaos of war.

As the battle raged, a new force entered the fray, emerging from the palace of Goldmoor like an omen of doom. Phoenix, Lyra, and Qellaun, formidable leaders of the Druchii, stepped onto the battlefield with an air of hostility that sent shivers through the hearts of the Eladrin defenders.

Phoenix, a figure of regal malevolence, led the charge. His obsidian armor gleamed with a cruel luster, and his sword, an instrument of death, radiated with a dark enchantment. With her icy beauty and cunning, Lyra was a sorceress of the highest order, her spells weaving a tapestry of destruction that left no quarter for her foes. Qellaun, a master of shadows, moved with a predatory grace, his daggers finding the chinks in enemy armor with deadly precision.

Their arrival turned the tide of battle, and a maelstrom of dark magic and malevolence enveloped the battlefield. With each swing of his sword, Phoenix cleaved through Eladrin's ranks ruthlessly. His every movement was a dance of death, and his eyes burned with a cruel fire that mirrored the inferno of war.

With her dark sorcery, Lyra conjured storms of shadows that consumed the very light around her. Her spells were an unrelenting storm, freezing the hearts of Eladrin warriors in their tracks and leaving them vulnerable to the impending darkness.

Qellaun, the shadowy assassin, moved with an uncanny stealth that seemed to defy the very laws of nature. His daggers were twin specters of death, finding their marks with a precision that was as terrifying as deadly. He struck from the shadows, a harbinger of doom that left no room for escape.

The battle now raged on multiple fronts, a chaotic symphony of clashing steel, roaring dragons, and the haunting chants of dark magic. Goldmoor's defenders, united in their determination, faced off against the evil might of the Druchii.

In the heart of this tumultuous conflict, Phoenix, Lyra, and Qellaun were the avatars of darkness, their presence an ominous specter threatening to consume Goldmoor in shadow. The realm's fate hung in the balance, poised on the precipice of salvation or destruction, and the battle raged on with a ferocity that would be remembered for generations to come.

Phoenix's gaze darted toward the heavens during the chaotic battle like a raptor spotting prey. There, he beheld a sight that both astonished and incensed him. Keisha, resplendent atop Kimras, the gold dragon, led her archers with unwavering resolve, raining fiery arrows upon the Druchii ranks.

A dark fury rose within Phoenix as he turned to Qellaun, his voice a thunderous proclamation of betrayal. "I thought you told me the noble dragons were gone!" His words were a bitter accusation laced with the venom of deception.

Qellaun, shadowy and enigmatic, met Phoenix's gaze with a hint of trepidation. He replied with a mixture of defiance and uncertainty, "I... I thought they were, my lord."

Phoenix's rage was palpable, his every word a condemnation of Qellaun's assurances. "And you wonder why I wanted Keisha captured!" His voice carried the weight of retribution, a testament to his mistrust and the dangerous repercussions of underestimating their adversaries.

The battlefield, already shrouded in chaos and conflict, seemed to hold its breath as the two Druchii leaders locked eyes, their unspoken discord a warning of further turmoil. The fate of Goldmoor teetered on a precipice, and the revelation of Keisha's presence among the noble dragons had thrown a new variable into the dark equation of war.

King Alex, once imprisoned and now freed, emerged onto the battlefield like a vengeful deity, his presence a beacon of wrath amidst the maelstrom of war. His unwavering gaze fixed upon Phoenix, the embodiment of torment for his beloved Queen Jeanne and the relentless oppressor of Goldmoor. Within him, an inferno of fury blazed, stoked by the injustices endured by his people.

"Phoenix!" His thunderous bellow rang out, cutting through the clamor of battle like a clarion call of reckoning. "For all the suffering you have inflicted upon my people and my beloved, you shall answer for your sins!"

King Alex's righteous anger propelled him forward, each step resonating with the weight of a kingdom's anguish. However, as he advanced toward his nemesis, a shadowy Druchii, insidious and evil, sought to exploit the fleeting opportunity. Before the treacherous blade could find its intended mark, a valiant Eladrin warrior, a sentinel of courage, interposed, taking the blow meant for the king. King Alex acknowledged the selfless act with a solemn nod, an unspoken pact of comradeship sealed in the crucible of battle.

Undeterred and fueled by an unyielding resolve, King Alex pressed on, an indomitable force of reckoning. He strode through the battlefield's chaotic tapestry, an emblem of hope and retribution, determined to confront Phoenix and ensure that justice, long delayed, would finally be served. The battle swirled around him, a storm of violence and courage, but he remained unwavering, embodying the spirit of unity in the face of a common enemy.

Amidst the raging battle, Lyra, the Druchii sorceress, was a specter of malevolence. Her icy beauty concealed a heart as frigid as the depths of the Abyss, and her spells wove a tapestry of destruction that threatened to engulf the Eladrin defenders.

As the battle's tempo quickened, Lyra's incantations grew more frenzied, her dark magic a storm of shadows and malice. Her sorcery summoned ethereal storms that twisted the very fabric of reality, freezing the hearts of Eladrin warriors in their tracks and leaving them vulnerable to the encroaching darkness.

But as Lyra raised her obsidian staff to unleash another cataclysmic spell, the Eladrin mages, riding atop their mighty silver and bronze dragons, coordinated their powers. With a synchronized burst of arcane energy, they unleashed a torrent of magical force that struck Lyra like a celestial hammer.

The sorceress's form convulsed with agony as the magical onslaught bore down upon her, leaving her injured and incapacitated. Her spells faltered, the storms of darkness dissipating into nothingness. Lyra's once-ferocious presence on the battlefield was reduced to a wretched figure, writhing in pain and unable to continue her evil assault.

The Eladrin mages, their faces resolute, had struck a decisive blow against one of the Druchii's most formidable assets. With Lyra incapacitated, the balance of power on the battlefield shifted once more, and the defenders of Goldmoor seized the opportunity to press their advantage. The battle raged on, but the sorceress, for the moment, had been defeated, her dark magic quelled by the unyielding determination of her adversaries.

The copper dragons, with their verdant and earthy scales, wielded the raw essence of nature with devastating finesse. As the battle surged toward the city's heart, they executed a calculated maneuver that pushed some Druchii forces into the labyrinthine crevices that scarred the landscape.

The battleground had shifted, and Goldmoor's destiny now hung in the balance within the city's heart. Phoenix, Qellaun, and the remaining Druchii forces were inexorably pushed back, trapped between the relentless tide of Eladrin warriors and the metallic scales of the noble dragons.

Amid this chaos, King Alex, the newly freed monarch of Goldmoor, pressed forward with unwavering determination. His presence was a beacon of hope for the Eladrin defenders, and his resolute strides took him closer to the heart of the conflict, where Phoenix awaited.

With each step, King Alex's resolve burned brighter, fueled by the injustices inflicted upon his people and the torment endured by his beloved Queen Jeanne. He had emerged from captivity as an avenging force, a righteous fury given form.

Phoenix, the embodiment of Goldmoor's torment and suffering, stood as the ultimate adversary. His cruelty and tyranny had held the realm in a vise grip of darkness for too long. Now, with the tides of battle turning against him, his ruthless determination clashed with King Alex's unwavering resolve.

The city's streets became the crucible of their confrontation, where the destiny of Goldmoor would be determined. The clash of their blades echoed through the heart of the city, a symphony of retribution and justice. The battle continued to rage around them, but the eyes of all who witnessed this fateful duel were fixed upon the two leaders, for their conflict would decide the realm's fate.

As they clashed with the Eladrin warriors, Phoenix, with his obsidian armor gleaming malevolently, led the charge with a relentless determination. His sword struck with deadly precision, his every movement a testament to his martial prowess. Beside him, Qellaun moved like a shadowy specter, his daggers finding the chinks in enemy armor with uncanny accuracy.

But the Eladrin warriors, bolstered by the archers and mages, stood firm, their resolve unyielding. Arrows, guided by expert hands, rained down upon the Druchii forces, finding their marks with deadly accuracy. Spells of arcane brilliance and elemental fury lanced through the air, seeking to repeal the dark magic woven by the Druchii sorcerers.

The clash of weapons, the crackling of spells, and the thunderous impacts of arrows created a tumultuous symphony of war echoing through the city's streets. It was a battle of attrition, where each step forward exacted a heavy toll on both sides.

A sense of desperation permeated their ranks as the Druchii forces fought to repeal the magic and arrows from the Eladrin mages and archers. The city's heart, where the final confrontation loomed, was now within sight. Goldmoor's defenders, united in their determination, pressed on, knowing that the outcome of this battle would shape the destiny of their kingdom.

King Alex, a symbol of hope and determination, led the way as they moved closer to the impending confrontation with Phoenix. Behind him, Ong, a stalwart protector, walked in solemn stride, his black hair ruffled by battle winds. Pumpkin, the fierce black panther, moved by his side with a predator's grace, her senses attuned to the dangers that lurked in the shadows.

As they advanced, a sudden assailant, a Druchii driven by desperation, leaped from the shadows with a dagger aimed at King Alex. Ong's protective instincts kicked in in a heartbeat, and he was interposed between the assailant and the king. Ong's blade intercepted the attack with a deft and decisive movement, thwarting the would-be assassin's deadly intent.

No less vigilant, Pumpkin lunged forward with blinding speed, her powerful jaws closing around the Druchii's throat. She held the assailant in an unyielding grip, her feral instincts honed by loyalty to her companions.

Ong, his heart pounding with relief and pride, gently stroked Pumpkin's sleek fur, whispering words of praise, "You're a good girl, Pumpkin." His voice, a comforting melody amidst the chaos of battle, carried the affection of a bond forged in adversity.

King Alex, his countenance unwavering, smiled at the display of courage and loyalty. With the threat neutralized, they resumed their course toward the confrontation with Phoenix, their resolve unshaken. The city's heart beckoned, and they moved forward, ready to face whatever trials awaited them in the crucible of destiny.

In the heart of Goldmoor, the stage was set for a climactic confrontation between Lord Karrenen, the Eladrin mage, and Phoenix, the malevolent Druchii leader. The tension in the air was palpable, as the kingdom's fate teetered on the edge of a precipice.

As Lord Karrenen advanced, Phoenix attempted to undermine his confidence with taunts and boasts about the power of darkness. However, Lord Karrenen remained steadfast, his focus on his goal unwavering. He moved forward, undeterred by Phoenix's words.

The dragons, their massive forms creating a protective barrier, landed around Lord Karrenen, and the Eladrin mages disembarked, ready to shield him from Phoenix's dark sorcery. The presence of these formidable allies added to Lord Karrenen's determination, for he knew that they stood united against the encroaching evil.

Phoenix's laughter echoed through the city's heart, but Lord Karrenen continued his resolute approach. The mages prepared their spells, their magic crackling in the air, and the dragons loomed protectively, their presence a testament to the unity of Goldmoor's defenders.

Amidst this charged atmosphere, Qellaun, Phoenix's loyal guardian, swiftly moved between Lord Karrenen and his target. With the grace of a masterful swordsman, Qellaun fended off the Eladrin warriors who attempted to breach their defenses. His blades became a whirlwind of deadly steel, a formidable obstacle to anyone seeking to reach Phoenix.

The battle for Goldmoor's soul had climaxed, with the kingdom's destiny hanging in the balance. The stage was set for a showdown, where the forces of light and darkness would clash in an epic struggle for supremacy, and the outcome would decide the realm's fate.

The battle at the city's heart reached a critical juncture as Phoenix unleashed his malevolent magic against the Eladrin mages who challenged him. Waves of shadowy energy surged, striking some of the mages and temporarily incapacitating them. The fallen mages lay on the ground, their magical abilities momentarily quelled.

Lord Karrenen, undeterred by the casualties, continued his advance, his magic radiating with brilliant intensity. With a commanding gesture, he conjured bolts of arcane energy that streaked toward Phoenix, creating a luminous counterpoint to the darkness surrounding his foe.

The clash of their magic was a spectacle of opposing forces, a tumultuous dance that threatened to tear apart the very fabric of reality. Phoenix's malevolent sorcery writhed and contorted, attempting to consume Lord Karrenen's brilliance. As the battle of magic raged on, even Lord Karrenen, with all his mastery, felt a flicker of concern. Phoenix's power was formidable, and the outcome remained uncertain.

However, Lord Karrenen's resolve remained unshaken, his determination unwavering. With each bolt of magic he hurled, he pressed forward, a symbol of hope and perseverance in the face of darkness. The heart of Goldmoor was the crucible of their destiny, and the battle of magic continued, a clash of opposing wills that would determine the kingdom's fate.

Amidst this magical showdown, a new force arrived to bolster the Eladrin's efforts. Riding atop Kimras the Gold Dragon, Keisha led a squadron of archers who circled above Lord Karrenen. Bathed in radiant light, their presence served as a striking counterpoint to the malevolence below. The arrival of Keisha and her archers added hope to the ongoing battle, a glimmer of light amidst the darkness.

Keisha's voice rang out with authority as she directed her archers to unleash their fiery arrows. With precision and grace, the archers nocked their arrows, their tips aglow with incandescent brilliance. In perfect harmony, they released their volleys, sending arcs of flame hurtling toward the ground.

As the fiery arrows descended, they ignited the streets below, forming walls of searing heat and flame that encircled the Druchii forces surrounding Phoenix. The malevolent Druchii warriors recoiled from the sudden inferno, their dark armor sizzling in the intense heat.

The strategic brilliance of the archers pushed the Druchii back, creating a protective ring around Lord Karrenen as he continued his unyielding advance toward Phoenix. The combined efforts of the mages, the dragons, and now the archers were gradually shifting the tide of battle, and a spark of hope began to kindle in the hearts of the Eladrin defenders.

The heart of Goldmoor had become a battleground where the elements clashed with dark magic, and the city's destiny hung in the balance. With each fiery arrow that streaked through the skies, the Eladrin's determination to reclaim their homeland burned even brighter. The battle raged on, a fierce contest of wills and magic, but the defenders of Goldmoor fought with unwavering resolve, determined to cast out the encroaching darkness once and for all.

As the battle raged at the city's heart, Ong, Pumpkin, King Alex, and the determined Eladrin and Crystal Vale warriors arrived on the scene. Their presence swelled the ranks of the Eladrin forces, forming a formidable wall of defenders.

Ong, drawing upon his wisdom and experience, quickly assessed the situation. He issued orders to the warriors, directing them to spread out and create a protective perimeter around Lord Karrenen. His authoritative voice carried the weight of command as he warned the warriors sternly: "Do not engage with Phoenix. He is a force beyond any warrior's reckoning."

King Alex, burning with a desire for revenge and eager to confront Phoenix, turned to Ong, seeking counsel. Ong, a staunch protector and mentor, shook his head solemnly and offered his counsel with caution, "Your Majesty, a warrior has no chance against Phoenix. Our priority is to protect you and Lord Karrenen. I advise you to stand back for now."

King Alex, though reluctant, recognized the wisdom in Ong's words. He nodded in agreement, his jaw set with determination. The battle before him was unlike any he had ever faced, and he understood that their best chance of victory lay in unity and strategic planning rather than reckless heroics.

With their forces consolidated and a protective barrier of warriors forming around Lord Karrenen, they stood resolute and ready to face the malevolent presence of Phoenix. The clash between light and darkness raged on, but the defenders of Goldmoor remained undaunted, their resolve unshaken as they fought to free their city from the suffocating grip of tyranny.

Phoenix's malevolent power surged like a storm, an unstoppable force of darkness. As the magic battle intensified, he focused his dark sorcery on the Eladrin mages and Lord Karrenen, pushing them back with relentless waves of shadowy energy. The mages struggled to maintain their ground, their protective spells straining against the relentless assault.

Phoenix wielded a sinister artifact in his hand, a dark staff forged in the depths of the Abyss itself. The staff pulsed with malevolence, its ebony surface etched with ancient runes of forbidden power. With each gesture, Phoenix channeled the staff's dark energies, amplifying his spells to a terrifying degree. Shadowy tendrils lashed out from the staff, snaking through the air like serpents of malice, seeking to entangle the Eladrin mages and drain their strength.

The ground beneath Phoenix's feet seemed to tremble in response to the staff's power, as if the earth itself had recoiled from its touch. He unleashed his dark magic with a malevolent grin, determined to break through the Eladrin's defenses and seize victory for the Druchii. The battle at the heart of Goldmoor had become a cataclysmic clash of light and darkness, and the outcome hung in the balance as Phoenix wielded his cursed staff with unholy zeal.

Lord Karrenen, though injured by the evil magic, refused to yield. Each step forward was a testament to his unwavering determination. Phoenix's laughter, cold and cruel, echoed through the streets as he reveled in the pain he inflicted. Qellaun, his guardian, repelled any Eladrin warrior who dared to approach, his blades a whirlwind of deadly precision.

Amidst the chaos, the Druchii sought to capitalize on the distraction caused by Phoenix's power. They moved stealthily, attempting to pick off the Eladrin and Crystal Vale warriors who formed the protective barrier around Lord Karrenen. Arrows and spells whizzed as the defenders fought to maintain their position.

The streets of Goldmoor became a battleground of shadows and light, where the very essence of magic clashed with brutal force. Lord Karrenen, wounded but resolute, continued his relentless advance toward Phoenix, undaunted by the hostility that sought to thwart him. The kingdom's destiny hung in the balance as the Eladrin defenders and the Druchii forces clashed in a desperate struggle to control the city.

As the battle raged, Keisha and her archers executed a brilliant maneuver, pushing the Druchii forces away from Phoenix and Qellaun. The archers' arrows whistled through the air, creating a protective zone around the evil leader and his guardian.

Now isolated with Qellaun, Phoenix unleashed his dark magic on the Eladrin mages. His sorcery struck with devastating precision, and some of the mages fell to the ground, their magic extinguished, their bodies wracked with pain. Lord Karrenen, wounded but resolute, witnessed this loss with a heavy heart. He knew he would have time to grieve later; now, he focused on stopping Phoenix.

Phoenix, with a sinister smirk on his face, taunted Lord Karrenen. "Do you wish to surrender, Lord Karrenen? Goldmoor and Vacari are mine!"

Lord Karrenen's response was unwavering. "No, we will never surrender Goldmoor or Vacari!" With determination burning in his eyes, he continued the battle of magic, pouring his arcane energy into the struggle against Phoenix's malevolence.

The streets of Goldmoor bore witness to an epic clash of light and darkness, hope and despair. As the Eladrin forces rallied around Lord Karrenen, they knew that surrender was not an option. Their kingdom's fate hung in the balance, and they would fight with every ounce to ensure that the darkness that had engulfed their city would be dispelled.

Phoenix's relentless onslaught of dark magic pushed Lord Karrenen to the ground, his body protesting the strain of the battle. But the indomitable Eladrin spirit refused to yield. An Eladrin warrior rushed to his aid, helping him back to his feet, their unwavering support a testament to the bond that united them.

With a sinister smirk, Phoenix proposed a nasty deal. "Give me E'vahona, and I will return Goldmoor to King Alex." Karrenen's response was persistent, rejecting the darkness that threatened to consume his city. "Not on my life."

Phoenix's smile turned cold and calculating. "It might just cost you your life."

With a surge of power, he pushed Lord Karrenen to the ground again, his dark magic overwhelming. Qellaun moved alongside Phoenix, his loyalty unwavering. Meanwhile, Ong, relentless in his mission to confront his enemies, turned to face Qellaun, ready for battle.

The clash between Ong and Qellaun was fierce and unrelenting. Swords clashed, and sparks flew as the two adversaries fought for supremacy. Qellaun, despite his loyalty to Phoenix, was not to be underestimated. His skill with a blade was formidable, and he fought relentlessly to protect his evil leader.

As the battle raged on, Qellaun's injuries began to accumulate. The Eladrin warriors, rallying behind Ong, pushed him to the brink. Despite his resilience, Qellaun could not escape unscathed. The toll of the battle was etched upon his face as he fought on, his loyalty to Phoenix unwavering even in the face of adversity.

As Lord Karrenen found himself on the ground once more, Keisha's swift command echoed through the ranks of her archers. They immediately acted, creating a protective path for their fallen leader through the chaos. One of the mages rushed to Karrenen's side, extending a hand to help him back onto his feet. The mages formed a protective circle around him, each determined to bolster their leader's strength in the face of Phoenix's relentless magic.

Caught in the throes of battle, Phoenix continued to unleash his dark sorcery upon the mages. His evil power crackled through the air, threatening to consume those who stood in his way. But then, his attention was drawn to the fiery path created for Lord Karrenen. His eyes locked onto Keisha, and he sneered, "You!"

The Eladrin archer met Phoenix's gaze with steely resolve, her bow at the ready. Though the confrontation seemed imminent, Phoenix held back for the moment, his malevolence simmering beneath the surface. The battle raged on around them, and the destiny of Goldmoor hung in the balance as the forces of light and darkness clashed in a desperate struggle for control of the city.

As Phoenix's malevolent attention shifted toward Keisha, Ong's heart sank with worry. He watched in horror as Phoenix unleashed his dark magic on Kimras, the magnificent gold dragon. Kimras, graceful and wise, attempted to evade the sorcerous assault, but the force of the attack dislodged Keisha from her dragon's back.

Time seemed to slow as Keisha began to plummet toward the ground, a look of terror etched upon her face. Ong's scream of anguish pierced the tumultuous battlefield, the sound echoing in the air. Turmoil contorted his face as he watched his comrade and friend falling toward what seemed certain doom.

But fate had not yet decided Keisha's destiny. As she descended from the skies, a moment of suspended animation held her in its grasp, the ground still distant, defying the inexorable pull of gravity. It was a breathless moment, a heartbeat stretched into eternity, as Ong and all who witnessed this harrowing sight held their collective breath, their hopes and fears hanging in the balance.

Phoenix's laughter echoed through the chaos of the battle as he taunted Keisha, claiming that she had chosen the wrong side. But his triumphant moment was short-lived. Kimras, the gold dragon, regained his composure and swooped down to intercept Keisha as she fell, his talons deftly grasping her and lifting her back onto his back. With her bow drawn and aimed squarely at Phoenix, Keisha unleashed an arrow that struck true, hitting him in the arm. The force of the blow was enough to disrupt his concentration, providing Lord Karrenen with the opening he needed.

With renewed determination, Karrenen channeled his magic, directing a powerful surge of energy toward Phoenix. The dark sorcerer staggered, his malevolent powers waning as Karrenen's magic overcame him. The relentless battle had taken its toll on Phoenix, and the realization of his imminent defeat replaced the once-arrogant demeanor that had adorned him.

As Karrenen's magic surged, it struck Phoenix with a force that shattered the dark staff the malevolent sorcerer had wielded throughout the battle. The staff fell to the ground in pieces, its dark enchantments fractured, causing Phoenix to lose a significant portion of his magic.

Disarmed and weakened, Phoenix was forced to the ground, his dark powers ebbing away. The Eladrin forces, emboldened by this turn of events, pressed their advantage, closing in on the fallen Druchii leader. The battle had reached a critical juncture, and Goldmoor's defenders could sense victory was within their grasp.

Qellaun, seeing his leader's dire condition, rushed to Phoenix's side, pulling him away from the ongoing battle. He whispered urgently to Phoenix, recognizing the severity of his injuries and urging him to surrender. Phoenix's defiance, once unyielding, had finally crumbled under the weight of his defeat.

Looking toward Lord Karrenen, Qellaun uttered the words of surrender, acknowledging their defeat in the face of overwhelming odds. The battle-weary Druchii had finally realized that their reign of darkness over Goldmoor had ended. Lord Karrenen and Ong exchanged glances, their faces bearing the weight of the arduous struggle they had just endured. With a sigh of relief, they knew that their forces, even with the dragons, had been vastly outnumbered, and the cost of victory had indeed been high.

The battle for Goldmoor had reached its climax, and the city's defenders had emerged victorious, their unity and determination prevailing against the forces of darkness.

Chapter 37

Phoenix's Banishment: The Fall of Darkness

In the aftermath of the grueling battle, King Alex embarked on a determined stride toward the heart of his beloved city, the grand throne room. With each measured step, his furrowed brow revealed the lingering frustration that clung to him like a shadow, a testament to his trials. "Cursed warlock," he muttered under his breath, the words tinged with the smoldering embers of irritation. "Changing my throne room without permission."

Intent on reaching the majestic throne that beckoned from the room's end, King Alex's footfalls reverberated through the chamber, a cadence of authority. Yet, amid this solitary journey, his senses were pricked by the distant symphony of turmoil that reached him through the massive chamber doors.

His advance stilled, like a sentinel at his post, he turned his gaze toward the imposing entrance, seeking the source of the growing tumult. Then, a vision of grace and resilience emerged, embodying his heart's longing—the radiant Queen Jeanne. Recognition flooded his eyes, widening them in awe, and without a second thought, he surged forward as if drawn by an invisible force, enfolding her in a fierce and protective embrace.

"Jeanne," he whispered a soothing balm amidst the chaos, reflecting the deep concern etched into his features. "How are you faring?" Though undoubtedly wearied by the trials she had endured, her response carried a glimmer of hope that danced in her eyes, and in that moment, he found solace in her presence.

With their reunion, King Alex and Queen Jeanne continued their journey towards the throne—an emblem of their enduring unity and the unwavering strength of their kingdom, where their hearts could finally find respite after the fierce storm of battle.

In the heart of Goldmoor, Ong, a storm of relief and affection coursing through his veins, drew Keisha close to him with an embrace that spoke of unspoken fears and unwavering devotion. Their lips met in a fervent kiss, a fervid communion of souls that bore witness to the depths of their love and the boundless comfort in knowing that she had emerged from the ferocious storm of the battle unscathed. Yet, beneath the surface of that passionate kiss, a subtle undercurrent, a hint of admonition that danced in his eyes and echoed in his words—a voice laden with both concern and the playful reprimand of a heart eternally tethered.

"Promise me," he implored with a fierce tenderness that mirrored the storm of emotions within, "that you will never subject me to the terror of seeing you fall from a dragon's back again."

Keisha, her laughter, a flowing melody that rang through the chambers of their shared history, responded with a wry smile that cradled the weight of shared experiences. "It wasn't exactly on my list of preferred experiences."

In that tender moment, Ong's gaze shifted toward Kimras, the steadfast and noble companion who had played a pivotal role in her rescue. With a profound gratitude that transcended mere words, Ong turned to the dragon, his voice a wellspring of emotion. "Thank you, Kimras, for bringing her back to me."

Kimras, his serpentine eyes reflecting their depth of understanding, responded with a dignified nod—a silent acknowledgment of the bond forged in the crucible of their shared journey.

In the sad aftermath of the battle that had raged through the heart of Goldmoor, a hushed and reverent solemnity descended upon the city. Lord Karrenen, the Eladrin mages, King Manard of Crystal Vale, and the brave Crystal Vale warriors moved with measured purpose through the battlefield strewn with fallen heroes.

Each fallen warrior, a testament to courage and sacrifice, was lifted with great care and reverence. Once animated by courage and unwavering determination, their lifeless forms were now still, their eyes closed in eternal slumber. The weight of their loss hung heavy in the air, a reminder of the price paid for the city's liberation.

Lord Karrenen, his regal countenance etched with sorrow, paid his respects to each fallen soul. He whispered gratitude and remembrance, an elegy to honor their sacrifice. The Eladrin mages, their expressions a tapestry of grief, channeled their magic to ensure that each hero's spirit would find its way to the embrace of the Evergreen, where they would join the ranks of the honored and the revered.

King Manard, a stalwart presence amid the melancholic tableau, directed his Crystal Vale warriors in the solemn task of gathering the fallen. His voice, tinged with the weight of responsibility, carried the resolve of a king who recognized the importance of honoring those who had given their all for the greater good.

As the fallen heroes were tenderly gathered and carried away from the battlefield, the air was filled with a profound sense of loss, an elegy for those who had paid the ultimate price. Yet, amidst the sorrow, there was also a deep appreciation for their unwavering commitment and the indomitable spirit that illuminated Goldmoor's history's darkest hours.

King Alex, having emerged victorious in the battle for Goldmoor, recognized the need to bring closure to the remnants of the Druchii forces that had once occupied Fel Thalor. With a sense of duty and resolve, he dispatched his warriors to the nearby city, their mission clear—to round up the remaining Druchii and bring them to Goldmoor.

Fel Thalor, once a place of darkness and oppression, now bore witness to a different kind of authority. The Goldmoor warriors, guided by their king's mandate, moved with precision and vigilance through the city's streets. They located the remaining Druchii, whose numbers had been greatly diminished by the recent events, and escorted them back to Goldmoor.

Upon their arrival in Goldmoor, the captured Druchii joined the ranks of those who had stood by Phoenix, Lyra, Qellaun, and their compatriots.

It was a stark reminder of the consequences of their actions, a moment of reckoning in the heart of the kingdom they had once sought to conquer.

As they were assembled, the Druchii faced a new reality—one where they stood together, outnumbered and defeated, in the presence of their adversaries. The air was thick with tension, and the once defiant Druchii now bore the weight of their choices.

The city's inhabitants watched this .procession with curiosity, resentment, and perhaps a glimmer of hope. Goldmoor had triumphed over the darkness that had threatened to consume it, and now, the final chapter in this saga was written as the Druchii faced the consequences of their ambitions.

"King Alex embodied sovereign authority, a symbol of regal command that surpassed mortal boundaries. Laden, with the weight of decisions made for the greater good, his gaze swept over the assembly of apprehensive Druchii, with each word he uttered carrying the gravity of a city's judgment."

"The time has come to deal with each of you," King Alex proclaimed, an unwavering echo of power and wisdom resounding through the chamber like a timeless decree etched in stone. It is within our rights to pass judgment. You could be executed for the suffering you have wrought upon our lands and people. The weight of your crimes cannot be denied; the darkness you brought upon Goldmoor will not be easily forgotten."

King Alex's words hung heavy in the air, a reminder of the vast power and authority he wielded as a sovereign ruler. The Druchii, their faces a mixture of fear, defiance, and resignation, listened intently, knowing their fate rested in his hands.

Phoenix, a defiant specter of his former self, dared to meet the king's gaze, his eyes aflame with a flicker of rebellion. "So, where do you intend to banish us?" he challenged, his voice a defiant tempest swirling against the monarch's authority.

Nonetheless," King Alex continued, his voice softening with compassion, "there has been enough death, enough suffering. Goldmoor and Vacari have paid a heavy price in this conflict, and we must strive for a different path leading to healing and reconciliation, even if it seems difficult to fathom now. Allowing you to remain in Vacari, even within the confines of our dungeons, would sow the seeds of revolt against Goldmoor and Vacari once more."

Phoenix, a defiant specter of his former self, dared to meet the king's gaze, his eyes aflame with a flicker of rebellion. "So, where do you intend to banish us?" he challenged, his voice a defiant tempest swirling against the monarch's authority.

In response, a wry smile curled upon King Alex's lips as if he held the key to their destiny within his grasp. His voice, as unyielding as the bedrock of the land, revealed their fateful destination—a sentence that would cast them into the murky abyss of the Afor, the treacherous swamps.

The air pulsed with electric tension within the throne room. A palpable force mirrored the turbulent history that had led them to this pivotal juncture. Lyra, a poignant echo of her former self, shattered the silence with a defiant cry, her words laden with the bitterness of defiance born of desperation. "I refuse to go!" Her proclamation was a discordant note of resistance as if her voice alone could change the course of their fate.

But King Alex remained steadfast, his resolve unwavering, his countenance unyielding in the face of protest. He responded to her dissent with a measured shake of his head, an unspoken rebuttal to her defiance. "I do not recall asking you what you wanted," he retorted, his voice a sad reminder of the duty that bound him to this solemn decision.

Phoenix and his compatriots listened to the sentence. Phoenix turned and looked at Ong and Keisha and cast one final, ominous remark toward Ong and Keisha. "Enjoy the time you have," he hissed, his words dripping with a venomous promise that lingered like a shadow, a foreboding echo of the battles that had shaped their destinies.

"Kimras, a celestial sentinel of the skies, spread his majestic wings and joined his draconic brethren in a symphony of soaring might, their collective presence casting a vast, looming shadow over the ancient lands of Goldmoor. Beneath this awe-inspiring aerial display, the warriors of Goldmoor diligently gathered the shackled captives, among them the defiant Phoenix and his Druchii followers. It was a solemn procession, a momentous march towards retribution.

Amidst this gathering of heroes and vanquished foes, Kimras, the resplendent Gold Dragon, emerged as a noble guardian of justice. With a regal inclination of his colossal head, he volunteered to convey these prisoners to the forlorn swamplands of Afor. Gratitude flowed through the ranks of the weary yet determined warriors as they accepted the dragon's assistance. They knew the daunting journey ahead on foot, fraught with peril and uncertainty.

With reverence and solemnity, the dragons executed their duty. Their colossal forms, adorned in scales that gleamed like the most precious of gemstones beneath the shining sun, bore the weight of justice upon their wings. It was a task of significance and gravity that would see the Druchii, led by their enigmatic commander, Phoenix, cast into the unforgiving heart of Afor—their fate sealed by the very land they had once sought to conquer.

In the heart of this accursed wasteland, Phoenix stood as an avatar of relentless hostility, his piercing gaze slicing through the desolate expanse that stretched before them. This forsaken landscape, a tableau of misery and despair, unfolded in all its wretched glory—a yawning abyss of treacherous swamps and forsaken settlements that resonated with the haunting echoes of forgotten sorrows. In the shadow of desolation, Phoenix, accompanied by his steadfast companions, Qellaun and Lyra, shared an unspoken communion.

Amidst the grim tableau of their surroundings, Phoenix's voice resounded like a clarion call, brimming with unwavering determination. "Vengeance shall be ours," he declared, his words a testament to a spirit undaunted by past defeat but steeled by the promise of future retribution. It was a pledge etched in the marrow of their souls. With each step, they embarked upon an odyssey into the uncharted depths of Afor, where shadows concealed enigmas, and the uncertain future beckoned with both trepidation and possibility.

And in this ardent pursuit of vengeance, Phoenix's thoughts turned toward those who had played a role in his exile. A sinister smile curled upon his lips as he vowed, "Ong and Keisha shall taste my revenge, for their part in our exile shall not go unanswered." The promise of retribution burned within him, an unquenchable fire that would guide their path through the desolation of Afor and beyond."

Within the walls of Goldmoor, King Alex and Queen Jeanne embarked on a solemn journey of assessment. The once-proud city bore the indelible scars of the recent conflict, its streets and structures marred by the ravages of war. Together, they traversed the cobblestone pathways, their steps a testament to the resilience of their spirits.

The grand towers that had once defined Goldmoor's majesty now stood as stoic sentinels, their walls bearing the memory of siege and strife. Crumbled battlements and shattered parapets whispered tales of courage and sacrifice, each stone a witness to the indomitable spirit of those who had defended their homeland.

As King Alex and Queen Jeanne surveyed the city, their hearts weighed heavy with sorrow and hope. Grief for the losses incurred in the battle to reclaim their kingdom and hope for the future ahead—a lot in which Goldmoor would rise from the ashes, renewed and glorious, like a phoenix reborn from the crucible of adversity.

Amidst the ruins, they glimpsed signs of resilience and renewal. Citizens worked tirelessly to rebuild, their determination a beacon of light amidst the shadows of destruction. The scars of war would linger forever, but so too would the indomitable spirit of Goldmoor, a city reborn from the crucible of adversity.

And as they gazed upon their beloved kingdom, King Alex and Queen Jeanne knew their journey was far from over. Together, they would lead Goldmoor into a new era of unity, strength, and the unshakable bonds of love and loyalty that had seen them through the darkest times.

Ong, filled with love and determination, pulled Keisha close to him. His eyes met hers, and in that moment, they shared an unspoken promise of a future that held the promise of happiness and unity.

With a voice filled with warmth and conviction, Ong made an announcement that sent a ripple of excitement through the crowd. "In one week," he proclaimed, "in the heart of the enchanting Purplefire Woods, we shall come together to celebrate our victory and love. Keisha and I invite you, our dearest friends and allies, to join us in a wedding ceremony and feast that will begin a new chapter in our lives."

The announcement was met with thunderous applause and cheers of joy. The prospect of a grand celebration amidst the magical splendor of

Purplefire Woods filled the people's hearts with anticipation and delight. It was a testament to the enduring spirit of unity and love that had triumphed over the darkness. It was a celebration that would bind them closer together as they moved toward a brighter future."

Chapter 38

Love's Triumph: A Wedding in the Forest

As the sun dipped below the horizon, casting a warm, golden glow over Vacari, preparations for Keisha and Ong's wedding ceremony and feast were in full swing. The realm of Vacari buzzed with excitement as allies from different corners of the land came together to contribute their unique touches to the celebration.

Goldmoor: Silver torches were carefully placed along the path leading to the heart of the Purplefire Woods. Each torch emanated a gentle, silvery light that lined Keisha's walkway, creating a shimmering aisle for her to traverse. The flickering flames whispered tales of love and unity, their glow reflecting in the eyes of those who had gathered, symbolizing the guiding light of their future together.

Crystal Vale: Tables adorned with intricate crystal decorations were set up for the feast. Their smooth surfaces caught and reflected the soft, ambient light, giving the dining area an ethereal quality. Delicate coverings graced each table, evoking an air of elegance. Crystal Vale's craftsmanship added a touch of sophistication to the gathering, with crystalline patterns and colors chosen to enrich the visual experience.

Eladrin: As twilight descended, the Eladrin stepped forward, their connection to nature evident in every move. With a wave, they summoned fireflies from the depths of Purplefire Woods. These tiny, luminescent creatures danced around the clearing, their delicate, natural light casting an enchanting and romantic glow over the ceremony. The Eladrin also used their affinity for flora to enhance the surrounding flowers, bursting them with vibrant colors and sweet, intoxicating scents. Soft melodies played on natural instruments added to the enchanting atmosphere.

Coraluna (Merfolks): Down by the waterfall, where Keisha and Ong had first met, the merfolk of Coraluna worked their underwater magic. They channeled their mermagic into the waterfall, causing it to shimmer like glass. The falling water refracted the dimming light, creating a mesmerizing spectacle. Soft, melodic sounds filled the air as the cascade flowed into a crystal-clear pool below, adding a touch of aquatic elegance to the occasion.

Dragons: The dragons roared their presence as the night sky unfurled its inky canvas. They lit up the sky with their mighty magic, turning it into a canvas of stars. Each dragon's breath painted radiant streaks of color across the heavens. The forest around them seemed to come alive, with trees and leaves aglow in an otherworldly radiance. Under this celestial canopy, Keisha and Ong's wedding ceremony and feast unfolded, bathed in the dazzling magic of their dragon allies.

Together, these contributions from the allies of Vacari wove a tapestry of love, unity, and magic. It was a testament to the power of friendship and cooperation in this enchanted realm."

"An ethereal beauty unfolded in the heart of Vacari's enchanted woods, a scene that transcended the realms of mortal imagination. Aligning a radiant gown woven with intricate starlight lace, Keisha moved with grace beneath the emerald canopy above. Her dress glistened like the moonlight filtering through the leaves, and her fiery strands of hair cascaded down like a breathtaking cascade of colors reminiscent of a setting sun.

As Keisha walked the path lined with silver torches, each step seemed to breathe life into the latent magic of the forest. The torchlight kissed the gemstones on her gown, igniting a dazzling display of iridescent purple and deep blue hues. She was a vision of celestial beauty, her attire a tapestry that mirrored the profound connection she shared with Ong.

At the heart of the woodland cathedral, Ong stood beneath the arched embrace of two ancient trees. Their gnarled and wise branches formed a natural canopy, framing the scene with venerable solemnity. The forest itself held its breath, as though the soul of Vacari had paused in anticipation of this sacred union.

With reverence befitting the sanctity of the woods, Keisha and Ong exchanged rings, a harmonious blend of purple and blue gemstones symbolizing their unique and exquisite bond. Their intertwined silver and gold rings mirrored their love, an eternal promise destined to shine brilliantly through the annals of time.

Under the soft, silvery glow of the torches, Keisha and Ong sealed their vows with a kiss. The forest responded with a crescendo of whispers and rustling leaves, a chorus of approval from the ancient trees. It was a union born of love, destined to be celebrated for eternity in the very heart of Purplefire Woods, a testament to the magic and enchantment that flowed through the land of Vacari.

With vows exchanged and a kiss that sealed their love, the enchanting ceremony drew to a close, and the celebration unfurled like a tapestry of wonder. The assembled guests, a kaleidoscope of faces from far-flung lands, gathered around tables adorned with a feast fit for legends. The spread unfurled before them was a cornucopia of culinary delights, a symphony of succulent fruits, vibrant vegetables, and rich dishes that seemed to sing to the senses."

"Beneath the iridescent shimmer of the stars and the beguiling charm of Purplefire Woods, the evening breeze rustled through the leaves, carrying the harmonious melodies of elven wind instruments and the dulcet tones of human musicians. Like an enchantment, this music wove its threads through the forest, invoking a sense of wonder and merriment that transcended the realm of mortal comprehension.

In the luxury and splendor of the forest, the guests converged upon a central focal point—the unity candle. This tall and elegant sentinel stood as a guardian of promises yet to be spoken. Within its serene flame, the hopes and dreams of two souls and the destinies of three realms would soon be ignited, illuminating the path to a shared future.

The radiant couple, their hands entwined in an unbreakable bond, stepped forth, commanding the reverence of all who beheld them. The forest breathed in profound anticipation as though the air had stilled to witness this momentous event.

Ong and Keisha approached the unity candle with a loving exchange of glances that spoke volumes without needing words. Ong's grasp enveloped a slender ribbon of golden hue while Keisha held another in her delicate hands.

Their hands, steady and unwavering, ignited the central candle together, their flames merging in a radiant union. The forest, bathed in the warm, flickering glow, seemed to awaken with dancing shadows that painted fleeting stories across the faces of the gathered guests.

The symbolism was as profound as it was unmistakable—the union of two flames to create one illuminated the love that bound Ong and Keisha and their unwavering commitment to Vacari. Their joining was not merely a fusion of two souls but a proclamation of their solidarity with the realms they represented.

This transcendent moment lingered in the air, a living testament to the timeless power of love and unity. The newly married couple, standing side by side, their hearts entwined in the enchantment of the evening, held the very essence of Vacari in their embrace.

The crowd erupted in a symphony of applause and jubilation, celebrating the profound love that bound Ong and Keisha and the alliance that had brought them together. In that luminous embrace of fire and unity, the destinies of realms and the promise of a brighter future intertwined, casting a radiant glow that would forever illuminate the pages of Vacari's history."

"Ong turned to gaze upon his beloved bride, and a timeless poem, woven from the threads of his soul, began to flow from his lips. His words were a symphony, a crescendo of emotions that surged like a mighty river in full flood, carrying the weight of his deepest feelings. Each utterance was a resounding note in a symphony of love, a magical incantation that resonated through the ancient trees, reaching every hidden nook and cranny, ensuring that none could escape the magnetic pull of his heartfelt confession.

Ong's resolute and unwavering voice embarked on its poetic odyssey in the boundless tapestry of life and love. "You, Keisha, are the star—a guiding light, a celestial constellation at long last."

A profound hush enveloped Purplefire Woods, the air pulsating with his words' vivid imagery. His verses painted a living portrait of their love, each line a brushstroke in the masterpiece of their shared emotions.

"With every heartbeat, every breath I draw," Ong's voice softened, imbued with a tenderness that held the forest in rapt attention, "My love for you, Keisha, slumbers not nor quivers."

As the poetic tapestry continued to unfurl, it became evident that Ong had poured the very essence of his soul into every word. He spoke of meaning, the joy he found in Keisha's presence, and the warmth that enveloped him in her embrace. His love was not a mere sentiment but a rich tapestry interwoven with threads of laughter, grace, and an unwavering commitment to the journey they had chosen to embark upon together.

"With each fleeting moment," Ong proclaimed, his voice resonating with a fiery passion that set the woods ablaze, "My love for you, Keisha, renews its brilliant hue."

Ong's heartfelt words held the forest spellbound, a potent magic that touched the hearts of all who bore witness as he concluded his poetic declaration. A tidal wave of applause erupted from the assembled guests, a harmonious crescendo acknowledging the profoundness of Ong and Keisha's love. At that moment, they shared a knowing, loving smile, aware that their union was not only celebrated by those in attendance but also by the very realms they represented under the towering, ancient trees of Purplefire Woods."

"Keisha, a vision of ethereal grace and elegance, stepped into the soft, otherworldly ambiance. Like a cascade of molten copper, her fiery mane caught the gentle glow that bathed the realm, framing her visage like a celestial halo of flames. With her eyes locked upon Ong, her groom, her heart swelled with abundant love and eager anticipation. The mellifluous timbre of her voice, as musical as the most enchanted of songbirds, filled the forest like a gentle breeze, carrying her sentiments to the farthest reaches of the magical woodland.

"In the luminescent cradle of starlight's tender embrace," Keisha's serenade began, each note resonating like a celestial melody, "Our love shall bloom—a fragrant blossom of joy to consume."

Her verses, like petals unfurling to reveal the vibrant core of a flower, were more than mere words; they were a solemn promise, a testament to the profound love that had taken root in the fertile soil of their hearts. The unity candle, nestled at the heart of the forest, bore witness to their passion, its twin flames dancing in synchronous harmony with the music that swirled around them.

"In the realms of Elven splendor, our journey finds its first step," Keisha continued, her unwavering gaze never straying from Ong's, "A love, boundless and eternal, etched in the marrow of Elven hearts."

Her verse painted a vivid tapestry of their shared path, a love that defied the boundaries of existence and a unity that transcended the realms they represented. As Keisha concluded her poetic declaration, a tangible sense of unity and purpose descended upon the forest as if the air itself were charged with the irrevocable promise of their union."

"In the enchanting ceremony within Purplefire Woods, a hushed anticipation settled upon the guests as King Alex stepped forward, his regal presence commanding the attention of all. With an aura of wisdom and gratitude, he extended his heartfelt words to the newlyweds, Keisha and Ong.

"Esteemed guests, allies of Vacari, and cherished friends," King Alex began, his voice resonating through the forest like a clarion call. "Today, we bear witness to a union that binds not only two hearts but also bridges realms, forging bonds stronger than any magic we have known.

"He turned his gaze towards Keisha, her radiant presence bathed in the soft forest light. "Keisha," he continued, "Thank you for your courage and resolve. On that fateful day when you first came to Goldmoor and chose to ignore Ong's warning, you altered the course of our history. Without your unwavering belief, my city would remain imprisoned in darkness. Like a beacon, your light guided us to a brighter future.

"He turned his attention to Ong, his expression filled with paternal warmth. "Ong, my friend and ally, you have found a partner whose spirit matches your own in Keisha. I implore you to cherish her, for in her, you have discovered a love that transcends time and space—a love that unites our realms."

With a regal nod of acknowledgment to both Ong and Keisha, King Alex concluded, "Today, we celebrate the union of two souls and the unity of our lands. May your love continue illuminating our path, and may the bond you share inspire us all. Thank you, Keisha, Ong, and to the radiant future you promise to us all."

"King Manard, a monarch whose genuine affection for Ong and Keisha was evident in every word, stepped forward to offer his wisdom. His voice, infused with the profound sincerity of a true leader, served as a bridge between realms, a testament to the boundless potential for unity embedded within this marriage.

"Ong," King Manard addressed the valiant warrior directly, his voice akin to a warm breeze that gently stirred the hearts of all those gathered. "From the moment Keisha graced my palace in your esteemed company, I perceived the radiant light in your eyes, the unwavering conviction that beats within your heart. You had unearthed the deepest desires of your soul. And Keisha, I have witnessed your metamorphosis into a beacon of hope and strength for your people."

With a gracious pivot, he turned his gaze toward the assembled multitude, a gentle smile gracing his regal countenance. "Today, as we celebrate the boundless love shared by Ong and Keisha, let us simultaneously exalt the unity of our realm. Humans and Eladrin know that we are not disparate entities. Rather, our shared aspirations, dreams, and love are the threads that weave our destinies together."

The guests, their hearts resonating with the profound sentiments echoed by King Manard, raised their goblets in unison, a collective toast not solely to Ong and Keisha but also to the cohesion and resilience their marriage epitomized for the realms they represented. It was a pivotal moment, and the celebration continued, permeating with a profound sense of unity and a genuine hope for the unwritten chapters of their shared future.

"Lord Karrenen, a paragon of noble and dignified presence, ascended to address the assembly. His gaze, a blend of sagacity and the warmth of deep understanding lingered upon Ong and Keisha—two souls whose arduous journey had led them to this profound moment of union and hope. He knew his forthcoming words bore the weight of deep gratitude and boundless optimism.

"My esteemed companions," Lord Karrenen began, his voice resounding with solemnity, his words like a clarion call that commanded the attention of all present. "Today, I stand before you with a heart brimming with memories of a time when Keisha was a solitary wanderer, burdened by the weight of her past. It appeared as though she was condemned to traverse the lonely path of solitude. Yet, as fate would have it, Ong entered her life—a paragon of strength, a wellspring of compassion, and an unwavering pillar of support."

He turned his discerning gaze towards Ong, a nod of profound appreciation for his silent tribute. "Ong, I extend to you my deepest gratitude for being the unwavering presence that Keisha needed when her world teetered on the precipice of despair. Your love, a radiant beacon that pierced through the darkest of nights, has illuminated her life, and in its radiant glow, it has touched our own. You have exemplified that love is a force that transcends the artificial boundaries of race and realm, and for that, I am profoundly grateful that you stand here today as both protector and beloved."

The guests, enraptured by Lord Karrenen's heartfelt oratory, hung upon his every word, for they recognized the profound significance of this marriage. This union bore the weight of Ong and Keisha's love and the collective hope of an alliance intertwined in a destiny fraught with trials and triumphant moments.

"As the husband to the bride of his most cherished dreams, Ong tenderly clasped Keisha's delicate hand in his own. They glided onto the forest floor, where the verdant grasses yielded to their touch. Beneath the celestial canopy of shimmering stars, they embarked on their dance. In the embrace of the enchanted woods, they twirled and swayed to the harmonious music of the night, their love casting a luminous aura that rivaled the very constellations above.

Before long, the infectious joy of this moment swept through the assembly, and the guests joined the newlyweds on the forest floor. Elves, humans, dragons, and creatures of the woodland all came forth to partake in this harmonious celebration. They danced under the expansive, starry tapestry of the skies, reveling in the enchantment of Keisha and Ong's union. This union had united two hearts and woven the essence of their fascinating world.

Even Pumpkin, their loyal and spirited companion, graced the celebration with her presence. She delighted in the enchanting ambiance of Purplefire Woods, her eyes gleaming with unbridled delight as she playfully pursued the luminescent fireflies that danced among the ancient trees. Ong and Keisha, bathed in the radiant glow of their love, shared a tender glance towards Pumpkin, acknowledging her as more than a mere pet; she was a cherished member of their family, a symbol of the enduring bonds forged on this magical night."

"Lord Karrenen, their steadfast friend and mentor, approached Ong with solemnity and purpose. Cradled in his hands was a set of glorious Eladrin armor, a profound testament to the enduring bond between Ong and Keisha and the newfound unity that now intertwined their worlds. The armor shimmered with an ethereal luster, its gleam a tangible symbol of their shared destiny and unwavering commitment.

Lord Karrenen, forever wise and discerning, guided them away from the jubilant revelry. He had a momentous revelation to impart. He spoke of a new sanctuary in E'vahona, where they could build a home that would bridge the realms of humans and elves, a haven filled with the promise of adventure and boundless love.

As Ong and Keisha contemplated the prospect of creating and adorning their house, the tapestry of their future unfurled before them. It was a canvas upon which the unwritten chapter of their magical lives would be painted with the vibrant hues of love, unity, and boundless possibilities."

"As the enchanting night in Purplefire Woods drew to a close, Ong and Keisha reluctantly prepared to depart from the mystical realm where their love had blossomed. Above them, Kimras, the glorious golden dragon, descended from the star-studded sky, a celestial steed offering them passage to their new home in E'vahona.

Filled with a profound sense of excitement, Ong mounted Kimras's regal back. His powerful arms enveloped Keisha in a tender embrace as he seated her before him. With a graceful touch, he ensured that her elegant gown remained immaculate, untouched by the brisk night air that caressed them during their nocturnal flight. As Kimras soared through the moonlit expanse, E'vahona loomed on the horizon, its mystical radiance beckoning them homeward.

Upon their arrival, Ong, still cradling Keisha in his strong arms, led the way up the grand staircase that ascended to their new abode. He gently carried her across the threshold with a whispered declaration of love that hung like a shimmering enchantment. "I love you," his voice murmured, rich with the promise of the shared future before them.

Keisha met his gaze, her eyes reflecting the depths of her affection. "I love you too," she replied, echoing their profound devotion to one another. Together, they embraced the anticipation of the countless adventures and joys that awaited them in the unwritten chapters of their shared life, ready to embark on the enchanting journey that awaited."

Epilogue

In the waning twilight of a world veiled in the enigmatic shroud of ancient secrets, a stubborn priest stood unwavering before the formidable portal of the sealed cavern. The atmosphere hung heavy with the hush of ancient eons as if the weight of countless centuries bore down upon his shoulders.

Inscribed upon the cavern's entrance were runes of forgotten power, their script a cryptic language known only to the priest. These arcane symbols served as the chains that bound the deity within—an entity of unparalleled might—imprisoned within the confines of this clandestine vault.

Cloaked in ceremonial vestments symbolizing devotion, the priest lofted a sacred relic high above his head. It emitted an ethereal luminescence, casting a radiant glow upon the foreboding entrance to the cavern.

With a voice that resonated like thunder, he commenced the recitation of ancient verses, invoking the blessings of the divine. The very earth beneath his feet trembled in response as if acknowledging the profound gravity of this moment. Above, the stars in the night sky seemed to manifest from nothingness, aligning in a celestial choreography that mirrored the intricate patterns etched into the stone.

As the ritual reached its zenith, a profound silence descended upon the land as if the world held its breath in anticipation. The runes adorning the cavern's entrance began to shimmer and pulsate, their power gradually yielding to the priest's sacred chants. The formidable barrier, which had steadfastly guarded its secrets for untold ages, weakened, and the cavern's obsidian maw slowly parted.

With a final, resounding intonation that reverberated through the very bedrock, the runes relinquished their dominion. The entrance to the cavern was fractured and shattered, crumbling into fragments like shattered dreams, unveiling the abyssal chasm that lay beyond—a fateful gateway to a realm long cloaked in mystery and shadow.

And from the profound abyss, a presence emerged—an imprisoned deity, released from its timeless captivity. Cloaked in a radiant divine aura, the god fixed its gaze upon the steadfast priest, its eyes bearing the weighty wisdom of epochs long past.

Inextricably linked by this momentous encounter, their destinies led them to exchange a solemn nod. The world stood teetering on the precipice of irrevocable change. As the priest lowered his eyes in deep reverence, he understood that the events unfurling this fateful night would herald the dawn of a new era. It would be an era marked by trials and tribulations, where ancient prophecies and long-forgotten truths would rise from obscurity to confront the present.

The priest, his voice reduced to a mere murmur, dared to break the hallowed silence that enveloped them. "Illustrious one," he implored, "I beseech you to heed my counsel. Your divine essence hunger for sustenance, a unique source that can stoke the eternal fires of your divinity, lest it fades into obscurity. Time, unforgiving and finite, demands that you seek a worthy tribute—a being of unparalleled potency and untarnished purity, whose very essence shall become the crucible of your dominion over this realm."

The god's gaze bore into the very core of the priest's soul, an unspoken covenant passing between them. It was a pact, birthed in the crucible of destiny itself, sealed with the weighty understanding of the choices and challenges that loomed on the horizon.

As the priest's words reverberated through the hallowed chamber, the god accepted his solemn charge, fully comprehending the gravitas of the tasks that lay ahead. In this pivotal juncture, where the world teetered on the precipice of profound transformation, the destinies of entire realms hung in precarious balance. They awaited the deft hand of the newly liberated deity and the shadowy ally they would seek amidst the labyrinthine uncertainties that unfurled before them.

With a nod of acknowledgment, the god embraced his divine mandate, keenly aware of the monumental challenges in his path. His form began to shimmer with a radiant light, his being transcending the physical constraints of the chamber as he started to move. He was drawn, inexorably, toward Afor, the realm of ceaseless desert.

As he departed, the priest watched with a profound sense of reverence, knowing that the god's journey would be fraught with trials and tribulations, yet also harboring the belief that the destiny of realms rested upon the steps of the deity as he ventured into the heart of the arid expanse—a world of shifting sands and unfathomable secrets, where the ally he sought awaited amidst the endless dunes.

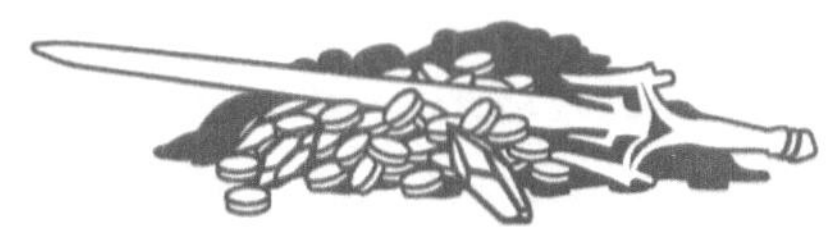

"AS THE SUN SET ON THIS chapter of their lives, little did they know that even greater trials and wonders awaited them in the pages of Shadows Unveiled, Book 2 from the series Elves of Vacari, where new allies would emerge, and ancient secrets would be unveiled."

Teaser from Shadows Unveiled

"It seems darkness is spreading in our lands," Lord Karrenen continued, his silver eyes reflecting the gravity of the situation. "Strange occurrences, sightings of dark creatures, and disturbances in the magical ley lines have been reported. King Manard has requested aid from allies he trusts, and you both are among them."

Ong's brow furrowed as he considered the implications. "Could Phoenix have found a way to extend his reach beyond Afor?" he asked, his voice edged with concern.

Lord Karrenen's gaze turned grave. "We cannot dismiss the notion entirely," he replied. "Though exiled, Phoenix is a cunning adversary. His thirst for revenge may have driven him to seek ways to sow chaos and darkness in our lands."

The weight of responsibility settled upon Keisha and Ong's shoulders. They grasped the importance of the mission and the potential consequences if they failed to act. The safety of Crystal Vale and Vacari depended on their courage and determination.

Keisha's grip on Ong's hand tightened, memories of their past battles resurfacing. "If he's responsible, we must be prepared for a formidable challenge," she asserted firmly.

"We'll need to be vigilant," Ong added, his warrior instincts awakening. "Even a possibility of Phoenix's involvement requires us to stay on guard."

Lord Karrenen nodded in agreement. "Your caution is wise. I trust that both of you, along with your loyal companion," he glanced at Pumpkin, "will bring courage and skill to aid King Manard in securing Crystal Vale from this looming darkness."

With renewed determination, Keisha and Ong exchanged resolute glances. They knew the journey ahead would be perilous but were ready to meet it head-on. As the sun dipped below the horizon, casting a warm glow over Vacari, Keisha, Ong, and Pumpkin bid farewell to their serene haven, the promise of their purpose guiding them toward Crystal Vale and thoughts of Phoenix lingering like shadows in their minds.

<u>Acknowledgment:</u>

There are a few individuals I want to thank:

Steven Thomas

A dear friend who took the time to read the drafts of the chapters. I appreciate your friendship.

Jean McEvoy

My dear mother. You and your red pen will never be forgotten. I also want to say thank you for always believing in me.

Pumpkin

I rescued my little black panther over five years ago. Her personality formed the basis of Pumpkin in the book.

About the Author

T. McEvoy was born in Corpus Christi, Texas, and has called Anderson, South Carolina, home for the past 12 years. She has been passionate about writing since high school and has recently embarked on a journey of self-publishing fantasy fiction novels. Her debut work, 'The Wicked Phoenix,' marks the beginning of 'The Elves of Vacari' series, with two more installments already in the pipeline.

In addition to her writing pursuits, Theresa holds an associate degree in paralegal studies and has gained over five years of experience working in a law firm in Texas. Since relocating to South Carolina, she has dedicated her time to being a caregiver for her mother.

Beyond the world of words, Theresa finds creative expression through painting and enjoys immersing herself in the world of video games."

"Thank you for reading The Wicked Phoenix. If you enjoyed the book, we would be immensely grateful if you could take a moment to leave a review at the location where you purchased the book.
Your feedback is invaluable to us and helps other readers discover our work.
Thank you for your support!"